Advance Praise for *The Facility* from the UK

"An unputdownable thriller . . . Apart from his storytelling skills, Lelic has two potent weapons in his armory, his dialogue which is scabrous and flint-edged, and his characters."   —*Daily Express*

"A startling vision of totalitarian Britain . . . Lelic creates a magnificent sense of place and deftly maintains the pace of his thriller plot. . . . Lelic's crystalline prose is frequently utterly seductive and his compassion deeply moving."   —*Metro* (Fiction of the Week, four stars)

"Lelic stormed on to the literary scene in January 2010 with his gripping debut. . . . [*The Facility*] proves he's no one-hit wonder. . . . Lelic has demonstrated again his talent as a storyteller, keeping his prose fast-paced, and always giving his characters distinct, believable voices. With *The Facility* he finds a niche as an author of solid, engrossing thrillers who could turn out to be a serial bestseller."   —*TimeOut* (four stars)

"The facility of the title is a mysterious prison to which seemingly innocent British citizens are renditioned. . . . As his first novel showed, Lelic can plot like a demon and write wonderful dialogue. . . . Lelic has real talent."   —*The Guardian*

"A journalist gets involved when ordinary people are 'disappeared' and incarcerated in a secret government facility where they are subjected to medical experiments. Already-existing terrorism legislation makes this story an unpleasantly plausible warning."   —*Literary Review*

"An elegant crime thriller about a falsely imprisoned man and his estranged wife, intent on finding the truth. They collide with a journalist investigating a secret government facility hidden in the countryside. Topical and fast-paced."   —*Red* (January 2011, "Top 3 Must-Read")

"Timely indeed . . . Lelic has written a thriller for our times, whose plot is driven by a political machine that's oiled and ready in the real world. . . . The plot grips not because of action scenes (although there are a few) but because we live in a world where feelings of mild guilt often slip into paranoia. This is Kafka meets Orwell in contemporary England."   —*Sunday Herald*

"This is a classic story of a race against time."   —*The Sunday Times*

"Clever, well-paced, and with a clear message, this is an ambitious and important novel with shades of George Orwell's *1984* at its core."
                                                    —*Edinburgh Evening News*

"A home-grown, high concept thriller . . . [*The Facility*] is set in a dystopian near-future, where the British government, seemingly through popular choice, has invoked unprecedented security powers. . . . All in all, this is a deeply unsettling read."   —*Daily Mirror* (Book of the Week)

"The book stands out for being resolutely unsensational, deriving its shock and horror from the truthlessness of the agents of government and the grim degree to which the 'good' characters, as well as the reader, become aware of their powerless fragility before the state. Lelic's prose is spare, concise, and fast-paced. The horror unfolds in a measured and inevitable flow, with the occasional surprising line of economically descriptive beauty. *The Facility* is an accomplished example of its type. And, in a world increasingly skeptical of the intentions of government, a book which is thoroughly of our time."   —*Morning Star*

"This Orwellian setup allows for several scenes of nightmarish strangeness. . . . Lelic's feverish imagination and expert plotting are qualities that suggest a future as a novelist."   —*The Observer*

Praise for *The Child Who*

"Simon Lelic's harrowing and haunting novel *The Child Who* has you utterly in its snares. A daring writer."
                                    —Megan Abbott, author of *The End of Everything*

"British author Lelic follows his acclaimed debut, *A Thousand Cuts*, with an equally gripping psychological thriller also inspired by a horrific real-life crime. . . . Lelic dares to make his lead less than Atticus Finch . . . and the plot unfolds in a way few readers will anticipate."
                                                    —*Publishers Weekly* (starred review)

"Lelic faces thorny issues of guilt and responsibility head on, and no one comes out unscathed."   —*Kirkus Reviews* (starred review)

Praise for *A Thousand Cuts*

"An electrifying first novel."
　　　　　　　　　　　　　　　　—*The New York Times Book Review*

"In his powerful, wrenching debut, Lelic takes a sadly familiar crime and delves into the equally familiar menace at its root: bullying."
　　　　　　　　　　　　　　　　—*People* (3 ½ stars)

"Outstanding . . . Artfully offering a range of perspectives on the events leading up to the fatal day, Lelic manages to make the murderer sympathetic as he sensitively explores the varying degrees of responsibility for the tragedy borne by others whose response to bullying was inadequate. This deeply human and moving book heralds a bright new talent."
　　　　　　　　　　　　　　　　—*Publishers Weekly* (starred review)

"Lelic, a former journalist, switches points of view between firsthand accounts of the event given by students, teachers, and parents and third-person narration of the investigation, an incredibly effective technique that gives his debut novel great immediacy and depth. Lelic wastes not a word in this searing indictment of a culture inured to cruelty: 'Why were the weak obliged to be so brave when the strong had license to behave like such cowards?'"
　　　　　　　　　　　　　　—*Booklist* (starred review; A Top Ten Best Crime Novel of 2010)

"A strikingly original debut: cleverly plotted, highly topical, told in spare prose with coiled intensity. Like Jane Tennison in *Prime Suspect*, police detective Lucia May is a powerful central presence and a wonderful creation. Simon Lelic is a remarkable and fresh new voice."
　　　　　　　　　　　　　　　　—Joseph Finder, *New York Times* bestselling author of
　　　　　　　　　　　　　　　　Vanished and *Paranoia*

"Each of the multiple narrators, from wary teenagers through embittered teachers through gossipy receptionists, is brought to life in deft, unerring detail. Their stories interweave to form a chilling, beautifully observed portrait of the monstrous cruelty that lies not only within human beings, but within our institutions, and the climate of absolute terror and helplessness it can create. *A Thousand Cuts* is ambitious, skillful, powerful, and hard to put down."
　　　　　　　　　　　　　　　　—Tana French, *New York Times* bestselling author of
　　　　　　　　　　　　　　　　Faithful Place and *The Likeness*

Simon Lelic is the author of *The Child Who* and *A Thousand Cuts*, which won a Betty Trask Award and was shortlisted for the CWA John Creasey New Blood Dagger Award and for the Macavity Award for Best First Mystery Novel; it was also selected as a *New York Times* notable crime book. He has worked as a journalist and currently runs his own business. He lives in Brighton, England, with his wife and three children.

SIMON LELIC

THE FACILITY

PENGUIN BOOKS

PENGUIN BOOKS

Published by the Penguin Group
Penguin Group (USA) Inc., 375 Hudson Street, New York, New York 10014, U.S.A.
Penguin Group (Canada), 90 Eglinton Avenue East, Suite 700, Toronto,
Ontario, Canada M4P 2Y3 (a division of Pearson Penguin Canada Inc.)
Penguin Books Ltd, 80 Strand, London WC2R 0RL, England
Penguin Ireland, 25 St Stephen's Green, Dublin 2, Ireland (a division of Penguin Books Ltd)
Penguin Group (Australia), 250 Camberwell Road, Camberwell,
Victoria 3124, Australia (a division of Pearson Australia Group Pty Ltd)
Penguin Books India Pvt Ltd, 11 Community Centre,
Panchsheel Park, New Delhi – 110 017, India
Penguin Group (NZ), 67 Apollo Drive, Rosedale, Auckland 0632,
New Zealand (a division of Pearson New Zealand Ltd)
Penguin Books (South Africa) (Pty) Ltd, 24 Sturdee Avenue,
Rosebank, Johannesburg 2196, South Africa

Penguin Books Ltd, Registered Offices:
80 Strand, London WC2R 0RL, England

First published in Great Britain by Mantle 2011
This edition published by Picador, an imprint of Pan Macmillan UK, 2011
Published in Penguin Books 2012

1   3   5   7   9   10   8   6   4   2

PUBLISHER'S NOTE
This is a work of fiction. Names, characters, places, and incidents either are the product
of the author's imagination or are used fictitiously, and any resemblance to actual persons,
living or dead, businesses, companies, events, or locales is entirely coincidental.

LIBRARY OF CONGRESS CATALOGING IN PUBLICATION DATA
Lelic, Simon.
The facility / Simon Lelic.
p. cm.
ISBN 978-0-14-312068-1
1. False imprisonment—Fiction.   2. Prison wardens—Great Britain—Fiction.
3. Political corruption—Fiction.   I. Title.
PR6112.E48F33 2012
823'.92—dc23   2012023398

Printed in the United States of America

For my mum, dad and sister

PART ONE

Welcome. Come in, sit down. Would you like some coffee? Muffin? They're yesterday's but they're fine. There's blueberry and chocolate and a lemon one with some kind of seed. Sesame, he thinks but his friend cuts in. Poppy, the friend says. Lemon and poppy seed. His personal favourite. Low fat too, he adds and he winks. And Arthur is saying, no, no thank you, and for the second time since entering the room he says, who are you? What is this about? And that is when they ask. They give him coffee even though he said no and they say, so, Arthur: do you like cock?

Arthur blinks and the skinny one, Sesame, smiles. He is seated across from Arthur and he leans in close and sniffs, as though expecting Arthur to emit some stench.

'What?' Arthur says. 'What did you say?' And he is smiling too. He cannot help it.

Poppy Seed, a big man in a double-breasted suit the same shade of charcoal as that of his colleague, appears at Sesame's shoulder. 'Cock, Arthur: do you like it? Rubbing it, chewing it, sitting on it? Is it cock that gets you hard?'

Arthur looks from one man to the other. From the expressions on their faces, they might have asked him if he wanted sugar or a drop of milk.

'This is a joke,' Arthur says. His smile, though, has grown stale. It is rigid and ready to crumble.

Sesame keeps his eyes on Arthur but angles his face up and towards his friend. 'Maybe it's our whatdoyoucallit. Our terminology. Maybe his lot refer to it as something different.'

Poppy Seed nods, as though his colleague has made a valid point. 'Let's see,' he says. 'Let's see.' And he turns and paces the length of the grey-washed wall. 'Choad?' he says. 'Schlong? Tool? Shaft?'

'Johnson,' says Sesame but Poppy Seed shakes his head.

'Not over here,' he says and Sesame rolls his eyes like yeah, of course.

'I'm leaving,' says Arthur. He stands and edges between the wall and the table, towards the steel-lined door. He expects to be stopped. Sesame, though, remains in his chair; his colleague is in Arthur's path but steps back and out of the way. Arthur keeps his eyes on Poppy Seed as he passes. His outstretched palm meets metal and his fingers fumble for purchase and only when he turns to look does he realise that there is no handle.

'Beaver cleaver,' says Sesame. 'Does that count?'

Poppy Seed nods. 'Shit dipper,' he says. 'Man handle.'

'Enough!' says Arthur.

'I'm running out,' says Sesame. Then, 'Cumstick.'

'Penis,' says Poppy Seed. 'You understand the word penis, don't you, Arthur?'

'I said that's enough! Who are you? Who the fuck are you?'

Sesame flinches. 'Please, Arthur. Language.'

'Take a seat, Arthur.'

Arthur glances at the chair he has vacated. He does not move from his position by the door.

'Sit down,' says Poppy Seed and Arthur, this time, obeys.

'You haven't answered our question,' says Sesame.

Arthur has shifted his seat as far back as the wall behind will allow. The room, though, seems to be contracting. It is a concrete cube, without windows, decoration or furniture other than the table and two chairs. There are Sesame and Poppy Seed and Arthur and there is Arthur's mug of coffee.

'I'm married.'

'No you're not,' says Sesame.

'What? Yes I am.' Arthur holds up his hand to show Sesame his ring.

'You're separated. And I'm married is not an answer.'

'I have a son, for Christ's sake.'

Sesame creases a cheek and shakes his head. 'That's not an answer either.'

'You haven't touched your coffee,' says Poppy Seed.

Arthur looks at him like he is joking but something in Poppy Seed's expression makes him lift the cup to his lips. Just the smell is enough to stop him drinking.

'That bad?' says Poppy Seed and Sesame smiles.

They wait.

'What do you want from me?'

'Answers, Arthur,' says Sesame. 'Just the one, for starters.'

'Who are you? Are you the police? This isn't legal, you know. You can't hold me like this.'

Sesame looks up again at his colleague. 'Maybe he didn't hear. Maybe we didn't ask loud enough.'

Poppy Seed nods and turns to Arthur and he is closing the gap between them and leaning forwards and grabbing Arthur's chin with one hand and tugging his ear up and out with the other. Arthur screams. He grips Poppy Seed's wrist but when he tugs it is like tugging on oak.

'Cock!' yells Poppy Seed. Sour breath and spittle slap against Arthur's cheek. 'Do you like cock!' Then Arthur's head spins free and drops forwards and the pain in his ear sinks into his jaw.

'Surely he heard that?' says Sesame and Arthur looks up in time to see Poppy Seed give a shrug.

'What?' Arthur says. He is drooling, he realises. He is slumping forwards and a rope of spittle has caught on his stubble. With the hand that is not clutching his ear, he wipes. 'What are you asking me? If I'm gay, is that it? What the hell does it matter if I'm gay? This is a free fucking country!' The pain is making him angry. He knows he should resist but he cannot. 'It's none of your fucking business if I'm gay!'

Then Poppy Seed is moving again, with the same rage in his eyes that Arthur feels, and Arthur is scrabbling backwards, sliding his chair but sliding off it, and before he knows how he got there he is a muddle of limbs on the floor.

'Is that a yes?' says Sesame and Poppy Seed stops his advance.

'What?' Arthur's eyes are on the man looming over him: on his forearms and his palms, just one of which would smother Arthur's face.

Poppy Seed reaches and Arthur flinches but he is only

reaching for the toppled chair. He sets it upright, angling the seat towards Arthur, and moves away.

'Your answer,' says Sesame. 'Is that a yes?'

Arthur does not respond and Sesame, for the first time, betrays his impatience. 'Get up,' he says. 'Sit down.'

Arthur totters as he stands but the wall catches him. He checks the palm he has been holding across his ear because the pain, surely, warrants some flecks of blood. He sits. 'I'm not gay,' he says. His voice is a whisper so he raises it. 'I have a wife. I have a son. I'm not gay.'

Poppy Seed tuts. Sesame rubs at his forehead with two fingers.

'His name's Casper. My son. He's three. He . . . he looks like his mother. Here.' Arthur pats his breast and locates his wallet. He draws it from his pocket and it flaps open. 'Here,' he says again but his fingers keep slipping from the photograph inside. He spies Poppy Seed moving and he holds up a hand. 'Wait,' he says. 'Look. I have a picture.' The wallet, though, will not let him have it. 'It's stuck,' he says. He laughs. 'Wait. Here. Look.' The picture is free but blank side up. He flips it. 'Look. That's him. That's my son.'

Sesame's hand is like the peak of a cap, directing his gaze towards the surface of the table. Poppy Seed is close now but he too ignores the photograph. 'Put it away,' he says.

'Here,' says Arthur. 'Look.'

'Put it away. I said, put it away!'

Before Arthur can respond, the picture and the wallet have been knocked from his grasp. They hit the wall and drop to the floor and when Arthur bends to reclaim the photo Poppy Seed lunges for Arthur's collar and hauls him upright.

SIMON LELIC

'It's sad,' says Sesame, finally looking up. Poppy Seed releases his grip and Arthur drops back into the chair. It takes a moment for him to shift his gaze. 'Truly,' says Sesame. 'It's sad.'

Poppy Seed snorts and turns away. 'It makes me sick.'

'You're the worst, Arthur. Do you realise that? You, people like you: you're the reason we're in the mess we're in.'

Poppy Seed snorts again, bobs his head.

'Because if it wasn't for you,' Sesame continues, 'this wouldn't be necessary. None of this –' he rolls his eyes upwards and around the room '– would be necessary.'

'I don't know . . .' Arthur says. 'I still don't know . . .'

'We want answers, Arthur. I've told you what we want.'

'I answered. Didn't I? I'm not gay. I'm not. I just don't see . . . I mean, even if I were . . .'

'Perhaps I should clarify,' says Sesame.

'Please! Please do!'

'We want answers,' says Sesame, 'but we also want the truth.'

Arthur's head slumps forwards. He grins at his lap and shakes his head.

'Sit up,' says Sesame. 'Look at me.'

Arthur looks. He is still shaking his head; he is still grinning.

'Stop smiling,' says Sesame. 'Arthur: stop smiling.'

Poppy Seed takes a step and Arthur raises his hands. 'Okay!' he says. 'Okay, I'm not smiling! I wasn't! It's just . . . All of this is just . . .'

'Unfortunate,' says Sesame. 'Necessary. And time-consuming. It's becoming time-consuming, Arthur.'

'Drink your coffee,' says Poppy Seed.

Arthur looks from one man to the other. 'Coffee? What? No, I . . . I don't want any coffee. I don't feel like drinking coffee. To be honest, the only thing I feel like doing is talking to my goddamn soli—'

Poppy Seed takes two strides and he is beside him. He grabs Arthur's hair this time and yanks back his head. Arthur makes to yell but the coffee cascades and flushes away his voice. He struggles, for breath as much as anything, and either the mug chips or his teeth do and his scalp feels like it is tearing from his skull.

The mug falls away. Arthur hears it clatter and crack on the floor. His scalp is still ablaze but Poppy Seed, he realises, has let him go. He coughs. The cough makes him gag. He hacks and he spits and he wipes at his face with a sodden sleeve. He tastes what he has been made to drink, as well as blood and something stronger. Like Windolene. Like Windolene might taste. He spits again and shrugs his shirt and slides upright on the chair. He glares at Poppy Seed but Poppy Seed has turned his back. He shifts his glare to Sesame but notices when he looks that there is something on the table.

'A friend of yours,' says Sesame, nodding at the photograph he has set in front of him.

Arthur looks, shakes his head.

'Pick it up. Look closer.'

Arthur leans in but keeps his hands in his lap. The image shows a man of about Arthur's age – thirty-ish, maybe younger – with hair as dark as Arthur's but longer, lanker, and with a narrower face tapering towards a cleft chin. He is seated at a table just like this one, in a room just like this one. The image has been taken from above and to the side, as if by a security camera. Arthur looks up and to his right and for the first time notices an air vent, grey like the walls and tucked into a corner.

Sesame sees him looking. 'Say cheese.'

Arthur spins the picture and slides it across the surface. 'I don't know him.'

Poppy Seed begins to pace.

'Funny,' says Sesame. 'Because he knows you.'

'I've never seen him before.'

'And yet he gave us your name. Told us where we could find you. He told us, in fact, that you stuck your dick in his mouth and your tongue up his arsehole.' Sesame turns to his colleague. 'What do they call that? They have a name for that, don't they?'

'Rimming,' says Poppy Seed.

'Right. Rimming. He said you rimmed him.' Sesame turns to Poppy Seed again. 'Can I say that? Can I use it as a verb?'

Poppy Seed does not answer. He twitches his shoulders, cracks his neck. He continues pacing.

'Why would he say that?' says Sesame to Arthur. 'Why would he say that if it wasn't true?'

'I don't know.'

'You don't know.'

'No. I don't. You could ask him. Why don't you ask him?'

'I'm asking you.'

'And I'm telling you I don't know. Ask him. Bring him in here. I'll ask him, for Christ's sake!'

Sesame smiles. 'I'm afraid you wouldn't get much of a response just now.'

Poppy Seed sets his hands on the table. The table creaks. 'Give us the names.'

Arthur leans away. He looks to Sesame. 'What names?'

'The names of the others,' says Poppy Seed. 'The others you've fucked.'

'What? What are you talking about? There aren't any others!'

'Just him then,' says Sesame and he spins the picture back across the table.

'No! Not him, not anyone! Jesus.' Arthur's hands find his head and he bows as if in prayer. 'Jesus,' he says again.

Poppy Seed mutters something to his colleague that Arthur does not catch. Sesame clicks his tongue. Poppy Seed mumbles again and Sesame continues clicking and there is a scrape of metal on concrete. Arthur looks up and Sesame is standing. He is as short as he is skinny but his size does not detract from his menace. He is like wire, Arthur thinks; like wire that would work just as well as a barb.

'What now?' says Arthur.

'Now I'm leaving,' says Sesame.

Arthur's gaze swings to Poppy Seed, who is standing beside his colleague at the door. Poppy Seed is smiling. 'Wait a minute!' says Arthur. He stands and thinks for a moment he has stood up too quickly. He sways. He takes a step and he stumbles. He reaches for the table but his focus fails him and he grasps only air. 'Wait,' he says again. He falls, on to his knees and then forwards on to his hands. Through a haze he sees his son, staring back at him from a different world.

'Wait,' says Arthur once more. He can talk still but his voice sounds distant. He tries to crawl but his hands are numb. He can hear, though. He can hear quite clearly. He hears Poppy Seed cracking his neck again and then Sesame's impassive voice.

'Try not to make a mess,' Sesame tells his friend. And then the door opens, then shuts again, and he is gone.

Henry Graves watches through the doorway as the man from the Home Office surveys the room. There is little to see – two bunks, two piles of bedding, a toilet, a sink, a narrow window with wire-mesh glass – yet Jenkins inspects what there is as though considering whether to make an offer. He taps a wall and seems satisfied, then taps again and gives a frown when his knuckle yields a thud. He peers in the toilet and behind it. He fiddles with a tap and turns it on and the ferocity of the water takes him by surprise. He arches his groin to avoid being sprayed and turns the tap off again. He moves to a bunk and presses a palm to the mattress. He sits.

'I'm no prude, Graves,' he says, after a moment. His attention is on the bunk opposite. 'But two bunks. In each cell.' He turns to face the corridor. 'Do you think that's wise?'

He is not the first to make the point. Graves's assistant, John Burrows, asked too, though in less delicate terms. 'The inmates will eat together, minister, and they will exercise together but they will only be required to share a room with a member of their own sex.'

'Quite,' says Jenkins. 'That's precisely my point. I'm not concerned so much about the women but the men . . . I mean, aren't most of them . . . That is, aren't they all . . .'

'They are not all homosexual, minister. And besides,' Graves adds, 'I do not see the harm. The harm, I would say, has already been done.'

Jenkins's lips give a twitch: not quite a smile but not far off it. He casts around once more. He stands. 'Good. More than adequate. So: is that everything?'

'Except for the grounds.'

Jenkins checks his watch. He squints behind him at the cell window. 'Is it still raining?'

Graves looks where the minister is looking. Through the wire and the dappled glass, he can make out only a pervading greyness. 'There is cover. We shan't get wet.'

Jenkins checks his watch again. 'Just quickly then. I've another appointment and then a long journey back.' He steps from the room and turns in the wrong direction. 'This way?'

'This way, minister,' says Graves. He gestures with an open palm towards the opposite end of the corridor, then follows at his guest's shoulder.

'You won't be staying for lunch?' Graves asks. 'We were told you would require lunch.'

'Perhaps next time.' Jenkins is scanning the walls around him as he walks. 'Could do with a lick of paint down here, Graves.' He pauses for a moment and points. 'Is that damp? You should get that seen to. The longer you leave it, the worse it'll get.'

Graves peers. 'Indeed. It does look like damp. I will ensure it is dealt with, just as soon as the budget allows.'

'Do it sooner rather than later,' says Jenkins, walking on. 'You have a budget, naturally, but it's a question of priorities. It's all very well having a forty-inch plasma screen in the recreational area but if that damp spreads any further, you won't have any power to run it.'

'Power, minister?'

'Power, Graves. I've seen it happen. The damp gets to the cabling and the whole damn fuse board ends up fried, especially in an old building like this. Where will your budget be then?' Jenkins turns his raised eyebrows towards his host but Graves has stopped three steps behind. He stands at the door to the stairwell.

'This way, minister,' Graves says. Jenkins retraces his steps and rumbles his thanks as he passes through.

'You are sure about lunch?' says Graves, returning to Jenkins's side in the corridor below. 'It would not be any trouble. In fact, I believe it has already been prepared.'

'Hm? What's that?'

'Lunch, minister. It's all prepared.'

Jenkins shakes his head. His jowls wobble. 'Thank you, no. I'm due to meet my sister. She lives in a village not far from here, as it happens. Although it's all relative, I suppose, in country like this. I say not far but it's forty miles at least.'

'Very sensible, minister. Combining business with a little pleasure.'

Jenkins glances at Graves as though to gauge his tone. Graves keeps his face expressionless and the minister gives a grunt. 'There'll not be much pleasure, Graves, I assure you. Aside from the company, I don't suppose the cuisine at the local brasserie is up to much. Given the choice, I would rather suffer the delights of your canteen.'

Graves inclines his head. 'I shall pass on the message,' he says. 'Our chef, I am sure, will appreciate the compliment.' He has gone too far this time but he pretends not to notice the minister's scowl. 'The door is just ahead. Please, allow me.'

The rain has indeed stopped. The clouds seem to have followed its descent, however, turning the courtyard into a basin of mist. Even from the edge of the covered walkway, they can barely see across to the arches opposite. Above them, the ragged line of the second-floor windows is visible but the pitched roof and corner turrets are nothing more than shadows.

Jenkins jabs his chin towards the centrepiece of the quad: a fountain, depicting Neptune in a chariot behind three horses. 'A touch extravagant, would you not say?'

'It is hideous, I know. The whole building, really, is an architectural chimera. His Majesty, for one, would not approve. There's Gothic here, Romanesque there, Palladian and Tudor in the outbuildings. None of it original, of course. Except for the staff quarters, which were built in the fifties.'

'You got it working, though. You left the damp but fixed the fountain.'

'It was no great expense, minister. We felt it would be beneficial. The sound of running water, a place for the men and women to gather. You understand, I am sure.'

'They are prisoners, Graves.'

'They will be imprisoned, minister. It is perhaps not quite the same thing.'

'Guff,' says Jenkins. 'Of course it's the same thing.'

Graves gestures to an opening in the grey-stone wall. 'We can pass around and through the gateway if you would like to see the rest. There is no shelter past the main building but from the passageway you will be able to see the layout of the grounds beyond.'

'No need.' Jenkins wipes a thumb across the face of his watch. 'I am sure it is satisfactory. Everything seems more than satisfactory. Except for that damp,' he adds, raising a finger. 'Be sure to see about that damp.'

'Indeed, minister. I will ensure it is attended to. And lunch. You are adamant I cannot persuade you?'

'Just my things, if you please. My overcoat is in your office. This way, is it?' Jenkins points the way he is facing.

'If you'll follow me,' says Graves and he leads off in the opposite direction.

Burrows is behind him, his pimpled nose pressed to the glass. He snorts periodically, a prompt for Graves to solicit his opinion. Graves is careful not to. He keeps his attention on the papers spread across his desk.

'Thirty minutes, would you say? Thirty-five?'

'He was here a good hour,' says Graves. He stacks a folder in the pile to his right, picks another from the pile to his left and opens it in the space between.

'Not including the time he spent on the phone, I mean. Thirty-five minutes, by my reckoning, at the very most. And we've been preparing, what? Six weeks if you count the renovations.'

'It's his prerogative.' Graves uncaps his pen, makes a note of a name on his pad. He closes the folder he has in front of him and sets it on the right-hand pile.

'We bought steak. Howard did. It's not as though they've given us money to waste.'

'It will not go to waste, I am sure.'

'You asked him, though? You told him Howard had prepared lunch?'

'Twice,' says Graves. 'Three times, in fact. It was beginning to sound suspicious.'

Burrows turns back to the window, though Jenkins's car is long gone. Graves glances at his assistant. There is a haze of condensation on the pane in front of him, thickening with each outward breath, ebbing as he inhales.

'Satisfactory,' says Burrows, still staring at the gravel drive. 'That's the word he used?'

'He said more than satisfactory, John. More than.'

'Did he mention anything else?'

Graves sighs. He shuts the folder in front of him and sets it on the pile to his right. He puts down his pen. 'Like what?'

'I don't know. Anything. There must have been something that made an impression.'

'The water pressure. In the accommodation wing.'

'What about it?'

'It made an impression.'

'What about the fountain? Did you show him the fountain?'

'I did.'

'And? What did he say?'

'He wondered whether it might be a touch extravagant.'

'Extravagant?' Burrows spins from the window. 'What's that

supposed to mean? It's running water! Did you say to him it was running water?'

Graves nods.

'And he understood the connotations? He understood the subtlety?'

'It's a fountain, John. It's a naked god, ten feet high. It's not subtle.'

'I meant the calming effect!'

'I know what you meant,' Graves says. 'And you are right to be proud of the idea. Let's leave it at that, shall we?'

Burrows frowns, turns away. He mutters something Graves does not catch. Graves can feel himself becoming infected with his assistant's irritation, though it is Burrows's petulance that grates on him the most.

'Really, John,' he says, knowing he should resist, 'what did you expect? A ribbon and some oversized scissors?'

'No,' says Burrows. 'Of course not.'

'What then?'

'Some recognition. That's all. We've done what they asked us to do and we've done it on time, in budget and without a single leak.'

'Which means we've done what we're getting paid to do. Nothing more. You knew the terms when you accepted this post. You knew and you accepted it anyway.'

'They barely gave me a choice.'

'One always has a choice, John.'

Burrows makes to answer back but Graves cuts him off. 'Enough,' he says. 'You've made your point. We have work to do.'

Burrows moves away from the window. He slumps into his boss's reading chair and tucks his outsized hands between his knees. His feet turn inwards and meet toe to toe. 'Everything's ready. What more is there to do?'

There are two more folders for Graves to check. He opens them in turn, content to let Burrows wait while he works. He adds one of the names to the list in his notebook, then straightens the pile of folders by his right hand and taps it with the pen in his left. 'These names,' he says. 'They will all be in the first batch?'

Burrows shrugs. 'I think so.'

Graves snaps before he can stop himself. 'Sit up straight, man. Answer properly. Talk to me properly.'

Burrows slides upright in the leather chair.

'These names,' Graves repeats. 'Will they all be in the first batch?'

Burrows nods once, rather precisely. 'Yes, sir. That's what they told me.'

'How many exactly?'

'Fifty-seven. Mostly men, a handful of women.'

'And how many to follow after that?'

'Twenty-nine, they said. But that may change.'

There are twelve names on Graves's list: ten men and two women. He tears the page from his notebook and slides it across the desk. 'Bunk these people separately. Just for the time being.'

'Separate from each other or separate from the rest of the prisoners?'

'Give them their own rooms. Keep them in the main wing but I don't want them sharing.'

'All right,' says Burrows. He stands and takes the list and checks the names but does not ask his boss's reasoning. Possibly he does not need to; more likely he is wallowing still in his sulk.

'Also,' Graves says, 'have someone take a look at the plastering outside room twelve. Probably there's a drain overflowing somewhere. Fix it, paint it. Check the rest of the corridor too.'

'Yes, sir. Is that everything, sir?'

There is a note to his assistant's tone that Graves does not appreciate. 'No, John, it is not. This project, this facility: it is not a game.'

Burrows draws back his shoulders. 'I realise that.'

'Well, then,' says Graves. 'I hope you realise too that when these people arrive here they will be angry. We cannot afford to let their anger get out of hand—'

'The staff are well equipped. They are well trained.'

'We cannot afford to let their anger get out of hand but we must respond with equanimity too.'

Burrows narrows his eyes. 'I'm not sure I follow.'

'Talk to the staff, John. Remind them that the men and women in our charge are human beings. They are not criminals. I would like everyone to remember that.'

'Yes, sir. I am sure it will not be a problem.' Burrows folds the list and sharpens the crease. He makes to leave.

'One more thing,' Graves says. 'They are dying, John. The people who will arrive here: they are dying. They might not know it yet but that's the truth of it.' He takes the cap off his pen and turns to a fresh sheet in his notebook. 'Please,' he says. 'Remember that too.'

'Who is she?'

'Tom, please. You're practically sitting on my lap.'

Tom edges away, careful not to forsake the cover of his colleague's monitor. 'Amy?' he says and he repeats: 'Who is she?'

The woman over at Tom's desk gives the impression of being annoyed with him even before she has realised he is in the same room. Her gaze does not settle but tugs her one way and then the other in her seat. Only her right arm remains anchored, to allow her fingertips to beat against his desk. The doors to the newsroom swing open and she turns, then turns back. The doors open once more and once more she glances across. She is like a spaniel, Tom decides, lurching every time its owner fakes to throw the ball. She is like a spaniel, more to the point, tiring of the game and just about ready to bite.

'She looks angry,' says Tom. 'Don't you think she looks angry?'

Amy peeks, then returns her gaze to her screen. 'She looks like someone who's been made to wait for an hour and a half.'

'She's been waiting for me for an hour and a half?'

'Uh huh.'

'That can't be good.' Tom slides behind the screen again as the woman turns his way. Amy jabs a bony elbow into his hip.

'I've got a deadline, Tom.'

'Did you get her name at least? What's her name?'

Amy's eyes find the gap between her glasses and her poker-straight fringe. 'I assumed she was a friend. You really don't know who she is?'

Tom starts to answer but Amy's question prompts a momentary panic. Does he know her? Usually he has a memory for faces, particularly young and attractive ones framed with blonde hair. If he were to pass this woman in the street, however, he would turn only because it would be a shame not to. Clearly, though, she knows him. Which means . . . Well. Which means there is a possibility that—

'You slept with her.'

Tom looks and Amy is reclining in her chair, arms folded and lips pinched. 'What?' he says. 'No!'

'You did. You got drunk and you slept with her and you said you'd call her and you never did.'

'That's not true!' Tom glances again at the woman, who is resting her forearms now on her clenched knees. 'Really, I'm almost certain that's not true.'

Amy makes a noise like he is something disgusting.

'I would remember. Believe me.' Tom's eyes drift from the woman's crossed ankles to her collarbone. 'I definitely would have called her.'

Amy tuts again. She returns her fingers to her keyboard and angles her chair away from him.

'Amy, please. Go and check. Ask her who she is.'

'I've got a deadline, Tom! Ask her yourself.'

'You let her in here! You could at least have asked her what she wanted.'

'She wanted to see you. Oh, and look. Now she has.' Amy gives him a shove and he steps to brace himself and there is no doubt when he looks that the woman has spotted him. She is standing and peering across. Amy nudges him again and almost as a reflex Tom is following his feet across the office floor and fixing his face with a wary smile.

'Mr Clarke?' says the woman as Tom draws near. 'Tom Clarke?' Her accent is American: east coast, Tom thinks. She is slightly frayed in her appearance – hair neat but not styled, skin pale and only lightly made up, clothes casual and inexpensive. She is no less attractive than he first judged, however. She simply seems the type who does not feel she has the time to waste with mascara and a set of hair straighteners. In her bearing and her tone, she conveys a sense of purpose that Tom has encountered before – with Amy, for instance, who has only ever reacted to his flirting with disdain; with Katherine Fry, his boss; with his sister, five years his junior but, even Tom would admit, a decade at least more mature – and that does nothing to set him at ease.

'Er, hi.'

'I hope you don't mind me waiting,' the woman says. 'Your assistant told me it would be okay.'

'My assistant?' Tom tracks the woman's glance towards Amy's desk. 'My assistant,' he repeats. 'Yes, of course. No, no problem.'

'I'm Julia. Julia Priestley.' The woman holds out her hand and Tom takes it.

'Hi,' he says again, more warmly this time. He does not know her. He told Amy he did not and he was right. 'Please.' He gestures to the chair behind her. She sits again and Tom looks around for a chair for himself. There is one at the desk opposite and he rolls it across. 'Can I get you some coffee? I could ask my assistant to fetch us some.'

'Thank you, no.'

'Water?'

'Nothing for me, really. I'd like just a minute of your time, if I may.'

'By all means,' says Tom. 'What can I do for you?' He props an ankle on his knee and he smiles.

'It's about my husband,' says Julia and Tom checks his grin. He adjusts his pose, dropping both feet to the floor and locking his hands in his lap. 'I was hoping,' Julia says. She pauses. 'I was hoping you could help me find him.'

Tom opens his mouth but he is not sure how to reply. A voice from above his shoulder interrupts before he can find his own. 'Hi,' it says. Then, 'Um.'

Tom turns and sees Terry Williams, sub-editor and serial snacker, standing above him. He holds a coffee and half a croissant and has scabs of pastry at the corner of his mouth.

'Hi,' Tom replies. He looks at Julia, then back at Terry. He waits.

'Um,' says Terry again. 'I think that's my chair.'

'Oh,' says Tom. 'Oh, right.' He stands. 'Sorry.' He wheels the chair back across to Terry's desk. Terry thanks him and takes a bite of croissant. As he chews he allows his eyes to slide across Julia's chest. Julia covers herself with the folds of her jacket and Tom flushes, as though he has been caught looking himself. He casts about and spots an empty meeting room on the far side of the office. He gestures towards it. 'We can talk in there.'

The *Libertarian*, the political news site for which Tom works, is only published online but still every corner of the office seems somehow to attract newspapers, magazines, scrawled-on Word files and website printouts. Tom clears a corner of the meeting-room table and they sit.

'I read these,' says Julia. She opens her bag and unfolds a clipping bearing Tom's byline. The headline reads, COMMONS CONSENTS TO POLICE CRIMINALITY. 'You wrote them, right?' Julia spreads another printout beside the first. LIBERTY INTERNATIONAL BANNED BY LAW IT FOUGHT TO QUASH is the six-month-old story, with an opinion piece stapled to the back: TERRORISM'S TRIUMPH: FEAR, FREEDOM AND THE BIRTH OF A POLICE STATE. Tom glowers in greyscale at the head of the topmost page, through glasses he borrowed from a colleague and beneath hair that was combed for the occasion and Photoshopped – at his request – to seem fairer than its usual fawn.

'I did.' Tom pulls the pages towards him and automatically begins to read. He is amazed that TERRORISM'S TRIUMPH turned out as well as it did. He wrote it on the tube, on the way back to the office after a whisky lunch with his favourite PR.

'They're good,' says Julia.

'Thank you.'

'You're right, too. What you say in there. You're absolutely right.'

'Well,' Tom says. 'I mean, yes, I suppose so. I would certainly hope so.' He is trying to recall what the first story was about. Katherine, the website's editor, liked it too, he remembers. The praise, though, is the only thing about it that stands out in his mind.

'They're the reason I'm here,' Julia is saying. 'These articles. I thought, well. I thought the man who wrote these might be able to help me.'

'Your husband,' says Tom. 'You're looking for your husband.'

Julia nods. Then she shakes her head. 'Not quite. I mean, yes, that's kind of right.' Tom frowns and she shakes her head again, as though to erase what she has already said. 'I know where my husband is, Mr Clarke.'

'Tom, please. Mr Clarke is what people call my father.'

'Tom, then. I know where my husband is. That is, I know he was arrested. I got them to admit that much, at least. I don't know why, though. I don't know where they're keeping him. I don't even know who has him, not really. I mean, it's not just the police, is it, in cases like this?' She looks, all of a sudden, as if she is about to cry. Tom frisks his pockets for something suitable to offer her but the only thing he can find is a packet of gum. When he looks up, though, her eyes are dry. She is upset, clearly, but more than anything else she seems angry. And she is waiting, Tom realises, for him to respond.

He offers her gum.

'Look here,' she says, ignoring his outstretched hand and reaching for one of the printouts. She traces the text with her fingertip as she quotes him back to him. '"The police are complicit. Sir Andrew Burns, the Metropolitan Police Commissioner, has long argued for an extension of police powers. Fourteen days was not enough, nor twenty-eight, nor forty-two, nor even the ninety days proposed – and rejected – in 2005. Now the police have been granted the de facto autonomy they campaigned for, and Burns finds himself invested with a concentration of powers not seen on this continent since the overthrow of the Nazi regime. The force that he commands is now the central cog in the machinations of a terrifying, countrywide security operation, involving not only the military and MI5, but also subcontracted and shadowy organisations whose true influence and agendas are not fully understood even by the men who help run them."'

It sounds even better read aloud.

'Those are your words, right?'

'Pretty much,' Tom says. He would have vetoed 'shadowy' if he had seen the subedited copy. He would have reminded Terry – and it was Terry, he would bet it was Terry – that grammar was his chief concern, not melodrama.

'This is it,' Julia says, waving the piece of paper in her hand. 'This is exactly it. They've got my husband. Someone's got my husband. The police won't help me. They won't tell me anything. They only admitted having him in custody when I confronted them with the video a neighbour took.'

'You have a video?'

'She was filming the teenagers outside her house. She was convinced they were smoking crack.'

'Jesus. Where do you live?'

'What? Ealing. We live in Ealing. And they weren't smoking crack, they were smoking roll-ups. But that's not the point.'

'No,' says Tom. 'Sorry. But you have evidence. The film, I mean. Surely if you show someone that—'

'Mr Clarke,' Julia says. 'This article you wrote.' She angles her head. 'Did you read it?'

'What? Yes. Of course. I mean . . .'

Julia waves a hand. 'Look. My husband was arrested. No one will tell me why. Because of these laws, these laws you wrote about –' and again she brandishes one of the printouts ' – they don't have to.'

'No,' says Tom. 'I guess not.'

'Which isn't right. Is it? It's not right.'

Julia is leaning towards him, imploring him with her eyes. Tom looks across from her towards the door. He wishes he had left it open.

'Did you talk to the US embassy? I mean, you're American, right? Is your husband—'

'He's British. English. I was born in Boston but I took dual nationality when Arthur and I got married. Not that my US passport seems to count for much. My husband, apparently, is not the American government's problem.'

'What about . . . I don't know. There are organisations, aren't there? There are people who can help with this sort of thing.'

'Which organisations?' Julia straightens her shoulders. 'Organisations like this one?' She slides the article on the banned civil-rights group towards him.

'Not that one, obviously. But there are plenty of others.'

'Not any more. Not after Drax. And those that are left are

inundated. I've tried them. Some say they can't help. Some say they won't.'

The packet of chewing gum is still in Tom's hand. He tears off a section of the wrapper and crumples it into a ball. 'Your husband,' he says. 'You don't know the details but you must have an idea about why he was arrested. I mean, I assume he was into something.'

'*Into* something? What the hell does that mean?'

'Nothing. I'm just asking. I have to ask.'

'This is anti-terrorism legislation, Mr Clarke. These are laws the police are supposed to be using to stop fundamentalists blowing up another power station.'

'I know. I realise that. All I'm asking—'

'My husband is not a terrorist, Mr Clarke. Whatever he's *into*, I can assure you it's not terrorism. He's a dentist, for Christ's sake!'

Tom raises his hands. 'Okay,' he says. 'Okay. So you've been to the police. Right? And you've spoken to Witness and Front Line and all the others. What about a lawyer? Have you spoken to a lawyer?'

'No, Mr Clarke. It never occurred to me to talk to a lawyer.'

'And?' Tom says, conceding the sarcasm. 'What did they say?'

'Forgive my tone, Mr Clarke, but what do you think they said? What do you think they all said?'

Tom sets the gum and the balled-up paper on the table and rubs one damp palm against the other. 'The thing is,' he says, 'that's sort of the point. Isn't it? None of these people – these people who know the law, who work with the law – feel they can help you. I'm a journalist. I'm just a journalist.'

Julia leans forwards once more. 'You have contacts. Don't you?'

'Of course but—'

'But what?'

'But they're contacts. That's all they are. They're people who might slip me a lead or an anonymous quote. They're not friends.'

'You could call them though. You could ask them.'

'Ask them what? Whether they've seen your husband?'

'Something like that.'

Tom scoffs.

'What's so ridiculous? All I'm asking is that you do what you tell others to. Listen,' she says and she reaches again for the words Tom wrote. '"National polls, the government tells us, show overwhelming public support for its Unified Security Act. The public, though, and not for the first time in recent years, has been grossly misled. The debate has been undermined; a ballot denied. For those committed to the ideals – nay, rights – this government is so willing to sacrifice, there are other ways—"'

'Please,' says Tom, taking the page from her. Julia, though, continues from memory.

'"—there are other ways in which we can act. March: in the capital if you can, in your home town at the very least. Speak out: in defence of those who have their freedom of speech denied. Fight: because if you do not, you must ask yourself – why should anyone else?"'

Julia's eyes meet his and though he tries to hold her gaze he cannot.

'I just work here,' he says. He is almost begging, he realises. 'I get up and I come to work and I write. Inevitably, I suppose, there's a certain amount of . . .' He rolls his fingers in the air.

'Of what?'

'Hyperbole,' Tom says. 'There's a certain amount of hyperbole.'

'Hyperbole,' Julia repeats and she grins. She somehow makes the grin look like a grimace.

'This is the *Libertarian*. Our readers have certain expectations. Look,' Tom adds, holding off her response with an open palm. 'Maybe if you spoke to the editor. I mean, she's busy but you never know. I might be able to set something up.'

'What would be the point? To convince her to write another story?'

Tom gives a dry laugh. 'That's kind of what we do here.'

'Forgive me, Mr Clarke, but really I was hoping for more than a paragraph or two that in an hour would be buried in your archive.'

Tom spreads his hands. Julia watches him with an expression of contempt. There is silence for a moment and then she stands.

'You look older,' she says. She starts to gather her things. 'In your photograph, you look older.' She shuts her bag, leaving the clippings on the table. Tom glances at his mugshot. When he looks up again she is already at the door. 'You look wiser too.'

No one speaks. They have been seated individually, in separate rows and away from the aisle, but it seems a needless precaution. The heads Arthur can see protruding from the seats around him do not turn; the pairs of eyes within range of his seem barely focused. He wonders, vaguely, whether his own expression is so blank but he does not reach any conclusion. His thoughts seem to glide. One moment he will fix on the knowledge that he is being taken somewhere, and his gaze will wander in search of some clue as to their destination. The next he will jolt as though from a trance, and be reminded by the stinging in his eyes that really he ought to blink.

He blinks.

In his periods of watchfulness there is not much to see. A seat-back fills the space ahead. It bears an advertisement, for National Express, promising care, convenience, comfort. The window to his right is shaded or painted or covered with something that admits a dim light but prevents Arthur from seeing out. It is scratched, though, at the corner, and Arthur can tell from his fissured view that it is raining;

that they are on a narrow road and travelling at a steady speed; that they are nowhere that anyone will see them. Once in a while the cabin darkens further and there is the sound of overhanging branches clawing at the glass, like the fingers of something just as curious to see in as Arthur is to peer out.

On the coach the rows of seats are offset and across from him there are two fellow passengers more visible than any of the others. They are both men, Arthur thinks at first, but he is mistaken. The one in front, the younger one, is a girl. She might be twenty; she might be a teenager. Her hair has been hacked into an androgynous, careless cut. Her clothes are filthy and the side of her face that Arthur can see is scratched, bruised, swollen. She has barely opened her eyes.

The man, seated in the row behind, is older – fifty-something, sixty – and he looks awake though no more aware. He is dressed in a suit and shirt, no tie, and is unshaven but otherwise presentable. He stares at the advert in front of him and moves his lips, as though soundlessly reciting the words. Care, convenience, comfort. Care, convenience, comfort. He could be praying, Arthur supposes. The prayer and the recital might even have become joined.

He blinks.

The engine noise is a drone. The sound is so constant, so unvarying, that Arthur begins to think it might not be a sound at all but rather the absence of sound. The sound is like silence: this strikes him as funny. He smiles. The smile produces a tingle in his cheeks and along his jaw.

He blinks.

There were two of them, he remembers. They offered him muffins.

He blinks.

Afterwards he saw Julia. He saw Casper. They were all together, at the kitchen table and eating dinner. Or breakfast. There was a large jug of orange juice, sweating on to the table-cloth, so probably it was breakfast. They were not alone, though. There were two men, maybe three, talking at his shoulder, and though they were talking in whispers it was enough to distract him from what Julia was saying. He told the men to hush but he did not turn. He did not see their faces. He just heard their hissing voices and became irritated and Julia became irritated too but at him. She was gesturing for him to drink his orange juice. She seemed to want him to drink it from the jug. He refused. He said it tasted funny. And Casper was laughing, not at him but at something the men were doing, the men behind him who were still whispering and hissing in his ear. And he was saying, ignore them, Cas, just ignore them. If you ignore them they'll go away.

He blinks.

He does not remember getting on the coach. How odd. He is on a coach and his hands are bound. He does not remember his hands being bound either. It is only now that he notices the plastic tie.

He blinks.

They offered him muffins. Right now, apart from the effort of chewing, he could eat a muffin. He thinks perhaps he would choose a chocolate one. He would not take a lemon one. The lemon ones, he suspects, would taste of Windolene.

He blinks.

He said, ignore them, Cas, just ignore them, but Casper kept laughing. He kept laughing.

He blinks.

The engine drones.

He blinks.

Care, convenience, comfort. Care, convenience, comfort.

He blinks.

He blinks.

He blinks.

There is a jolt and he opens his eyes. The engine is shifting gear. They are turning. Arthur checks through the crack of uncovered glass but there is just another narrow road, more rain, the same lack of people, of buildings, of trees now too. He sees grass and he sees mud, extending to a damp-sugar sky.

He looks across from him. The girl with the bruises continues to sleep. Her position is as it was: hands tucked between her skinny thighs, shoulders sagging, chin cushioned by a tight roll of skin. Arthur turns to the older man behind her, expecting him to be praying still, or sleeping like the girl, but when he looks the man is looking back at him.

And then he is not. He turns away. For a moment Arthur continues to stare but then he too returns his gaze to the seat-back in front of him. Care, convenience, comfort. The words overlap and intertwine. He glances again across the aisle but the man has his eyes shut now, as though he has long been dozing.

He should say something. Should he? He wonders what

would happen if he were to say something. Whether he would be able to talk, first of all, and who would be listening if he did. Who would answer, and how.

They are turning again. This time when Arthur looks he sees a wall, low and crumbling. It guides them up an incline and round another corner and then falls behind. The road they join is quieter, smoother than the road they have left but possibly this seems so only because they are slowing. His view is blocked and they are in darkness for a second, two, and then there is light again and open space and Arthur imagines they have passed through an archway. The coach slows further, almost to walking pace, and from below there is the slow grind of tyres on gravel.

They stop.

For a moment the engine idles and the sound, as much felt as heard, is somehow reassuring. Arthur would like it to continue. He knows that when the engine cuts out someone will tell him to move. He is not sure he will be able to, for one thing, but most of all he does not want to. He wants just to sit. He wants the engine not to cut out. He wants just to sit but then the engine cuts out.

A door opens, up ahead. Arthur cannot see it but he hears the hiss. There is no extra light, though, until a curtain is drawn back and then there is. It is not a bright light but it is brighter than he has become used to and Arthur flinches. For the first time the presence of those around him is audible. There are groans, as one might expect from a roomful of sleepers who have been woken in the middle of the night. There is coughing, from several places at once, but most immediately from across the aisle. Arthur checks and it is the girl. She has her eyes closed but both hands across her mouth, as though she were trying to force a cough back inside. Arthur glances at the man behind her. It seems ridiculous but he is wary of once again meeting his eye. He is imprisoned, on a coach with blacked-out windows, his hands cuffed and his senses confounded, but meeting the eye of a stranger – a fellow captive but a stranger above all – would still feel awkward. The man is looking forwards, however: to the front of the coach and the drawn-back curtain. Arthur watches the man for a moment, then follows his gaze.

A figure has appeared in the aisle. Arthur assumes it is a man but it could just as well be a woman because all he can really see is a silhouette. It stands motionless, facing them or towards the front Arthur cannot tell. The figure moves and Arthur strains to see but then the overhead lights flick on and he is once again compelled to look away. When he looks back the figure is gone.

People are standing: in the row nearest to the curtain, the row behind, the row behind that. Tops of heads become shoulders and then torsos and soon everyone at the front of the coach, it seems, is on their feet and shuffling into the aisle. Arthur feels a surge of adrenalin as movement cascades towards him. Where are they all going? Why are they going, when Arthur has heard no instruction? It would be better to wait, wouldn't it, because maybe they are not supposed to be moving, not yet. But then the woman in the seat in front of his rises, and the man in the suit across the aisle, and Arthur is standing before it occurs to him to worry again about whether he is able to. The girl, though. The girl remains seated. Her head is raised and her eyes are open – on one side of her face at least because on the bruised side her eye is a slit – but she does not follow the others. She barely seems to notice the others. Arthur is in the aisle now and inching forwards and as he passes the girl he hesitates. He opens his mouth. Get up, he should say. Excuse me. Hey. As he would if he were on the tube, at Ealing Broadway, when the train is emptying and the guard is already making his way along the platform and turning out the carriage lights. But there is pressure from behind, breath on his neck from the man in the suit, and Arthur moves on without saying anything. And in fact the girl is not the only one. A passenger here, another there: they seem awake, aware, but slump where they sit, as though boneless.

Arthur concentrates on the set of shoulders in front of him. He passes through the curtain. He squints and with a stagger steps from the bus.

When he was eleven years old he kissed a girl for the first time. He had to wait in line, behind Jason Parker and Christian Rafferty but ahead of Brendan Marsh and Stanley Jessop and the boy all the other kids knew as Morbid, who admittedly was only in line because he followed Stanley Jessop like a pet. Samantha Bartlett, when it came to Morbid's turn, made puking noises and shoved him away but Arthur was granted a full six seconds. He knows because Stanley Jessop timed it. And it would have been longer, Arthur is sure, had he known what to do with his tongue. He did not, and six seconds was all he got, but still it was a victory of sorts, a milestone even, and it made the excursion to Devonshire Manor almost worthwhile.

It is the same building, Arthur is convinced. But it is only the courtyard that makes him think so: an expanse of pale gravel, walled in but otherwise featureless, which might have been landscaped with coach parties and school kids on field trips in mind. The building itself is at once generic and unique. It is a castle but not one that would repel an army. It looks, rather, as if it has been modelled on a child's drawing and then modified to satisfy the caprices of its owner. There is a rose window above the main door, glassed in hues of red and too small to resemble anything other than a pimple. The staircase that spills from the entrance might be the building's tongue; the oversized windows on the second floor its goggling eyes. There are crenellated towers at each corner of the main wall, protruding like splintered horns. The face the building presents is stark enough to be imposing but it is faintly ridiculous too. It leers, mocking those who would regard it and heedless of what they might think.

'Walk!'

Arthur looks for the source of the voice.

'I said, walk!'

Before he can locate it, the voice finds him.

'Get in line! Follow the man in front!'

There is a face in his, a hand between his shoulders. It shoves him and he stumbles and he falls before he can catch himself. His hands, still bound, land on gravel; his knees too. There is pain but he barely has time to register it before he is being hauled to his feet and shoved forwards once again but this time

and long division would be unbearable, this is harder. Because he knows the answer. He already knows the answer. Which means he cannot work it out; he cannot start from the beginning and reckon forwards. He has to delve back, when his memory is a fog and his sense of where to look is anyway—

There is no context. That is the clue. There is no context because they have never met. The face is just that to him. It is the face they showed him; the face in the photograph. It is the face of the man who put him here.

Already she has the phone in her hand. 'Tom? Are we done?'

'What? Yes.' Tom stands. He picks up his notepad. He puts the plastic lid back on his cup of coffee and scrunches the empty sugar packet that lies next to it. He looks at Katherine, who is frowning at surnames beginning with D. He sits back down.

Katherine lifts her head.

'There was something else,' Tom says. 'It's nothing, probably, but I just thought . . . I mean, while we're talking . . .'

'I've got a dozen calls to return, Tom. What is it?' Katherine does not replace the receiver but reaches and cuts off the dial tone with a finger.

Tom slides his coffee cup further on to Katherine's desk. 'Someone came to see me this morning. A woman. She was looking for her husband and she wanted help.'

'We're the media, Tom. We're not the local constabulary.'

'No. Quite. That's why she came here.'

'Tom.' His boss says his name the way his mother used to.

'It's the police who have him. He was arrested and they won't let her see him.'

'What did he do?'

'Nothing. She says he did nothing.'

Katherine gives him a look. Her arm is still outstretched; the receiver is still in her hand.

'The man's a dentist. And they arrested him under Unified Security.'

Katherine sighs. She sets the receiver in its cradle. 'They can do that. They can hold you under Unified Security for failing to pay a parking ticket.'

'I know. That's my point.'

'I did wonder whether you had one.'

Tom shuffles forwards in his chair. 'There's a film. A neighbour was videoing some kids and she got the arrest on tape.'

'And? What happens in the film?'

Tom frowns. 'What do you mean? He gets arrested. They arrest him.'

'They arrest him. That's it.'

'They don't kick the shit out of him, if that's what you mean. At least, I don't think they do. I haven't actually seen it.'

Katherine holds up a hand. She shuts her eyes, opens them again. 'Can this wait, Tom? Is it essential that we talk about this now?'

'No. Of course not.' Once more Tom stands. 'I don't see why it can't wait.'

Katherine smiles with her lips pressed tight. She reaches for the phone.

'Except,' says Tom, turning back on his way towards the door, 'we have some time before the evening news cycle, right?

If I were to knock something together, we could squeeze a head-line and a standfirst on the home page?'

Katherine lets her hand drop. She smiles again, at the desk and then up at Tom.

'And a picture. A still from the film, maybe, which could link to the mpeg.'

'On the home page,' says his boss. 'A headline and a stand-first and a still from the film.'

'Not as a main story, obviously. If we're pushed for space, we could run it below the fold.'

For a moment Katherine does not react. She exhales, then turns to her screen and brings up the *Libertarian* home page. 'Okay,' she says and she nods. 'Okay, Tom. You win.'

'Really?' Tom takes a step towards her desk.

'Sure. Why not? What we'll do is, we'll drop the lead on the Middle East. I mean, it's the same old shit, right? Israel, Palestine; Palestine, Israel. Everyone knows it's a waste of breath.'

Tom looks to his feet.

'And this banner ad. It's sitting right where you'd have me put the still from your Zapruder sequence. That's fine though,' Katherine says, waving down Tom as he is about to speak. 'We'll just kill it. It's only a grand or two and it's not like we're run-ning a business. I'll tell Apple we'll put it back up next week. It's timed for a launch but they won't mind.'

'Katherine—'

'The archive. We'll stick it on the stories in the archive.'

'All I was saying was—'

'It's fine, Tom, really – it'll work just as well.'

Katherine falls silent but Tom does not speak. He has a feeling she is waiting for him to say something in order that she might interrupt.

'I only thought—' Tom says, after a moment.

'Is she pretty?' says Katherine, interrupting.

'What? Who? No. What?'

'This woman who came to see you. Is she pretty?'

'She's married! And anyway that's not the reason—'

'You have a history, Tom.'

'I'm suggesting it because it's a story!'

Katherine looks to the ceiling, then back at him. 'It's not a story, Tom. There is no story.'

'Of course there's a story! A man disappears. The police admit arresting him only after being caught on film. They hold him without charge, without informing his relatives, without – and this goes without saying – giving him access to a solicitor. How is that not a story?'

'It's old news. It's the way of things now.'

'Right. And this is the *Libertarian*. I mean, this is the *Libertarian*, right?' Tom makes a show of looking around the room. 'I didn't get off in Wapping by mistake?'

'We've made our position clear, Tom. You, very eloquently, have made our position clear.'

'So that's it? We write a column or two, vent some steam, then shrug our shoulders and move on? That's not us, Katherine. That sort of thing: it's the reason you left the *Sunday Times*. It's the reason you set up this website in the first place.'

'We pick our battles,' says Katherine. 'No,' she adds. '*I* do. *I* pick our battles. And we're not fighting this one. Not on the say-so of a pretty girl who knows how to spot a sucker and a home-made video showing the police acting to the letter of the law.'

'An innocent man is in prison, Katherine. And even if he's not innocent—'

'There!' Katherine stands. 'There it is! That's exactly what I'm saying. You don't know if he's innocent. You don't even know what he's supposed to have done.'

'That's because the police haven't told—'

'You haven't seen the film, Tom! You're asking me to run a film you haven't even seen! Just think about that for a moment.'

Tom has his hands on his hips. Katherine has her weight on her palms and her eyebrows raised. She waits.

'I'll get a copy,' says Tom.

Katherine says nothing.

'And I'll do some digging. I'll talk to Julia again. The woman who came to see me.'

'I don't know, Tom,' says Katherine finally. A corner of her mouth curls upwards. 'That sounds an awful lot like actual research.'

Tom swallows. 'Yeah well. I suppose it had to happen eventually.'

A silence follows. Tom is not sure whether to fill it.

'Listen, Tom,' says Katherine. She sits. 'I meant what I said. About picking our battles. Our readers trust us but only so far. If we start crying wolf every time we catch the scent, soon enough there'll be no one to listen.'

Tom clears his throat.

'Don't waste your time on this, Tom. Please.'

Tom reaches to collect his coffee cup from Katherine's desk. 'I understand,' he says. 'I do.'

'Good,' says Katherine. 'Now,' she says and she picks up the phone. 'Are we done?'

He does not know why they come here. The drinks are over-priced and watered down. There is never anywhere to sit except at the one table everyone else ignores, so close to the toilets it might as well be housed in a cubicle. The staff are rude and slow and incompetent, and the food – if they get drunk enough to order any – tastes of month-old frying oil. But it is close by. That is the reason they come here. An inability to venture more than twenty-five yards from the lobby is the reason they, and the architects from the floor below, and the accountants in the offices above, waste their evenings drinking piss at the Florist.

'Where are the flowers?' says Josh from the seat opposite. He is talking to Tom but Tom ignores him. He has his hands round his pint of Foster's and his eyes on the dwindling head.

'What flowers?' says Alisha.

'It should have flowers,' says Josh, turning. 'Shouldn't it? On the tables. On the bar at least. A freesia here and there. A daffodil.'

There is a tap against Tom's knee. He does not need to look to know that Gilbert, seated to his left, is trying to pass him something under the table. He shakes his head.

'It's called the Florist,' says Alisha. 'It's not called the Flowers.'

'Okay,' says Josh. 'So where's the florist? If you see him, remind him what it is he does for a living.'

Alisha just sips her vodka-tonic.

'It could be a woman,' says Amy. 'The florist. You said he but it could be a she.'

Josh is about to reply but Gilbert interrupts with a laugh. He always begins his jokes with a laugh. 'It would explain the lack of flowers,' he says and he grins. 'Right? It would explain why she forgot the flowers.'

Only Amy bothers to respond. 'What?'

Gilbert is still grinning. 'It would explain—'

'No, I heard what you said, Gilbert. It was very funny. Sophisticated too. Bigoted and misogynistic but really quite sophisticated. Well done.'

Gilbert sniffs. He wipes at his nose. He glances around the table but the others avoid his eye.

There are five of them. The usual five. They are all in their mid to late twenties but earn their rent and beer money in different departments. Gilbert and Alisha are in sales; Josh does something involving technology that only he and Katherine seem to understand. Tom and Amy are the only journalists in the group, which means, as far as they are concerned, that they work the hardest for the least reward. Generally they are still in the office when the other three have already logged off – except on Wednesdays, when only breaking news of a national disaster will keep Tom and Amy from joining their friends after hours at the Florist. Although even amid a national disaster, they have been known to head out with their laptops.

Free wi-fi: that is the other reason they come here.

Gilbert is tapping him again, more obviously this time, and frowning at Tom when once more he shakes his head. 'What's up with you?' Gilbert says, forgetting himself and his fear, too, that a bouncer – or Amy – will catch them with a wrap of coke. It is early, though; Gilbert is two or three lines from noticeably gurning and probably Amy assumes he is only asking from curiosity at Tom's sullenness. She picks up the theme.

'He's sulking,' she says. 'Aren't you, Tom?'

'Shut up, Amy.'

'He is,' she says. 'He's sulking because Katherine wouldn't run his story.'

'What story?' says Josh.

'Amy,' Tom warns but the conversation is already beyond his control.

'He won't say.' Amy grins at Tom. 'But it's something to do with a size-eight blonde he can't stop thinking about.'

'Seriously, Amy.'

'I didn't know you liked blondes.' This from Gilbert. He is leering.

'What? I don't. I'm going to the bar,' Tom says but when he looks at the table he realises no one is ready yet for another drink. He has barely started his own.

'He's blushing,' says Alisha. 'That's so sweet.'

'What does she look like?' says Gilbert, all teeth. Josh leans into the table.

Tom shakes his head. He slides his pint away and drops his hands into his lap. He turns away.

'He's sulking!' says Amy. 'He's genuinely sulking!' She is goading him. He knows she is goading him.

'Come on, Tom,' says Gilbert. 'What does she look like?'

'Amy,' says Josh. 'What does she look like?'

'Blonde,' says Amy. 'Skinny. Too skinny, really,' she adds, turning to Alisha. 'And I'm fairly sure her hair was bleached. Pretty though,' she says, shrugging and looking again at Josh. 'Oh, and she's exotic. She's from Massachusetts.' She smirks. 'Tom took her for a private interview.'

'Oh yeah?' says Josh.

'She's married,' Tom says. He cannot stop himself. 'She's fucking married.'

'So?' says Gilbert and Alisha thumps him.

'Thwarted love,' says Josh, nodding. 'That would explain it.'

'Explain what? I'm not sulking!'

'You are,' says Amy. 'You're sulking right now.'

'I'm not. I'm not sulking. I'm thinking. I'm allowed to sit and think, aren't I?'

Amy shakes her head.

''Fraid not,' says Josh. 'Not under this government.'

'Not since Unified Security,' says Amy and Josh nods.

'I'll just sit then,' says Tom. 'How about you let me just sit?'

Amy winces. She sucks air between her teeth. 'What do you think, Josh?'

'It all depends where,' he says. 'And how. You wouldn't want your sitting to be construed as some form of non-sanctioned protest.'

Alisha laughs. Tom would too, ordinarily, but not today. Instead he falls silent. He returns his attention to the glass in front of him and waits for Amy to say something more.

She does not. In deference to his mood, perhaps, she changes the subject. The conversation turns to plans for the weekend but Tom finds this no less irritating. They leave him alone, though, and that is something, until Gilbert starts once again to tap at his leg.

This time Tom stands. 'For fuck's sake, Gilbert.'

Gilbert attempts a meaningful look. 'I was just—'

'I don't want any. Okay? I don't want any fucking cocaine!'

Gilbert shrivels in his seat and Amy glares and Tom is angrier for having snapped. He curses. He picks up his coat.

'Where are you going?' says Josh. 'Tom?'

Home, he is about to reply. He is about to say home but he stops himself.

He watches from the window in the darkening room. There are lights on only in the northern wing and the impression Graves has is that the building has its back turned; that he observes it unnoticed. Or that it knows he is there but acts as though it does not: an errant child that makes an outward show of obedience but conceals more despicable plans within.

The inmates will be eating. The lights are from the accommodation wing and, directly below, the canteen. The budget is tight and the food is not fancy but it is nutritious. Low fat, limited sugar, rich in vitamins and protein. Fibre too. Fibre is important. It is astonishing the institutions he has visited where diet is ignored, where digestion is ignored. It is the simplest, and about the cheapest, remedy Graves knows for aggressive behaviour: satisfy a man's stomach, keep his bowel movements regular. Like these teenagers causing trouble at school. Look to the parents, yes. Improve teaching standards, certainly. But think about what these children eat, first and foremost. If they do not eat what they should, they cannot concentrate. If they cannot concentrate, they become bored. If they become bored, they look for entertainment elsewhere, and that is when trouble manifests itself. It is common sense, plain and simple.

Although he is one to talk. His own dinner – rubberised vegetables and some kind of flesh topped with cardboard cut to look like pastry – sits where he left it, in its tin on a plate, balanced on the arm of the sofa. His fork protrudes like something reaching from a grave. Other than three mouthfuls, he has not eaten since breakfast. He should be hungry. He is hungry, probably, but not for the food he has in the cottage. Which is what? Three more pies and a box of All-Bran, as well as half a packet of rich-tea biscuits in the cupboard under the kitchen sink.

Ordinarily he would have eaten at the facility – in his office or with the other staff. Today, though, he wanted to read, away from the distractions of other work. He wanted to make a call, more importantly, away from anyone who might hear. He should have stayed at the facility. Jenkins was not available; only his assistant, who promised Graves the minister would call him back. Presently was the term the assistant used, which Graves took to indicate a matter of minutes. Two hours later, he is still waiting, unable to concentrate on reading and feeling sick from the odour of his festering meal.

He turns from the window and collects his plate. On his way into the kitchen he switches on the overhead light – the only light in the room and as yet without a lampshade – but rather than improve matters, the bulb casts the room and its bare walls in a jaundiced haze. The monitor wired to the computer emits a more decisive glow.

In the kitchen the light is better. There is a strip light: far too big for such a narrow space but at least Graves can see without squinting. He slides the pie, tin and all, on to the centre pages of a week-old *Times* and wraps the newspaper around it. He opens the bin and is about to drop in the bundle but then remembers that the bin is not lined. There is a carrier bag, in the cupboard next to the packet of biscuits, and Graves uses this instead. He ties the handles and looks again at the bin but thinks about the smell and decides to leave the pie on the porch instead. But then he thinks about foxes from the woods, wolves too, even though the thought is ridiculous, and he sets down the bag beside his shop-clean hiking boots on the doormat.

The light fitting hums. He did not notice before but, returning to the lounge, there is an audible fizz. Given the likely state of the wiring in the cottage, the sound is not comforting. Graves flicks the switch again, so that the only light now comes from the kitchen and from his computer. For the time being he needs to see his screen and nothing more. Later he will slide a dining chair into the kitchen and read there. Unless he just goes to bed. He has not slept well recently and really he should try to catch up. Although he knows that his chances of doing so are poor. He will fall asleep easily enough; he always does. But then he will wake: two hours later, three if he is lucky. The earlier he goes to bed, the longer the night will seem.

He has an email from his daughter. The subject is 'Well?!?', which makes Graves apprehensive about opening it. He double clicks but too slowly. He tries again and the email bursts and fills the screen.

Well?!? it reads. *Were you going to tell me??*

Just that.

He did not think. That is, he would have told her, of course he would, but the point was he could not tell anyone. He did not think it would hurt, leaving it for a couple of weeks, just until things settled. Although it has been well over a month now, he realises. Almost two. Which actually proves his point because clearly she has only just noticed he is gone.

He hits reply.

Darling,

He hits backspace.

Rachel,

How are things? I hope the job is going well. And Nick – I hope you are both happy and enjoying life in the city. Please send him my love.

He hits backspace.

my regards.

I am sorry that I could not see you before I left. Something came up in a hurry and I had no time, really, except to pack and catch a train. I meant to call, but

But. But what?

but I know how busy you are and I didn't want

He hits backspace.

but there were a million and one things to do here and

He hits backspace.

but I forgot. I am sorry.

There is not much I can tell you except that I have accepted a new post. Really, that is all I am allowed to tell you. I cannot say where I am, or why I am here, and I cannot give you a number by which to reach me. Email is best for the time being, so do please reply and tell me how you are.

SIMON LELIC

*I am perfectly well myself, so please do not worry. And I am
sleeping much better, before you ask, which is one benefit I suppose of working such long hours.*

Take care, darli—

He hits backspace but then re-types.

Take care, darling. Please write.

Dad

He reads through his email and runs a spellcheck. He hovers
the cursor over send. He clicks and the email disappears and
the screen returns to his inbox, empty now of unread mail.

He should have seen her before he left. He wrote that he
forgot but the truth is he allowed himself to. Because there
was time. He could have made time. But had he seen her
before he left she would have asked him where he was going
and he would not have been able to answer – not in a manner
that would have satisfied Rachel. He could not have been
honest, for one thing. And even if he were, she would not have
understood. She would not have accepted that some things –
like war, for instance, or politics or capitalism – are necessary
evils. She would have prodded at the knots in his conscience
and he would have bridled and probably he would have said
something that would have damaged their relationship when,
over the years, he has allowed it to become damaged enough.

He was afraid, then. Is that the truth also? He is fifty-five
years old; he has run maximum security gaols full of rapists
and murderers and prison guards too, many of whom are no
less sadistic than their wards; he has faced riots and strikes
and public inquiries; he has been spat at, strangled, stabbed.
He has done all of this and yet he is afraid to confront his only

58

daughter, a woman – a girl, really – half his size and age because of the questions she might ask. Because, more to the point, of the answers she might compel him to consider.

He opens the email he has sent her. It is evasive and for-mulaic and he wishes he had not written it. He reads it again. He is halfway through when he notices an envelope has appeared beside the clock at the bottom of his screen. He clicks back to his inbox and sees his daughter's name against a new message. She is online. She is sitting at her computer, which means she is sitting beside her telephone. She is aware, more to the point, that he is beside his. What excuse does he have for not calling right now?

He opens her answer.

Are you a spy now??

You don't have to tell me where you are. It would have been nice to know that you were going, that's all. It feels like ages since I saw you. Since I spoke to you, in fact. It's my fault too – I'm not blaming you.

Anyway.

Call me.

020 7403 3888

x

PS You can't fool me. Try Nytol. They make a herbal one. What can it hurt??

He knows the number. She has included it as though he did not already have it. Is that a rebuke? It feels like a rebuke but maybe she is offering him an excuse. That it is so hard to tell reminds him how difficult he finds it to read her. He looks at the phone beside his keyboard, then once more at his daughter's number. He re-reads her email. He looks again at the telephone and he thinks maybe he will pick it up but then it rings.

What will I say? he thinks. What will I say to her?

But it could not possibly be his daughter calling.

He reaches. 'Henry Graves,' he says into the mouthpiece.

'Graves.' It is Jenkins, of course. 'What is it?' the minister says. 'I haven't got long. I'm due at a reception for the prime minister of . . . Christ. The prime minister of . . . of . . . Simpkins. Simpkins!' Graves holds the phone away as the minister hollers for his aide. He hears a palm muzzle the receiver at the other end of the line and the muffled bass of the minister's voice. Then it is booming once again into his own ear. 'Of Slovenia. Part of old Czechoslovakia. Wait a minute. That's Slovakia. What the hell was Slovenia a part of?'

'I believe it was Yugoslavia, minister,' Graves says but Jenkins is already yelling once more for his aide.

'Yugoslavia,' he says, returning to the phone. 'Slovenia was part of Yugoslavia. Not that it matters to anyone who doesn't live there. But get to the point, Graves. What do you want? Has something happened?'

'No, minister. Nothing untoward.'

'The blue one, Simpkins. Not that one. You'll have people thinking I'm a socialist.'

'I only wanted to ask you, minister, about some of the paperwork we've received. Relating to some of the inmates.'

'I said *blue*, Simpkins. Are you colour-blind, man, or just obtuse? What paperwork, Graves? What about it?'

'They have been tested, sir.'

'Who? The prisoners? Of course they've been tested. Why

wouldn't they have been tested? Simpkins. Simpkins! Here. Look here. This is blue. This, over here: this is purple. I want the blue one. Yes, that one. The blue one, yes. Hallelujah.'

'It's not—'

'Now that you've mastered your colours, maybe tomorrow we'll start on your ABC.'

'It's not that, minister. It's the results that concern me.'

'What? What about the results? You've been briefed, surely. You know the risks . . .'

'Forgive me, minister. I'm not being clear. The results: some of them appear to be negative.'

Simpkins is talking in the background but he stops midsentence, as though Jenkins has signalled for silence. 'And?' says the minister. His voice seems suddenly closer.

'And,' says Graves. 'And, well. And I was wondering, I suppose . . . I mean, if the results are showing as negative . . .'

'They are not positive.'

'That's correct, minister. For twelve people in the first batch and six in the second, the results are showing as—'

'They are not positive, Graves. It is not the same as being negative.'

Graves hesitates. He has the paperwork in a pile on his desk and he opens one of the folders. 'It says negative, minister. I have the paperwork right here and—'

'You understand the distinction, I assume? Regardless of what the paperwork says, you understand the distinction?'

'What? Yes. I suppose so.'

'Because the testing: it is not infallible. For one thing, there is a whatdoyoucallit. What did they call it? A window period.'

'But I thought—'

'This is something new, Graves.'

'Yes, minister.'

'And every one of these men and women has had contact. Contact is the common factor here.'

'Of course, minister.'

'We cannot afford to take risks, Graves. You understand that, don't you? You understand the risks?'

'I do, minister. I was only wondering . . . With the people who have shown up negative . . . I assume at some point they will be re-tested?'

The palm again, across the mouthpiece of Jenkins's phone. Graves waits. There is a mumbled exchange that he does not catch, before Jenkins returns with a rattle of phlegm.

'Has Silk arrived yet?' says the minister.

The name means nothing to Graves. 'Silk? I'm not sure I . . .'

'Dr Silk,' says Jenkins. 'Is he there yet?'

'No,' says Graves. 'Although I don't believe we've been expecting a Dr—'

'Expect him, Graves. Talk to Silk about the testing.'

'Yes, minister. I'll do that. Dr Silk, you say? May I ask—'

'Is that all, Graves? I wouldn't want to miss the champagne.'

'Of course not, minister. That's all. Thank you for your—'

The line goes dead.

Graves sits with the receiver in his hand. He only sets the phone on the hook when the tone on the line changes and nudges him from his daze. His hand reaches to his forehead and slides into a pinch across the bridge of his nose. Really, he should have spent his evening at the facility.

He stands and walks again to the window. The building atop the hill is hardly visible now so he continues past. He enters the kitchen but the light is too bright; his reflection in the glass above the sink too clear a picture of himself: pallid skin, marbled eyes, black hair mired in the grey. He turns from the sight of him and drifts back towards the lounge.

Bed, then. What else to do but go to bed?

He checks his watch. It is not yet half past eight. Which means, if he is lucky, he will sleep until twelve.

He collects his glasses and a memoir he has been trying to start and carries them through to the room in which he sleeps. It is the spare room really but the main bedroom is large and damp and cold. The room he has chosen fits a single bed and a chest of drawers and a rail to hang his suits, which is all the space he needs. He sets his book on the bed and changes without haste into his pyjamas.

He is brushing his teeth in the kitchen sink – the bathroom, situated beyond the kitchen, is colder still than the main bedroom – when the telephone rings once again. Graves spits and wipes his mouth but by the time he reaches his desk and lifts the receiver, the caller has already hung up. Seconds later, Graves's mobile lights up. It quakes and begins to chime in its spot beside the keyboard. Before the ringtone reaches its second bar, Graves has answered the call. 'John. Is that you? What is it?'

'We've got a problem, Henry,' says Burrows. 'You'd better get up here.'

'What do you mean? What kind of problem?'

'There's a . . . a disturbance. You should get up here, Henry. Right away.'

She prods at the cake as though it were something dead. The icing topples in a hunk, exposing a slab of stale sponge beneath. Julia pushes the icing one way on the plate, then back again, then sets down her fork alongside it. She slides the plate to the centre of the table.

'That bad?' Tom says.

'I'm not hungry, that's all.'

'Have you had dinner yet? You really should eat something.' It strikes Tom right away how ridiculous he must sound saying it. But Julia gives him a look, then looks away, and Tom can tell that in fact she agrees with him. Because probably she has not eaten. Certainly she looks as if she has not slept. She has a black coffee laced with sugar and the manner of someone who has already had too much of both today.

'It's a nice place,' Tom says, glancing around the cafe. 'Quirky.' There are prints of Italian-American movie stars on the walls, mixed with signed football shirts in patterns and colour combinations Tom has only ever seen on late-night cable sports shows. There is an old woman with a dog and a bowl of soup in one corner and a couple sharing pizza in another and seven or eight foreign students crushed around a table meant for two in between. The owner, a fat man with more hair on his knuckles than on his crown, watches the students from behind the counter, aggrieved, clearly, that only two have ordered drinks.

'It's just a cafe. It was the only place near the tube still serving coffee.'

'No, I know. But it's, you know . . .'

Julia dismisses what he is saying with a shake of her head. 'You said you had something to tell me.'

'I do.'

'So? Tell me.'

Tom is unsure how to begin. Because it is not the news she is hoping for: that is part of it. Also, because it is not, in the traditional sense, news at all. 'You have to read between the lines,' he says. 'Just to warn you.' Possibly, too, he may have led her to expect more. In retrospect, there is definitely that possibility.

'I'm tired, Tom. I'm not in the mood for riddles.'

Tom slides his cup forwards an inch and leans in. 'I spoke to my boss,' he says. 'Katherine Fry. She said we couldn't help. The site, I mean. She told me we didn't have enough for a story.'

'You told me that, Tom. You said on the phone.'

'Right. But after that, I thought: what the hell. So I spoke to a few contacts, called in a few favours.' He likes the sound of that: the what the hell and also the idea that people – prominent people – owe him favours.

Julia does not seem impressed. She sits impassive, impatient.

'Anyway,' says Tom. 'There's a bloke I know in the Met. He's an important bloke. Superintendent level.'

'And? What did he say?'

Tom reaches for the spoon beside his coffee. 'Nothing,' he says. 'He said nothing.' He glances to gauge her reaction but her expression offers no clue. She is waiting for whatever comes next.

'Next,' says Tom, 'I spoke to a guy in the Home Office. A civil servant. This guy, he likes to brief. I pay him – the website does – and he's got tastes, shall we say, that require investment. So usually I pay him, assuming he comes up with something I can use.'

'Did he?' Julia says, in a tone that suggests she already knows the answer.

Tom meets her eye. 'No. He didn't. But listen,' he adds. 'These are my best sources, Julia. These are the *Libertarian*'s best sources.'

Julia does not seem encouraged. 'That's good, is it? The fact that your best sources haven't told us anything?'

'But they have!' Tom is grinning. He checks around, conscious that his words will have carried. 'The fact that they didn't say anything: it tells us something.'

'Like what, for instance?'

'Well,' says Tom. His smile fades. 'I don't know exactly. But I had assumed your husband's was a routine arrest—'

'They arrested him under anti-terrorism legislation. How could you possibly have considered that routine?'

'But that's my point! These days it is routine. Or it can be, at least in terms of how information is fed to the press.' Tom shakes his head. 'Look,' he says, 'my point is, the Met, the Home Office, the entire law-and-order apparatus: they rely on us to report these things. They leak information because they want us to have it.'

'I'm not following, Tom.'

'They'll tell us why. If we notice an arrest, and we ask about it, ninety-nine times in a hundred they'll give us something we can write well before any charges have been made. Because if we're asking, it's in the public domain. If it's in the public domain, they have to guard against any form of backlash.'

'By saying what exactly?'

Tom shrugs. 'If it's a terrorist they're holding, they might say the arrest was made in conjunction with the ISI and leave us to fill in the blanks – just as an example. If they don't give us something, they know we'll cry human rights.'

'So why not just come out with it? If they're effectively telling you anyway . . .'

'It's part of the game. They can't just come out with it, not until they press charges. If they press charges, they are obliged to make a case, which very possibly they will lose. Besides,' Tom adds, 'they don't need to. They tell us what they want us to know and we make the case for them. We legitimise their actions, justify the time for which these people can be held by making them seem more dangerous, sometimes, than they really are.' Tom reaches for his coffee spoon again, twirls it clumsily between his fingers. 'We insinuate and incriminate and incite and the more we do the better the police look.'

'And you do this?' Julia's expression is one of disgust. 'You, your website. Despite everything you've written, you still do this?'

'Not us so much but . . . I'm talking about the press in general. The media in general. It's just how things work.'

'You mean it sells papers. It gets traffic.'

Tom shrugs again. 'I suppose.'

Julia turns away. Tom watches her for a moment, then drops his gaze. At the sound of raised voices, he lifts his head. There is an argument developing between the cafe owner and the group of students. One of the girls wants the key to the toilet but she is not one of those who has bought a drink. The cafe owner has his arms folded, the girl her palm outstretched. Her friend, a boy, intervenes, by offering the girl a sip of his Coke. She drinks and smiles triumphantly and once more holds out her hand. The cafe owner continues to refuse, however, which sparks a blaze of abuse from the rest of the group. Tom does not understand German, or any language except English, but there are certain words he has picked up somewhere and the students are using these now. The cafe owner responds in Italian and Tom is able to follow the exchange quite readily. In the furthest corner of the cafe, the dog begins to bark, and the old woman strains to keep it under control. Only the couple in the corner nearest seem undisturbed: they do not turn to watch but remain huddled and holding hands. In the end the students leave, in a clamour of scraping chairs.

Tom faces Julia and rolls his eyes. Julia seems hardly to have noticed the commotion.

'Don't think I'm not grateful, Tom,' she says. 'When I say what I'm about to say, don't think I'm not grateful. Because I am, I truly am, but I'm tired too and I'm frustrated and I'm worried about Arthur more than anything.'

'It's okay. I understand.'

'But your news,' says Julia, her tone colder. 'Your news,

basically, is that you have none. Right? And that you have none somehow implies that things are worse than I thought they were. But,' she adds, interrupting Tom as he is about to speak, 'you're not sure how much worse.' She tips her head. 'Is that fair?'

'Well, I suppose you could put it like that . . .'

'Or,' says Julia, 'and forgive me again if this sounds rude, but is it possible that your sources . . . I mean, they're good sources and they're senior people and for whatever reason – and I don't want to think about why – but for whatever reason they owe you a favour. But could it be that they simply don't know why my husband was arrested?'

'Absolutely,' says Tom, leaning in again. 'But what I'm saying is, these people are senior enough that they should have been able to find out. That they couldn't, or that they told me they couldn't . . .'

'You still think it means something.'

'I do,' says Tom. 'It's something different, Julia. I really think this is something different.'

With the students gone, the cafe is quiet. The dog is sleeping and its owner digesting and the lovers giggle once in a while but barely speak. There is a television behind the counter, tuned to Eurosport and with the volume set low. Tom's eyes drift to the screen but only because he is looking anywhere now but directly at Julia. She is staring at the ceiling, water pooling in her eyes but yet to spill. She blinks, though, and a tear runs free.

'I'm not upset,' she says, when Tom shifts. 'I mean, I am but that's not why I'm crying.' She turns to face him. 'I'm pissed off,

Tom. I'm crying because I'm fucking pissed off.' She says it in a hiss but with evident relish and Tom cannot help but smile.

'You've a right to be. Christ, Julia. I'm pissed off and I barely know you. I've never even met your husband.'

Julia drags the heel of a hand across each cheek and clears her throat. 'Thank you. You've done what I asked you to. You didn't have to and I'm grateful that you did.' She unhooks her bag from the back of her chair and checks its contents. 'I'm sorry if I was rude to you,' she adds, talking to her handbag now. She looks up. 'You didn't deserve it.'

'Wait,' says Tom. 'You're not leaving?'

'We've finished.' Julia stands and picks up her coat. 'Haven't we?'

Tom coughs out a laugh. 'Hardly. I'd say we were just getting started.'

Now Julia laughs. 'Tom. You've done what you can. I appreciate it, I really do. But I can't ask you to—'

'You don't need to ask.'

Julia sits again, on the edge of her chair. She smiles, with genuine warmth, and it is the first time since they met that Tom feels he is looking at her – that he has been granted a glimpse of *her*. She reaches across the table and takes his hand. 'You're kind,' she says. 'You're just being kind.'

Tom shakes his head. He pulls his hand away. 'That's not it.'

'What then? What else do you think you can do?'

'Keep digging,' Tom says, knowing before he speaks that this is not an answer.

Julia smiles again. 'You have a job, Tom. You have your own problems. I appreciate you wanting to help but—'

'I'm not doing it to help you, Julia.' This does not come out the way Tom intended. 'I mean, I am. Of course I am. But this, whatever this is: it's a story. If it's a story, it *is* my job.'

'Really?' Julia raises an eyebrow. 'And your boss. Katherine, was it? She would agree with you?'

This time Tom does not reply.

'I have to go,' says Julia and again she stands.

'You're still going?'

'I have to pick up my son. I told my cousin I'd be there by eight.'

'Your son?' Tom has forgotten that she has a son. 'How old is he? What's his name?'

'He's three. Almost four. His name's Casper.'

'Like the ghost,' says Tom, before he can stop himself.

Julia's lips tighten. 'Like my grandfather.' She glances at the clock on the wall. 'I have to go.'

Tom slides back his chair. 'I'll walk with you.'

Julia looks like she is about to protest but does not. 'Fine. Let's go.' She moves towards the door and Tom follows. Julia is already on the pavement when Tom turns back.

'Wait,' he says. 'My coat.' He returns to their table to collect it. It is on his chair and he pulls it free, then hurries again towards the door. On the step he turns once more, to check whether he has forgotten anything else. Except for their abandoned cups and Julia's cake, their table is empty. The cafe, in fact, is now deserted, but for the lovers ensconced at their table. Tom glances at them and then away and catches up with Julia outside the door.

'What is it?' she says, noticing Tom's expression.

'What? Nothing. Let's go.'

Julia leads and Tom lags. He looks behind him, towards the couple still visible through the glass of the door. They are giggling again and gazing at each other, which is exactly what they have been doing the entire time. Except for that moment when Tom glanced back; when he checked again that he had left nothing behind. Because for a second – for a fraction of a second really – he was convinced that they were both watching him.

Arthur eats. The food is bland and anaemic but it is the first meal he recalls eating since . . . Since what? A tuna sandwich in the surgery, which he did not finish because the bread had turned soggy. A KitKat, after that, and a cup of coffee. Does that count as a meal? Before that there was breakfast – or did he skip it? Before that was dinner, the night before he was taken wherever he was taken, and dinner was probably something in a plastic tray. So perhaps this is his first proper meal in months, in a year – since he separated from Julia. Drooping vegetables and dry chicken and rice that has been scraped from the bottom of a pan, as well as a hunk of bread so stale it feels toasted and a glass of warm milk, slightly sour. Bland then, anaemic then, but delicious nonetheless.

So Arthur eats. His head dips as his fork lifts, in the way his mother always told him it should not. He starts with the chicken but it takes too long to chew so he scoops the rice instead, unashamedly using his fingers to stop the grains falling from his fork. He swallows too quickly, as though he were drinking, and gulps the milk to flush his throat.

He is conscious that there is someone beside him and across from him and behind him but he has barely looked yet to see who they are. The people from his coach, Arthur assumes, because they eat the way he does: with a sprinter's focus and without exchanging a word. There is no conversation anywhere in the hall, in fact, just the sound from Arthur's table and the one behind of scraping and shovelling and swallowing and the snap, periodically, of plastic cutlery not up to the job. Arthur wonders vaguely why the rest of the room is so quiet. Not all the prisoners can be as hungry as the new arrivals but rather than eating perhaps they are watching; it is the first time, after all, that they have all been assembled. Between mouthfuls, Arthur glances to check. He looks up and he sees and what he sees makes him stop. He lowers his laden fork to his plate.

Disgust. Abhorrence, even. Over the penitent shoulders of the man sat beside him, Arthur has an unobstructed view of the half-dozen tables beyond, of the people – men, for the most part, though a handful of women too – around them, of their faces, their expressions. It is as though they were watching the new arrivals eating something other than food: something that only savages would eat, or animals. Or perhaps it is how they are eating. Perhaps it is the ferocity with which they gorge themselves. The man opposite Arthur is licking his plate. Something has stuck to it and he scrapes at it with his fingernail, his tongue again. Arthur looks back to those watching and though their countenances seem barely to have changed, he has missed something, he realises. He thought it was disgust but it is that and something more. It is shame too.

The people watching are disgusted but also they are ashamed, as though it were not strangers they were watching but themselves.

Arthur slides his plate away. He is famished still but all of a sudden he cannot eat. The man opposite – a youngish man, slim but not skinny, dishevelled like the rest of them but with the look of someone who might usually take care over his appearance – notices and catches Arthur's eye. He regards Arthur warily, gauging him for a moment, then takes hold of Arthur's plate. He pulls it towards him, slowly at first, all the while watching Arthur and tensed for him to react. He might be dragging a discarded bone from the twitching muzzle of a dog. When the man seems reassured that Arthur is not going to protest, he smiles and stacks Arthur's plate on top of his. He picks up the piece of chicken and bites, smiling still, watching Arthur. He takes another bite, then drops his eyes to his second course.

There is a voice from across the hall. Arthur looks for its source and the woman who spoke is easy to spot. Other than the guards along the walls, she is the only person in the room on her feet. The inmates around her are seated as before, their trays untouched and their hands clasped or cupped across their foreheads or under the tables in their laps. Except, that is, for the man across from her. He is jabbing at his plate, loading his fork and hoisting it towards his bulging, undulating cheeks.

'Look around you,' says the woman, glaring at the man eating. She is short and slight but her voice has weight. 'You're the only one eating.'

The man takes another mouthful. 'I'm hungry.' He jabs again, focuses on his tray.

The woman shakes her head. Revulsion creases her eyes and her mouth hangs open as she searches for her voice once again. 'Look.' She points towards Arthur's table. 'Look at the state of them. Look at the state of you.' The new arrivals are dressed in their own clothes still but the others wear a uniform of shirt and trousers: both blue, both ill-fitting. 'It's disgusting,' the woman says. 'You. You're disgusting.'

This time the man looks up. He finishes chewing and dabs at his lips with a baggy sleeve. 'Watch your mouth, love.'

There is muttering from the rest of the table. Eyes narrow and train on the man eating. 'Watch your own,' says someone. 'Leave it out,' says someone else. There is another, slightly older woman seated to the left of the first and she reaches a hand to her younger companion. The man seated to the standing woman's right scrapes his chair back, as though preparing to rise at her side.

'You!'

Heads turn; Arthur's too. There is a guard striding through the aisle towards the woman who is on her feet. As he walks he draws his baton from the holster at his side.

'Sit down! Right now!'

The woman angles herself to face the guard. She remains standing. 'I'm done. I've finished eating this slop.'

'Take your seat! I said, take your—'

The guard closes the gap and seizes the woman's arm but before he can force her down the man across from the woman – the man so intent before on finishing his meal – is standing too. 'Let go of her! Who the fuck do you think you are?'

There is another guard, approaching on the man's side of the table. Like his colleague he has his baton drawn. Unlike his colleague, he has it raised above his shoulder. The woman is struggling and the male prisoner is reaching and before he even notices the threat at his shoulder, before Arthur can register what is about to happen, the guard strikes on a downward arc, catching his victim on the back of the thigh. The prisoner yells and the guard swings again and this time strikes at the point behind the man's knee. The prisoner crumples, falling back and down and against the metal table. He yells again but his yell is cut short by a crack. The guard makes to swing again, at the body that is at his feet now, but he gets no further than lifting his baton. Like those around him, he stares at the man he has struck. He is still staring when a prisoner at the table behind launches himself from his seat and grabs the guard's throat.

Arthur stands. The prisoners around him stand. There is yelling from all areas of the hall, and people moving, and chairs scraping. The guards rush forwards to rescue their colleague and their advance breaks on a wall of blue. A table topples and three, four, five of the prisoners closest dart behind it and beneath it and charge with the table raised towards a guard caught alone against a wall. The guard dives and the table strikes brick. The prisoners try to turn it but they are turning in different directions and one at least gets struck with a baton by an onrushing guard. Something is in the air above him and Arthur ducks. When he looks up, whatever has been thrown has already landed. It has hit someone perhaps because just a few feet away another body is on the ground: a guard's this time, her arm twisted beneath her and her baton adrift. As Arthur looks, a prisoner snatches it up. He pauses, testing the weight of his find, then disappears amid the melee.

They watch. It is all they can do. They are the only ones static: the new arrivals, wondering where on earth they have arrived. But then a guard advances from the wall behind them, dragging with him two colleagues, and points at the man beside Arthur. The man backs away, into Arthur, and Arthur stumbles. He catches his feet on the legs of his chair. The chair tips and Arthur falls but he grabs at the table and somehow hauls himself free. He looks behind him. All those round his table have scattered. The guards are closing though, and closing on him, and Arthur finds himself scurrying the only way open to him: into the midst of the skirmish.

It is mindless. It is fighting for the sake of fighting. Arthur lurches and weaves and no one around seems any surer than he about what they are doing, or why. Even the guards. Especially the guards. They hit and shout as though hitting and shouting were all that mattered. The prisoners too: Arthur sees a cluster of women back to back, spiralling wide-eyed from the fighting, but among the men anger appears the only manifest emotion, the single factor that drives them. It is a state of mind Arthur has witnessed just once before in his lifetime, at the march against the Unified Security Act – an event, several years back, that brought him on to the streets out of curiosity mainly, out of having a Saturday with nothing to do and a flat within walking distance of the protestors' route. With his waterproof and his rucksack and his camera, he followed a crowd larger, so they said later, than the Stop the War March of 2003. The camera ended up in pieces, the rucksack torn from his back. The waterproof became his mask, as he cowered in a doorway from the missiles and the smoke.

Something strikes him. It does not hit him hard and for a moment there is no pain but all of a sudden he cannot see. Whatever it was struck him on his forehead and it is as though the impact has triggered a cascade of tears. It is warm though: whatever blinds him. It is thicker than tears too because he cannot blink it away. He stops and crouches and wipes at his eyes with his palm. When he looks again he can see, long enough to realise that his hands are crimson, but then his vision blurs once more and pain drips from his hairline. He wipes his eyes again and staggers forwards. He collides with something, someone, who shoves him away. He spins and trips and this time he falls. He lands on his knees and one elbow. Someone cries out, right beside him, but when he turns to the voice he realises it was his own. He crawls. He bumps into something again and wipes his eyes and sees an upturned table blocking his way. He stands, or tries to, and clambers over it. A siren is sounding now, a single screeching note drowning the cacophony of voices and piercing Arthur's skull as though it has found a route in through his wound.

'You!'

Arthur slips again, rights himself, flounders on.

'You! Stop!'

The voice is closer, closing.

'On the floor! Right now!'

Arthur drags a sleeve across his eyes and the guard is only a yard or so away from him.

'Get down! I said, get down!'

Blood curtains Arthur's vision but he sees enough to see the baton. He wipes again and he sees the baton rising and he wipes and the baton is falling. He raises his arms above his head. He tries to scamper backwards but there is an obstruction at his heels and without meaning to he sits, on a chair it feels like, and he is sitting on a chair with his arms raised, waiting to be struck.

The baton falls. He feels it fall more than he sees it, or senses it rather, anticipates it. There is a yell, a scream of pain, and Arthur assumes it is his own voice again, that he has been struck and struck numb. He moves, though, and finds he can. He wipes his eyes. He sees the guard but it is the guard's back. He sees the baton rising again but when it falls this time it falls away from him. The yell that follows is not his own. He knows this time it is not his own because he cannot be yelling if he is also sobbing.

Someone grabs him. A hand on his wrist, gripping tight and tugging him back to the place he was fleeing. He resists and breaks free but the hand finds him again, finds his sleeve this time, pinching at the flesh on his arm as it grasps. Still Arthur fights to pull away. Whoever has hold of him is stronger, though, and ready this time for Arthur's resistance. There is a voice but Arthur cannot make out what it is saying. He struggles and claws at the hand on his arm but now there is another hand, under his shoulder, pulling him back, down, and he is falling.

He has fallen. On top of someone, it feels like, because there is movement beneath him. Then Arthur is moving, or being moved, and he is sitting, almost, and leaning against something.

'Here.'

The arms around his body loosen. He feels something soft – a rag perhaps, a balled-up shirt – being pressed against his forehead.

'Here,' the voice repeats. It has to shout to make itself heard. 'Take it. Hold it firm.'

Arthur takes it and uses it to wipe his eyes again.

'Hold it against the wound,' the voice says, almost angrily. The rag is snatched from him and forced against his head. Arthur winces. He takes hold of the rag and presses it above his eyes. He blinks. He looks.

He sees a wall. He sees his own feet and another pair and there is a man beside him, angling his head up and away from Arthur and peering over the upturned table against which they lean. Arthur takes the rag from his head, which turns out to be someone's sleeve, and sees it is heavy with blood. He feels the wound above his eyes begin to leak and returns the rag to his forehead. He turns and sees his companion looking at him.

The man is not old but he is no longer young. He is dark-skinned, with coiled black hair and stubble that is dusted with grey. He looks at Arthur and he grins. He tips his head to the scene behind them. 'Personally,' he says, 'I didn't think the food was that bad.'

Arthur opens his mouth but does not know how to reply.

The man looks at Arthur's clothes. 'Just got here?'

Arthur croaks. 'What?' he manages to say.

'I said, just arrived?' The man checks again over his shoulder. He looks at Arthur. 'Here,' he says, gesturing around him. 'You've just arrived here?'

Arthur nods. He lowers the rag and looks once more at the blood.

'Hold it up,' the man says. He guides Arthur's hand towards his forehead. 'Try to keep your head still too,' he adds but as he speaks something hits the table on the other side and both men duck towards their knees. The man gives a wry smile. 'As still as you can.'

The alarm shuts off. A drone fills the vacuum in Arthur's ears. The effect, too, is that the volume behind them has been turned up: the fighting, the bawling, the clash of baton and bone feels as close, all of a sudden, as it really is.

Arthur's companion, though, seems encouraged. He lifts his head and glances to the ceiling, like a holidaymaker sensing breaks in a heavy sky. He grins again and extends his hand. 'I'm Roach.'

Arthur is holding the rag with his right hand. He reaches awkwardly with his left. 'Arthur.'

'Arthur, is it?' Something else hits their barricade and Roach ducks again, pokes his head around to see. 'Well, Arthur,' he says, turning back. He spreads his palms. 'Welcome to the facility.'

He treads and he treads on something, in something; he lifts his foot and there is rice stuck to his sole by what looks like a glue of pulped vegetables. Graves lowers his foot and drags it across the ground like a bull preparing to charge. When he moves on, the lump beneath his shoe makes it feel like he is walking with a limp. Satisfy a man's stomach: that is what he told himself. There is a chicken breast on the ground in front of him and he nudges it away with his toes.

Burrows is behind him and from the curse Graves hears, the groan, he assumes his assistant has trodden in the same mess he did. He knows it is churlish but he is gratified. It is hardly Burrows's fault but it is someone's fault and for the time being Burrows, as a focus for Graves's ire, will have to do.

The expense: that is what he keeps coming back to. It is not the most important issue but in the role to which he has been appointed he cannot help but worry. Broken chairs, broken tables. Trays, crockery – although the plastic items can perhaps be saved – uniforms for the inmates, for the guards, as well as a light fitting here, a pane of glass in the window there: all will have to be paid for. Not to mention the clean-up. He shudders to think what the cost will be for the clean-up. Something will have to give, that is for certain. The food budget perhaps. This seems appropriate.

'It looks worse than it is,' says Burrows.

Graves glances across his shoulder and his assistant is standing on one leg, poking at the sole of his shoe with a plastic fork. The fork breaks and Burrows wobbles, almost topples. Graves walks on.

'It's all this food everywhere. It'll clean up, though. The tables are fine, look.' Graves turns again and Burrows is setting a table the right way up. 'There,' he says and he pats it and the legs snap, splinter, and the table collapses and almost crushes Burrows's toes. Burrows leaps backwards. He lands and he slips. This time he does fall, as though someone has kicked his heels away, and when he hits the ground something tears: his trousers perhaps. He has torn the seat of his trousers and he is sitting in a puddle of purée and really it should be funny. It would be funny. If this man were not his assistant – his deputy, no less; his second in command – the sight of him sprawled on his backside would, quite possibly, make Graves laugh.

He does not laugh. 'I want updates,' he says. 'Twice a day. And any time in between if there's some change.'

Burrows is back on his feet. He is wiping at his suit as he scampers to catch up. 'On Lambert?'

Lambert. The guard. The man who started this by resorting so readily to his baton and will soon enough be wishing he had not.

'On the inmate in the infirmary. Prior. You can send Lambert to see me just as soon as he can walk. No,' says Graves, stopping. 'I don't want to see him. You see him. First thing. Debrief him, remind him of the Official Secrets Act, then watch as he packs his things. If he can't walk by himself, carry him and drop him on a train. Or in front of one,' he mutters.

'Yes, sir. Although I don't think . . . I mean, the inmate, Prior: I don't think the prognosis is good.'

Graves gives his assistant a look.

'But I'll keep you informed. Of course I will. If there's any improvement in his condition, I'll make sure you're the first to know.'

Graves is at the centre of the hall now. The space is large enough to take thirty tables, a handful more at a squeeze, and the ten or so that were set up were grouped at one end. No longer. The debris is everywhere, the scene a product of three hundred rampaging prisoners, you would think, not seventy. Graves shakes his head. He surveys the hall again, then checks his watch. 'You put the inmates in the courtyard?'

'The ones who were here during the riot. The sickest are still confined to their cells. Do you want me to assemble them too?'

'No, of course not. How long have the rest of them been out there?'

Burrows looks at his own watch. 'Twenty minutes or so.'

'Long enough then.' Graves turns towards the exit.

Burrows is in his way and he scuttles aside. 'You'll need your coat,' he says but Graves ignores him. Graves leads and his assistant follows, across the hall and along the corridor and to the door at the far end that opens on to the courtyard.

It is colder in the night air than he thought. On his way

SIMON LELIC

from the cottage to the facility he barely noticed the temperature, partly, he imagines, because he was walking so quickly,
partly because his mind was on matters more pressing than
the likelihood of an October frost. No matter, though. The
weather will help the inmates to cool off. It will remind them
of their status in this facility; that they cannot expect to behave
as they have and not suffer the repercussions.

Except, as Graves crosses the lighted square and sees the
inmates packed on the floor beside the fountain, he recalls
the distinction he drew when Jenkins visited the facility:
between prisoners and those who are imprisoned. It is a distinction he has been trying to convince himself to disregard
but looking at these people now – the dozen women, in
particular, huddled together to the rear of the sixty or so men
– he cannot help but notice how obviously different they seem
from the criminals with whom he is used to dealing. The people
gathered before him look more like refugees than prison inmates. In the sense that they have been both persecuted and
displaced, that is exactly what they are.

Graves has a speech prepared, one he has used in similar
circumstances before, but all of a sudden it feels inappropriate. Not inappropriate. It feels unjust, rather. Unjustifiable.

'Fetch some blankets,' Graves finds himself saying. Burrows
twitches at his shoulder and Graves turns to face him. 'Bring
them some blankets,' he says again. 'And you.' Graves points to
the nearest guard. 'Remove their bindings.'

The guard opens his mouth and looks to Burrows.

'Sir,' Burrows says. 'I'm not sure—'

'Do as I say.'

The guard moves to obey; Burrows too. The other guards are standing in a cordon around the prisoners and several step out of the circle to help.

Graves watches and waits. He sees the guards in turn watching him as they move from inmate to inmate, surprised no doubt at his show of compassion and suspicious of it too. The blankets arrive and the guards toss them towards the prisoners – at the prisoners, really – and Graves realises as he witnesses this exhibition of spite that it is not the prisoners, nor Burrows, but the guards with whom he is most angry. The guards, and what they represent.

But he cannot let this show. To do so would undermine not only the guards' authority but his above all. The speech, then. He has no choice but to say what he is expected to say.

He faces the inmates. They are seated on the ground before him, cross-legged for the most part now and their shoulders covered by blankets. One or two rub at the marks the plastic ties have left on their wrists; others cradle injured arms, hands, shoulders. The new arrivals, Graves sees, have clustered together just like the women. They are first years summoned to a school-wide dressing down, anxious and uncertain about what comes next.

'Your friend,' Graves begins, 'is being cared for.' He is talking too quietly and he injects some robustness into his tone. 'He is being cared for. That he is injured is unfortunate but what's happened has happened and that's that.' Graves pauses. He has an urge, all of a sudden, to shy away from the prisoners' stares. But, 'That's that,' he repeats. 'That is the end of it. There will not be an investigation and there will not be an

inquiry because the usual rules, at this facility, do not apply.'
He pauses again – for effect, he tells himself. He takes a breath.
'I will repeat that. The usual rules, at this facility, do not apply.
There is no board, no oversight committee. There is just me
and the rules I set. So you will behave, please, as I instruct you
to behave or you will suffer the punishment I choose.'

Please. He has never before said please.

He hurries on. 'Tonight you will not be punished. Your
rations will be curtailed and your privileges will be restricted
but in comparison with what I have licence to do to you, you
are not being punished at all. This,' he says and he straightens his shoulders, 'is a warning. This is your only warning.
I will not go into what will befall you next time because as far
as I am concerned there will be no next time.' He holds up a
finger, a gesture that has rarely felt so obviously part of the
act. 'Again, I repeat,' he says, '*there will be no next time.*' He
emphasises each word in turn and the effort of doing so drains
him.

He falls silent, even though he still has a verse to go. The
speech varies of course but the gist is the same and the next
few lines would serve to give the inmates something to aim for.
Rehabilitation. Training, an education. Early release. Which
does not seem appropriate at all.

He cuts it short. He says, 'You are human beings.' He says,
'Do not demean yourselves by behaving like animals.' Then he
signals to Burrows, who signals to the guards, and the inmates
are ushered to their feet. Graves starts to walk away. He shuts
his eyes and fills his lungs but a voice stops him before he can
savour the feeling of emptying them.

'Why are we here?'

Graves halts. Immediately he realises this is a mistake but it is too late to walk on.

'Why are we here? What are we supposed to have done?'

The man talking stands apart. He is refusing to be led away and there is a guard – one male, one female – on either side of him. The female guard – Thorne, as Graves recalls, Thorne or Thorpe – has her baton drawn. In spite of everything that has happened tonight, she has her baton drawn.

The prisoner waits. Thorne and her colleague too. The entire courtyard is still, expectant. Even Burrows is looking to see how Graves will respond.

'You are here for your own protection,' Graves says. It is the answer he has been authorised to give, the answer he has rehearsed, but it is feeble and he knows it.

'I don't feel protected.' The prisoner seems to have anticipated Graves's reply. 'And the man who hit his head. The man you called our friend. I don't know him so maybe it's not for me to say but I don't imagine he feels protected either. He didn't look like he was being protected.'

Graves noticed this man when he approached the fountain, he realises. Standing, he seems thin, frail; tall but too tall, as though his body were liable to snap. There is strength, though, in the set of his features; a rigidity at odds with his physique. He is someone Graves would ordinarily single out as a man to watch; a man, if necessary, to subdue. Ordinarily, that is what he would do.

'What is your name?'

The prisoner lifts his chin. 'Simmons.'

Graves recalls the file. A photographer, based in Shepherd's Bush.

'Whether you feel protected is not my concern, Mr Simmons. As you do not know what we are protecting you from, I would suggest your judgement is flawed. You are here because it is safer for you to be here than anywhere else. It is safer for others that you are here too.'

'What does that mean?' Simmons steps forwards but the guards haul him back, grip his arms. 'That means nothing. It tells us nothing!' He shrugs to free himself. One of the guards – not Thorne this time but the other one, clearly as mindless as his colleague – seizes his wrist and wrenches it up and between his shoulder blades. Simmons struggles and the guard slides an arm around his neck. Left alone, he would no doubt take pleasure in crushing the prisoner's windpipe. This time Graves cannot hide his irritation. He signals for Simmons to be released. The guard hesitates and then obeys. He shoves Simmons forwards and Simmons stumbles. He coughs, spits, raises a hand to his throat.

'You know what year this is, don't you? You know this isn't the nineteen-thirties?'

'Mr Simmons,' says Graves, 'date and time have nothing to do with this. You are here and that is the end of it. I suggest you come to terms with that fact because there is every chance you will remain here until—'

You die. He is about to say, until you die.

'—until I decide otherwise.' Graves signals to Burrows. 'That is all,' he says, addressing the other inmates now. 'If you are in need of medical attention, make yourselves known. Otherwise . . . Otherwise, get some rest.'

Graves moves quickly away. He hears Burrows behind him, issuing instructions to the guards, and his intention is to be inside before his assistant can catch up. If Burrows had any sense about him, he would recognise this and let Graves go.

'Henry!'

Common sense, then, is not his strong point. That much was clear already.

'Henry, hang on!'

And it is only Henry, Graves is learning, when Burrows wants something or regrets something or feels the need to make amends, as though invoking his boss's Christian name will addle in Graves's mind the nature of their relationship. His assistant is only a young man but he is old enough for Graves to expect better. Better discipline. More respect. Although tonight, it is true, he hardly feels worthy of respect.

'What is it, John?'

'I . . . I owe you an apology,' Burrows says, drawing level. 'I hired the guards. I briefed them. They did not behave properly tonight. They let me down, which means they let you down. Which means that . . . Well. That I let you down too.'

For a moment Graves is unsure how to respond. He is confronted suddenly with the likelihood that he has judged his assistant too harshly and the realisation does nothing to repair his self-regard. 'Thank you, John,' he says. 'Apology accepted. I appreciate you offering it.' Graves hesitates. He nods, then continues on his way.

'You're not angry then?' says Burrows, hurrying to catch up.

Although, it must be said, this constant need for approval is growing a little wearing. 'I'm not angry, John. Not at you.' Graves veers towards the door and Burrows has to drop behind and around him to keep level.

'Can I do anything though? I'll organise the clean-up, shall I?'

Graves stops. Burrows stops too but a fraction too late to avoid bumping into his boss.

'The clean-up?'

Burrows points. 'Of the canteen. I'll get some of the guards, fetch a few mops. It shouldn't take more than a couple of hours.'

'A couple of—' Graves shakes his head. 'Think, John. Think about what it is you are planning to mop up.'

Burrows looks perplexed. 'What do you mean? It's just food. Food and milk and maybe a few drops of—'

Graves watches as understanding dawns. 'There is a procedure, John. When blood is spilled, there is a procedure we need to follow. I wouldn't have thought it necessary to remind you.'

'No. No, of course not.'

'The guards, John. See to them first. If any of them have suffered lacerations, treat them, isolate them and we'll have to see about getting them tested.'

'Yes, Henry. I mean, sir.'

'And while you're at it, perhaps you might have a word with them. Perhaps you might remind them that there are less forcible ways to deal with dissent than clubbing a man senseless with a truncheon.'

Burrows nods. Graves regards him for a moment. On any other occasion he might be tempted to take him to task. Instead he reaches for the door that leads inside. He is about to let it close behind him when he stops again, turns. His assistant is studying the ground at his feet.

'John.'

Burrows looks up. 'Yes, sir?'

'The name Silk. Does it mean anything to you?'

'Silk?'

'Dr Silk. I was on the phone to Jenkins before and he mentioned the name. Told me to expect him.'

'Oh,' says Burrows. 'Yes. That's right. He's arriving Monday, I believe.'

'Monday?' It is Friday. 'You didn't feel the need to mention—' Graves shakes his head. 'Never mind.'

'I assumed you knew. I assumed someone had told you.'

'Who would tell me, John, if not my assistant?'

Burrows opens his mouth but no sound comes out. He shuffles his feet.

Graves exhales. 'Monday, you say?'

'Yes, sir. That's what the message said. They are arriving on Monday. Dr Silk and his team.'

His team now. Dr Silk and his team.

Graves is suddenly exhausted. In body, in mind: he is ready to shut down. Goodnight, John, he would say but he does not have the energy. And anyway it hardly seems appropriate. Regardless of how tired he feels now, he knows already his chances of getting any sleep.

There is no pattern. That is the problem with research: the more you find out, the more confused things become. Give him white or – preferably, for the sake of a story – give him black; shades of grey create an unwelcome fog.

'There's no pattern.' Tom taps his pen against his notepad. He chews the end for a while and then taps it again on the pad. He turns. 'Amy,' he says. She has her eyes closed but he knows she is awake. 'Amy.' He throws a Skittle from the packet on his desk. It misses so he searches for another green one and throws that too. It hits her nose. Amy opens one eye.

'There's no pattern. How can I tell how a law is being used when the whole point of that law is to prevent me finding out?'

Amy's eye closes.

'I mean, they only admit to a handful of arrests, and usually only then because someone confronts them. Like Julia did, for instance. Although if it hadn't been for that video she would still be phoning round hospitals.' Tom flicks with his mouse from browser to browser. He settles for a while on the only high-profile case he has found of an arrest where Unified

Security is even mentioned, that of a Muslim man from Leicester who was detained for ninety-seven days before being released without charge. The episode made the nationals, including one or two front pages. It did not help the police that their operation from the start was so clumsy: Samal Khan was seized on the steps outside a mosque, on his way home from the Maghrib prayer. A campaign was launched against the police's right to hold Khan and for almost a fortnight Unified Security became a topic of debate. It was the first time, really, the act had made headlines since the Freedom Marchers lost the moral high ground by trapping, inadvertently, a mother and her baby in a burning car. Once again, though, the sympathetic segments of the press grew twitchy and aligned themselves with the tabloids and public opinion instead. Khan was ambiguous in his devotion to his new homeland. He did not, more to the point, photograph well: his beard was long, his left eye squinted. The debate shifted from why Muslims were so often victimised to why the hell should they not be? Unified Security became a sidebar, then a footnote, then a story consigned to the archive.

So there is the Khan case and nothing that is any more helpful. There are one or two NIBs in the local press, some independent sites on the web – maybe twenty instances in total of an arrest where Unified Security is the focus of the coverage, almost all of which relate in some way to accusations of terrorism. Which leaves Tom no further along than where he started: with no idea whatsoever about why or where Arthur Priestley is being held.

'Guess,' he says. 'Have a guess how many times they've used

Unified Security and the general public has been none the wiser.'

Amy makes no sign of having heard him. She still has her eyes closed, her feet on her desk and her head on a balled-up jumper against her chair.

'You can't,' says Tom. 'Can you? There's no point even trying because I wouldn't be able to tell you whether you were right or not. Which is why,' he adds, raising a finger, 'the law is so effective, from the government's point of view. And it's why they're winning. No one opposes the act any more because no one can see how it's being used.'

'They've never opposed it, Tom.'

Tom is looking at his monitor again and at the sound of Amy's voice he turns. She is sitting upright now, yawning. She rubs at her eyes with her fingers, then tenses in a half-extended stretch. Tom checks the clock on his screen. It is almost midnight. 'Go home,' he says. 'It's Sunday tomorrow, remember? You're the only one still here.'

'You're here.' Amy swallows and grimaces as though there is the taste in her mouth of something unpleasant.

'I'm not tired. If I were tired, I'd go to bed. I wouldn't be sleeping at my desk.'

'I'm power-napping,' Amy says. 'I don't sleep any more. If I power-nap, I don't have to commute.' She wiggles her mouse and her computer clicks and whirrs into life. 'Also, I have like a million words to write. And at the moment I'm on . . .' She squints at her screen and taps a key on her keyboard. 'Eighty-two.'

'And anyway you're wrong,' says Tom, ignoring the digression. 'Two million people camped outside the gates to Downing Street: that's how I know you're wrong.'

'Two million out of sixty-five. Which leaves sixty-three million sitting on their sofas with a copy of the *Daily Mail* and a nice cup of tea.'

Tom shakes his head. 'Just because they didn't march, doesn't mean they supported the bill.'

'Every poll, Tom, even ours: they all put support in the high sixties. As for the other thirty-odd per cent, they probably weren't that bothered either way. That's why the press doesn't report on it. That's why Katherine wouldn't let you write about your friend.' Amy stands. 'By the way,' she says. She is smiling and edging towards Tom's chair. 'How is the dazzling Mrs Priestley? How are things, you know: *between* you?'

Tom scowls, waves a hand. 'It's not like that.'

Amy leans in close. When she talks he can feel her breath in his ear. 'But oh, how you wish it were.' She reaches and plucks a Skittle from his desk. 'Write my story for me.'

'What? No.'

'Go on. It's right up your street.'

'Why? What's it about?'

'Thwarted love,' says Amy and she flutters her eyelids. She reaches for another Skittle but Tom clamps his hand on top of the packet.

'I'm working,' he says. 'I'm trying to work.'

'I'll help.' Amy pulls up a chair and sits beside him. 'Seriously. No more jokes, I promise.'

'I thought you had an article to write.'

'I do. That's why I'd rather be sitting here. Tell me,' she says, tugging the bag of Skittles from beneath Tom's hand. 'What have you got?'

'Sore eyes,' says Tom, rubbing them. 'RSI in my wrist. An aching head from banging it against a brick wall.' He stands. 'I'm getting coffee. Do you want some?'

Amy's attention is on his screen. She shakes her head. Tom picks up his cup and carries it through the darkened office to the kitchenette. The hum of the fridge greets him, as well as the smell of the food that has been left to fester inside. He flicks on the overhead light. There is coffee in the jug but no heat from the plate underneath. He fills his cup anyway and blasts it in the microwave. He does not give it long enough and the coffee is tepid as he sips it on his way back to his desk.

'What are you looking for exactly?' says Amy. She has moved from her seat to his. 'How is all this stuff supposed to help?'

'It doesn't.' Tom gestures for the return of his chair but Amy shoos him away. He frowns, sits in hers. 'I thought it might but I was wrong.'

'You should speak to what's his name.'

'Stanford? At the Met? I have already.'

'What about—'

'Maynard? In the Home Office? Him too.'

Amy turns from the screen to face him. 'Nothing? They couldn't help?'

'Couldn't or wouldn't.'

'That's unusual,' Amy says. 'Especially for Maynard.'

'That's what I thought.' Tom chews a Skittle and washes it down. The coffee is not improved by the twist of synthetic lime.

'Have you found anything of any use? What's all this stuff?' Amy tips her chin to the pile of printouts on his desk.

'Missing-person reports. Online appeals. Rewards offered. That sort of thing.'

'You think they've been arrested?' Amy lifts a corner of the pile nearest to her and allows the pages to fan out from under her thumb. 'You think these people are being held somewhere and their families don't know?'

'Not all of them. Some of them. Maybe none of them. I don't know. I was just looking for . . . I don't know. I don't know what I was looking for.' He presses his palms to his eyes. 'I'm tired. I am. I said I wasn't but I really am.'

'Ten minutes,' says Amy. 'Trust me. Just ten minutes with your eyes closed. If Katherine's around, stick your headphones on and it'll look like you're listening to an interview.'

Tom shakes his head. 'Coffee,' he says. 'Confectionery. That's what works for me.' He slaps his cheeks, rather harder than he intended.

'And self-harm. Ingenious.' Amy points at another pile on the desk, smaller than the first and topped by a Post-it note scrawled with a question mark. 'What does this mean?'

'It's a question mark. It means I don't know what it means.'

Amy peels off the Post-it note and scans the top sheet. There are only five pages in the pile and she looks at each in turn. 'Okay,' she says, turning from the last page to the first again. 'So?'

'I don't know. I really don't know what it means. But I was looking at people who've been reported missing. And there are a lot of them, as it happens. About two hundred thousand new cases in the UK every year.'

SIMON LELIC

'Wow.'

'I know. But that's mainly kids, right? Narrow it down to white male professionals in their late twenties or early thirties and it drops to a few thousand. Restrict it by date and it's hundreds. Look for those who are still missing after a week, it's fewer still.'

'And these . . .' Amy gestures to the pile in Tom's hand.

'These,' says Tom, 'are the white male professionals in their twenties and early thirties who went missing about the same time as Arthur Priestley. None has been found and none has a profile, as far as I can tell, that suggests any good reason why they should have vanished.'

'Such as?'

'I don't know. I'm just guessing, really. But financial troubles. An estranged family. Drug abuse. That sort of thing.'

'Are they all from London?'

'Mostly. One's from Brighton.'

'But they're all gay. All the cases you can find that bear any resemblance to Arthur's—'

'Involve gay men. Right. There's another three in this pile here and I don't know whether they're gay or not. They don't have Facebook pages, there's nothing obvious in the coverage—'

'Like what? How do you know the other five are gay?'

'It says. Either they have a partner called Toby or Jonathan or something, or it just outright says. These other three, though: they're not married, they don't have kids. There's nothing to suggest they're straight but that's not exactly confirmation that they're gay. So they get their own pile.'

100

Amy reclines in her chair. She takes the printouts from Tom again and skims each page one more time. 'So you've got five, maybe eight, men who went missing at the same time Arthur did, all fitting Arthur's profile except for the fact that they're gay. Right?'

'Right.'

'What about Arthur?'

'What about him?'

'Is he gay?'

'He's married. He has a son.'

'So?' says Amy. 'He could still be gay.'

Tom smiles, shakes his head. 'I don't think so.'

'Why not? Just because it's Julia he's married to?'

'She would know.'

'Not necessarily.'

'You would know, don't you think? If you were married and your husband turned out to be gay, don't you think you would know?'

'I would hope so. But I couldn't be certain. If my husband wasn't certain himself, for example, how could I expect to know better than him?'

Tom snorts.

'What?' says Amy. 'What does that mean?'

'If your husband wasn't certain. How could your husband not be certain? If he had a thing for other blokes, I would think he would probably be aware of it. Men get . . . You know. Signs.'

Amy tuts. 'That's so typical.'

'All I'm saying is—'

'I know what you're saying, Tom. The problem is, not everything in this world is black and white. There are shades of grey, you know. There's such a thing as ambiguity.'

Tom finds himself smiling. 'I don't think I can really argue with that.'

Amy has her arms crossed now. She is staring at the screen-saver on Tom's computer screen. Tom tugs at a thread that is loose on the upholstery of his seat. He winds the thread around his finger but when he pulls to try and snap it off it only gets longer.

'They're separated, you know.' Tom looks at Amy. 'Julia and Arthur. They're still married but they've been apart for about a year.'

Amy raises her eyebrows. She does not say what she is think-ing but she does not need to.

'I know,' says Tom. 'I know. But even so, I don't think he's gay. I don't think he's that interesting, to be honest.'

'How do you mean?'

'I did some digging, spoke to some friends of his. He runs his own dental practice and that's basically his life. He earns good money but he doesn't spend it. He plays golf once in a while but not very well. He likes wine but only ever drinks in moderation. I guessed his password on Amazon—'

'His wife's name?'

'Close: his son's. Anyway, he once bought some porn. Nothing very racy and it was straight porn, before you ask. That's it, though. As far as I can tell, that's as wild a thing as he's ever done.'

'Maybe he's repressed.'

Tom laughs. 'Maybe.' He drops his gaze. 'There's your answer, though.'

'Answer to what?'

'To what you asked me before.'

'You mean about you and Julia.' Amy is smiling, not unkindly.

'She didn't tell me they were separated. Right from the start she made it sound like they were living together when in fact he's got his own flat. I think that makes things pretty clear.'

'Oh, Tom. It doesn't mean anything. It means she was embarrassed, that's all. At first she had no reason to tell you and after that she was embarrassed for having not. I mean, it's a bit forward, isn't it? "By the way, Tom, my husband and I are separated. Which means I'm available, in case you're interested."'

'She still loves him, though. Obviously she still loves him because why else would she be going to so much trouble?'

'Because they were once in love even if they aren't now? Because he's the father of her son?'

Tom just grunts.

'Men,' says Amy. 'Honestly.'

They sit for a moment without speaking. There is only the drone of Tom's computer and the creaking of the building bedding down for the night, until a light flicks on behind them and they both turn. It is the porter bringing in the early editions of the Sundays. He notices Tom and Amy and lifts his hand. Amy waves back. 'Over here okay?' the porter calls and Amy gives him the thumbs up. The porter offloads the papers, then waves again and rattles his trolley back into the corridor.

'It's late,' Amy says. 'I'm kidding myself that I'm going to get any writing done tonight. Wanna share a cab?'

Tom shakes his head. 'I think I'll stick around for while. I've still got a bag of M&Ms.'

Amy narrows her eyes. 'Regular or peanut?'

'Peanut.'

'Then I'll let you off for not sharing.'

Tom knows what is coming and he ducks but Amy is quicker and she ruffles his hair. 'Don't stay too late,' she says. There are two Skittles left next to the crumpled packet on Tom's desk and Amy takes the purple one. She grins triumphantly.

Even when Amy has gone, Tom does not shift back into his own chair. He has no intention of doing anything more tonight but he has no desire to go home either. His flatmate – Craig, an ex-banker, who is two weeks into a compulsory redundancy that is turning into an early-life crisis – will be there, playing Nintendo probably or stoned on the sofa in front of Movies for Men. In which case Tom would escape conversation anyway but he would much rather be here and alone. So he sits and he stares and he watches the swirling colours on his screen until even his computer becomes weary and clicks itself off.

After staring at his own reflection for a while, Tom gets up. He drifts towards Amy's desk, stopping at Terry's on the way to inspect the contents of his top drawer. It contains tea bags and the carcasses of a dozen devoured pens, as well as an unlikely quantity of snack bars and individually wrapped processed cheeses. Amy's desk is no more diverting. Tom does not go as far as prying in Amy's drawers – Terry, in this regard like so many others, is a special case – but it is clear from the chaos that consumes the surface that Tom would only be appalled at what he found there.

He decides to read the papers instead. Glance at them, at least, because that is all he ever seems to do with newspapers these days. Since he followed Katherine from the *Sunday Times* he has become used to reading and writing news that feels far more immediate. At the *Libertarian*, for instance, stories are published as soon as the copy is written – while it is being written, sometimes. Anything that appears the following morning in the printed press reads to Tom like news that is no longer that.

And the tabloids. Just on principle, he can barely bring himself to look at the tabloids. He lifts the *Sunday Mirror* and tosses it down again. He ignores the *Sport* and the *Star* and only picks up the *News of the World* to see what is on the back page. Another spat, probably. An engineered story about someone saying something about someone else rather than a report about football – the game, twenty-two men kicking a ball – which is, after all, what the sports page should really be—

When he sees the front page, his grip tightens; the newspaper creases in his hands. There is a picture of a man's blacked-out face, the proclamation of a World Exclusive. There is a headline – GUANTANAMO UK – and a line beneath promising 'an insider's shocking revelations' about a 'secret government prison'. There is another reminder that the story is a *NOTW* exclusive and there, right there in the first paragraph, are two words that cause his frantic eyes to lock: Unified Security.

He reads as he walks. He has his phone in his right hand and he is thumbing through his contacts and he collides with a desk and he is doing too many things at once. He stops. He focuses on his phone. He finds Julia's number and he hits call and he is beating the newspaper against his leg as he listens to the dial tone in his ear.

PART TWO

'**Everyone recognises someone** in here, my friend. It's part of the whole, you know. The whole mystery.' Roach wiggles his fingers and widens his eyes, as though the mystery were also some frivolous game. 'Like what's his name. What's his name and the other guy. Before they lived here, they lived together. Had rings like they were married. Which they don't wear no more, by the way. They don't even talk to each other no more.'

Arthur stops digging. 'Why not?'

Roach shrugs. 'You had a little chat, right? Before they sent you here? Small room, big bloke, rancid cup of coffee?'

'Something like that.'

'So probably they did too. And probably they found out some stuff. Probably they discovered their relationship wasn't quite so monolithic as they thought.'

'Monogamous.' Arthur scrapes at the earth with the blade of his shovel.

'Right. Monogamous. Same thing. And there's another couple too. Like, a straight couple. Man and wife. They're not talking to each other either but, thinking about it, maybe there's nothing so unusual about that.' Roach lets his spade drop and bends to test the weight of the bag the two men are filling. He heaves it on to the wheelbarrow. 'Me,' he says between breaths, 'I've seen a face I'd sooner forget. Thought I had forgotten it, actually. Thought I was too drunk to remember it in the first place.' He coughs. He drags a muddy cuff across his forehead and stares down at the trench in front of them. 'What the hell are we digging here anyway?'

'Something to do with drainage, they said. Something to do with rising damp.'

'Looks like a goddamn grave.'

'Maybe it is,' Arthur says. 'Maybe they're planning to shoot us when we're done, toss us both in.' He is only half joking but he smiles nonetheless.

Roach gives him a look. 'I always knew you dentists were sick sons of bitches.' He picks up his shovel. He breathes, exhales, coughs again. 'Not that they're gonna have to shoot me. This, just digging: that's what's gonna kill me.'

A guard approaches their section of the trench and they fall silent. The guard stops at Arthur's shoulder but Arthur does not turn to look. He keeps digging, Roach too, until the guard decides to move on. They are quiet still after he has gone. Arthur finds himself working to the rhythm of his companion's breathing.

'It's different,' says Arthur after a moment. 'This isn't some bloke I met in a bar.'

'Right,' says Roach. 'You told me. The same time you told me you weren't gay.' He looks Arthur up and down. 'Like I couldn't work that out for myself.'

'It's a mistake. My being here is a mistake.'

Roach leans on his shovel. He laughs and it sounds like a wheeze. 'Whereas the rest of us, particularly us faggots: we *deserve* to be locked away.'

Arthur shakes his head. 'I didn't mean it like that.'

Roach grins, picks up his shovel. 'You're lucky you're pretty, Arthur. You're lucky I've taken a shine to you.' He winks and Arthur, for a moment, does not know what to say. This time when Roach laughs, he laughs so hard he starts coughing and cannot stop. 'Man,' he says, spluttering. 'You should see your face.' He is delighted with himself and Arthur is suddenly annoyed. He scowls but this only makes Roach laugh harder.

'I get it, Arthur,' Roach says. He is chuckling still; grinning. 'I do. You reckon he knows why you're here. Not the rest of us necessarily but with you there was some kind of mix-up and this bloke, you reckon, was the cause.'

'Right.' Arthur stabs at the earth.

'Well then,' says Roach and Arthur, in spite of his irritation, looks across.

'Well what?'

'Well let's have a chat. Let's talk to your friend and see if we can't convince him to share.'

'How?' says Arthur. 'When? I've watched him in the canteen. I've followed him in the grounds. He eats alone and exercises alone and every time someone comes near he veers towards one of the guards. It's like he's afraid. Terrified, rather. More so than the rest of us, I mean.'

Roach shrugs. His grin has faded but only to a smile. 'So we'll be gentle,' he says and again he looks at Arthur and winks.

*

He walks with his arms hanging straight at his sides, as though he were carrying heavy shopping. His shoulders are rolled forwards, his chin tucked close to his chest. He stares at his feet, or seems to, and makes no sign of having noticed them following.

Roach tracks the man from the opposite pathway. Somehow he manages to convey nonchalance, whereas Arthur, walking alone on his side of the grass, feels like his purpose is as plain to see as the orange waterproof he was issued with at the door.

He is just being paranoid, he tells himself. Other inmates are walking in the grounds too, in singles or pairs as mandated by the guards, and drifting as Arthur might appear to be doing. That Arthur dallies, lingers once in a while in a particular spot, can hardly seem unusual. What else is there to do here, after all? The gardens might once have been impressive but now, in a soggy autumn and after seasons of neglect, they are ragged and rundown and as inhospitable as the building they surround. In the section to which the prisoners have been confined there are greys and yellowed greens but mainly browns. The trees and rows of bushes have mostly been cut back, and mercilessly – not with any design in mind but to clear sight lines, Arthur suspects, for the guards stationed along the fence. Between the inmates and the woodland beyond there are two fences, in fact: an inner boundary and an outer one, like in the prisoner-of-war films Arthur remembers watching as a boy. He thinks of Steve McQueen – was it Steve McQueen? – tossing a ball into the space between them and defying the Nazi guards by daring to retrieve it. The thought does not encourage him. It makes him feel craven, rather; cowed. It reminds him how distant such images are from reality, from his own particular reality: here, in a cordoned patch of earth that is mainly mud and weeds, among men and women as powerless to defy their captors as Arthur and surrounded by guards with licence, it would seem, to channel their own anger at being here in any way they please.

Up ahead, the man they are trailing has stopped. Arthur does too and immediately feels awkward once again, exposed. He shuffles. He stoops to tie his lace. Halfway to the floor, he remembers: their laces were taken from them. He feels hot all of a sudden, even though it is damp and maybe six degrees and his uniform is only polyester and the waterproof an unlined sheet. He cannot think what else to do so he removes his shoe, tipping it and frowning as though a stone from the gravel path had lodged itself inside. But then the man walks on, more quickly than before it seems, and Arthur is left standing on one leg with his shoe in his hand. He hurries to replace it, feeling even more exposed now, and in his fluster he wobbles and has to step to stop himself falling. He lands sock first in a puddle. The puddle fills a hole and the water is deep enough to cover Arthur's ankle. He curses and tries again to ram his foot back into his shoe but it is harder now that his sock is wet and it takes him two attempts, three. When he looks up the man is gone.

Arthur hurries forwards. He sees Roach hurrying too, still on the path parallel but a dozen yards or so in front. There is a line of conifers bisecting the lawn ahead of them, spared the shears perhaps because they run perpendicular to the fence and are visible to the guards from either side. The two men, though, approach them head on, so that the conifers loom like a wall. The man is behind them; it is the only place he might have gone. Arthur draws level with Roach and does not slow his pace as he approaches the trees. He does not think to.

'What? What do you want?'

As Arthur rounds the corner the man is up and hissing in Arthur's face. He is shorter than Arthur, slighter too, but he is angry and presses his advantage. Arthur takes a step back.

'You're following me. Stop following me!'

'What?' says Arthur. 'I wasn't . . .'

'I saw you! You and your friend!' The man looks around but Roach is nowhere in sight. 'I watch films, I read books: I know how it works in these places and I'm not interested. Got it?'

'What? No. That's not what . . . I just wanted to . . .'

'Don't think I won't fight you.' The man shows his teeth. He has a chip on one of his incisors, Arthur notices. He has a scar from a cleft lip too and whether it is that or just his expression, his features beneath his lank hair seem somehow misaligned. 'I mean it,' the man is saying. 'I may be small but I can fight!'

And he is ready to, Arthur can tell. He is so focused on trying to intimidate Arthur, in fact, that he does not notice Roach emerging from the trees behind.

'Relax,' says Roach and the man spins. Arthur looks towards the fence but the guards he can see have not yet noticed the three prisoners standing together.

'Get away from me!' The man backs into the conifers and a raises a finger as though in warning.

'Take it easy,' Roach says, edging forwards. 'We just want a little chat.'

'I'll yell. I will. You come any closer and I swear to God I'll yell for a guard.'

Arthur advances. He cannot help himself. 'Who are you? What's your—'

The man draws breath and opens his throat but Roach's hand is across his mouth before the cry can escape. He forces the man backwards, as deep into the conifers as the branches will allow.

'Now, now. There's no need to raise your voice.'

The man struggles but he is powerless to escape Roach's bulk.

'Who are you?' Arthur says again and Wilson's eyes meet his.

'Answer the man,' says Roach. 'And remember: shouting's not gonna do anyone any favours.'

The man writhes but Roach holds him tight. He has his left hand across the man's mouth and is gripping with his right down below. He squeezes and the man squeals.

'Well?' says Roach. 'What's your name?' He eases his left hand away. His right remains in place.

'W . . . Wilson. My name's Wilson. Who are you? What do you want from—'

The man interrupts his own sentence with a yelp.

'Just answers, please,' says Roach. 'Save the questions.'

'How do you know me?' says Arthur. 'Why did you give them my name?'

Wilson looks from Roach to Arthur. 'What? I don't. I . . . I didn't.' He tries to pull away again but Roach holds him firm.

'Keep still, Wilson, or I'll twist it right off.'

'They showed me your picture,' Arthur says. 'I know you know me!'

Wilson shakes his head and again Roach tightens his grip.

'Please! I don't! Honestly I don't!' There is no bluster about Wilson now. If anything, he seems close to tears.

'Priestley,' says Roach. 'My friend's name is Arthur Priestley. Think hard now, Wilson, because my hand: it's beginning to cramp up.'

Arthur watches for Wilson to react. He only whimpers, though, and shakes his head.

'Priestley,' Arthur repeats. There is a branch between him and Wilson and he shoves it aside. 'I saw your picture! You gave them my name! Arthur. Priestley. I live in London. In Ealing. I . . . I have a wife. A son. I'm a dentist. You gave them my—'

But there is no need to go on. Wilson's eyes draw wide. He looks at Arthur and his lips fall apart. The only sound he makes now is a guttural rasp, as though he were struggling all of a sudden for breath.

'What?' says Arthur. 'What is it?'

Wilson is staring. His head moves barely perceptibly from side to side.

'What?' Roach echoes. He gives Wilson a shake and grips again with his right hand. As though wrung free, the tears that have been threatening spill across Wilson's cheeks.

He starts to mutter. 'Sorry,' he says. 'I'm sorry!'

Arthur and Roach share a look.

'I didn't know.' Wilson is still shaking his head. He sniffs. He rolls a shoulder to his cheek but under Roach's weight it does not reach. 'I didn't know. I'm sorry!'

'What are you talking about?' Arthur reaches past Roach and

grabs two fistfuls of Wilson's shirt. Again Wilson whimpers. He seems to go limp, as though he would crumple were Arthur not there to hold him up.

'They wanted names. I didn't have any! I told them and they didn't believe me. They said they knew I was gay but I'm not! It was just one time. Just one time with a stranger in a club!'

'So you gave them my name? You didn't have any so you gave them mine? What the fuck did I do to you! I don't even know you!'

'I'm sorry!' says Wilson again. 'I didn't think they'd . . . That it was . . . I mean, I had to tell them something!'

'Why me though! Why my name!'

Wilson cowers as though from a blow. 'I was looking for dentists,' he says. 'For my tooth.' He retracts his upper lip to reveal again his chipped incisor.

'Dentists?' Arthur feels his grip on Wilson's shirt slacken.

'That morning. The morning they came for me. I remembered your name. I don't know why. I wouldn't have told them anything but they . . . they . . .'

'They made you tell them something.' Arthur lets go of Wilson and the man staggers. He slumps.

'You were just a name,' Wilson says. He is seated on the ground now, gazing up at Arthur through bloodshot eyes. He reaches out a hand. 'They broke my finger. The big one, he . . . he cracked my rib. They wanted a name. I had to give them a name!'

Arthur takes a step back and Wilson's hand falls away. Arthur is shaking his head now. He can feel the look of disgust on his

face. Roach is beside him, staring at Wilson too, and for a
moment there is just the sound of the man sobbing.

'Hey!'

Roach turns. Arthur, an instant later, does too.

'What the fuck are you three playing at?' The guard is striding towards them, elbows jutting from his hips.

Arthur feels Roach tugging at his wrist. 'Arthur. Let's go.'

Arthur looks back at Wilson. The man is snivelling. He legs
are coated in mud; his face in tears and snot. 'Get up,' Arthur
tells him. 'Get going.'

Wilson, though, just sits there.

'Arthur. Come on.' Once more Roach tugs Arthur's arm. He
glances towards the approaching guard. 'Let's go,' he says again.
And this time when he pulls, Arthur allows himself to be led.

They file in silence back to their rooms. Neither man has spoken
since they left Wilson in the grounds but Arthur reaches now
and prods Roach in the kidneys. Roach glances to check no
guards are watching and half turns.

'That's it then,' Arthur whispers. 'Right? I don't belong here.
Wilson knows that, you know that, I know that.'

A guard up ahead snaps her chin to her shoulder. 'Quiet
back there!'

Roach faces forwards and both he and Arthur drop their
heads. They walk on.

Further along the corridor, Arthur checks to see whether the
guard is looking. He prods Roach again and again Roach turns.

'I just tell them,' Arthur hisses. 'Right? If I just tell them,
they'll have to let me go.'

He is speaking too loudly. The guard stops. She hollers for quiet again and stands with her shoulders to the wall, glowering at each inmate who passes by. Roach and Arthur draw close but there is time still for Roach to answer. He looks at Arthur and Arthur waits and then Roach turns away.

'**Where is it?** Is it on British soil?'

Tom cannot see the man who is speaking but he knows the voice. The *Sun*'s political editor has an Eton drawl entirely antipathetic to the audience he represents.

'It's on British soil,' the home secretary replies. 'That's all I can tell you, other than to point out that the locations suggested in Sunday's *News of the World* were based on nothing more than the paper's own uneducated guesswork.'

'But their source—'

'Their source – whoever their source is – would not know where the facility is located because not even the people who work there could tell you that. The *News of the World* got two things right and two things only: first, that the medical facility exists; second, that the patients there are very sick indeed.'

'The source did not refer to them as patients,' the *Sun* man persists. 'He did not refer to it as a medical facility either.'

'As I say, the source was not very well informed. The facility is a fully equipped, fully staffed medical institution. It is a secure hospital, not a prison.' The home secretary points to another raised hand. There is movement beside him and Tom sees Julia's arm in the air. He curses and tugs at Julia's sleeve.

'What are you doing?'

Julia ignores him. She pulls her arm free and raises it once more. It is lost in the forest of shirtsleeves around them and anyway Julia is half hidden by a pillar. The home secretary calls on a journalist in the second row, close to the seats Tom would have been assigned had he asked for them. Instead, at Tom's insistence, they are positioned towards the rear, in the seats *Libertarian* reporters would typically have been assigned just a year or two ago – before Katherine's single-mindedness and a flurry of high-profile scoops set the publication's readership, and reputation, on a par with that of the smaller broadsheets. Tom is relieved now that, when he gave Julia Amy's pass, he ushered her away from the podium and did not give in to her protests. Sit still, keep quiet, don't attract attention. He asked Julia to promise and she promised. Not that he can blame her for rescinding. Given what they have already heard, he is amazed she has managed to keep quiet for so long.

'In your statement you described the disease as a previously unidentified sexually transmitted infection. What does that mean exactly? Can you give us any more details?'

'Right now, very few.' The home secretary adjusts the microphone in front of her. She is a short woman, wide too, with enough hair for several heads. Political cartoonists have united in drawing her as an over-inflated balloon, bobbing at the prime minister's shoulder and tethered by party colours to his pinkie. It is this image that occurs to Tom as he watches her, though he is aware too that her political opponents know better than to take her so lightly. Margaret Myers is bright, shrewd and ruthless, and has positioned herself at the razor tip of her party's right wing. 'I can give you some anecdotal comparisons,' she says in her saccharine, girlish voice. 'That's all.'

'Comparisons with what?' asks the journalist in the second row.

'With HIV, for example. The chance of contracting HIV during unprotected sex is somewhere between one in three and one in a hundred thousand, depending on the manner of intercourse and, of course, which study you read. For this virus, transmission rates are demonstrably higher.' Myers checks her notes. 'Similarly,' she says, reading now, 'infection can be detected within weeks, whereas the window period for HIV is as wide as six months. Most worrying, it attacks rapidly. Even without medical intervention, by contrast, HIV can lie dormant in the bloodstream for years, decades even.' Myers looks up. 'With the virus we are facing now, death typically occurs within six months.'

There is a collective murmur and the journalist uses the commotion to follow up once more. 'So this is HIV? This is some kind of . . . what? Some kind of super HIV?'

'No, it is not. At least, we do not think so. We can treat HIV, to a degree. Against this virus no medical intervention has so far been successful.'

'So what is it? Where did it come from?'

'Please,' the press officer interrupts. 'One question, one follow-up. You know the rules, everybody.'

The journalist in the second row acknowledges the rebuke but the home secretary answers anyway. 'It is too early to say.

Our scientists, however, are exploring a range of possibilities and they are confident they will be able to pinpoint the disease's origins relatively soon.'

'Relatively soon? You don't know, then. Is that what you're saying?'

'Hector,' says the press officer, 'this isn't a one-on-one. There are other journalists present and most, I am sure, would like just a single question answered, never mind half a dozen.'

The home secretary curls her lips and gestures for the press officer to stand down.

'We do not know *yet*,' she says. 'These things take time, Hector. HIV has plagued western society for decades but still there is no fixed consensus on where it came from. With the contagion we currently face, the matter is complicated by the fact that no other cases have so far been reported anywhere else in the world. Which is not to say,' the home secretary adds, raising her voice above the fizz of pencil movement, 'that the disease does not have a foothold in other countries. The likelihood is that other governments have simply been less successful in identifying pathological threats to their citizens.'

There is a show of hands but the home secretary ignores them. She raises one of her own. 'Which brings me to the good news,' she says, casting a reassuring smile towards the cameras at the back of the room. 'The carriers of the disease in this country have been isolated. The risk to the general population is precisely zero. The disease has been confined to a group of men and women characterised by their high-risk behaviour and aggressive promiscuity: homosexual men, for the most part, but also a small number of intravenous drug users, as well as several sex workers and their clients, all within a sixty-mile radius of central London. Patient zero – that is, the first person to have died from the illness – was a bisexual man from Croydon: it was by analysing his immediate social network and extrapolating the contagion's path that we have reached our current position of containment. So far, seven people in total have died as a direct result of infection. Eighty-six others have been tested and confirmed as carriers, and every one of them, as I say, is now a patient at the facility I have described.'

Myers does not signal for a question but one comes anyway.

'What about the blood supply? Is there any chance—'

'There is no possibility whatsoever that the UK's blood supply has been contaminated.' Myers affects an expression of motherly calm. 'This is not the 1980s. In fact, the western world's response to the HIV crisis is an interesting parallel. In the United States, Europe – even Britain, I am ashamed to say – it took us years to recognise the extent of the HIV epidemic. By contrast, in response to what could well have become a public-health crisis on a scale even greater than that of HIV/AIDS, we have acted with alacrity and resolve.'

Myers allows her hand to hover for a moment before aiming it at another journalist.

'Can you talk us through the timings, Home Secretary? When did patient zero, as you refer to him, die? At what point did you first become aware of the disease?'

'Patient zero's death occurred three months ago. But we had been monitoring the disease and tracking the vectors of transmission for a month before the man's death: since the very first reports from the medical front line that patients were exhibiting symptoms that did not fit with any known contagion.'

'And this – ' the journalist who holds the floor looks to his notepad ' – this facility. When was that created?'

The home secretary draws back her shoulders. 'The decision to build the facility was taken long before this disease manifested itself. It has, for some time now, stood empty – but ready. The facility was a core aspect of this government's strategy to prepare our country for any and all external threats – the known unknowns, to borrow a wise man's phrase. Our foresight, I am sure you will agree, has been rewarded.'

'What about the detainees? How long have they been there?'

'The first group of *patients*,' Myers says, 'took up residence a fortnight ago, once each and every carrier of the disease had been assembled.'

Tom and Julia share a glance but the home secretary continues before either one of them can speak.

'There will be questions, I realise, about our decision to impose a media blackout on the story until now but I make no apologies for this. This government believes in governing, not scaremongering.'

For a moment the home secretary turns away. There are six or seven people to the rear of the stage and they cluster around her. Tom recognises only a few of those to whom Myers talks: the press officer, of course, and his deputy, Annette, who is as aggressive in bed, Tom can testify, as she is with the media. Rupert Jenkins, the Home Office minister of state, is on stage too, though he seems to be excluded from the discussion. He adjusts his tie and glances towards the press and does his best to convey the impression that he does not need to hear what is being said because he knows already what to expect.

The home secretary nods at whatever she is being told. She returns to the podium. 'Which brings me to the second purpose of this briefing. The previous administration left this country massively exposed to globalised health threats. It did not learn the lesson from HIV, nor from SARS, nor avian flu, nor swine flu. Since the general election, we have worked to dramatically strengthen our disease-surveillance systems, as I have said, and our success in this most recent crisis demonstrates just how far we have taken this country on the road towards unified public-health security.' She pauses, allowing time for the phrase to resonate.

'We intend on going even further,' she continues. 'First, we will be fast-tracking legislation that will clarify the legal situation regarding sexually transmitted infections. There have been cases in the past of prosecutions brought against carriers of, for example, HIV, who have knowingly put their partners at risk by soliciting sexual encounters without disclosing their infection. Not all of these cases have been successful, however. Our proposal is to create a legal framework that fully protects the victims of what, by any standard of decency, is a heinous and malicious crime. Furthermore,' Myers says, lifting a finger, 'ignorance of infection will no longer be a defence. Put simply, if you have unprotected sex with someone and you are carrying a sexually transmittable infection, you will go to prison. The British public can be assured: no one in this country is infected with this new disease who we do not know about. It is extremely unlikely that this legislation will be brought to bear in the present situation but it is good, responsible policy regardless. Those who indulge in a high-risk lifestyle have a moral obligation and this government plans simply to remind them of that.'

'There it is,' Tom whispers.

Julia turns her head but not her eyes. 'There's what?'

'This government's core constituency: the moral high ground. You'd never guess there was an election due next year.'

'Second,' Myers says, 'and again we are looking to the future as much as to the present situation, this country's immigration controls will be selectively tightened. We have the outbreak in this country completely under control but, as I say, it is highly probable that the disease established itself in other territories either before or at the same time as it arrived here. As soon as the first case of infection in another country is acknowledged, we will put in place stringent immigration controls. Nobody from the countries concerned will board a plane to the UK without presenting at check-in a certificate of health validated by the British embassy. What's more, they will not leave Heathrow without undergoing both a further test and a period of quarantine, the cost of which will be borne by the individual in question, unless of course they are a British citizen. The same rules will apply with regard to any country that fails to establish comparable safeguards in their own immigration arrangements.'

Hands are raised and Myers accepts a question.

'What about British citizens?' says the man from the BBC. 'Will they be subject to punitive immigration controls imposed by other nations?'

'We are confident that won't be necessary, Ravi. The disease is under control: let me re-emphasise that. The international community, I am pleased to say, has shown every sign of being reassured by the containment procedures we have put in place. They have every faith in this government.'

Myers points to another raised hand.

'On the issue of the media blackout,' says the man from the *Daily Express*, 'don't you think the public had a right to know? Should there not at least have been a public-education campaign about the disease?'

The home secretary indulges a show of irritation. 'Do you really need me to answer that, Trevor? Do you think, if we had told you, you would have confined yourself to reporting the facts? Do you think if we had come to you without absolute assurance that the disease was under control you would have presented to the public a balanced, responsible, reassuring message?' She flicks a finger towards a journalist in the front row. 'Next question.'

'Home Secretary, how can you be certain that every case in this country has been isolated? You claim the disease is most likely present in other countries but that it remains undetected. If that's the case, then surely—'

'No other country in the world has the unified security network that we do, Jessica. No other country has the legislative framework that, in effect, saved our own from disaster. Infection rates, I can assure you, would almost certainly have spiralled had our security services not been able to call on the powers granted to them by the Unified Security Act.'

'That's all very well, Home Secretary,' the journalist says, 'but does the use of anti-terrorism measures in the field of public health not prompt the usual questions about civil liberties? You accept, surely, that there will be criticism.'

'You are right,' Myers says. 'They are the usual questions. They are questions we have answered time and time again. The utilisation of anti-terrorism measures in what was potentially a public-health *crisis* suggests one thing and one thing only: the Unified Security Act has made this country safer for its citizens than it has been for generations. Two more questions and then I am afraid I will have to leave you. Yes.' She points to the PA's correspondent.

'You say the disease is currently untreatable. Is anyone working on a cure?'

'The chief medical officer will be conducting her own briefing within the hour and she will be able to answer that question more fully. Suffice it to say for the time being that an extensive research budget has been allocated and that a team, led by Dr Leopold Silk, is already making significant headway. Last question, please. Yes, Ravi again.'

The man from the BBC lowers his hand. 'Um . . .' Ravi glances at his colleague beside him. 'What do we call it?' he says at last. 'I mean, you say the disease doesn't yet have a name. That the virus doesn't even have a designation. But our viewers . . .' He gestures to journalists that surround him. 'Our readers, too. I mean, we have to call it something.'

There is sniggering scattered in the crowd yet every eye in the room trains on Myers. Notepads are raised, pens readied.

The home secretary, though, disappoints. 'I'm not here to write your headlines, Ravi. I'm not here, either, to second-guess the scientific community. If I gave you a designation, you would ignore it. If I gave you a name and it contained too many syllables, you'd come up with something snappier.' Again there are sniggers and Myers indulges the journalists with a complicit smile. She shuffles her notes. 'Which brings me, ladies and gentlemen, to my final remarks. I would like to take a moment, if I may, to remind you of your responsibilities in reporting this story . . .'

'That's it?' Julia turns to face Tom. 'What about Arthur? What about all the others? Nobody even asked!'

'They're not the news any more. She moved it on. She did it very well.' Julia scowls and Tom gives an embarrassed shrug. 'Listen,' he says. 'It's over. We should go.'

'What? No!' Julia looks to the front. The home secretary is wrapping up and the journalists around them are gathering their things. Julia thrusts her hand in the air.

'Julia,' Tom says but this time he does not try to stop her. He does not need to. The home secretary, if she notices Julia's hand, makes no sign of it. The journalists close by simply laugh. Julia flushes and Tom waits and Julia's arm falters. She allows it to drop. Let's go, Tom is about to say but then Julia stands. She shouts.

'Ms Myers! Home Secretary!'

There is no doubt that Myers sees. But she turns away quickly and the press officer moves past her to the front of the stage.

'What about the prisoners, Ms Myers? What about the people you've locked up?'

Myers has her back turned. The press officer is at the podium. 'No more questions now, thank you. This briefing is over.'

'Julia.' Tom stands. He tugs at Julia's elbow. 'Christ, Julia.' He pulls again but Julia shrugs him off.

'What about my husband, Ms Myers? What have you done with my husband?'

This time the home secretary reacts. It is a fraction of a movement – a tension along her spine: no more than that – but there is no question in Tom's mind that she has heard. She does not turn, though. She smiles at a colleague and a procession forms behind her and she exits without a glance.

It is the only television in the main building. Graves watches from the back of the room, his hand curled around a mug of cold coffee and his shoulder against the wall. Burrows is ahead of him, seated in one of the chairs and with his feet propped on the arm of another.

'I don't know if it's just the size of the screen,' Burrows says, 'but Myers really does look like a balloon. Don't you think?' Burrows is focused on the television. As he speaks, the coverage cuts to an advertisement, for shampoo or hair dye or something anyway that requires a young woman to toss her hair a great deal, to flash her teeth a great deal. Graves checks his watch. The inmates will be returning soon from their morning exercise and today, for the first time, they will be allowed to mix freely in the recreational area.

'Turn it off, John. They'll be needing the room.'

Burrows stretches. The remote control is in his uppermost hand and he flicks standby at the apex of his stretch. He swings his feet from their perch and topples himself upright and takes a step towards Graves. Graves gestures him back.

'What?' Burrows looks behind him and he sees: the *News of the World* is still balanced on the arm of his chair. He grins awkwardly and reaches to pick it up. He is about to move away again and Graves is about to send him back once more when Burrows remembers of his own accord about the television. He turns it on and sets the code that will block everything but the movie channels. He flicks off the television, tosses the remote control back down. As he crosses the room, he studies the front page of the newspaper.

'It was Lambert,' he says. 'Wasn't it?'

'It doesn't matter now,' says Graves.

'Maybe you were right. Maybe we should have dropped him in front of a train after all.'

Graves glances at Burrows but does not reply. He leads the way into the corridor. A few paces on they pass the canteen. The room is being cleared of the remnants of the inmates' breakfast and the sound of plates being stacked is as though someone were hurling them against the wall. Burrows checks through the doorway but Graves keeps his eyes on the floor and continues. He is thinking about what the home secretary said, about Dr Silk and his research. About why Silk would be coming here.

'What did you make of it?' says Burrows, catching up.

For an instant, Graves assumes Burrows is thinking about the same thing he is. 'The press conference? It's just politics.'

Burrows gives a sniff. 'I suppose.'

They walk on.

'It's funny, though,' Burrows says. 'What she was saying about the timing of it all. Because if you remember—'

'It's politics, John. It's not our concern.'

'I know, I know. But there was the thing about the testing too. Didn't you say that some of the prisoners—'

'John,' says Graves, stopping. 'It's not our concern.'

He holds open the door to the stairwell and Burrows passes through. Graves is about to follow when movement further along the corridor catches his attention: someone he does not recognise carrying a white cardboard box towards the empty wing of the building.

'You there!' Graves turns from the stairwell, allowing the door to trap Burrows inside. He walks towards the stranger. 'Wait a moment, please. I said, stop!'

The man and the box have disappeared around the corner ahead. Graves increases his pace, not knowing whether the man has heard him. He reaches the corner, sensing Burrows trotting behind him, and does not slow as he turns.

The man is waiting and the box is in front of him and Graves walks into it stomach first. It drops and it lands on the floor. The noise it makes is quieter than a smashing plate, less dramatic, but no less definite. Graves looks down at the box. The man does too. Graves looks up and the man looks up and then Burrows rounds the corner and is unable to stop himself either. His momentum propels Graves forwards. Graves stumbles and he trips and whatever is in the box this time has no chance.

'Oh,' says Burrows. 'I'm sorry, Henry, I . . .'

Graves extricates his knee. He can feel Burrows's fumbling hands under his shoulders and shrugs himself free. He staggers upright. He glares at Burrows and then at the man whose box he has just flattened. 'Who are you?' He turns to Burrows. 'Who is this?'

'His name is Wood.' The reply comes from further along the corridor. Graves looks and sees another man approaching, not hurrying but covering the ground briskly under his long stride. 'A promising virologist,' the man says, 'but a hopeless removal man.'

The man who was carrying the box turns. 'I'm sorry, Dr Silk. It wasn't my fault. I—'

Silk cuts him off with an upraised finger. The box is at his feet now and he checks it from every angle, as though the damage were not plain to see. He stands to his full height – three inches at least above the men around him – and allows air to vent from his nostrils. 'Fix it,' he says. He places a hand on Wood's shoulder and his assistant squirms under his touch. 'If you cannot fix it,' Silk says, 'you will have to replace it.' Wood ducks from Silk's grip and gathers the box. He scuttles away.

'You're Dr Silk?' says Graves.

'Mr Graves, I assume.' Silk shows his teeth and extends his hand. Graves takes it, allowing his knuckles to be enclosed by the doctor's long fingers. A pianist's fingers, Graves's ex-wife would have said; or, had she not been taken by the man's mist-coloured eyes, his blond, almost white hair: a strangler's.

Silk allows his gaze to drift to Graves's brogues and up across the pale-grey fabric of his suit. 'You look exactly as I was led to expect.' He speaks as though issuing a compliment. Graves is not at all sure whether to take it as such.

'I wish I could say the same,' he replies. 'I'm afraid you have me at a disadvantage, however. I was told only that you were coming, and that only belatedly. Had I known sooner, or indeed your purpose . . .'

Silk raises a pale eyebrow.

'Well,' Graves says. 'I suppose . . . I suppose we might have provided you with some assistance. With the unpacking and such forth.' Graves clears his throat. He is fairly certain he has never used the phrase 'such forth' before in his life. 'Your equipment,' he says. 'It was entirely my fault. Please don't blame your assistant.'

'These things happen,' Silk says. 'Although it does seem to happen to some people more often than others, do you not find?' He glances over Graves's shoulder.

'Oh,' says Graves. 'Forgive me. This is John. John Burrows.'

Silk returns Burrows's nod. 'Well,' he says, addressing Graves again. 'Perhaps you would like a tour?'

Graves feels his lips give a twitch. '*I* would like a tour?'

'Unless you are too busy? I realise you have your hands full. With the . . . disturbance. The man in the infirmary. And the leak, of course.' The doctor's tone is conciliatory, conspiratorial – not obviously insincere but somehow precisely that.

Graves shifts. 'Not at all.'

'Excellent,' Silk says and he beams.

'But a tour of what exactly? Forgive me, Dr Silk, but when did you arrive?'

'Several hours ago.' Silk leads the way along the corridor. He glances at his watch. 'Eight hours ago, in fact.'

Graves checks his own watch. 'You arrived in the middle of the night?' He turns to Burrows and Burrows shakes his head, shrugs.

136

'Or early in the morning,' Silk replies. 'Depending on how you look at it.' He stops at a door and gestures Graves and Burrows ahead. 'Please.'

'But this wing's empty,' Burrows says. 'We were told to keep it empty.'

'You were indeed,' says Silk. 'Pending my arrival. Please.' He opens the door himself.

They enter another corridor, newly skimmed but not yet decorated. It has a smell that is familiar to Graves from his time at the facility but one that seems to have faded in the rest of the building: of fresh plaster masking old damp; of stale air and decades-old dust; of bleach and cleaning products not quite as pungent as the odour that still emanates from the drains.

'We'll have to see about getting these walls painted,' says Graves. 'They weren't a priority before but if you plan on being here any length of time . . .'

'It's clean,' says Silk. 'It's heated. For the time being, that is enough.'

There is a set of double doors ahead and the sound from the other side of something heavy being dragged across the concrete floor. There are voices, too: not conversation but instructions and directions and questions being asked and answered. There must be at least a dozen people working in the room beyond.

'It sounds like quite an army,' says Graves. 'I did not expect a research team to comprise so many.'

'There are four of us,' Silk says. 'Myself; Wood you met; also Perkins and Doyle. The army you can hear is your own. I hope

SIMON LELIC

you don't mind but I press-ganged some of your guards. Just to help us get set up.'

Graves feels his jaw tense. 'Of course.'

Silk smiles. 'They are off duty,' he says. 'I can assure you, the prisoners have not been left to roam free across Dartmoor.'

This time Graves cannot repress his irritation. 'Dr Silk. We have a policy not to discuss our location. You understand the reasoning, I am sure, particularly in view of recent events.'

Again Silk smiles. 'Come now, Henry. You know where we are. Your assistant here knows where we are. Certainly I do.' Silk makes a show of checking the empty corridor. He affects a whisper. 'Our secret, I would say, is safe.'

'Perhaps,' says Graves. 'But there is a principle. It is safer to stick to a hard and fast policy than to risk—'

Silk brings his finger to his lips. They have reached the threshold to the room and Silk reaches to open one of the doors. 'After you.'

Graves flushes. He steps inside.

Quite what he expected, he could not say. Test tubes and Petri dishes and conical flasks, with pipes joining one to the other; white coats, too, and plastic goggles and possibly the odd Bunsen burner: these, in Graves's mind, are the essential elements of a medical-research laboratory. Instead there are eight cots, spaced across the room, and the kind of equipment – drip stands, ventilator tubes, heart-rate monitors – that Graves would consider more befitting an intensive-care unit. Guards – men mainly, dressed in jeans and jogging bottoms, T-shirts and football tops – are bearing boxes and unloading them and

138

even, in the furthest corner, making up the cots into beds. Silk, it seems, has Graves's staff working as chamber maids and apparently without complaint. It is scandalous, of course: they should be resting; they should be switched off from work in order that they return to their posts this afternoon prepared for it. Graves, though, cannot help but feel a measure of respect, not least because Silk also seems to have convinced them to take their instructions from a civilian – and a female civilian at that, when most of the male prison guards with whom Graves has ever worked seem unable to respect a woman even when she has earned the same uniform as them.

'You met Wood. Over there, directing your men, is Doyle. And Perkins . . . Perkins, I assume, is about somewhere. Ordinarily I would not have included two women in a team to be billeted in a facility such as this but, given the sexual proclivity of the majority of the male prisoners, they are probably safer than you or me.' Silk allows his lips to curl at one corner. 'Wouldn't you say so?'

Graves is watching Doyle. She seems young, no more than twenty-eight or so, which is older than Graves's daughter but not much. Rachel is, what – twenty-five now? Still a teenager, practically, and certainly nowhere near old enough to be working in a place like this. Graves wonders whether Doyle's father knows of his daughter's whereabouts. If he doesn't, he should. If he does, well. Either way Graves would like a talk with the man. But then he thinks of Rachel. He thinks, Rachel could be working in a place exactly like this and there's no guarantee she would tell me about it either.

'Henry? Did you hear me?'

'Sorry? What?'

'I was saying to Dr Silk here: we already have an infirmary.'

Graves glances about the room again. 'Right. John is quite right. The inmates, as their health deteriorates, are being cared for in their rooms but we have an additional four beds set aside for medical emergencies. We even have a small team of nurses.'

'Yes,' says Silk. 'Although from what I understand they already have their hands full.' This time the sneer is visible in his smile. Graves bridles. He is about to reply but Silk does not give him time. 'Nevertheless, I am not here to gather the overspill from your dinner-table altercations. I would have thought Rupert would have made that at least quite clear.'

'Rupert? Who is Rupert?'

'Rupert Jenkins,' says Silk. 'The minister of state.' His tone is one Graves has on occasion resorted to himself – with employees, usually, who struggle to grasp what should be obvious. Again he feels himself reddening. 'The point,' Silk continues, 'is that this is not just another infirmary. Rupert – Mr Jenkins – is not inclined to waste my talents treating grazed knees and tickly throats.'

'In which case,' Graves says, 'may I ask how your talents, as you describe them, are to be directed? The home secretary said you were working on a cure. Why would you need to come here unless—' Graves stops. Silk smiles.

'Unless what?' says Burrows. 'Henry?'

'Unless he already has a cure. Or thinks he does.'

'Really?' says Burrows, turning to Silk. 'You have a cure?'

'We are not there yet. But we have made progress, to the

point where we have certain interventions ready for trial. There is every reason to believe—'

'I cannot allow it.'

Silk looks to Graves. Burrows turns too.

'I am sorry, Dr Silk, but if you are here for the reason I think you are here, I cannot – will not – allow it.'

'Henry—'

'John, please,' says Graves, raising a hand. He is waiting for the doctor to speak. Silk regards Graves as though he were observing the side effect of some experiment: an unforeseen side effect, and curious for it, but of little more than passing interest.

'I don't understand,' says Burrows. 'If the doctor is working on a cure, Henry, what could you possibly—'

'For pity's sake, John.' Graves glares at his assistant. 'He is here to experiment. This isn't an infirmary. It's his laboratory. These beds: they're for his lab rats.'

Gently, Silk laughs. 'Please, Henry. These people are dying. It is my intention to heal them, not to hasten their demise.'

'I understand very well your intentions, Dr Silk. And I repeat: I will not stand for it. I will not allow you to deceive these people, to mislead them, to experiment on them without their knowledge.'

'Really,' says Silk and he tuts. 'What do you take me for? I am not some modern-day Mengele. The inmates will not be misled. They will not be tricked or coerced. They will be asked to volunteer and they will do so. They will, I would imagine, be clawing at the chance to participate in trials that may very well save their lives.'

'They do not know their lives are in danger! They do not know why they are here!'

'Ah. You are right, of course. But that is one thing, at least, we can remedy immediately. It is a task, in fact, you might perhaps take on yourself.'

Graves folds his arms. 'My orders do not allow for that. On the contrary, I have been instructed to insulate the inmates entirely from news about why they have been interned.'

'Those were your orders, Henry. I am changing them.'

'With respect, Dr Silk—'

'With respect, Mr Graves,' says Silk, finally betraying his impatience. 'I do not care what your instructions are. I do not care what you will and will not stand for. You are the gover-nor of this facility but that is all you are. Talk to Rupert Jenkins, by all means. Talk to the prime minister if he will take your call. They will say to you what I am saying now. You. Are no longer. In charge.'

Graves opens his mouth to reply. He looks around him. Burrows is watching. Doyle, the doctor's assistant, is watching. The guards – his own guards – are watching too.

'Now,' Silk says. 'If you would be so kind, Henry. My instruc-tion to you still stands. Tell the prisoners.'

The Price We Pay

by Tom Clarke

So what have we learnt? That there's a virus out there and it's a killer. That there's no cure. That seven people have died so far and scores of others will die too. That we faced disaster but . . . it was averted. We're in safe hands. We elected this government to do a job and, by God, they've gone and done it. Move along, folks – there's nothing to see here.

All's well, then. What a relief. What a relief to know that Margaret Myers has our best interests so close to what passes for her heart. I don't know about you but I for one will sleep better tonight knowing that, to quote the home secretary, 'the carriers of the disease have been isolated'. That the risk to me and to my friends and to my family is zero because this disease, whatever this disease is, has been confined to men and women characterised by their 'high-risk behaviour' and 'aggressive promiscuity'. My sense of rectitude will keep me warm. The Unified Security blanket will keep me snug.

Because this is what we do to such people, is it not? It's what we've always done. When a person is careless enough to fall ill with a disease they've clearly brought upon themselves, we moralise them into a corner. We round them up and shut them away (physically if we can; figuratively if it's the best we can manage) and turn the other cheek. As long as it's a stranger, not a friend or a relative or – perish the thought – *you*, what does it matter what fate befalls them? It is a question of the greater good, after all. It is sacrificing the immoral few on behalf of the enfranchised many.

Never mind, for instance, that 'aggressive promiscuity' is meaningless drivel; that it is a moralistic turn of phrase intended to misinform, mislead, misdirect. Never mind, too, that 'high-risk behaviour' implies a convenient disregard of the policies, espoused by Myers and her cronies, that have helped generate such behaviour in the first place: shutting down needle-exchange programmes; slashing public-health spending; promoting abstinence and 'family values' and ignoring real-world sexual behaviour; fostering an economic climate that rewards the rich for being rich and flushes the poorest, the most in need of help, into society's gutter.

Never mind all that.

What matters is that we're safe. What matters is, *I* am safe. Eighty-six men and women have been apprehended and incarcerated, as though they were criminals; denied legal representation or even advice, as though they were terrorists; stripped of their civil rights and torn from their families, as though they were anything but human beings. But just keep repeating: *I am safe*.

It's a price worth paying, I hear you say. Because it's a valid argument, isn't it? I mean, regardless of who the victims of this disease are – of what narrow sociological term the home secretary chooses to define them – it's the right policy regardless. It's the best way to safeguard this nation. It's what we'd do to eighty-six citizens of any stripe or creed, even if they happened to be . ... I don't know. Civil servants, let's say. Members of parliament.

Wouldn't we?

Eighty-six Muslims, perhaps, because no doubt the government would find a way to spin some spurious link to the threat of terrorism. But any group but the most readily castigated, the most morally maligned, the most politically isolated? Please. Do not be fooled. *We* are the victims: every one of us. The people locked away in this so-called facility are our neighbours, our children, our loved ones. The truth is in the headline the *News of the World* used to break this story (and there's a phrase I never thought I would find myself typing): GUANTANAMO UK. This facility – wherever it is, whatever it truly is – is our disgraceful, inexcusable equivalent. The greater good is no defence. The facility, rather, is this government's greatest wrong.

So, that question again: what have we learnt? That disaster was averted. That we're in safe hands. That we elected this government to do a job and, by God, they've gone and done it. Move along, folks. Hold your nose and avert your eyes. There's nothing to see here.

She has finished reading. Her eyes have settled on the final line and for some time they remain there. Tom waits. He does not look at her directly but he is watching for her reaction. His gaze moves from his fingers knotted in his lap to the pages in Julia's hands to her expressionless profile and back again. It takes a squeal and then a wail from the sandpit ahead of them to jolt Julia into movement.

'Casper,' she says. 'Casper!' She drops the clutch of pages on to the bench. She is two steps on to the sand when her son spies her approach. Without waiting to be told, he returns the spade he has stolen to the girl playing next to him. He picks up a stick and starts burrowing with that instead. Julia hesitates. She makes to say something, to issue some reprimand, but Casper is paying her no attention. He jabs with his stick and gouges at the sand and he does so with his chin tucked against his collarbone. He is not smiling. He has not smiled, as far as Tom can remember, in the time Tom has been with them.

'Do up your coat, Casper.' Julia's voice is gentle. She tugs at Casper's zip but he continues playing as though she were not there. She stands over him for a moment, then retreats.

'He seems . . .' Tom says but he is wary of finishing the sentence.

'He's okay.' Julia sits again, hunching her shoulders as though mindful suddenly of the cold. 'He doesn't even know anything's wrong. Not really.'

Tom watches the boy. He is a rustier blond than his mother but his skin is as fair and his eyes the same grey-green. When he frowns, as he is doing now, he does so with the same fervour. 'I just meant, I don't know. That it must be hard on him. This. Seeing you upset.' Tom hesitates. 'Also,' he says, 'the separation.' For an instant he meets Julia's eyes.

'You know about that?'

Tom nods. Casper has abandoned the stick and is instead piling sand across one of his outstretched legs. The sand is damp and it clings to the boy's shin as readily as a plaster cast.

'It doesn't change things, you know,' says Julia. 'The fact that we're apart doesn't make me any less determined to find him.'

'Of course not. I didn't say that.'

'What then? You're annoyed that I didn't tell you?'

'No. Not at all.'

'It sounded like you were accusing me of something.'

'I wasn't.'

'What then? Why mention it?' Julia seems angry but unduly so. Tom bridles.

'Just . . . I don't know. Just so you know I know. And so you know that you could have told me if you wanted to. Because, well.' Tom knows he should not say what he is about to. He says it anyway. 'It might have helped. That's all.'

Julia smiles, open-mouthed. It is not a kind smile. 'What difference does it make? How could it possibly have helped?'

'I was looking for clues,' says Tom. 'I was looking for patterns.' Julia scoffs.

'Is there anything else you haven't told me?' Tom did not mean to start an argument – does not mean to continue one now – but the release of emotion is intoxicating.

Julia folds her arms. 'Like what, for instance?'

'Like, I don't know. Like anything that might have helped.

147

Like . . . Christ. Like why the two of you split up. I mean, if the reason is connected somehow to this disease . . .'

'Are you asking me whether Arthur is gay?'

'No. Of course not.'

'Or whether he took drugs? Whether he slept with hookers?'

'That's not what—'

'Let's say he's gay, that we split up because Arthur's gay. So what? So bloody what?'

'Wait,' says Tom. 'What does that mean? That he is gay?'

'No!' Julia tilts her head and, with one hand, grips the skin above her eyes. 'He's not gay. Okay? He doesn't do drugs and as far as I know he hasn't had sex since he and I split up. I mean, he still . . . He won't even accept that he and I . . .' She drops her elbows to her knees, her body folding in on itself, but then reaches suddenly and picks up the printout of Tom's column and tosses the pages towards him. 'He's not dying, Tom. He hasn't got this . . . this *thing*.' She slumps forwards once again. The curve of her back betrays a tremble.

Tom opens his mouth to reply. He shuts it again, swallows. He did not think. He was preoccupied with the article, with everything he had been obliged to leave out. Arthur, in particular, was not mentioned because Katherine had refused to allow it. There was, in fact, nothing expressing particular concern about the prisoners anywhere else on the site, nor in any of the major newspapers. Their fate was being ignored, except by a senior churchman whose comments had made it to page three of the *Telegraph*: debauchery, he maintained, was a sin, and homosexuality a precursor to paedophilia, so perhaps it was no bad thing that these people were locked away with their demons. As far as Tom could see, the dearth of sympathetic coverage was the problem.

'Listen, Julia. He doesn't have it. I'm sure he doesn't.'

Julia does not answer. Her head is still in her hands and she angles it away.

Tom reaches to place a hand on her shoulder but pulls it back before it settles. 'We don't even know if he's there. I mean, why would he be? There's no reason for them to have taken him there.'

Now Julia looks across. Her eyes shine and the tracks of her tears are sketched with make-up. 'He's there. Of course he's there. There's no reason for them to have taken him there but that's what they did. You heard the home secretary. The timing fits exactly.' She drags a hand across one cheek, then the other. She slides her fingers into her hair and grips. She pulls herself straight and immediately her face crumples. 'Casper. Oh, Casper, honey.'

Tom looks and sees what Julia sees. Casper is watching his mother cry and he is crying too: not the tears Tom would expect of a three-year-old boy – tears, for instance, like the little girl shed when Casper took her spade, which dry quickly and are anyway more heard than seen – but steady, silent, rolling tears. The boy drops his head again as his mother moves to his side. Julia crouches, then kneels in the sand. She lifts the boy's chin. She runs a thumb across his cheek and gathers Casper to her. She says his name again. She strokes his head. She says his name.

Tom watches but in spite of himself. He turns away but it feels wrong to turn away too so he turns back. He slides forwards on the bench. He thinks perhaps he should stand. He looks at his feet and then at the boy and now the boy is watching him. Tom attempts a smile but the impression it creates, or so it feels, is of a shrug. The boy stares and his own expression does not change: blank, emotionless – reproachful. Again Tom looks to his feet.

'We should go home.' Julia has the boy in her arms. She is standing at the edge of the sandpit and facing Tom. Casper's chin is hooked over her shoulder, his arms draped around her neck. 'I shouldn't have brought him.' Julia carries Casper to the buggy but does not put him in. She whispers and runs her fingertips up and down the boy's spine.

Tom gets to his feet. 'I'm sorry,' he says. 'I didn't want to . . . I didn't mean to . . .'

Julia lowers her son into the buggy and bends to fasten the straps. She reaches into one of the canvas pockets and pro-duces a parcel of tinfoil. She opens it, offers whatever is inside to the boy. Casper shakes his head. He turns to one side. Julia strokes his hair. She kisses his temple.

'I should have told you.' Julia is crouched beside her son and it takes a moment for Tom to realise that she is talking to him.

'What? No. It makes no difference. Just like you said.'

Julia stands. 'I still should have told you. I didn't because . . . I didn't at first because it sounded complicated. This thing, this situation, it was complicated enough. I was coming to you – to a stranger – for help and . . . I don't know. I didn't want to confuse things.' She smooths away a tear. 'After that,' she says. 'Well. After that I suppose I just felt . . . I just felt . . .'

'Julia. You don't need to explain. Really. You should just ignore me.'

'It didn't work,' says Julia, looking up. 'Arthur and me. There was no great secret, no betrayal, no melodramatic break-up. I came to this country to study and Arthur was virtually the first person I met. We became friends. Somehow, later on, we convinced ourselves we were more than that. I mean, we knew, when we got married, that we were mainly doing it so I could stay. But we told ourselves we loved each other enough.' Julia smiles. 'It was the accent: that's what Arthur always said. That I was just a sucker for his home-counties accent.'

Tom studies his hands.

'Now we're friends again. Maybe we should only ever have been friends. Although I can't tell you how glad I am that we took a chance.' Julia rolls her fingers around her son's ear to tidy a loose strand of hair. Casper does not move. He has his eyes closed and breathes as though asleep. 'So that's our story,' says Julia. She laughs. 'Not a very exciting one, I'm afraid.' She looks at Tom. 'But I should have told you. I'm sorry I didn't.'

Tom is about to reply – to apologise again, to tell her it is none of his business – but Casper shuffles and they turn to look. The boy's eyes are wide now but directed away from their own. They are focused on the inside of the buggy's hood.

'We should get going,' says Julia. She moves behind the buggy and holds its handles. She pushes, struggling to get it moving on the uneven grass.

'Julia.' Tom steps towards her. He reaches, then hesitates – then reaches again and takes Julia's hand. Her fingers coil willingly into his. 'I haven't given up.'

Julia nods. She smiles and the smile brings more tears. 'I know.' Her grip on Tom's hand tightens. 'Neither have I.'

'**It had to be.**' Roach grins. He shakes his head, as though astonished at himself for missing what should have been obvious. 'Didn't it? Either that or something, you know. Political.' He laughs, shakes his head again. 'And it was never going to be anything political. I mean, I don't even vote. Never have. Not once. No,' he says and he holds up a finger. 'I did vote once but only because the bloke who was standing was openly gay. I thought, good on him. I thought, he deserves a bit of solidarity. But I couldn't tell you what party he was. Monster Raving Loony, probably. Hah, yeah. Probably he was a Monster Raving Loony.' Roach paces, covering the length of Arthur's cell and then turning. 'So I'm not exactly an activist. Right? I'm not exactly a revolutionary, though Lord knows we could do with a bit of revolution in this country. I'm just an ageing, unemployed black man who happens to be homosexual. For them to even notice me, it had to be something like this.' He shakes his head once more, still smiling. There is spittle at the corner of his mouth and he wipes it. He stops pacing. He stops grinning too, as though his momentum had somehow been

152

powering his facial muscles. The rest of him, likewise, seems to droop – his arms, his shoulders, his chin. 'Fuck,' he says. He sits. 'Fuck.'

A spear of sunlight from the narrow window severs the room, tracing a path to the open door. Arthur is on one side of the line, perched on his bunk; Roach sits on the other, on the bare mattress of the unassigned cot. He has lodged himself between Arthur's discarded nightclothes and the rest of his scant belongings: his wash kit, in a mesh bag that has already begun to fray; a golf magazine, illicit and insipid; his outdoor coat; a deck of cards he has drawn himself, still arranged in an abandoned game of patience. Arthur has his forearms propped on his knees and the beam of light warms a narrow strip of skin below his rolled-up sleeves. He notices how pale he is, as well as how raw his wrists and hands are. From the soap, Arthur imagines, which comes in blocks that look like the bricks they toss into urinals and is so harsh it might indeed be solidified disinfectant. Also, he is used to hand lotion. Atrixo was his brand – that or Neutrogena. He would fuss, he recalls, were Julia ever to bring home anything else.

'Who told you?' says Roach and Arthur looks up.

'Sorry?'

'Who told you? Who was there? Was it Graves? That's his name, right? The bloke in charge? And his assistant. Burrows, is it?'

Arthur nods, lets his gaze drop.

'In a group, right? Like, ten of you?'

Again Arthur nods. 'Something like that.' He looks at Roach. 'Wilson was there. You remember Wilson?'

'Mr Wilson,' says Roach. 'Your would-be patient.'

'He didn't look well.'

Again Roach gives a grunt. 'No. Although I don't expect any of us did. Bit of a shock to the system, isn't it?' His voice adopts a tone. 'Sit down, everyone. Got a bit of news for you. It's a bit of a doozy this one, so brace yourselves. Basically, what it boils down to is this: you're all going to die. So, er, yes. Sorry about that. Next!'

Arthur attempts a smile. He can do no better than a grimace. 'I suppose. Although what I meant was, he didn't look well on the way in.' He glances at Roach and Roach catches his eye, his meaning, and both men look away.

For a moment they are quiet. Roach coughs and it is just a cough but he has been coughing, on and off, for more than a week now. But it is just a cough. Roach smokes, Arthur knows, or did smoke before they arrived here – as good a time as any to give up, Roach told him – so probably the cough is something to do with that. Roach, though, sees Arthur looking. 'I need a cigarette,' he says, as though also having tuned to Arthur's thoughts. Then, as though to substantiate them: 'Every time I try to give up I start drowning in phlegm.' He coughs again, gestures to his throat in apparent annoyance. 'Let's go for a stroll. I'll cadge one from one of the others.'

They walk together along the corridor. Roach affects nonchalance, as though such freedom of movement were nothing unusual, were in fact his absolute right, but Arthur remains wary. It is only today – since lunchtime, following the announcements in the morning – that security has been relaxed enough for them to be able to go where they please within the main compound, and with whom. Although relaxed is the wrong word. Security, rather, has been distanced. The guards are there still but they stand further back. The regulations, the procedures: nothing has altered, they have been told, except for the element of trust. It feels almost respectful – as though the prisoners were being afforded the space to mourn. It is not, though, what Arthur would have expected. On the contrary, he would have anticipated tighter restrictions, more isolation, limitations on opportunities for them to confer. Why address the prisoners in groups, after all, if there had been no expectation of trouble? It was more compassionate, certainly, than addressing them all together but inadvertently, Arthur is sure. Like the security, which seems kind-hearted but more likely is calculated: a concession that concedes nothing. The people here have been told they are going to die. Who among them is likely to have any hunger left for a fight?

Certainly the prisoners Arthur and Roach encounter seem stunned. As they make their way along the corridor, they see men and women lying on their bunks. One or two appear visibly unwell – just the flu, they all assumed; it is that time of year, after all – and too weak perhaps to do anything else. Others, though, seem simply to lack the will to stand. They lie with their hands behind their heads and their eyes gazing sightless to the ceiling. One man is on his side, his fists drawn to his throat and his knees to his stomach.

The recreational area, when they reach it, at first appears almost empty but the prisoners inside have gravitated to the dimmest corners. There is little movement. Some people have gathered in groups, their toes touching in the centre of the circles they form, their conversation low, intermittent, interrupted occasionally by bursts of hushed, nervous laughter. There are several couples – a man and a woman, two pairs of men – and they seem intimate. Most of the inmates, though, sit alone. Three share a table – a man at either end, a woman in the centre – and each is hunched over a sheet of paper. The men scrawl as though running out of time in an examination; the woman has her pen poised but seems frozen, as though the blank sheet of paper were an approaching set of headlights. Or perhaps the woman suspects what Arthur thinks he knows: that the paper and envelopes they have been offered will, regardless of what is written on them, never actually be sent.

'Arthur,' says Roach and Arthur feels his friend's touch on his shoulder. 'Let's go outside. I'll ask someone outside.'

They return the way they came, continuing past the stairs until they reach the door to the courtyard. They step outside and into the shadow of the covered walkway. The sun, though, is directly overhead and the square itself is a prism of crisp autumn sunshine. There is a group of ten or so men draped around the fountain and, in defiance of the lingering chill, several have removed their shirts. They could be pink-skinned tourists just off the coach in an Italian piazza. Or soldiers: fatigued and frightened but fuelling themselves while they can for the battle that lies ahead.

Roach has spotted a man smoking and he drifts from Arthur's side. Arthur waits in the shade cast by the nearest column. It is the first time the sun has broken through since their arrival and any other day Arthur would probably be seated in the square himself. Today, though, he would rather linger in the shadows. The sunshine feels cruel rather than convivial. Like the expression on the face of the guard who stands behind him, it seems smug somehow; gleeful but also spiteful. Roach, though, has his cigarette and is waving Arthur to his side. Arthur squints and shuffles into the sunshine.

They sit apart from the group of men. Roach reclines, crossing his ankles in front of him and propping himself on his elbows. Arthur faces him, his knees to his chest and his shoulders to the sun. He scoops a handful of gravel and shuffles it in his fist as though it were dice. He tosses it, then brushes the dirt from his palm.

'I got two,' says Roach. 'I know you don't want it but I'm gonna offer you one anyway. It would be rude not to.'

Arthur shakes his head. 'They turn your teeth yellow. Apart from anything else.'

'That they do.' Roach tucks the second cigarette behind his ear. He drags on the first, pauses, then sends a cloud towards the pale blue sky. He coughs and his cough sounds looser. He taps his chest with a fist. 'Better than Benylin.'

They sit in silence while Roach smokes. When he is done, he grinds the cigarette on the ground and piles a cairn around the filter. He unbuttons his shirt and reclines again and angles his face skywards. He shuts his eyes. In the daylight, Arthur thinks, he looks older. He has told Arthur he is fifty-something – fifty-what? Arthur asked; fifty-and-some, Roach replied – but Arthur found it hard to believe. Looking at him now, though, he could be sixty, sixty-five. The sun casts him in a harsh light. Arthur notices the lines running like cracks from the corner of his eyes, the greyish tinge to the bags beneath them, the rash of what look like liver spots on his forehead. His chest, once powerful, Arthur can tell, sags. The hair – sparse, tight coils – is greyer here than at his temples.

'There's an optimist and a pessimist,' says Roach. He still has his eyes closed but he is smiling slightly, anticipating perhaps his own punch line. 'The pessimist says, the situation's awful. It's terrible, he says. It couldn't possibly be any worse! The optimist says, oh yes it could.'

Roach laughs and Arthur smiles, as much at his friend's delight as the joke itself. 'That's old,' Arthur says. 'I use that one on my patients.'

They fall silent again but the silence is interrupted by a splash. Roach opens his eyes and Arthur turns and they see a man standing in the fountain. He is naked but for his boxers and clearly freezing but he holds his arms aloft as though triumphant. The men around him grin, clap, cheer. Roach gives a hoot and beats a palm against a thigh. Arthur looks for guards. He sees one edge towards the fountain from beneath the walkway, then another move to his side and place a hand on his arm. Both men draw back.

'Lunatic,' says Roach, beaming. 'Lunatic!'

The man does not hear. He is marching around the fountain, lifting his knees and stomping his feet and dousing those too slow to leap aside. Arthur watches, thinking about the paddling pool he bought for Casper on a visit to Julia's place the previous summer. It took him an hour to blow it up because he forgot to buy a pump, then another thirty minutes to fill it – and when it was ready his son refused to go in.

His neck begins to ache from craning and he turns away from the impromptu entertainment. He watches Roach watching, until his friend's attention drifts too. A cloud covers the sun momentarily and Roach looks up, then around the courtyard. His gaze settles in his lap.

'What about these trials? What do you think?'

'I think . . .' says Arthur. 'I think I don't know what to think.'

'You wouldn't consider it? If you had this . . .' Roach rolls a hand in the air. He does not finish the sentence.

'I'd consider it. Certainly I would. But they're asking you to trust them.' Arthur meets Roach's eye. 'Do you?'

There is jeering from the centre of the square. A guard – the guard, Arthur thinks, who was straining to intervene earlier – is dragging the prisoner from the fountain. He has hold of the man at his elbow and tugs him so he stumbles against the concrete surround. The prisoner half crawls on to the gravel and the guard lifts a finger and says something to the prisoners close by. The jeering stops. The guard turns his back and, with his thumbs on his belt, saunters to his post in the shadows.

'It's different,' says Roach. 'Don't you think? It's not like they have anything to gain by lying. Not about this.'

'Maybe,' says Arthur. 'But, well . . . I don't know. For one thing, you don't even know if you have it. This disease, whatever this disease is. You don't even know if it's real.'

Roach smiles but it is a tired smile. 'It's real, Arthur. Why the hell would we be here if it weren't? And anyway,' he says. 'I've got something.'

'What? What do you mean? If you mean the cough—'

Roach shakes his head. 'Forget the cough. The cough's smoking, like I said. But I've got, you know.' He nods to his lap. To his groin. 'Something.' He grins suddenly. 'Want me to show you?'

Arthur does not smile back. 'I'll look. If you want me to look, I'll look.'

Roach laughs. 'Now that is a true friend.'

'What? I'm a dentist, remember?'

This time Roach laughs so hard that a guard turns in their direction. 'Stop,' Roach says. 'Please.' He is crying, Arthur realises. He is pressing the heel of his hands to his eyes as though trying to force the tears back inside but a bead of water rolls to his chin. Arthur draws back his shoulders. He waits. Roach catches sight of his expression and he holds up a hand. His laughter slows to a trickle. 'I'm sorry.' There is a visible swell of glee within him but he contains it. He wipes at his eyes again. 'Man,' he says and he chuckles. Arthur keeps his expression rigid. Roach, though, looks at him with genuine warmth and Arthur feels the tension in his jaw ease.

'I'll spare you. It's very kind of you to offer, Arthur, but I'll spare you. Look here though,' Roach says and he shows Arthur the inside of his elbow. 'And here, on my forehead.' He points to the marks that Arthur assumed were liver spots. 'It doesn't hurt yet and they said it would hurt, I think, but it only came up a few days ago.' Another laugh escapes him but it is a splutter. It is like the final rasp from an empty aerosol.

'That's just . . .' Arthur leans to look at Roach's cheeks. 'It could be anything.'

'That's what I thought. Yesterday, that's what I thought.'

'What then? You're going to put your name down?'

Roach shrugs. He opens his mouth to answer, then closes it. He shrugs again.

They sit for a while. In spite of the sunshine, Arthur begins to feel chilled. He shivers and shifts himself around so that he is at Roach's side and the sun is on his face.

'What about you?' Roach says. 'Have you made any progress?'

Arthur flicks at a stone beside his feet. 'It depends what you count as progress. Last time I asked, I got this.' He angles his head to show Roach the knuckle mark behind his ear. 'He drew blood. The guard did. I think he was going for something less visible but he looked pretty pleased with himself nonetheless.' He glances at his friend. 'I don't know. I think ... I think maybe you were right.' He sees Roach about to protest and cuts him short. 'I know: you didn't say anything. But you didn't need to.' He picks out another stone, tosses it away. 'But after today. After what they've just told us. They're not about to call me a taxi.'

'What about Graves?' says Roach. 'You should talk to Graves.'

'That's what I've been trying to do. He won't see me.'

'So,' says Roach, 'go and see him. Now's the time, right? They said we can go where we please.'

'I don't think they meant—'

'Arthur. Seriously. Go and see him. Because everything they've told us today – it's good news for you. You realise that, don't you?'

Arthur feels disgust crease his face.

'I'm not kidding, Arthur. Don't get all noble on me.'

'Jesus Christ.'

'You have a family, Arthur. You can't take no for—'

Arthur snaps before he can stop himself. 'Do you think I've forgotten? My wife, my son: do you think my family has slipped my mind?'

Roach drops his head. Arthur glares, then drops his too.

'I'm sorry,' says Roach. 'I didn't mean . . .'

'Forget it.' Arthur sighs. 'It's not like I'm angry with you. And it's not like I'm the only person in here with a family.'

Again they are silent but Roach, after a minute or two, breaks it with laughter. He sniffs, then he snorts, then there is the sound like sobbing and Arthur turns. His friend is grinning. '"I'll look,"' he says, parodying Arthur. His voice goes high. '"I'm a dentist!"' He sniggers, snorts again, and Arthur cannot help but smile.

'I would have looked,' he says and Roach howls.

'And I would have let you. Only, well, I didn't want you getting a complex.' Roach beams. 'You being a white guy and all.'

Graves has half a mind to leave. His arms are crossed and he angles his wrist to see his watch face. He does not register the time but as he does not know what time he arrived it does not seem important. It is the gesture rather. It is his obvious impatience. It is the fact that Graves is the governor of this facility but Silk seems determined to treat him as just another of his assistants.

He steps forwards. 'Dr Silk.'

This time Silk does not even look. From across the room, he shows Graves the sleeve of his white coat, his upraised index finger. 'Just a moment, please.'

The doctor is fussing over a piece of machinery – a monitor of some kind. He gives a solid impression of a man enjoying himself. It is science. It is life and death. It is a serious business, you would suppose, but watching Silk you would not know it. He bustles and badgers and buzzes from bed to bed, as though he were preparing to throw a party. He seems as eager to begin as his guests, in fact: from what Graves understands, thirty-three inmates had signed up for the trials by the

SIMON LELIC

previous evening, within hours of having been told that anything was wrong with them. Now, barely twelve hours later, the
lucky eight who have been selected fill the beds, ready to imbibe
whatever cocktail of drugs their eager host passes round.

'He looks like he knows what he's doing,' says a voice. 'Don't
you think?'

Graves turns. The prisoner on the bed nearest is propped
upright against the headboard. Like Graves, he is watching Silk.

'Pardon me?'

'The doctor,' the prisoner says. 'He looks like he knows what
he's doing.'

Graves follows the prisoner's line of sight. Silk is frowning at a clipboard. He scribbles. He ticks. He scribbles again.
He holds out the clipboard for one of his assistants to take
from him, then moves on to his next task. 'Yes,' says Graves.
'He looks like he knows what he's doing.'

The prisoner seems not to catch the cynicism in Graves's
tone. 'Do you think he's found it, Mr Graves? The cure, I mean.'

He is a thin, oily man, who would look ill, Graves suspects,
even if his face were not quite so blotched, his eyes not quite
so bloodshot. He has the look of a man children might avoid
in the street but there is also something of a child about his
demeanour. He shoulders are hunched, his forehead creased.
With his left hand he grips his right thumb, worrying at the
skin as though it were a surrogate for a shred of blanket or a
lost childhood toy.

'What's your name?' says Graves. He leans to read from the
chart at the foot of the bed at the same time as the prisoner
answers.

164

'Wilson,' the prisoner says. 'Pleased to meet you.'

He seems to say this last almost as a reflex – as a result of the same conditioning, perhaps, that taught him please or thank you or may I get down from the table?

'Do you though?' Wilson is watching Silk again. 'Do you think he's found the cure?'

'I'm afraid I couldn't say. There is always that possibility, I suppose.'

'Because if he has,' Wilson says, as though Graves had not spoken, 'then I don't think I should be here. I don't think I deserve to be.' The thumb that he grips is now quite bloodless. He persists at wrenching it as though determined to work it loose.

Graves angles himself towards the man's bed. 'What makes you say that?'

Wilson does not answer. He shrugs. He swallows. He looks down at his nervous hands.

Graves leans again to read from the chart. 'Your Christian name,' he says. 'Benedict. Do you know what it means?'

'Only my mother ever called me Benedict. It's religious, I think.'

'That's right. It's Catholic. It means blessed, Mr Wilson. It means your parents were asking God to protect you.'

For a moment Wilson's hands stop working. He opens his mouth to say something. The voice that follows, though, comes from across Graves's shoulder.

'Not upsetting my patients I hope, Henry?'

'Dr Silk,' says Graves. He turns to Wilson. 'Excuse me,' he says and Wilson responds with an emphatic nod. Graves steps away from the bed and Silk follows. 'I'd like a word with you, if I may.'

'Will it take long? I am rather busy, as you can see.'

'It won't take a minute. Shall we?' Graves gestures to the double doors that lead into the corridor and takes another step. With a sigh, Silk follows.

'I must say,' says Graves once they are outside, 'you are not wasting any time.'

'Certainly not. There is very little time to waste.' Silk checks his watch.

'No. Of course. And I shan't keep you long. But there is a matter, I feel, that is relatively urgent. I have discussed it with the minister of state and he advised me to bring it to your attention.'

Silk nods impatiently. He is yet to let go of the handle on the door behind him.

'It concerns the testing.' Graves tries to keep his tone even, unhurried. 'Of some of the prisoners. Their test results, in fact. Their negative test results.'

The doctor rolls his eyes. He actually rolls his eyes. 'There is a window period, Henry. I would have thought, by now, you would have understood that a person can be infected without—'

'It has elapsed, Dr Silk. It had elapsed, in most cases, before the initial testing was undertaken. Not only that: these people – there are eighteen altogether – have shown no signs of infection since.'

Silk is shaking his head even before Graves has finished speaking. 'It means nothing. The disease may lie dormant for months before manifesting itself.' Graves is about to interrupt but Silk holds up a hand. 'It tends not to, it is true, but this is new, Henry. We cannot take any chances, at any stage. And besides,' he says and he smirks, 'given the lifestyles the majority of the prisoners have chosen; given their . . . proximity, shall we say, to others who are carrying the disease, it is highly likely they have been tempted into behaviour since their arrival here that has once again put them at risk. In which case, the window period begins anew.'

Now Graves shakes his head. 'They have been kept apart. They have not had the opportunity to put themselves at risk. What's more,' he says and he feels the leash on his temper growing taut, 'they are human beings. They are not mindless, rutting animals, for heaven's sake.'

Silk lifts his eyebrows. His lips slip sideways.

'They should be re-tested,' Graves says, more aggressively than he intended. He takes a breath. 'They could be re-tested. That is all I am asking. Because there is a chance isn't there, that . . . I don't know. That they used protection, for instance. That they didn't have contact in the first place. That they are only here because a mistake has been made.'

'A mistake? What kind of mistake?'

'They were rounded up. Weren't they? Perhaps – in the confusion, in the understandable haste to ensure the virus was contained – perhaps some of these people were detained when they did not need to be. Perhaps the information that led to their incarceration was somehow . . . tainted.'

'Tainted?' Silk smiles. 'It is a quaint theory, Henry, but it does not change things. These people are here because, no matter what the test results say, there is every chance they are carrying the virus. That, as far as I am concerned, is the end of it.'

'Dr Silk,' says Graves. 'Please. We are dealing with people's lives. All I am asking—'

'There,' says Silk, locking his arms across his chest. 'You said it yourself. We are dealing with people's lives. Not just the prisoners' lives. Thousands, millions of people's lives. Testing takes time. Analysing the results takes time, it takes resources. My mandate is clear, Henry. My purpose here is clear. Perhaps you should re-evaluate yours.' And with that he turns and opens the door and allows it to slam in his wake.

Burrows is at his desk, in the room adjoining Graves's office. Graves walks past. He ignores his assistant's greeting, the note in his tone suggesting there is business to be dealt with, and he does not turn as Burrows gets to his feet. He strides into his office and he shuts the door with a bang. He leans on his desk. He exhales. He breathes in. He exhales. He takes another breath and he moves round the desk and he drops his weight into his chair.

It is hot. Is it hot or is it him? Yesterday was an aberration and today there is no sun – the sky, rather, is the colour of an unlit light bulb. But it is hot, humid, as though it were August rather than November. Unless it is just this damned office, with its windows that do not open and its blinds so tangled they do not draw. He removes his jacket, which is too damned thick any-way. He wipes at his forehead. He reaches for the mouse to his computer and he wiggles it and wiggles it again and he wiggles it and wiggles it and still the damned screen remains blank. He hits the spacebar on his keyboard, the return key, all the keys. He wiggles the mouse again, then slams it on the surface of the desk, once, twice, a third time. He shoves it away and it collides with his telephone. 'Damn,' he says. 'Damn damn damn!'

There is a click and a squeak of rusting iron and the door to his office slides ajar. His assistant's nervous features poke through. 'Mr Graves?' Burrows says. He dare not risk a Henry, Graves notes. 'Is everything . . . It's just, there are a few things . . .'

'Come inside for pity's sake, man. Don't talk to me through the keyhole.'

Burrows opens the door more fully and slips into the office. He closes the door behind him but, like Silk, clings to the handle as he talks. 'How . . . How did it go?' He seems to notice Graves's expression. 'Never mind. Sorry. Um.'

'What is it, John? What do you want?'

Burrows clears his throat. 'There are some messages. Nothing urgent for the most part but there's one from the Home Office.'

'From Jenkins?'

'Indirectly, yes.'

'And? What's the message?'

Burrows shuffles. 'Well,' he says. 'I emailed you. It's all in my email. I think, basically . . . I mean, I don't think you need to call the minister back but . . .'

'Never mind. I'll take a look. What else?'

'There's a prisoner outside. Two, actually. One named Priestley, the other named Roach. Although only Priestley says he wants to see you.'

Graves waves a hand. 'Not now,' he says. Then, 'What does he want?'

'He wouldn't tell me. Just another request to see his family, I would imagine. It would be about the fifteenth today.'

'Where are they? Are they in your office? I didn't see—'

'They're in the corridor. They're sitting on the floor. There's a guard with them but, well, you said . . . That is, you gave instructions . . .'

'Let them sit there,' says Graves, wiggling his mouse again. He clicks the left button, then the right, then both together until he ends up slamming the mouse again on the desk. 'For heaven's sake, what's wrong with this infernal contraption? Why can't I see my screen?'

'I don't know.' Burrows takes a step forwards. 'Is the computer switched on?'

Graves looks under his desk. The light on the stack is, quite clearly, off.

Get a grip. For heaven's sake, man, get a grip.

'Never mind,' Graves says. 'I'll deal with it. It's probably a . . . a loose connection or something. Is that everything?'

'Other than the usual matters,' Burrows says. He points to Graves's computer and starts forwards once more. 'Are you sure you don't want me to take a—'

'I can manage.' The words come out with a snap. 'Thank you,' Graves adds.

Burrows gives a tentative nod. He walks backwards to the door and shuts it gently behind him.

*

It takes several moments for Graves's computer to boot up. As he waits, he turns away from the screen, from his reflection. He checks through the papers in his in tray. He sighs and tosses them back. He scans his desk and realises what a mess it has become. He is no slob but the lack of space even to prop his elbows is an unwelcome reminder of how quickly he is falling behind on matters that require his attention. Over here, for example: a stack of invoices and accounts awaiting his signature. And here: staff rosters and schedules – blank still – for the upcoming weeks. There are unopened letters, both incoming and outgoing, though the truth of course is that the outgoing ones are going nowhere. Graves feels obliged to read them, though. It is an intrusion, he acknowledges, but the net benefit to the inmates' welfare, if he knows what is on their minds, outweighs the infringement. As for the incoming letters, these are more bills probably, more problems, more sheets of paper to shuffle to other piles: here, here, here.

And here. Here are the files of the eighteen men and women who should not, in all likelihood, be under his charge at all. Graves reaches and as he does he remembers. Priestley. A; something beginning with A. Arnold? Arthur? Arthur. Arthur Priestley. The man in the corridor and one of the names on the folders in the pile. Graves slides off the top folder, the next one, the one after that and then he finds it. Priestley, Arthur James. He pulls the file free and sits back in his chair and hooks one leg over the other. He opens the folder and reads. Not that he needs to, he realises. He remembers the details: married but separated; one child – a young boy; not obviously gay but not necessarily straight; a doctor, wasn't it, or . . . no, a dentist.

Linked to the disease by a man named . . . Yes, of course. Wilson. Graves gives a snort at the coincidence. He turns to the final page and flicks backwards to the front, until his eyes settle again on Arthur's name.

For a moment he just sits, tapping the file against his knee. There is only the tapping and the ticking of his computer, until a chime sounds from the built-in speaker and a picture of a distant beach appears on his screen. Graves reaches for his mouse and clicks to open his inbox. The folder is in his other hand still and he moves at the same time to place it somewhere on his desk, somewhere apart from the others so he will remember to look at it properly later. There is nowhere. There is no space whatsoever. He has an urge to yell to Burrows, to instruct his assistant to find him a bigger desk, an extra desk, a set of shelves for pity's sake. He has an urge to yell but he resists. It would not help. The yelling might, for an instant, but surface area, he knows, is not the problem. It is all about control. That is what his ex-wife would tell him. She would tell him he is neat because he is a control freak and he gets irritated when things get messy because it is a sign he is losing his grip. In his mind, that is. A bit of mess is normal, Carol would say, to most people; it is a sign of life, of living, of not being beholden to work. And that is about as far as the conversation would get because then he would raise his voice or she would and one or other of them would throw up their hands and leave the room.

She has sent him an email. As though in anticipation of when his reading it would irritate him the most. And he does, of course, and it does irritate him, although he feels a little smug as well because who is the control freak now? She is worried about Rachel. About Rachel's job and Rachel's boyfriend, Nick, and where Rachel lives and why she so rarely calls. She thinks Graves should speak to her. She does not suggest what he should say. Change your job, change your boyfriend, get a new flat, call your mother. That, it seems, should be the gist of it because Lord knows Rachel takes such interfering well. About as well as her father does, in fact.

Graves closes the email and remembers about the message from the Home Office. He opens one of Burrows's emails but it is the wrong one so he closes it and clicks on the next. It is a single paragraph. Burrows could have told him in a sentence what the message was but Graves understands now why he opted to be so vague. There is another coach coming. They did not say when and they did not say with how many but Graves has been instructed to expect another coach. Which means the policy, the facility, has not worked, not yet. Which means his job here is far from finished. Which means . . . Which means . . .

Which means that Silk was right. His wife too, though he is just as loath to admit it. Because it is true that Graves has been stepping beyond his mandate. It is true that he reacts badly when his sense of control is undermined – which is exactly what happened the moment Silk arrived at the facility. Although more than anything Graves has brought this on himself: the frustration, the unattended piles on his desk, the sheer unprofessionalism of it all. What is he doing, wasting a day addressing the prisoners in groups when they could have been informed all together of their affliction in a matter of minutes?

Graves told Burrows it was a question of security but it was never that. The news, however many inmates were assembled, was always likely to be as effective as a blow to the solar plexus, a truncheon to the back of the knee. And look. Look at the time. It is gone eleven and what has he accomplished today? He has squandered the morning. More than the morning. He has squandered hours, studying these files and pondering these people's lives and caring whether Arthur James Priestley is a doctor or a dentist. And the single cells. Keeping Priestley and the others apart. How is that an efficient policy? How is that an effective allocation of the facility's limited resources? It is not and it will have to change. Because when the next coach arrives there simply will not be space.

He blames his age. In the past, at Wandsworth for example, or Liverpool, he never allowed personal frailties to infringe on his professional responsibilities. He had a thousand prisoners under his charge, more, and never was his desk in the state it is now. He is softening, that is the trouble. He knew he was and it is the reason he gave up permanent postings. But he is becoming more proprietorial, too, and that surprises him. Because after the break-up, after living on his own, he thought he had matured, not regressed; not succumbed to what is usually a younger man's failing. He thought – he would often think – she does not know me. She does not know the man I am now. If she knew how my life, my way of living, has changed . . .

Well. So much for that.

Quite: so much for that. For God's sake, man, pull yourself together. Silk has a job to do and he is doing it. Do yours.

It is that simple. It is your last post, probably, and what a hash you are making of things. What a way to crawl into retirement.

He calls for Burrows. Not in anger but with purpose – a purpose, he feels, that has been sorely lacking. He has Priestley's file still in his hand and when Burrows enters he passes it to him. 'Take this,' he says. 'Take those.' He gestures to the seventeen other folders. 'Put them with the others, in the proper order – there is no need to keep them apart.'

'Yes, sir.' Burrows picks up the stack from the desk. It leaves a foolscap-sized hole of laminated beech and just the sight of it gives Graves heart.

'Bring me some coffee, John, if you would. And lunch: I'll take lunch at my desk. Just a sandwich will be ample.'

'Of course,' says Burrows. 'I'll see to it.'

'One more thing.' Graves gestures with his chin towards the door – towards his assistant's room and the corridor beyond. 'Take Priestley and his friend back to their cells. Take all the prisoners back to their cells. They've had enough time now, wouldn't you say, to come to terms with why they are here?'

Burrows nods. 'Yes, sir. If you say so, sir.'

'Good,' says Graves. 'Good.' He picks up his pen. 'And see to it that I'm not disturbed. I've a stack of things to catch up on.'

He ignores the doorbell. It will be Craig, his jobless flatmate, too depressed to summon the energy to frisk his pockets to locate his key. If it is not Craig, it will be someone selling something – double glazing, dishcloths, a political candidate, God – and the only thing Tom needs is a clean pair of socks. Because he has none. None, at least, that match. Again he blames Craig because before Craig arrived socks were never an issue. These days they go missing. Tom will do a wash and hang out the damp clothes and there will be two pairs, three, of socks that are definitely his. But Craig steals them. Craig never does a wash, or not that Tom has ever seen, so when he runs out of socks he steals Tom's. It is the only possible explanation. Tom has had it in his mind to say something, to tell Craig to buy his own frigging socks, but if he were to start on socks he does not know where he would stop. The state of the bathroom. The bicycle that blocks their hall. The unwashed Weetabix bowls. Rent.

The bell rings again and Tom curses. He crosses the room and trots down the stairs to the front door. He squeezes past

Craig's bicycle and unhooks the latch and is already turning away as the door swings open. 'You've got a key, Craig,' he says as he climbs back up. 'It fits the lock and everything.'

'Er . . . Hi. Tom?'

Tom turns. He stoops so he can see. 'Julia. Hi. God. Sorry.'

'Is this a bad time?'

'No. God.' Tom scurries to the bottom of the stairs and pulls the door wide. 'Come in. Come up.' He sees Julia glance at what he is wearing: a T-shirt with a hole at the neckline and a pair of frayed pyjama bottoms. 'I'm up,' he says. 'I'm just . . . I was just sorting out a few things. But come in. It's fine, really, come in.'

Julia steps across the threshold but tentatively, as though wary that the floorboards beyond might be about to give way. She catches her jacket on the handles of the bicycle and unhooks it and slides past. Tom babbles as he leads her upstairs. He asks her what she is doing here but does not wait for her to answer. He offers her coffee. He warns her they may be out of milk. He says it is only instant too but they have tea if she would prefer, would she prefer tea? It would have to be black though. Does she mind black tea? And Casper. He asks after Casper but again does not give her time to respond. He thought she was Craig, he tells her. He thought she was his flatmate. He's been made redundant. He's depressed and it affects his ability to remember his key. But what is she doing here?

'I tried your cell phone but I got your voicemail. So I called the website and they said you weren't coming in.'

'I've taken holiday. Just a couple of weeks. Here. Sit.' Tom clears a stack of newspapers from an armchair in their cluttered living room. He crosses to the window to open the curtains. 'And my phone: I switched it off. If I don't, they call me every two minutes.'

'You're that important?' says Julia, sitting. Tom cannot tell if she is teasing.

'We're that lazy. Journalists are. It's easier to pick up the phone and ask than to look for a file or a contact or a paper-clip or whatever yourself.' He lowers himself on to the arm of the sofa across from her. 'Is something wrong?'

'No. I mean, nothing new. I was just, I don't know. I wondered where you were, that's all.'

'I'm here. I've not gone anywhere.' Although from where he is sitting, he can see the open bag on his bed, the stack of clothes beside it. Julia looks where he is looking.

'But you were about to.'

'Well,' says Tom. 'Kind of. But I was going to call you. From the road. When . . . When I had something to tell you.'

'From the road? Where are you going?'

'I don't know. Not exactly. What I mean is—'

Julia shakes her head. 'It's fine, Tom. Really. It's none of my business. You don't have to sneak out the back door if there's somewhere you need to be.' Her tone is composed, reasonable, hurt.

'No, no, no. I'm not sneaking out anywhere. Well, I am, a bit, but not because of you.'

Julia stands. 'I'll let you get on. I'm sorry, I shouldn't have just turned up like this.' She checks her bare wrist. 'I should be leaving anyway. I have to collect Casper from nursery.' She smiles, unconvincingly. 'I'm always late. They always have him waiting for me in the office. Really, I don't know what the staff there must—'

'It's to do with Arthur.'

Julia is at the living-room door. She turns.

'I'm going because . . . I mean, it could be nothing. It's almost certainly nothing, in fact, which is why I didn't call . . . But I'm going because of Arthur.'

'What about Arthur?' Julia steps back into the room. She stands with her thigh against the arm of the chair, the finger-tips of her left hand grazing the upholstery. 'Did you find something? What did you find?'

'Nothing. Really.' Tom sighs at Julia's frown. 'This is why I didn't tell you. I didn't want you thinking I'd found out more than I have.'

'But you've found something. Tell me, Tom, please.'

Tom hesitates. He glances again through the doorway towards his bag. 'Take a look.' He steps past Julia and leads her through the hallway and into his bedroom. 'Excuse the mess,' he says but Julia is not looking at the mess. Her eyes are on the stack of printouts Tom pulls from his holdall.

'What are they?'

'Expenses claims,' says Tom. 'Ministerial expenses claims. Think moat cleaning, duck islands: that sort of thing. The Freedom of Information Act is about the only civil-rights legislation the government has had to extend. You remember what happened in 2009.'

'Why though? I don't understand.' Julia takes the stack from Tom and flicks through the pages. Her gaze lingers on the lines he has highlighted.

'Just a hunch. I thought it would probably be a waste of time but I didn't have much else to go on.'

'It wasn't though.' Julia looks up. 'Was it?'

Tom takes back the printouts. He sets the pile on his mattress and flicks until he finds the right page. 'Almost. But then I saw this.' He passes the sheet to Julia. There is an item highlighted and, unlike the other lines he has daubed in yellow pen, this one has an asterisk beside it, a tick, an underline. 'Ignore my markings. I was tired and it was late and probably I got over-excited. But I still think it's worth looking into.'

'Ninety-three pounds and seventy-six pence,' says Julia, reading, 'at the Market Place Brasserie in Camelford. Where's Camelford?'

'The middle of nowhere. The middle of Cornwall, rather.' Tom points. 'But look here. Look at the name.'

'Rupert Jenkins,' Julia reads. 'Wasn't he—'

'At the press conference. Right. Doing nothing, saying nothing. Standing beside the home secretary looking like an eight-year-old nursing a smacked bottom.'

'You think he was responsible? You think he made the leak?'

'I think it happened on his watch. I don't think he was responsible but I think he was in charge at the time. Of the policy, I mean. Of the facility.'

'What makes you say that?'

'It's just a hunch, like I say. Probably I'm wrong. But he's the right level: senior enough to carry some clout, junior enough that the government can cast him to the press should they need to. And he's in the right place, politically speaking, and at the right time: it would be his remit and he's not exactly a liberal.

Also,' Tom says and he gestures to the expenses claim, 'there's this.'

Julia frowns. 'I still don't get it. He went to Camelford; he had lunch. What's the big deal? Maybe he was visiting his sister. His mother. A doddery old aunt.'

'Right the first time. But that's the point: it was a jolly. He's hardly likely to have travelled down to Camelford for the sake of a ninety-quid lunch. He was in the area, rather. More to the point, he was in the area and it wasn't on his itinerary.' Tom shuffles in his bag for another clutch of papers. 'I got hold of a copy of his schedule for that week and according to his press office Jenkins was never there. He was in London, supposedly, in "meetings". The only thing that links him to Camelford on that particular day is his lunch receipt.'

'The day,' says Julia. 'The date. It's the day they arrested Arthur.'

'That's right. You're right. I didn't realise that.'

Julia reaches for the stack of papers on the bed and flicks through. 'What then? The facility is in Camelford, is that what you're saying?'

Tom laughs. He cannot help himself. 'I doubt it. I doubt very much it will be that easy. But it seems as good a place to start as any. It's British soil, after all. That's what the home secretary said, right? That it was on British soil?'

'That could mean anything. It could mean the facility – Arthur – is in . . . I don't know. Gibraltar, for instance. Bermuda. It could be in the Antarctic – don't you guys own some of that too?'

'True. But Jenkins didn't order steak in the Antarctic. And

his staff – ' Tom shuffles the pages in Julia's hands until he comes to another highlighted section, another sprawl of asterisks and underlines ' – his staff didn't take a train trip once a week from Paddington to the south pole; they went to Bodmin Parkway instead. A guy called Simpkins did. Another one called Cooke.' He looks up and catches Julia's expression. 'It's not much, I know, but it's all I can find. It's a pattern, at least. You know how I like to look for patterns.'

Again Julia studies the papers in her hands, as though looking for something more than Tom has given her. She glances at Tom's half-packed holdall. 'So you're going to Camelford. Based on a hunch. Based on a lunch receipt and half a dozen train tickets.'

'I told you,' Tom says, 'it's not much. But look at it this way: if I'm wrong – if Jenkins went solely to have lunch with his sister – at least I know the local restaurant will be worth the trip.'

Julia fails to laugh. She is chewing on her lower lip. 'What's it like?' she says, after a moment.

'What? The restaurant?'

'Camelford. What's it like? Good for kids, do you think?'

'What? No. Julia, no.'

'We could do with a vacation, Casper and I. A fortnight away, some place quiet.'

'You're joking. You are joking, right?'

Julia's gaze drifts to Tom's feet and back again. 'You should get changed. Finish packing. We don't want to get caught in traffic.'

*

Tom grips with his left hand at the handle above the door. His right is under his thigh, clawing at the tattered leather of his low-slung seat. 'I had a car, you know. It was all arranged.'

Julia shifts down a gear. She pulls into the inside lane of the dual carriageway, then drifts left again once the caravan is behind them. 'It's November. Who the hell goes caravanning in this country in November?' She glances at Tom. 'What car?'

'A hire car.' He unsticks his hand from the leather and points. 'There's a—'

'I see it, Tom. Relax, would you? You're making me nervous.' There is a car joining the road from a lay-by and again Julia eases the BMW round it. 'I meant, what type of car?'

'I don't know. The cheapest type.'

Julia gives a sniff. 'Like a Fiesta? Like a Micra or something?'

'Maybe. Probably.' Tom angles himself to see the speedometer, then looks behind him. Casper is curled in his car seat, his eyes closed and his hands clasped at his chest. 'I thought you lot all drove at fifty-five. How fast do you go when Casper isn't on board?'

Julia rolls her eyes. 'You sound like Arthur,' she says. Then, as though to cover the momentary awkwardness, 'I'm going eighty. I'm not going fast.'

'Eighty's fast. Eighty's three points and a fine.'

'Eighty's what the speed limit should be: here, back home. Eighty – ninety, even – is what modern cars are designed to cope with. The Germans have got the right idea.'

Tom runs his eyes across the dashboard: its antiquated dials and laminated-wood panelling. 'This isn't a modern car, Julia. It's old – you said it yourself.'

'I said it was a classic. There's a difference. And anyway, it's a BMW. BMW have always been ten years ahead of the curve. You're safer than you would be in a Nissan Micra, I promise you that.' Then, as if to prove it, Julia brakes sharply, as a Volkswagen Beetle older even than the BMW cuts across the road from the opposite carriageway. She curses and Tom drives his heels into the foot well. Behind them, Casper stirs. They pass the Beetle and Tom turns. Casper moans, as though about to cry, but then falls silent again. His eyes remain closed. Tom looks towards Julia and sees her watching her son in the rear-view mirror. They seem to slow. There is a Honda estate ahead of them and they tuck in behind it. Tom glances once more at the speedo and the needle this time points to just below seventy. Julia notices Tom looking. She shrugs. 'We wouldn't get there any sooner.'

Tom laughs. 'You don't believe that.'

A moment later there is a roar and a motorbike, then two more, speeds past them. Julia murmurs, as much in frustration perhaps as appreciation. Tom laughs again.

'What?'

'Nothing.' Tom directs his grin towards the passing countryside.

'Motorbikes,' says a voice behind and both Tom and Julia turn.

'Hey, honey,' says Julia. 'Are you okay?'

But Casper is asleep again. He sleeps on until they reach Camelford, his mother watching him as much as the road and driving inside the speed limit the rest of the way.

*

It is dark and it is drizzling as they pull into the village. There seems at first to be little to Camelford but mist-shrouded street-lamps and curtained cottages. The main road is also the only road, as far as Tom can tell: high street and bypass all in one. Eventually the cottages give way to a truncated row of shops: a cafe, a hairdresser's, a post office, all closed. They pass the Market Place Brasserie too and the number of empty tables in the window confirms in Tom's mind that the minister of state was unlikely to have been lured by the restaurant's reputation. After the brasserie it is cottages again and Tom is about to suggest to Julia that they turn around. There must be a B&B somewhere, he is about to say; maybe they passed it. But ahead the road widens and splits and wraps itself around a pond and a patch of grass. There is a pub, larger than the church next door and with a car park the size of the village green it over-looks. Rooms available, a sign proclaims. Families welcome.

They fool no one, Tom is sure. A man and a woman and a child seated for an early dinner but it is clear, surely, that there is something amiss about their group. Tom shuffles; Julia prattles; Casper says nothing and prods at his baked beans. He glances at Tom periodically but only as though to check Tom has not edged any closer since the last time he looked. Tom attempts conversation. He asks Casper how his dinner is. He asks him twice, in fact, forgetting the second time that he has asked once already. The first time Casper is non-committal. The second time he ignores Tom completely.

As they finish their meal, the dining area of the pub begins to fill up. There are couples, mostly, of about the same age as Tom's parents. They have the look of locals, regulars, who do not need the menu and whose drinks appear apparently without being ordered.

Tom asks for the bill and makes to pay. Julia protests and they argue for a while but settle on splitting it fifty–fifty, which satisfies neither of them. 'So,' Tom says. He suggests a walk. A drink maybe? 'A Coke, I mean,' he says when Julia glances at Casper.

'It's been a long day,' says Julia and Tom takes the hint. He accompanies the two of them to their room. Casper is asleep in Julia's arms even as they climb the stairs.

'He's worn out,' says Tom because it is the type of thing, he thinks, that responsible adults say.

'He hasn't been sleeping. Neither of us has.'

Tom waits outside the doorway as Julia parcels Casper in the duvet of their double bed. She kisses him and strokes his head and then she stands. She checks about the darkened room, as though uncertain what to do next.

Tom holds his own key, to the room two doors down. He taps the fob against his thigh. 'You sure you don't fancy a drink? I mean, the bar's just downstairs.'

'I would,' says Julia. She looks at her son.

'Right. Of course. Well. Sleep tight.'

'Wait,' says Julia. She reaches into her handbag. She pulls out her mobile and crosses to the bedside table. Beside the clock-radio there is a phone: a three-decades-old hunk of Formica with tangled wires and a rotary dial. Julia hovers one hand over the receiver and with her other hand keys her mobile. The room phone barely has a chance to ring before Julia has snatched up the receiver. She sets it down, at the edge of the table and angled towards her son's parted lips, and sets her mobile to speaker. She holds it aloft and smiles at Tom. 'Better than a baby monitor.'

They take a table in a corner of the bar area, out of the light but close to the failing fire. Julia insists on getting the drinks and Tom asks for a pint of the local ale. They sit and raise their glasses to their lips.

'I don't think he likes me,' Tom says. He laughs, like it is no big deal.

Don't be silly, is Julia's line. Of course he likes you. 'Are you surprised?' she says instead.

Tom stares for a moment. He shrugs with his eyebrows. 'No. I guess not.'

'So how do we do this?' says Julia, after a pause.

For an instant, half, Tom thinks she has in mind the same thing he does. 'The facility,' he says, catching up. 'How do we find it, you mean?'

Julia sips her beer at him. She folds her lower lip across the top one to catch some foam.

'I don't know. Just drive about, I guess. Look for likely spots and head to them.' He tips his chin towards the regulars at the bar. 'Maybe chat up a few of the locals, see if they've heard any rumours. You know what these villages are like.'

Julia shakes her head. 'We need a plan. We need a system.'

'Like what?'

'Like, talk to the locals – that's fine. But we can't just drive about. I grew up in countryside like this. We'll get lost and get nowhere and spend the rest of our time trying to find our way back to Camelford.'

SIMON LELIC

'I thought you grew up in Boston?'

'I was born in Boston. I grew up in rural Massachusetts. Which is even worse. Or better, depending on how you look at it.'

'How do you look at it?'

Julia has beer on her nose now. She wipes it with a knuckle. 'Worse. Definitely worse. These days Ealing is about as rural as I can handle.'

'Right. I know what you mean. A break from the city for me is a ride on the Northern Line to zone four.'

Julia smiles. 'So we're agreed: there's no place like home. All the more reason we need a plan.' She reaches into her handbag and pulls out a map. It has been folded so that Camelford is at the centre of the topmost page. 'I bought this at the gas station. Also, these.' This time she takes out what looks like a child's stationery set. 'Ruler, highlighter, compass and . . . er . . .'

'Triangle thing.'

'Right. Triangle thing.' She sets it aside. 'We decide on a perimeter,' she says, demonstrating with the compass as she speaks. 'Camelford is the hub and the roads are the spokes. We drive up one spoke, down another, taking the occasional detour as we go. That way, we don't miss anything. We don't go round in circles.'

'We go round one circle instead.'

'Right. But it's our circle. Once we've covered it, we draw a new one, further out. Then we start again.' She reclines in her chair and picks up her glass.

Tom stares at the map. 'What do you do?' He looks up.

'I mean, you're a mother, I know that. But before. What did you do?'

Julia tilts her head. 'You mean your research didn't cover that?'

'I wasn't researching you. I was researching Arthur.'

Julia looks for a moment like she does not believe him. 'I came over here to study politics,' she says. 'I ended up training as a teacher.'

'You teach? What age?'

'Reception.'

'In London?'

Julia nods. 'Acton.'

'Was it a good school?'

'It wasn't private, if that's what you mean. It was just . . . I don't know. A London school. The good comes with the bad.'

'Are you going back? You were good at it, I bet.'

'I'll have to,' says Julia. Then, 'Are you mocking me?'

Tom shakes his head as he drinks. 'Not at all. You're good with kids. I can see you are. Me, I never know what to say to them. In my mind I sound either patronising or boring.'

'You're young,' says Julia. 'You probably haven't been around kids much.'

'Young? Who's young? I'm your age.'

'Gee, thanks.'

'I didn't mean . . . I'm not saying you're . . .'

Julia smiles. 'You're what? Twenty-seven?'

'Twenty-eight, actually.'

'That's young,' says Julia.

'Who's being patronising now?'

Julia makes a face.

'So how old are you?' says Tom. 'You must be—'

'Careful.'

'—twenty-nine?'

'That'll do,' says Julia.

'What then? Thirty? No way you're older than thirty.'

'Wow. You're smooth.'

'Thirty-one?'

'Try thirty-two. Then add one.'

'Thirty-three? No way. You're thirty-three?'

Julia takes another sip of her beer. Tom drops his gaze to his, arithmetic running through his mind. He looks up when Julia laughs. 'I'm flattered, Tom. You genuinely seem surprised.'

'I just thought, I don't know. I figured you were the same age as Arthur. He's thirty, right?'

'Thirty-one. His birthday was two weeks ago.'

'Well,' says Tom, looking at his beer again. 'At least I know you go for younger men.' It takes a second, less than that even, for him to realise what he has said. He can feel the burn on his cheeks as he lifts his head. He opens his mouth to say something – to apologise, even though he knows that is the last thing he should do, or to explain perhaps, make a joke of it – but Julia is facing away. She is blushing too, he realises – and when she blushes, she could easily pass for twenty-five.

Neither of them speaks, for a minute at least. When Tom finally says something, Julia does too.

'Another drink?' says Tom, even though neither of their glasses is empty.

'It's nice with the fire,' says Julia, even though the fire is almost out.

'It is.'

'I shouldn't.'

They smile. 'Sorry,' says Tom.

'I shouldn't,' Julia says again. 'I can hear Casper stirring. I don't want him waking up alone in a room he doesn't know.' With two hands, she slides her glass to the centre of the table. 'Walk you to your door?'

'Thanks,' Tom says. 'I might sit a while. Finish this, maybe have another.' He coughs, pulls himself straight. 'I'll see what I can wring from the blokes at the bar.'

'All right.' Julia stands. 'Goodnight.' She touches his arm as she passes.

Tom resists the temptation to watch her walk from the room. He hears his name, though, and turns. Julia is standing in the doorway.

'Engines,' she says. 'Cars, trucks, diggers. Stuff with engines.' Tom frowns and Julia smiles. 'Casper. Talk to Casper about engines.'

'I don't know anything about engines. I'm the bloke who was planning to tour Cornwall in a Nissan Micra, remember?'

'He's only three, Tom. You don't need to get technical.'

'Oh. Right.' Tom smiles. 'Thanks.'

Julia smiles back. She nods and she says goodnight again and she drops her chin as she turns. A full minute after she has gone, Tom is staring still at the empty doorway.

'Sheets.'

Arthur turns his head.

'Sheets, towels. Or lie in your own filth for another fort-night, s'all the same to me.'

He said the same thing last time, seemingly unaware that his suggestion is not bad advice. Because, since more of the other inmates have begun to fall ill, the laundry he has offered in return has been no cleaner. It is stained, in the way Casper's bibs were stained even after they had been soaked and boiled – although the red on the sheets, Arthur knows, is not ketchup; the brown is not chocolate. And the laundry smells: of mildew, if you are lucky; of something worse, something that makes the towels and the pillowcases unusable, if you are not.

Baggins, so called among the prisoners because of his stature, his stunted limbs and furry knuckles, stands with a palm out-stretched at Arthur's door. He gives the impression of leaning across the threshold, his weight anchored by his other hand to the cart in the corridor beyond. 'Well?' Baggins says and he claps one-handed. He plucks a bundle from the stack and raises it to his nose, shutting his eyes as he inhales. 'Ahh,' he says and he grins. 'Meadow fresh!'

Arthur is sitting on the spare bunk in his cell, his legs crossed and his shoulders hunched. He is shuffling his home-made deck of cards. The paper has warped, though, and the edges have bent so he can manage only one, two more, a fourth and fifth shuffle before the stack jars and crumples and drips into his lap. His goal is ten shuffles, in quick succession and without cheating by spreading the deck. Every time he fails, however, he bends the cards further and makes it more difficult for himself the next time. When it gets to the point that he can shuffle no more than once or twice, he will go through the deck and stroke each card flat against his leg. Then he will start again.

He glances at Baggins. He glances at the bundle. Even from six feet away, he can tell he is better off sticking with the sheets he has. 'No, thank you,' he says. He waits for his door to close, for the bolt to slide home, in order that he can continue his game. Instead, there is a dull thump as something lands on the bunk and bounces against his thigh. He looks at the bundle beside him and then up at Baggins. 'I said no,' he says. 'Thank you.'

'Those ain't for you.' Baggins holds a tattered sheet of paper six inches from his eyes. He lowers it and, with the tip of his tongue between his teeth, makes a mark on the paper with a pencil stub plucked from behind his ear. 'You're gettin some company.' Baggins looks at Arthur and he grins again. 'Someone to keep you warm at night. It don't seem fair, does it, that the others have someone to play with while you have to make do with just your pecker and your pack of cards?'

Arthur sits straighter. 'Who? When?'

Baggins makes to leave. 'Dunno. Don't care.' He is in the corridor and reaching to slam Arthur's door. He always slams it. He does not have to but always he does, just as he will slam the next door and the next and the one after—

Arthur drops the stack of cards and shuffles forwards. 'Wait! Baggins, wait!'

Baggins pauses but only to glower.

'Francis,' says Arthur. 'Wait, Francis, please. Just for a second.'

Baggins opens the door a fraction wider. His feet remain rooted in the corridor.

'You can help me,' says Arthur. 'It's just occurred to me that you can help me.' Already Baggins is sneering. 'There's a bloke. A friend of mine,' says Arthur and Baggins's sneer turns into a leer. 'Not a friend like . . . I mean, he's just a . . .' Arthur shakes his head. 'He's sick and they won't let me see him. He's not at meals and he's never in the grounds and I'm guessing he's so sick now he's confined to his room.'

Baggins sniggers. 'You could be talkin about a dozen of your fairy friends.'

Arthur slides to the edge of the bunk and drops his feet to the floor. 'His name is Roach. He's tall, black, greying around the ears. You'd know his laugh. It's sort of booming, like . . . I don't know. Like the kind of laugh that travels through walls.'

'Sounds quite a catch.'

'You could take a message to him. A note. You could put it in a bundle or something. No one would see.'

Baggins's expression has settled into a smirk. 'What would the note say? I mean, just so's I know if I was to get caught.'

'I don't know,' Arthur says. Baggins is humouring him, he realises, but he has not left yet and that is something. Arthur scrabbles on the bunk for the pen that cost him a ration of cigarettes. He finds it and looks for paper. 'It would say . . .' Arthur is hunting still for something on which to write. He spreads the deck of cards and plucks out the first ace he finds. 'It would say . . . Let's see.' He hovers the pen nib over the white space beside one of the corner diamonds.

'You want the ace of hearts, surely,' says Baggins. He has edged into the room and is angling his head to see. 'Or the ace of spades. You said he were a coon, right, so you could use the ace of spades.' He sniggers.

Arthur has got as far as writing Roach's name. He gnaws his lower lip, then his thumb nail. He glances up at Baggins.

'Lost for words? Don't look at me. I ain't exactly Billy Shakespeare. More's the point – ' Baggins turns away ' – I ain't got time to sit around writin love letters.'

'I'm writing. Hang on, I'm writing.' Arthur lowers the pen but again his movement stalls. What should he say? What can he say?

'Ta-raa.' Baggins is at the door.

'You can come back.' Arthur stands. 'Can't you? I'll write it and you can pick it up later.'

'Sure,' says Baggins. 'Sure I'll come back. Next week. The week after maybe.' He is grinning again. He reaches to close the door.

Arthur opens his mouth to say something, to say anything that will stop Baggins leaving. 'I'll pay you,' is all he can think of. 'Please. I'll pay you.' He searches around his cell but he knows without looking that there is nothing of value. He does not even have any cigarettes. Other than those he used to bargain for the pen, he gave his entire ration to Roach. Baggins, more to the point, is not a prisoner; he can get all the cigarettes he needs, from the inmates' supply if nothing else. 'Please,' Arthur says again, just to say something. He looks up and expects Baggins to be gone. The door, though, is open wide. Baggins steps back into the room.

'What?' says Arthur because from the look in Baggins's eyes it seems he has settled on a price. Arthur again checks his cell, to see what he has overlooked. 'What?' He holds up the pen in his hand, not to offer it, more to reconsider its value.

Baggins glances into the corridor, then closes the door. When he speaks he speaks in a rasp. 'Toss me off.'

Which is what Arthur heard but cannot be what Baggins said. He lowers the pen. 'Sorry?'

Baggins edges forwards. 'Toss me off,' he repeats. His shoulders are hunched and one hand grips the other. 'Just with your hand.'

Arthur can feel his lips curl, his nostrils flare, his eyes narrow. His head gives an involuntary twitch.

'If you do it,' Baggins says, 'I'll do better than take him a message.' He steps closer. 'I'll take *you*. I'll take *you* to him. I could, you know, if I wanted to. If you made it worth my while. I could say you were helpin me. They said to choose someone to help and I could say I chose you.' As he makes his pitch, his eyes widen. He could be a salesman in a forecourt, willing his client to reach for his wallet. 'Just imagine you're doin it to yourself. That's what you do all day anyway, right?' He smiles, winks. 'It wouldn't take long, I promise.'

Arthur finds his gaze drifting downwards. The trousers Baggins wears are stretched tight, as though the only pair he could find that were short enough were also too tight for his thick thighs, his swollen waist – his bulging groin.

'It's not like you don't make a habit of it.' There is a note of impatience in Baggins's tone now. 'It's not like you've never done it before. That's why you're here, right? Because you like doin it. You can't get enough of it. You're all the same, I know you are, but every faggot in here acts like they're Snow friggin White.'

Arthur has been backing away without realising he was moving. His heel hits the skirting and he stops. Baggins, though, continues to edge forwards. He treads gently. He is smiling again, his hands level with his waist and one ahead of the other. He might be reaching to pet a timid animal, coaxing it forwards so he might snatch at it, grab it, hold it tight. Arthur feels an urge to spring forwards. He feels an urge to shove Baggins away. He feels his knee flex and his heel brace and almost he starts to move.

But then he thinks of his friend. He thinks of him suffering. He thinks of him dying and dying alone. He thinks of his friend and he asks himself: what would Roach do?

'Take it out.'

Baggins stops his advance. His eyebrows join.

'Take it out. If you want me to, take it out.' Still Baggins hesitates and Arthur takes a step towards him. 'Quickly. Before

I change my mind.' He glances across Baggins's shoulder, to check the door is still pushed to. He looks at Baggins and Baggins looks back.

And then he is moving. He is scrabbling at the buckle around his waist like an escape artist who has been shackled and dropped into water. He tugs at his shirt and a button flies free. He finds his zipper and unzips and he bends to yank down his trousers. Something rips and Baggins laughs. He giggles and carries on, until his belt is a coil at his feet and his trousers are a bundle at his knees. He hooks his thumbs behind the elastic of his pants. He hesitates, just for a moment, and looks at Arthur. Then he smiles and sets himself free.

As Arthur moves forwards, Baggins shivers. He swallows and Arthur does too. There is a noise in the corridor beyond but it is some way distant and neither man takes any notice. Arthur forces himself to look where he is reaching. He swallows again. He thinks, what would Roach do, and his hand continues to float from his side. Baggins closes his eyes. His lips are parted, his chin raised up. Arthur's fingers touch flesh and it is warm and harder than he expected and he thinks to himself, what would Roach do?

He grips. Baggins groans. He grips harder and Baggins moans. The moan, though, changes pitch and Baggins opens his eyes. He looks down and his hand closes on Arthur's but Arthur is gripping and twisting now and wrenching and he is surging forwards and forcing Baggins back. Baggins stumbles and almost falls but Arthur accelerates and slams Baggins against the cell door. His free hand is across Baggins's mouth but the man is whimpering, wincing, and clawing at Arthur's fingers down below. He is scratching and Arthur feels it but the pain, if anything, drives him on. He has to stop himself, in fact. He has to remind himself to stop. Because it is exhilarating and invigorating and a release, after all this time, to finally exert some control.

The smell knocks him back. It is sweet; sticky. Not like honey. More like rotting fruit, or the bins at the back of a restaurant. The stench, moreover, has layers: sweat and urine and vomit and something, buried deeper, like rusting metal. Like blood.

Arthur turns his face and opens his mouth and forces himself across the threshold. Baggins is beside him and Arthur hears him curse. 'It gets worse every time,' he says and he swears again. He drops back. 'Ten minutes,' he says. It sounds like he is holding his nose now. 'You've got ten minutes and if you ain't ready when I come back, you can find yourself a place to kip in with them.'

Arthur ignores him. He takes another step and hears the door close behind him. Something has been draped across the narrow window and the only light in the cell comes from the gaps around the makeshift curtain. Arthur steps again and looks left, right. Each bed is a bundle. Roach, Arthur knows, shares with a younger man named Gardner and neither one of them has been outside the cell, as far as Arthur can tell, for the best part of two weeks. Roach's bunk is on the left but there is movement to Arthur's right and he turns to look. Gardner has his blanket pulled high and beneath it he writhes and groans. He rolls on to his back and his face emerges from the blanket. Arthur peers. He edges towards Gardner's bunk. The man has his eyes shut but, looking closer, they seem swollen shut. His cheek bulges too, giving the impression he is sucking on a golf ball. Arthur leans in and immediately recoils. The man stinks, or his sores do. They glisten and Arthur cannot tell with what but he thinks of the stains on the laundered bedclothes and decides he does not want to know. Gardner groans again and his mouth opens with a sound like something unsticking and even in the dark Arthur can see that the man's gums are black. Several of his teeth are missing too: his upper laterals and the central incisors on the lower jaw. Arthur reaches a hand, a finger, but suddenly Gardner coughs – a wet, wheezing cough, which Arthur feels in his chest as though it were his own lungs toiling – and something hits Arthur on the cheek: a spray of saliva but also something hard. Whatever it is lands on the floor with the soft tap a falling button would make. Arthur drags a sleeve across his face and bends to look. Gardner has lost another tooth.

'Don't tell me dentists believe in the tooth fairy.'

Arthur turns. Roach is on his back and propped on his elbows.

'I can't say I believe in anything much right now.' Arthur moves to Roach's side and kneels. He studies his friend's face and for a moment he is encouraged: he has his teeth, for one thing. There is no swelling either and nothing like the sores afflicting Gardner. His skin is blotched but only as much as it was the last time Arthur saw him. There is something odd, though, about Roach's eyes. The left seems clouded across the white; the right is almost totally black. Or red. It could be red. Arthur shifts and only Roach's left eye follows his movement.

'How did you get in here?' Roach's voice is a whisper. Arthur looks and sees an empty beaker on the floor beside the bed. He takes it to the sink and fills it, then returns to Roach's side. He makes to raise the glass to his friend's lips but Roach adjusts his weight and takes hold of the cup himself. He has sores, Arthur sees, on his fingers and knuckles. The skin is split and weeping, as though he has punched through glass. Arthur watches as Roach drinks. He sips at first and then gulps. Water runs from his cracked lips and Arthur wipes it away with his thumb.

'Baggins brought me. He told the guards I was helping with his rounds. Said he needed some help now that everyone was getting so sick.'

Roach frowns. 'Baggins? Now why would Baggins do that?'

Arthur lifts a shoulder, a corner of his mouth. 'I exerted a little pressure.'

Roach laughs. His laugh turns into a cough. 'You sound like Roger Moore. You sound like James Bond.'

Arthur makes a gun shape with his finger. 'Dentistry is just my cover.'

'Licensed to drill, right?' Roach laughs again, coughs again.

Arthur nudges the cup of water towards Roach's mouth. 'You're obviously not that sick. Looks to me like you're just shirking; like you're tired of digging holes.'

Roach grunts. 'Maybe they can use me to fill one instead.' He drinks again and sighs as he sinks into his pillow.

There is movement once more in the other bunk and both men turn to look.

'He stopped speaking,' Roach says. 'Two days ago maybe. He

201

barely eats and he doesn't drink, except for when they force him to. They stop by,' he says, looking at Arthur now. 'Once in a while.'

Arthur glances towards the door. 'I haven't got long.' He puts his hand on Roach's forehead and winces at the warmth. 'What can I do? Can I do anything? What do you need?'

Roach shuts his eyes. He smiles and shakes his head. 'You shouldn't be here at all. Remember? You should be gone.'

'I'm not going anywhere.'

Roach makes to raise himself up. 'Don't get me started, Arthur. You have to tell Graves. Go to his office again, or—'

Gently, Arthur forces his friend down. 'Graves knows, Roach. He's always known.' Roach frowns and Arthur shrugs. 'I'm in a cell on my own and I'm fine – right? I'm not sick. All the other prisoners on their own: they're fine too. Maybe they weren't sure what to do with us at first but now they're making us share. Which means I'm staying. Which means we're all staying.'

Roach opens his mouth. He closes it again, his eyes too. He turns his face to the wall.

'What about food? Are you hungry? What can I bring you?'

Roach swallows. He rolls his head back towards Arthur. 'Some kind of miracle cure would go down a treat. Maybe on granary? With a little mustard?'

'I'll see what I can rustle up.'

'Talking of which,' says Roach. 'How go the trials? You can put my name down now, if you like. I'm willing to put aside my doubts.'

'No one knows. No one's heard. I think . . . I think if there were good news, someone would probably have heard.'

Roach exhales through his nose. He shuts his eyes again and for a long while he keeps them shut. When he opens them once more, his good eye is pooled with water. He turns his head towards Arthur and a tear spills across his cheek. Arthur rolls his lips between his teeth and reaches to take Roach's hand. His friend grips and grips hard. 'I can't see, Arthur. I can't see out of my right eye. And the left – I don't know. It comes and goes.' He looks at Arthur and he swallows. Then he sniffs and barks out a laugh. 'You want the truth?' He reaches his cracked fingers to wipe his cheek. 'The truth is I'm scared, Arthur. Don't tell anyone for God's sake – ' he attempts another laugh ' – but the truth is I've never been so scared.'

Arthur reaches with his free hand to brush at his own cheek. He does not know what to say but he opens his mouth to speak anyway. Roach, though, shakes his head.

'Don't say anything. What can you say? I'm glad you're here, that's all.' He squeezes Arthur's fingers. 'I'm glad you came.'

For a moment Arthur holds his friend's gaze, then he lowers his eyes to his lap. He says nothing. He could not talk now if he wanted to. He just sits and holds his friend's hand.

He cannot, it feels like, stop shaking his head. 'Yes,' says Graves. 'I realise that, minister, but—'

Burrows is watching and Graves holds his assistant's eye as he listens to Jenkins's rumbling voice.

'It is not July, you are quite right. But even in November—'

Now he shuts his eyes, raises the heel of his left hand to his forehead.

'Obviously they're not going anywhere but—'

He is shaking his head again and faster than before.

'We were told, though, that arrangements had been—'

He won't snap. He will not. Not even listening to this pompous, overbearing, over-fed bureaucrat who cannot seem to get it into his head that they are talking about—

'Dead bodies!' Graves says. It just comes out. 'For heaven's sake, minister, we are talking about dead bodies! We cannot simply leave them to rot. We cannot simply shift aside the frozen peas and stuff them into our Frigidaire!'

Burrows's eyes have grown wide. He is holding out a hand,

palm down, and it quakes in time with his head. He steps closer. Graves screws his eyes tight and gestures him away.

'They must be collected, minister. They must be disposed of. Apart from the question of what is decent, the bodies in my basement are a health risk. They are a threat to the welfare of my staff.'

Why they are even in this situation is beyond him. Call it what you like: a prison, a hospital, a facility if obfuscation really must prevail. But the disease, no one disputes, is a killer. Scores of people have been infected and there is no treatment yet available that is any more effective than a dose of Nurofen. So the inmates will die: it is as obvious as it is regrettable. One might have assumed, therefore, that someone, somewhere – the brains who conceived the strategy in the first place, perhaps – would have thought things through to their logical conclusion. One might have assumed, hoped, prayed they would have half a plan, at the very least, for dealing with the single inevitable consequence of this infernal operation.

'Yes, minister. Yes, minister. Of course, minister. Well, for that I apologise, but when one is dealing with dead bodies, with diseased dead bodies—'

He lets his jaw hang. He looks to the ceiling.

'No, minister. No, minister. Of course, minister. If you would just allow me to—'

But Jenkins hangs up.

Graves listens to the drone in his ear and he counts. One. Two. Threefourfive. He does not slam down the receiver exactly but he uses more force than is necessary and upsets a cup of cold coffee. Liquid spills on to a stack of folders and Graves

SIMON LELIC

curses. He stands and looks about him for something with which to wipe but there is nothing on his desk now because he has cleared it. There are just the folders of the people soon to arrive and the coffee mug and no tissues even, not a serviette or a paper towel or something, anything, that he might use to—

A tissue flutters at the edge of his vision. He turns and plucks it from Burrows's fingers. He makes a grunting noise, which is as close to a civil tone as he can manage, and he wipes: the folders first and then the phone and finally the underside of the cup. He balls the tissue and searches for somewhere to throw it and now he cannot see his bin. Where is his bin? It was under the desk but someone has obviously moved it and not told him and he wishes that people wouldn't—

Burrows's hand appears once more in front of him. This time Graves growls his thanks. He watches as Burrows leans and drops the tissue into Graves's bin, which is at the wall behind Graves's chair – in the very place that Graves put it when he set about tidying his desk.

For a moment Graves focuses on breathing. He checks behind him and sits back down. He looks at the bin, at Burrows, at the telephone. He reaches, adjusts the phone so it is set straight, then reclines in his chair and clasps the arms. 'What is it, John? What is it about this place?'

Burrows pulls his lips tight. He looks to the floor.

'It's one thing and then another and then another after that,' Graves says, as much to himself now. He shakes his head again. He stares at nothing. Then Burrows shuffles and Graves stirs. 'Well.' He pulls himself straight. 'At least we know where we stand. At least things cannot possibly get any worse.'

Burrows offers a tentative smile. 'There's an optimist and a pessimist,' he says. 'They're sitting down, having a cup of coffee—'

Graves frowns. 'What are you talking about?'

'It's a joke. I heard it from one of the guards. There's an optimist and a pessimist and they're sitting down, drinking coffee—'

'Not now, John, please. I have six dead bodies to dispose of and a government ministry to placate. But if you're making a pot . . .'

'A pot? No, no. That was the joke. In the joke, they're drinking coffee, that's all. Although I don't know why they're drinking coffee. They don't have to be drinking anything.' Burrows sees the expression on Graves's face and reaches to collect his cup. 'Biscuit?'

'Just the coffee, John, thank you.' Graves watches his assistant to the door.

He opens the post while he waits and he files. His in tray empties and his mood lifts slightly, and the coffee, when it comes, soothes Graves further. That is all it takes: an empty in tray and a cup of fresh coffee. Which just goes to show how ridiculous it is that he allows himself to get so worked up. Because how many times recently has he lost his temper? Twice today, for a start: just now, talking to the minister, and this morning, shaving, of all things. He scalded himself, first, on the hot tap, then threw his razor blade away before checking whether he had a new one. He had to empty the rubbish bag to recover the old blade and when finally he reapplied the cream and started shaving, he took a slice from his Adam's apple. He bloodied the basin and his towel and then the shirt he had just finished ironing. So, in an act of retribution, he balled the shirt and tossed it towards the sink – but knocked a bottle of cologne and the bottle broke. Which made the cottage reek, and him too once he had finished cleaning up, of a scent he disliked intensely and only kept because it was a gift from his daughter. After that he was late and he is never late, although perhaps he would have been better not coming in at all. Certainly it would have been better not to have shouted at his employer. But he did of course, which made it twice in just a few hours that he lost his temper, when he promised himself only last week that he would *keep a sense of perspective.*

The bodies. Yes, they are a problem, but he is here to resolve problems, not to whinge about the lack of resources. And really it is quite simple. They will have to be buried, at least until alternative arrangements can be made. The bodies might need to be treated in some way, or a coffin constructed, or something done anyway to safeguard against the spread of disease but that should be straightforward enough. Silk could help. Could he? Why not, after all? He could talk to Silk, or have Burrows do so, and find out how the cadavers should be handled: how to treat them, where to bury them, how deep and so on. Who knows, the doctor might actually prove to be of some value. And razor blades. What a fuss because of a razor blade, when he can borrow a disposable from the inmates' supply and have Burrows order some of his own brand the next time they plan a delivery. Problem solved. Two problems, in fact, in the time it takes to drink a cup of coffee.

He is tired. Not to make excuses for himself but he is sleeping badly still – worse than ever, as it happens – and it does not help. He thinks perhaps he should take something, which brings to mind his daughter – her email, specifically, to which he still has not replied. She asked him to call her and he has not done that either. He has been putting it off: he can admit that much to himself at least. There is no longer any need, however – if, indeed, there ever was. He has built up talking to Rachel as being akin to a reckoning with his conscience. His conscience, though, is at peace. She is his daughter; he is her father. Even were she somehow to learn what he is involved with, she would simply have to come to terms with it, just as he has. Their relationship is fragile, yes, but it is hardly likely to toughen if they shy from exposing it to the occasional knock.

He opens Outlook. He finds Rachel's last message and he reads it again and he drags the telephone towards him. He reaches for his coffee mug too and finds that the mug is empty. He needs a top-up. And this had better be the last one because the caffeine can hardly be helping, with his sleep or with his temper. The last cup then and perhaps . . . Yes, why not? Perhaps he will have that biscuit after all.

He is chewing the custard cream still as he trails Silk's assistant down the stairwell. He is panting and asking questions and trying to swallow all at once, and it feels like his mouth is clogged with glue. Burrows is at his shoulder and at one point his assistant's foot clips his heel. Graves stumbles and has to grab at the banister to keep from falling. He glowers at Burrows, who winces an apology, and both men hurry to keep up with Wood. At the bottom of the stairs they turn right, then jerk to a stop when they see Silk's assistant heading left.

'Where are you going, man?' says Graves. 'The ward is this way.'

'Dr Silk isn't on the ward,' says Wood. He strides on.

'But there's nothing along here.' Graves directs his frown towards Burrows. 'Is there? I thought there was just . . .'

Burrows nods. 'Another stairwell.'

Graves quickens his pace and pulls level with Wood. 'Will you please tell me what this is about?'

Wood shrugs, not because he does not know, it seems to Graves, but because he will not say. 'He told me to fetch you. He told me to hurry. I think it would be better if . . . That is, if Dr Silk . . .'

Graves gestures towards the approaching doorway. 'You are aware, I assume, of where you are leading us? You are aware what is down there?'

Wood does not answer. He gives Graves a look, then lowers his gaze. It is like they are rushing to the scene of an accident, Graves thinks; like someone up ahead is bleeding and this young man feels somehow responsible.

They reach the doorway and Graves goes ahead: down the first flight of stairs – narrower and less well lit than those in the rest of the building – and then back on themselves and down the second. There is another door at the bottom and the hinges groan as Graves tugs the handle. He ducks his head and wipes a cobweb from his face and steps into the room beyond.

He is braced for the stench but there is only the smell he would have expected had the basement not also become their morgue: rising damp, rotting timbers, air that has been trapped here since the building was constructed. He hesitates, though, in the gloom. There are three strip lights running along the central beam but only the middle one emits a steady glow. The light nearest has blown; the strip at the far end fizzes and flickers. Graves peers towards the furthest corner of the room. There are two figures standing upright and a number of bundles at their feet. Six, Graves assumes, because the far corner is where he instructed his staff to lay the bodies of the six dead inmates: Prior, the man from the riot who finally succumbed to his wounds, plus four victims of the disease and another of his own despair.

'Over here,' says Wood and he steps around Graves's shoulder. Graves and his assistant follow.

The strobe effect seems to intensify the closer they get. As they walk under the light itself it buzzes so violently that Graves ducks his head and Burrows, next to him, scuttles sideways. In the flash, Graves gets another glimpse of the scene ahead. There are in fact three figures standing: bunched tight and whispering. And there are more than six bundles on the floor. There must be, what? Ten? Twelve? 'My God,' Graves says.

Wood clears his throat and the tallest of the figures turns. Silk steps forwards and out of the shadows.

'Henry. Thank you for coming.'

Wood scurries around Silk and huddles beside the doctor's companions: Perkins and Doyle, Graves can see now – the doctor's two female assistants. They are tight jawed and pale and unable to meet Graves's eye. Graves looks from them to the bundles. This time he is able to count properly and finally he understands. He moves forwards and past Silk. He looks at the corpses, eight men and women lying next to the six inmates who were here before, and he turns to face the doctor. 'You killed them.'

'Come now, Henry. There is no need for melodrama.'

'What then?' Graves looks from the doctor to the dead bodies. They are wrapped in blankets but shoddily. A hand protrudes here, a foot there. One face is completely uncovered and Graves knows it. Wilson's eyes are pinned wide and his teeth are bared. It is not an expression Graves ever contemplated seeing on a dead man. 'What then?' he says again. 'They're dead. Aren't they?' Graves looks and once more he counts. He made no mistake, however. There are fourteen bodies, which means every one of the prisoners who volunteered and was accepted for Silk's trial is now a corpse. Graves stares again at the doctor. He opens his mouth and tries to speak but even when he shakes his head he cannot dislodge the words.

'The intention,' says Silk, 'was to cure them, as you well know. Their reaction to the treatment, however, was . . . unfortunate. It was unforeseen.'

'Unforeseen?' Graves manages to say. He is smiling, he realises. 'What in God's name did you give them?'

Silk leans with his head and he hisses. 'This isn't the common cold, Henry. The virus we are dealing with is as hardy as HIV. It is as vicious as Ebola. In instances like this, it is a case of fighting fire with fire. Echinacea, I can assure you, would not have cut it.'

'Unforeseen, though? How could this possibly have been

unforeseen? How the hell,' Graves says, raising his voice, 'did you get it so wrong? Didn't you test it?'

Silk makes a face. 'Of course I tested it. That's what a medical trial is! I was testing it on them.'

'But mice, man! Rats! And . . . and . . . they're *all* dead.' Graves is looking again at the bodies. 'Every one of them. Shouldn't half of them have been taking a placebo? I thought the whole point of a trial was to have a control group!'

'We are beyond mice,' says Silk. 'We are beyond control groups. The virus, as I keep reminding you, has not afforded us the luxury of time.' The doctor lifts his chin and drops his shoulders. 'It was for precisely this reason that I decided an extended trial process would not be ethical. It hardly seems fair to treat one person and not another.'

'But this,' Graves says. 'This *is* fair? This *is* ethical?' He looks to Wood, to Wood's colleagues. Wood already has his eyes on the floor; Perkins and Doyle lower theirs.

Silk is shaking his head now, as though suddenly irritated. 'I didn't summon you here for a biology lesson, Henry. I asked Wood to fetch you because I hoped you might be of some service.'

Graves is distracted momentarily by Burrows. His assistant is crouching beside Wilson's body, peering at the dead man's face. He reaches a finger and guides it close but draws it back and springs upright when he notices Graves looking.

'First things first.' Silk is pondering the bundles at his feet. 'The bodies can remain here for a day or so but after that they will need to be disposed of. I assume the appropriate arrangements are in place?'

Graves does not reply. He clamps his teeth.

'More important, we will need to keep this quiet. I don't want—'

'You're worried about your reputation?' Graves says. 'You're worried what people will think?'

'Not at all,' says Silk. 'My reputation is burnished enough that the odd scratch here and there will hardly be noticed. No, I am worried about the next eight volunteers. I am concerned they might prove less amenable should they become aware what fate has befallen their predecessors.'

Graves feels his lips part. He looks to Burrows, who is staring wide-eyed at the doctor. 'The next eight?' Graves smiles again. 'You aren't serious.'

'Their disappearance can be explained readily enough,' says Silk. 'We shall say that they have been moved to another facility, to a hospital perhaps. If the implication is that they are in the final stages of recovery, we may in fact see some benefit in the next trial.' Silk allows his mouth to curl at one corner. 'You will be aware, given your expertise on such matters, Henry, that an expectation of improved health among the participants is often a precondition to success with the intervention itself.'

'You would poison eight more. You would lie again and poison eight more.'

'It is not my intention to poison anyone. But if another eight have to die in order for me to find the cure, then so be it. You seem to be forgetting, Henry, that they will die anyway. You seem to be forgetting what is at stake here. You have another coachload of detainees on their way. What does that tell you?'

Silk pauses, tilts his head. 'That your facility is working? That all we need to do is shut these people in a room and hope that the disease goes away, that someone else discovers the cure while we sit picking at our fingernails?'

'You are,' says Graves. 'You're worried about your reputation. You don't want anyone else to find a cure before you do.'

Silk flicks a hand. 'Nonsense. I'm worried – the government's worried – about what will happen if nobody finds a cure. We are worried about what will happen if the facility fails, if *you* fail, Henry. But I have no intention of letting this beat me, if that is what you mean. In my entire career, I have never let anything beat me.'

'This isn't a game, Silk! This isn't some fiendish Sudoku! You told me before – you said quite explicitly – that none of the participants would be misled, that none of them would be lied to!'

'And they weren't! Every one of these people – ' Silk gestures to the row of corpses ' – knew the risks. They knew precisely what they were signing up for.'

'And now? How do you justify lying now?'

'Now, Henry, the situation has changed. As far as I am concerned and the government is concerned and the patients, for that matter, should be concerned, finding a cure will be justification enough. For anything.' Again Silk waves a hand. 'But we are wasting time. All this talk is a waste of my time.' He paces. 'The guards,' he says, as though Graves had not interrupted. 'They will need to be briefed. I have spoken to those who were in the room at the time, obviously. It cannot harm, though, for you to talk to them also.' He stops and faces

Graves. His ashen hair seems to come ablaze every so often in the flickering light, his pale eyes too. 'I have reasoned with them,' he says. 'Perhaps you should adopt a firmer line. A stick to my carrot, as it were. Effecting discipline, from what I hear, seems to come naturally to you, Henry. I'm afraid the staff here regard me more as something of a "good cop".'

Graves is still. He is silent. He notices Burrows looking again at the bodies but his own eyes are transfixed by the doctor's.

'Of course,' says Silk, 'you may wish to speak first to Rupert Jenkins. You may wish to gauge his opinion of my plan. I am sure he will regard any suggestion you might have as being equally worthy of consideration.' The doctor does not quite keep a straight face as he talks. With his eyes still glinting in the light, he waits for Graves to respond.

Graves blinks. He shifts his gaze once more towards the bodies. It is Wilson's face that commands his attention: that expression, so like a snarl – or a grimace, perhaps, as though the man had been bracing himself against the pain when he died.

'Cover them up,' Graves says, talking to Wood now.

Wood looks to the doctor.

'Cover them up, I said! They are human beings. Afford them some dignity, for pity's sake.' Graves stares until Wood starts to move, then glances at Silk, who is regarding him with an expression of amusement. Graves ignores the doctor and turns to Burrows. 'John,' he says and he takes a step. Burrows does not need to be told twice. He follows, as Graves strides past Wood and past the doctor and away from the fourteen dead bodies on the basement floor.

Engines do not come into it. Tom points and coos every so often at a passing motorbike, a plane overhead, but Casper seems wise to his tactics; it is as though he can sense that Tom is a phoney. Casper, more to the point, does not need to be prompted. He spots the planes before Tom does. He hears the motorbikes and is already tracking their approach by the time Tom catches on and spins his head and says, 'Wow, Casper, check it out!' Which is almost the worst part about it: the wow and the check it out. Even Julia cannot keep from laughing. It was her idea, so really she ought not to ridicule. She would be advised, in fact, to keep her suggestions to herself in future because engines, in the end, do not come into it. Tom's triumph, instead, is teaching Casper to pee standing up.

Although it is getting to the point that he wishes he had waited until the end of the second week. Julia had Casper squatting, or sitting if they were anywhere near a petrol station, and in male circles, Tom told her, it is not the done thing. Teach him then, said Julia, so Tom did. To his surprise – and Julia's too, Tom suspects – Casper let him. But peeing standing up,

SIMON LELIC

Casper has decided, is the coolest thing since . . . Well. Since motorbikes. And now, less than a week into the trip, he wants to pee every six minutes.

'You've just been,' says Julia. She keeps her eyes on the road as she talks.

'I need to, Mum. I really need to. Tom does too.'

And that is the other thing. Every time Casper pees, he expects Tom to stand beside him and pee too. The pressure is intense. It is worse than standing between two strangers at a communal urinal.

'Tom's fine, honey. And if you're old enough to pee standing up, you're old enough to wait until we find somewhere to eat. It should only be a few more miles.'

'But I really need to go, Mum. Really really.'

Julia sighs and looks at Tom. She is thinking, Tom can tell, about her ancient – and by now porous – leather seats.

'We can stop,' says Tom. 'I'm not sure I can squeeze any out myself but it'd be quicker to stop now than to have to pull over and clean up later.'

'Listen to you,' says Julia. 'Talking like a battle-scarred parent.' She looks for Casper in the rear-view mirror. 'Can you hold on until we reach the next lay-by? I can't stop here, honey. The road is too narrow.'

Tom assumes from Casper's silence that the boy has acquiesced. He smiles and rolls his eyes at Julia but she does not see. She is looking in the mirror still and she is frowning. Tom frowns at her frown and checks across his shoulder. Casper is reclined in the booster seat, looking bored perhaps but

218

content enough as he stares at the hedge-lined roadside. Tom turns back. 'What is it?'

Julia twitches her head. 'Nothing. Driving madness, that's all.'

'I'll take over if you like. Give you a break.'

'You will not.' Julia shuffles in her seat, sets her hands at ten to two. 'You're on lookout, remember?'

Tom faces the window. There is nothing very much to see. Every so often the hedgerows yield to the scene beyond but it is mainly clouds and fields and more fields, and once in a while a hamlet. There are wind farms, too: towering alabaster pylons spread generously between the road and the horizon; their industrial presence seems only to confirm that no one else thought much of the view either. The most engaging sight, after so many hours staring, is the rain beading then racing down the glass. Tom expected forests and hills and roads carving through them; some green once in a while, not such relentless brown. When he said as much to Julia at the end of their second day, she reminded him that it was late November. She chastised him, too, together with every other Brit, for his appalling knowledge of his own little island. He was thinking of Devon, she said. Devon or perhaps Middle Earth.

Tom was consoled by the thought that their search, given the topography, might prove easier. But even that assumption, four days later, seems misguided. They have heard rumours but none that has come to anything worthwhile, other than an extended delay one lunchtime at a creamery in Davidstow. They staked out an airfield for a morning but moved on when an employee mistook them for enthusiasts and offered them a guided tour. One old lady selling pasties suggested they visit Lanhydrock, which fitted the description of a remote country estate Tom had given her but turned out to be a National Trust site, complete with cafe, souvenir shop and children's adventure playground. Casper, understandably after being tethered for so many hours to his car seat, was delighted with the discovery, Tom and Julia less so. Today they are heading east – towards Dartmoor and, on the say-so of a Pencarrow publican, a nineteenth-century manor house that was used during the war to lodge German airmen. It is a monstrosity, the publican warned them. Whoever built it, he said, must have been blind or mad or just having a bit of fun. It is way out of their circle too but when the publican said he thought the building was still government owned, they hitched their eyebrows and gathered their things. Not that either of them holds out much hope. They are barely halfway into their search and Tom has about as much hope left as liquid in his bladder.

He points. 'Lay-by!' he says, with more enthusiasm than the finding perhaps warrants. He is delighted, though, finally to have found something.

Julia pulls in and Casper bounces, as though just the sight of the bushes has made him desperate. He is scrambling from his seat even as Tom unfastens the buckles and he scurries to the edge of the grass. He grins as he pees. Tom stands beside him but has to dance to save his shoes when Casper is distracted by a tractor heading the way they came. The boy finishes and reaches for Tom's hand as they trudge back towards the car. Julia is leaning on the open door, watching the tractor as it dissolves into the drizzle. She has on the frown Tom caught her wearing before. This time, though, she does not wait for Tom to ask.

'They should have passed,' she says. 'Did you see them?'

'What? The tractor?'

'Behind us. Not the tractor. There was a car.'

'I didn't see a car.'

'It was an Audi, I think. Dark grey. It was behind us today and I could have sworn I saw it at the airfield.'

'There was a grey car at the bed and breakfast. Maybe they're on their way to Dartmoor too.'

Julia shakes her head. 'That was a Mondeo. This was an Audi. There are no turnings on this road, so it should have passed.'

Tom shrugs. 'They could have turned round.'

'They must have. If they didn't, they'll have to this time. There's no way they're squeezing past that tractor.' Julia looks at Casper and she smiles. 'All set?'

Casper presses his lips tight, as though considering whether he might need to go one more time.

'In the car, please,' says Julia. 'You can certainly wait until lunchtime now.'

By the time they reach the next village Casper is asleep. They pull into a car park behind a church in the central square. The car park is empty so Julia picks her spot: tucked against the side of the church and overlooking the river that ambles along the gully below.

Tom reaches for Casper's foot. 'Shall I wake him?'

'Don't you dare!'

Tom snatches back his outstretched hand as though from
something hot.

'The sun's coming out,' says Julia. 'We can picnic here. There
was a sandwich place on the green that looked open.'

It is open but that is the best that can be said for it. The
coffee is instant and the sandwiches anything but. By the time
the girl behind the counter has assembled three ham-on-whites,
the coffee is already cold. Tom picks out a chocolate bar for
Casper. He hesitates, wondering whether Julia would like one
too, then chooses a second just in case. He pauses again and
thinks what the hell and takes down a Snickers for himself.
He pays and staggers with his stash across the square.

It is black, Tom thinks, not grey. But then the car emerges
from the shadows and it is clearly grey and definitely an Audi
this time, not a Mondeo. And he has seen it before. At the airfield maybe, as Julia said, but somewhere else too, Tom is sure.
Back in Camelford? Before that even: at the service station on
the motorway. When they headed for the pumps, he saw the
Audi veer right towards the restaurant.

Tom drifts towards a tree and lingers below the branches as
he tracks the Audi's progress. It seems lost. It slows at a side
road, the road leading to the car park, but does not turn and
crawls on. At another turning further on it pauses again but
once more continues around the square. It is heading back
towards Tom now, on his side of the green, and Tom rolls round
the trunk of the tree to keep out of sight. The engine is powerful – even Tom can tell that from the sound the car makes
as it passes. The motor rumbles and the tyres hiss and then
there is a snarl as the Audi accelerates. Tom steps from behind

the tree but too late. He sees the back of the driver's head, the passenger's too, but they are nothing more than silhouettes. The Audi turns again, back towards the main road. As it rounds the corner the sun hits the rear windscreen and, with a wink, the car is gone.

They perch on the bonnet while Casper sleeps. Their lunch, only half eaten, is discarded; their coffees sit untouched on the wall before them. Tom has not mentioned the Audi. What is there to say, after all? The driver got lost and turned round. And grey Audis. How many grey Audis must there be in this country, in this county? They are on edge, he and Julia, that is all. It is understandable, given what they are involved in. It is natural that they should feel a little paranoid. Better not to indulge it, Tom reasons. Better for Julia not to have to worry about anything more than she already does.

He focuses on the water below. He is staring still when he feels Julia's hand come to rest on his shoulder.

'You look like you're thinking about jumping.'

Tom attempts a smile. 'Just thinking,' he says. 'That's all.'

'Care to share?'

'It's nothing. Just getting twitchy, I guess.'

Julia's hand is still on Tom's shoulder. She lifts it and reaches her fingers towards his forehead. She barely touches his skin but the sensation cascades and fizzes towards Tom's collarbone.

'The wind will change,' says Julia. 'You'll set like that.'

Now her hand settles on his cheek. Tom covers her fingers with his own. He turns towards her and Julia is already leaning in. Her lips meet the corner of his mouth. Again her touch is gentle – it is barely a touch at all. She pulls away. She looks down. Tom watches her for a moment. Her hand slips from under his and Tom reaches and lifts her chin. She smiles and he smiles back. This time when they kiss, they linger. There is nothing, in that moment, to prise them apart.

Julia whispers Casper awake. She takes him for a walk while Tom stays at the car and studies the map. Casper pees and then eats and then pees again, and then they are reversing from the car park. Julia points the BMW the way they came. Tom suggests sticking to the back roads. 'Just for a change.'

It is hard, from the passenger seat, to check the road behind without seeming to. Julia senses him fidgeting, Tom is sure, but she only smiles and reaches to lace her fingers into his. She holds Tom's hand and entertains Casper as they drive, singing and reciting stories from memory. It is Julia, nevertheless, who spots the Audi first.

She withdraws her hand and reaches to the rear-view mirror. Tom leans, angling for a view behind.

'Is it a motorbike?' Casper says, raising his head.

'I thought it was.' Tom smiles at the boy. 'I guess it isn't.' He faces the front and says nothing and Julia adjusts her grip on the steering wheel. She accelerates but has to slow again as they reach a bend. Tom is glad for all their sakes that she did not let him drive. The road has narrowed and coiled and the hedges at the edge of the tarmac have given way to dry-stone walls. If Tom were at the wheel they would be crawling, or else lodged bonnet first in a farmer's field. Even with Julia driving, however, the Audi is closing.

'What is it?' says Casper. He cranes to look where Tom is looking.

'Nothing.' Tom attempts another smile. 'I think . . . er . . .' They round a corner and Tom has to grab at the headrest to keep from toppling. 'I think we might have taken a wrong turning. That's all.'

'We're lost?' Casper beams. 'Tom got us lost again, Mum!'

'No, I . . .' Tom stops himself. He grins at Casper and gives a guilty shrug.

'What shall we do?' Julia hisses below Casper's cackle.

'Drive. Just drive. I don't think we have any other option.'

They are at the edge of Dartmoor and there was a farm half a mile back but nothing since. There was a wood and there are hills and the roads are certainly carving but Tom would swap it all if he could for a petrol station or a traffic jam or just the sight of another car. He wonders how he could have been so naive. He wonders how he could have convinced himself that a *Libertarian* reporter and a detainee's wife would not attract attention – would not, given what they are looking for, attract reprisal. He wonders, most of all, what possessed him to drag Julia – and Casper, for pity's sake! – along with him.

Tom checks behind them again but the Audi, this time, is lost round a bend. He looks at Julia. 'They were in the village,' he says. 'They were there when we stopped. They didn't see me and they drove off. They . . . I don't know. They looked lost. I tried to tell myself they were just lost.'

Julia keeps her eyes on the road. 'Who are they, do you think?'

Tom opens his mouth but ends up shaking his head. He sees Julia glance again in the rear-view mirror and he makes to look too but stops when he feels pressure on his arm.

'Don't. You'll scare Casper. I can see.' Julia checks once more in the mirror. 'I know where they are.'

'Are they gaining? How close are they?'

'Tom got us lost again, Mum!'

'I know, honey. It's fine, though. We'll go a little faster and we'll be back on track in no time.' Julia tips her chin towards Tom's foot well. 'Check the map,' she tells him. 'See what's ahead.'

'Julia,' says Tom. 'How close are they?'

'They're close. Check the map.'

Tom reaches between his feet but is tipped backwards as the BMW accelerates. He looks up and sees they are on a long, dipping straight. There are walls either side still and fields beyond and nothing in the distance but the crest of the straight and an open swathe of moorland. Tom tries for the map again but by the time he has it spread on his lap they are swerving again. His fingertip slips from the page and the map slides back on to the floor.

There is a roar. It sounds likes an aeroplane overhead and instinctively Tom looks up. He looks around. 'Jesus,' he says because he cannot stop himself. The Audi is a car's length behind.

'There's two of them,' says Julia. 'Can you see them? Who are they?'

The BMW swerves and Tom is toppled sideways. He rights himself. 'I can't see. I can't tell.' The Audi roars again and it

226

seems suddenly that its bonnet has been swallowed by their boot. 'Christ Almighty! What are they trying to do?'

'Casper? Sit tight, honey. Are you buckled in? Is he buckled in?'

'What's wrong, Mum? Are they motorbikes? What's that noise? I can't see the motorbikes.'

'He's buckled in.'

'I can't see the motorbikes, Mum. Mum. Mummy. I can't see the—'

'Just sit tight, Cas! Please, honey, Mummy's driving!'

The Audi hits them. It is just a nudge but the sound is like the BMW is splitting in two.

'Jesus Christ!'

'Shit! Shitshitshit! Casper, are you okay? Tom! Tom! Is Casper okay?'

'He's okay! Jesus Christ! Are you okay, buddy?' Tom has his cheek pressed to the headrest. He is watching the boy's face as it crumples. 'It's okay, Casper, I promise you. Just hang on.'

'Just sit tight, honey!'

The impact, this time, hurls Tom towards the dashboard. The seatbelt catches him and yanks him back and drives his skull into the headrest. The pain, when it comes, is in his neck, across his chest. He needs to breathe and he opens his mouth and he realises his mouth is already open. He hears Julia scream her son's name and he looks up and the windscreen is filled with wall. He yells, or tries to, but Julia is already turning.

'Shit! Shit! Tom! Are you okay? Tom!'

'I'm okay.'

'Tom! Shit! Tom!'

Tom says it louder. 'I'm okay!'

There is another roar. Tom turns and it is like a knife slits his spine. He spots the Audi before jerking back. It is close but falling away, as though it lunged again but this time missed its target.

Casper is wailing now and Julia is trying to comfort him. She is shouting though, almost screaming. Tom reaches and ignores the pain and his hand closes on Casper's foot. The BMW swerves and the jolt makes Tom yell but he shuffles back in his seat and holds tight. He feel Casper's fingers scrabbling to find his and leans further until their hands join.

'They're dropping back!'

Julia is smiling into the rear-view mirror – grinning, in fact, like someone touched.

'They are!' she says. 'They're dropping back!'

Tom twists. There is nothing beyond the rear windscreen but road and a brightening sky.

'What they hell were they playing at? Did you get the registration, Tom? I can't see it.'

'No, I—'

Julia is not looking at the road. She is looking in the mirror still as Tom turns towards the front and she is not looking at the road and she does not see what Tom sees.

There is no time even to say her name. There is no time to point or to brace himself or to tighten his grip on Casper's hand. He has an instant only and time for just a single thought: this is going to hurt.

PART THREE

Graves counts as they disembark. He counts again as they file towards the entrance. There are only twelve, he is about to say. But then the thirteenth and final prisoner appears. She has to be carried from the coach. There is a guard either side of her, bearing an arm and a leg each, and the prisoner slumps in her makeshift throne. She is a big woman and the guards, despite their own size, have to pause halfway across the courtyard to adjust their grip. They jerk the woman to get a better hold but they jerk too violently and they stagger. Another guard hurries forwards to catch their balance. He tries to help with the carrying but there is no limb for him to hold. He moves to the rear and then the side and then the front. He grabs a trouser leg but his colleague shakes his head. Possibly he says something, snaps something, and the guard who was trying to help moves aside. He stands for a moment, looking as useless as he no doubt feels, but then he yells at the line of prisoners and points as though with purpose and gives one of the men a shove and feels, Graves suspects, much better.

He should be hiking. He stopped at the office to collect some

SIMON LELIC

paperwork but he has on the boots he has not yet worn and today is his day off – the only day off he has taken – and he promised himself he would put it to good use. Instead, for the time being, he watches the scene in the courtyard below from his window. Burrows is beside him and Graves, for once, feels gratified by his presence. It could simply be that the man is not bleating. He is not talking for the sake of talking or knocking something over or breathing through his mouth as he so often does. Burrows watches as Graves watches and it feels like they are thinking about much the same thing.

Graves looks at his assistant. He looks away. When he talks, he talks to the glass. 'Why are you here, John?' He hesitates. 'You said before you hardly had a choice. What did you mean?'

For a while Burrows does not answer and Graves begins to think that maybe he will not. 'I needed the money,' he says at last. Like Graves, he keeps his eyes on the row of prisoners. 'I had debts. Gambling debts, if you want the truth.' Burrows says this last with a hint of a challenge but when Graves remains silent he carries on. 'Not fortunes. I mean, to you it wouldn't sound like a lot of money at all, I'm sure. But they had to be paid.'

'And?' says Graves. 'Did you pay them?' It is the kind of question an interfering father would ask; the kind of question he has never dared ask his daughter.

'They did. It was part of the deal.' Burrows takes a breath and speaks as he exhales. 'Now I have new ones.'

Graves parts his lips. He feels reproach tug his gaze but resists. How? he does not say. With whom?

Burrows sighs. He answers as though Graves has asked. 'We

232

play cards. Poker, mainly. Me, Baggins sometimes, a few of the guards.'

Graves bobs his head. 'I'd heard rumours. I even had an invitation once, from a guard who didn't know, I think, who I was.'

Burrows turns. 'You should come,' he says, forgetting the debts evidently and talking now as though about a drink at the pub. 'It's only for pennies, really.'

Graves turns too. 'Pennies?'

'Sometimes pounds.' Burrows lifts a shoulder. 'I haven't been lucky.'

The last of the prisoners has disappeared from view. In the courtyard, the coach is turning. Graves has a glimpse of the driver and he wonders momentarily about the man's life. Where he lives and with whom and what he said to his wife, if he has a wife, when he left for work this morning. Although of course the driver would have said nothing. He is army, probably, or something similar, and he is trained to say nothing, to think nothing, to follow orders.

'What about you?'

Burrows's tone is brave, brazen almost, and Graves shifts. He is tempted to assert his authority and avoid answering but that, he tells himself, would not be fair. What, after all, would he really be avoiding?

'I was bored,' he says. 'It was important, a service to the country: they made that clear. But to me, mainly, it was something to do.' He finds himself snorting because although the answer comes readily it is not something he has previously acknowledged. Even to himself, he has only ever admitted an adulterated version of the truth. 'I was retired, supposedly. I retired myself. But I don't play golf and I don't have an allotment and I was sitting at home for most of the day building my tolerance to caffeine.'

'You do drink a lot of coffee.'

Graves cannot help but smile. His smile, though, quickly sours. 'This is me, John. This is all I can do. It's all there is for me to do. I don't have friends. I don't have family. I have a daughter but she . . . Well. My daughter has her own life. I missed my chance to be a part of it.'

'You have a daughter? I didn't know that.'

'No. There's no reason why you would.'

'What about your wife? I mean, I noticed you wear a ring. Is she . . . That is, does she still . . .'

'She's alive. We're divorced. I wear the ring because I can't get it off.'

Burrows swallows. He seems to be searching for another question. All of a sudden, though, Graves wants not to be here. It is not Burrows that makes him feel so, nor even the conversation. It is as though he has realised suddenly that he is late for something; that the day he has given himself seems quietly to be stealing itself back.

He turns and collects the paperwork for which he came. 'You should get on,' he tells Burrows. 'Dr Silk will want to know the prisoners have arrived. It wouldn't do to keep him waiting.'

'No. I guess it wouldn't.'

Graves puts a hand on Burrows's shoulder. 'I'll see you tomorrow, John. I'm going for a walk.'

*

234

He hikes until he can no longer see the facility, which is not particularly far but far enough that he develops blisters. He stops at the summit of a tor and finds a rock on which to sit. He is breathing heavily and his fingers are thick from the cold and he cannot work an opening to unknot his laces. After a minute he gives up. He does not have the energy and anyway the pain round his heels is subsiding. If he stretches his legs and takes the weight from his soles, it is nothing more than a memory of an ache. He puffs, slouches. He shifts his feet but then the pain returns so he shifts them back and gives another puff.

He had no idea he was so out of shape. The doctor, on the other hand, clearly had some inkling. It would be an idea, Henry, he said, if you were to take some exercise. Have you tried just walking? As though for the past five decades Graves had negotiated life balanced on his hands. But those were his words: it would be an idea. Firm but not alarmist. A suggestion, not a prescription. So Graves had not taken it particularly seriously. He promised to make an effort but his effort was a trip to buy some walking boots – even though, at the time, the only place he envisaged walking, if at all, was Hyde Park.

Needless to say he did not make it that far. He should perhaps have listened to what the doctor did not say; he should have acknowledged that he deigned to treat Graves like an adult. But Graves only went to see him in the first place at his daughter's insistence, after he made the mistake of admitting to her about the palpitations. As far as he was concerned, he did not sleep because he could not stop thinking. It was that simple. And his heart: it was just the occasional flutter, nothing serious – the doctor said it himself. A lifetime of stress was the cause and a walk along the Serpentine would not cure that. So, yes, he is out of shape and of that he is a little ashamed. But he is too old now to start worrying about his health. His life is too far gone.

He looks at his hand and worries at his wedding ring. He thinks of his conversation with Burrows and considers how easily he lied. He twists the ring and pulls. The ring slides from his finger.

His wife, he recalls, had him jogging once. And it was just once: out of Wandsworth gates and down Trinity Road and to the common. That was the route she planned for him. He made it as far as the second set of traffic lights. Then he turned and walked back, apace with the crawling traffic and through the gates again and past the smirking guards.

The grief Carol gave him. Like she was a paragon of vitality. She ate muesli, that was her claim to healthy living. Muesli and then biscuits and sugared coffee at ten. How was that any better than a bacon sandwich? Apparently, though, it was different for men. Particularly, Carol said, for men of a certain age. And besides, it wasn't just about keeping fit. It wasn't just about sleeping. It was about de-stressing, which to Graves did not even sound like a real word. It was about learning to take some time out and just, for twenty minutes, *letting go*.

Would it have helped? he wonders. Would jogging and eating less bacon and making the effort – at weekends, she pleaded; on Sundays even – to ignore the telephone: would doing those things have saved his marriage? Certainly, in the months after their break-up, he regretted not having at least given them a try. But he has no such regrets any more. Those things on to which his wife latched were symptoms, it is clear to him now, of a character flawed but immutable. Like his wife's, in fact. So exactly like his wife's and that was the other problem. Graves's only real regret, the one thing time has not pardoned, is that he behaved, when the end came, so perfectly like a child. Carol did too, he can say that now without prejudice, but his offence – their offence – was to expect their daughter, barely a grown-up, to be the adult.

He wears the ring still because he cannot take it off. That is what he said. And it is true, in a sense. He loves his daughter and he even loves his wife still and he cannot take off the ring because he does not deserve to.

He stands. It is beautiful. He has not considered – he has not, in his time here, had cause to consider – quite how stunning the moorland is. Not picturesque. Not quaint bridges and clipped hedges but jagged rock and thick-stemmed grass and trees that dance in the wind. It is raw. It is uncontrolled, uncontrollable. That, Graves feels, is the source of its beauty. The land in front of him and behind him and in every direction in which he looks is the world left just to get on with things. It is nature, unredacted.

He starts to walk, back the way he came. Gloves and plasters: he should have thought to bring gloves and plasters. A thermos of coffee would have been nice too, perhaps one or two of Burrows's biscuits. What would the doctor, Graves wonders, say to that?

He aches and it is a worthy ache but that does not lessen his desire for a bath. A bath, ideally, he has to ease into, one square inch of skin at a time. After that a meal, involving mashed potato and gravy. Instead he braves the tepid shower and heats up another pie.

He eats as much as he did last time. Tonight, though, he does not wait before resorting to the rich teas. He gobbles one whole, snapping it against the roof of his mouth with his tongue, then carries the packet into the living room, to the chair he has positioned to catch the outer glow from the kitchen light. The papers he collected from his office are at his feet. He sets aside the uppermost file, his pretext – to Burrows, to himself – for going to the office at all, and lifts on to his lap the stack below. He nibbles the circumference of another biscuit as he reads. Crumbs patter on the pages and he dabs at them with a fingertip.

He learns nothing new but he did not expect to. He tracks the words and the pictures in the files but it is a trick, really, and one he acknowledges, that he is playing on himself. It is a delaying tactic. It is reading the brochure one more time after deciding already to place a deposit. Because he has decided, he knows he has. He knows and yet when he finishes the final folder he flips the pile and starts again from the beginning.

The curtains are drawn. It is not a curtain so much as a bed sheet but the important thing is that it covers the window. It blocks his view and that is the point, except it leaves him with nothing, after the folders, at which to stare.

He turns on the television. He does not expect it to work but it does. Coat hangers and snow, he remembers, are a relic of another age. He finds the news. There seems to be none.

It is too early for bed so he watches for a while anyway.

It is sport, which he does not follow, then entertainment, which he does not understand. After that it is business, which he encourages himself to find interesting, and finally it is the weather. Some cloud, some sun, some rain, the occasional gust of wind. Comprehensive, then, but hardly enlightening. After the weather the headlines roll again. Graves missed them on the previous cycle but he no longer cares to watch. He turns off the television and listens for a moment to the silence. It is not a comfortable silence, however, so he turns the television back on.

In his bedroom he lays open a case on his mattress. He does not fill it. It is open though and that is a start. It is an acknow-ledgement, of a kind. But then he shakes his head and shuts the case and slides it back under the bed. He returns to the lounge. The folders are still on the chair and from his position at the door he considers them. This is the problem, he tells himself. This is his other problem. He is better not having the opportunity to think. Put him on the spot, rather. Ask him for a decision, quickly now please, and he will make one and usu-ally a good one. But give him time – days and, most especially, nights – and he will prevaricate. He will second-guess. He will decide and then undecide and it is no wonder that he can never sleep.

And this woman's voice. Honestly.

Graves turns to the television and the newsreader is a man. Which is all well and good but does not make the voice any less irritating. He crosses the room and reaches for the switch on the set. He presses it but then he is holding it. He bends. Still holding the button, he watches the screen. Because the newsreader, finally, has said something worth hearing. Just a name but it is enough. It is enough to keep Graves watching: the image of the mangled car, the television reporter hunched against a rain shower at the roadside, the faces in the photographs on the screen. He watches and he keeps watching, even as his finger aches and his knees creak and the blisters on his heels chafe against his socks and begin to bleed. And even after the report is over, Graves does not shift. He remains in front of the television, waiting for the news cycle to begin again, knowing that his decision has finally been made.

Dear is too formal and hi is too glib and Casper, Julia is too stark. But that, as far as he can see, is his choice: a letter of complaint, an email or a memo. Unless he just starts with the start? But then he could be writing to anyone.

He digs and tries not to think about what he is digging. He tries not to think about the last time he was digging, and with whom. About whose body might be the first to lie where Arthur's feet are now.

The end is easier: love always. He does not have to sign it. He was stuck on that for a while: how to sign it. Dad or Daddy but then it would have to be Dad/Arthur, Daddy/Arthur, which is ugly and unnecessary because it is not like they will not know. So love always, nothing more. Which leaves him still with how to start.

It is just another drainage ditch, he tells himself, even though the thought is ludicrous given the dimensions they have been instructed to follow. Eight by eight, the first guard said. Or, said the second through a grin, if it's easier: imagine four people lying side by side.

He would experiment, see what the words look like written down, but the act of writing it once might be all that he can stand. Better to decide now and then just write, without having to think about what he is writing. Like the digging, in fact.

Looks like a goddamn grave. Isn't that what Roach said last time? And he said, maybe it is. Maybe they're planning to toss us both in when we're done.

Ignore the start. Come back to the start. He is only obsessing about the start because he is struggling at the moment to think beyond it.

It is just another drainage ditch. Even though there are four separate teams, four separate holes; even though they are fifty yards beyond the outer fence and in a clearing between the trees and there is nothing whatsoever that could possibly need draining; even though the prisoners are dying and their bodies . . . Roach's body . . .

It is a drainage ditch. It is just another drainage ditch. And the point is to concentrate on the letter.

He should say sorry, above all else. That, then, is how he should start.

I'm sorry.

To you, Julia, he will write, for a hundred thousand things. Most you've probably forgotten and I'm doing myself no favours by bringing them up. But the Gower, for instance. Not that I didn't enjoy it and I'm fairly sure you did too but it was the fact that we went there at all. That I made us go. That you wanted to go to Sardinia and I said – like I always said – maybe next year. Which is actually the point I'm trying to make because it's not the Gower, as such, that I'm sorry

242

about. It's the maybe next year. It's insisting on Chez Pierre because we know it's reasonable and the food is decent and it doesn't take an age to get served. It's arguing about the car even though you won the argument about the car. It's the two-for-one deals on wine that neither of us likes. It's spending Saturday morning shopping around for cheaper insurance. It's buying insurance, for everything. It's never, not once, even though you insisted I would like them, ordering oysters.

He knows what he means. She will too, probably, but he will have to limit the letter to a page or two and the Gower, oysters: do they really deserve to take up half of it?

I'm sorry that I made you marry me. I'm being succinct now so there's no space to argue because we both know the truth and I did. And now you're arguing even though I've already told you there isn't space. You're saying, how dare you? I seem to be implying that your mind is not your own. But that's not what I'm saying. I'm saying it was always my plan. That's how despicable I am. Right from the day we met – or maybe the week after, because it took me a while to reconcile myself to those dungarees you were so fond of wearing – my plan was to make you marry me. You didn't seem so immediately convinced but that was only, I told myself, because you didn't know me. So I became your friend. I wanted to be your lover so I became your friend. To be near you, mainly, but also so you'd never be far. And I plotted and I planned and I dreamed and I schemed until finally I convinced you to take a chance. So I did. I made you marry me. So stop arguing, please, and accept the fact that I am sorry.

Which is all very well because he is, in one sense, but in

another sense he is absolutely not. Because if they had never been married they would not have had Casper and how could Casper possibly engender regret? So he is sorry but he is not and there will certainly not be space enough to be equivocal.

I'm sorry we did not stay together. You know how sorry I am and you're sorry too, in your way, but I think – I know – that if you had given me one last—

It is Arthur's turn to rest and just as well. He has taken that paragraph as far as it ought to go.

There is water but it is brown. He drinks anyway, filtering out the larger clumps of soil between his teeth. The man who replaces him in the hole will soon be filling one, Arthur can tell. Only the well work – the well men – but the man is not well. He claims to be, he claims to be fine, just give me the shovel, but there is a rash on his forearms that Arthur could recognise now in the dark, through a bandage, beneath seeping ulcers and scabs of blood. The man – Taylor, his name is – must know what he is digging but still he insists on working. If it were Arthur, he would take the opportunity to be excused. Or perhaps not. Being excused means sitting in your cell, on your bunk, reckoning the hours until . . . Well. Until whatever comes next. So probably Arthur would dig too.

The three men in the trench nearest to theirs work shirtless. It cannot be more than seven degrees but the sun is dripping through the branches and the ground, given the time of year, is surprisingly firm. Some gloves would help. Some clean water too. Arthur looks to the nearest set of guards, three men stationed beside his trench, and maybe if he were to catch one's eye he would ask but none sees him looking so he turns away. And in fact he cannot be bothered. He knows how the conversation would go. He knows how it would end.

So: to you, Julia, for a hundred thousand things.

And something more.

And then move on.

To you, Casper, for not being there: now and tomorrow and every day after that. For not being there to watch when you learn to balance your bike, to tie your laces, to pee standing up. To walk you to school. To help with your homework. To drop you off and pick you up and embarrass you in front of your friends simply by being your dad. To teach you to shave. To teach you to drive. To give you money and say, what happened to the last lot? To watch you graduate. To meet Chloë, Christina, Cleo and then your fiancée. To shake you by the hand at your wedding and to slip into your pocket a cheque for the honeymoon. To watch you, just watch you, and not be able to speak past the lump in my throat.

But he would have to write it, not just think it. What kind of message would it send if the letter were stained with tears?

The guards are laughing. Arthur looks behind him to see what is funny. He turns back and realises they are laughing at him. He wonders why. He drinks and they laugh again and it is the way he drinks: siphoning and then spitting and then slurping again. One of the guards makes a rabbit face, rabbit noises. Arthur watches. He takes another scoop from the bucket and raises it to his lips. No way they are getting clean water now.

Some advice perhaps. Something that will stand his son in good stead. Which is a suitably responsible phrase in itself and possibly, Arthur thinks, worth using.

But the advice.

Don't be a dentist. The money's good but it's boring as hell—

He cannot say hell.

Don't be a dentist. The money's good but you should choose a career that has the potential to be more fulfilling—

Can he say fulfilling? It sounds like a pun but possibly one only dentists would get. Dentists, and Roach. Roach would have got it. He would have insisted, too, that Arthur use it. He is grinning, in Arthur's memory, and that he is grinning makes Arthur smile too. It is a painful smile, though, and he swallows it down.

—more fulfilling, like painting or composing or writing or even teaching, like your mother.

Julia, though, might have something to say about that. Teaching, she would point out, is noble and worthwhile and, yes, it can be fulfilling but it can also be frustrating and exhausting and heartbreaking, and probably it is those things on more days than not. And painting, composing, writing: they are hardly the basis of a steady income. How can he in good conscience advise his son to turn his back on a decent credit rating? Whoever follows Chloë, Christina, Cleo will need a home. She will need a car. She will need the knowledge that the children she bears will not suffer because of what their father cannot afford.

Be a dentist, then. It can sometimes seem dull but the money's good. Don't, whatever you do, become a painter or a composer or a writer. You might consider being a teacher but talk to your mother about that.

He does not want Casper to be a dentist. He is not sure he

wants Casper to be a teacher either, not after seeing the pain it caused Julia.

Be yourself. Be what your heart tells you to be. Listen to your head too because sometimes it might be necessary to be a little bit less yourself than is comfortable but, when in doubt, listen to your heart.

That is not bad. He will use that. Unless it is a trifle throwaway? Be yourself: it sounds as though Arthur could not be bothered to think of anything more meaningful. It is evasive too. It is exactly what someone would say if they were worried about being held accountable. Throwaway, then, and evasive: not, on reflection, an impressive distillation of thirty-one years of accumulated wisdom.

He would like to ask Julia. Julia would know what he should write. She would smile and slip behind his chair and wrap her arms around his shoulders and nestle her cheek against his. And she would say . . .

His break is over and he returns to the ditch. They are thigh deep now, which does not seem bad going, although it strikes Arthur that he has no idea, actually, how long they have been digging.

Taylor lets his shovel drop. He crawls from the trench and he sits, slumps, with his head sagging and his elbows jutting. It is not his turn to rest but Arthur and the other man, the third in their team of three, have an understanding, somehow, that they will each take only one break in two – for Taylor's sake. The guards have not noticed. Or, if they have, they do not care. The excursion is a jolly for them, a chance to smoke and chat and ridicule.

He should say something about his state of mind. Obviously it will not reflect well that he felt it necessary to write the letter in the first place but he should include some words of reassurance.

Although part of him thinks, why should he? The same part that says, when he thinks about how frantic Julia must be, good. I'm glad. I hope she cannot eat or sleep or breathe from all the worry. With any luck she blames herself and she should blame herself because it is her fault. Because if they had not been separated, would he be here? If he had been in his home, with his wife and his son, would they have dared to take him away? And then another voice joins in, and this one tells him that she is glad he is gone. That she has been waiting for it, *planning* it somehow. And though neither voice sounds quite like his own they are compelling and convincing and Arthur, through his shame, finds it hard not to listen.

Some days. On some days he listens. Today he will not because he knows, he *knows*, that the worst part for Julia when she reads the letter will be trying to imagine what Arthur would have gone through.

Don't worry about me, he will write.

But it will be too late, of course, because she will have, so he cannot say that.

It's not so bad here, he will write.

But it is, of course, so he cannot say that.

I have a friend, he will write.

When, of course, he no longer has. So he cannot say that.

His state of mind, then. How best to sum up his state of mind?

A state. But what kind of message would *that* send?

He stops digging and plants his shovel. A guard calls his name so he picks the shovel up again. He digs, even though he is so tired now that when he stabs with the blade it ricochets from the earth. He hears his name again and tries to dig faster. When he hears the guard shout a third time, Arthur turns.

'Jesus Christ, Priestley, are you deaf? Get out here.'

Arthur hesitates. He looks at Taylor, who looks right back.

'Either he's deaf,' says the guard to his colleagues, 'or he soon fucking will be.' He rests a palm on the butt of his truncheon and directs his smile towards Arthur. The smile is a warning: he does not expect to have to ask again.

Arthur leans his shovel against the side of the trench and checks for the easiest point from which to climb out. He presses his palms to the earth and swings his leg but falls back down. He tries again and this time keeps his balance. He drags up his back leg behind and clambers to his feet.

'Come with me.' The guard turns away but not before Arthur recognises his face. It is the guard with the knuckles – the one who took such offence when Arthur last asked for a chance to see Graves.

Arthur looks at Taylor, still slumped at the edge of the trench. 'What about the hole?'

The guard is already walking away. 'Don't worry,' he says. 'We'll save you a space.' The other guards laugh and Knuckles turns to show his sneer.

They are halfway to the outer fence, Arthur being made to walk in front now and the guard directing him from behind, when they hear a shout. Both men stop and look. Arthur sees only what was there before: the prisoners, the guards, the graves in progress perforating the ground. The guard, though, peers in a single direction, frowning slightly as though vaguely amused. Arthur tracks his gaze.

Someone is running: one of the inmates who removed their shirts. The guards are giving chase but the prisoner has a head start and he is flying, above the roots that try to trip him and beneath the branches that reach to grab him. The trees thicken ahead and all he needs to do is get that far. And he will. The guards yell and stumble and curse and move like they are tethered by elastic. One has a rifle and he fires. It is just a warning shot though and the crack, if anything, acts like a whip at the fleeing prisoner's back. There are cheers and even Arthur finds himself muttering, wishing the man on, and it works because he is, he is flying, and he is only yards now from the—

He falls. There is another crack. In that order, which is why Arthur thinks that perhaps the shot has missed. He is not alone either because the cheering among the prisoners continues. They think he knew the shot was coming so he dived and in a second he will be on his feet again, running again. But the guards know. They stop and why would they stop if they did not know? When they start forwards once more they take their time. They wade through the foliage like holidaymakers paddling along the shore. By the time they reach the man's body, the forest is silent.

Arthur feels a hand at his back. The guard shoves and Arthur stumbles.

'Move,' says the guard. 'Keep moving.'

Arthur cannot help but look round. He can no longer see the body, just the guards who are clustered around it. The guard with the rifle is there, the weapon slung now across his back and the hand of another guard resting on his shoulder.

'Keep walking!' Knuckles gives Arthur another prod.

What is the point? The letter: why even bother? It will not bring his friend back. It will not make his absence seem any less present, even temporarily. And Julia, Casper: what hope is there that they will read it? What chance that they will be allowed to? There is no point, then: that is the truth of it. In every respect, writing the letter would be futile. It would be an exercise to distract him from the pall that is over him, to convince himself that his fate – like Roach's, like that of the man who ran – was not long ago decided. And if his fate has already been decided . . . Well. Why leave it in somebody else's hands?

'Pick up the pace, Priestley. I didn't ask you along for a gentle stroll.'

He would not be the first. There was the man in the cell three along from Arthur's who hung himself from the frame of his upturned bunk. He was ill, it is true, and in that sense his choice was easier but there is the inmate, too, whom Arthur has just seen shot. And he was well. Well enough to work, at least. Well enough to run, and to know that he could never run far.

'I'm not kidding, Priestley. Jesus Christ. Anyone would think you were ill.' Knuckles sniggers at his own wit.

Well or not, though, what difference does it make? The point is, there are ways. The point is, everyone has their reasons. And without Roach; without Julia and without Casper. Without the prospect of seeing them or speaking to them or to anyone, ever, who is not another human being condemned, it is a reason to carry on that Arthur lacks.

The guard pauses to light a cigarette. There is a flick of flint and the sound of Knuckles exhaling, followed by bootsteps as he marches to catch up. Then, between smoking and sniggering and digesting the fact he is a witness to murder, he manages to give Arthur another shove.

He remembers everything. He remembers thinking it would hurt and then the pain itself: in his neck and behind his skull and then in his arm as if it was ripping in two. And the noise, like a bottle bank being emptied from a height. After that, screaming, and the thought that screaming was a good thing because it meant they were all still alive. They were his screams, though. They were only his screams. He screamed and the car slid and when the car stopped he did too. Silence followed, until he remembered to breathe. He tried to turn but could not. He was facing the passenger-side window and he had lost all feeling in his limbs; he could move his head but only a fraction and he was straining his muscles but only thought he was because in reality, he felt sure, he was paralysed below the chin.

He shouted for Julia. He shouted for Casper. He was shouting so much he would not have heard them had they replied. They did not. They might have jumped from the car before it hit for all the sound they were making after it had. Screaming was good: the thought returned. So he shouted and he screamed again and still he could not break the silence.

And it dragged on. The waiting was almost the worst part of it. He waited and he waited and all he could do was stare at the same piece of sky. He stared at a cloud, which seemed to have interrupted its journey in order to stop and stare right back. Then it left, just as the ambulance arrived, as though it had dallied too long already and had no desire to get caught up in the commotion that was to follow.

No one would talk to him. He was shouting once more, asking questions, pleading to be told whether Julia and Casper were all right. The answers he got in return, however, were barely answers at all. They told him everything was fine, they would all be fine, that it was important he keep calm and try – as though he were bucking and writhing – not to move. They asked him his name and kept asking until he answered. They asked him what day it was, what month, what year. The only real clue he had as to what was happening behind him were the curses and exhortations of people he could not see.

Welcome back, someone said. A nurse, holding out a plastic cup. You've had a lucky escape, she said. He tried to speak but his mouth was stitched shut. He tried to take the cup with his left hand but found he could only lift his right. It's just a fracture, she told him. It will heal. She held the cup to his lips and gradually they eased apart. He tried to speak again and managed a croak. The nurse smiled and fed him sips and finally set the cup to one side. I'll fetch a doctor, she told him. I'll be right back. And in seconds, it seemed, she returned, following at the doctor's heels.

The doctor said, hello. He said, it's Tom, isn't it? He said, you've had a lucky escape. And after some prodding and not a little head bobbing, it was the doctor who gave him the news.

He sits at her bedside. He is not alone. Beside him is Julia's cousin; Casper is balanced on Tom's knees.

'Please, love.' Julia's cousin has an accent as English as her Laura Ashley dress. She reaches for Casper's foot. The boy lets her take it but does not so much as turn.

'Casper?' says Tom. 'I think you should go with Pippa. Just for a little while. You're hungry, aren't you?'

'Tom,' says Pippa. Just that. Just his name and a look. Tom leans back and Pippa slides forwards, angling her head to try and catch Casper's eye. 'Come on, love. It's time to go. Your mummy would want you to eat something.'

Tom glances at the figure on the bed. He can see only the right side of Julia's face and from this angle, ignoring the tube to her nose and the bandage covering her crown, she might simply be sleeping. She does not look hurt at all, from this angle.

Pippa is standing. 'Let's go, Casper. Come on, please.'

Still the boy ignores her. He does not shift; he just stares at his mother's prone form. Only when Pippa reaches again, and this time takes hold of Casper's arm, does Casper make any movement at all. He twists and he clutches at Tom. Tom recoils, wincing at the pressure on his cast and clinging with the balls of his feet to the floor to stop his chair from toppling. He smiles, as much in surprise as anything, but his smile withers when he catches sight of Pippa's expression. She glares, as though it were Tom's grip and not the boy's that were keeping

Casper tethered to his mother's side. Tom tries to indicate his helplessness but Casper is pinning his shoulders. He smiles again instead, with one corner of his mouth, but from Pippa's reaction the smile might just as well be a sneer.

She looks to the ceiling. 'I'll fetch some sandwiches then, shall I?' She tuts as she turns, leaving Casper with his head buried and his hands locked around Tom's neck.

'Tom! Is that you?'

'Amy. Hi.'

'Where are you? Jesus. Are you all right? We heard what happened to you. What happened to you?'

'I'm fine. I'm in Exeter.'

'Are you all right though? We've been so worried.'

'I'm fine, really. Just a few scrapes and bruises.'

'What about Julia? What about . . . Casper, is it?'

'Casper's fine. A bump on the head but otherwise not a scratch.'

'And Julia? How's Julia?'

'She's . . . not so good.'

'Oh. Oh, Tom.'

'But she's tough. She'll pull through. They're doing everything they can. I mean, obviously they are but . . . Well. You know.'

'Are you sure you're all right, Tom? You sound . . . I don't know.'

'I'm fine. I am. I'm just tired, that's all. They let me out and I moved in down the corridor and this might actually be the first time I've stepped outside the hospital since the accident.'

'You should get a hotel. Or come home. Maybe you should come home and get some proper rest. They have telephones at these places, you know. They'll keep you informed. Do you want me to . . . I could come down there and pick you up?'

'No, no. It's fine. Really. Thanks, though.'

'What happened, Tom? Do you remember?'

'It was just an accident. The roads down here can get a little hairy.'

'They said you hit a tractor. Is that right?'

'We hit a trailer on a tractor. Which was good news for the bloke driving it.'

'How? I mean, it was going the same way as you – that's what they said. Did you not see it? How come you were going so fast?'

'Jesus, Amy. You sound like the police.'

'Did you speak to the police? What did you tell them?'

'Just what I told you.'

'And?'

'And what?'

'And what happens now?'

'I don't know. They're waiting to speak to Julia.'

'Oh. I see. Of course. Listen, Tom – are you sure you don't want me to pick you up? Or I could just drive down. Just to sit with you.'

'Really, Amy. It's sweet of you but I'm fine. Julia's cousin's here. She's . . . she's keeping me company.'

'Oh. Okay. Good. I'm glad there's a friendly face.'

'Yeah. Uh huh. Anyway, Amy, could you do me a favour? Could you talk to Katherine? They're moving Julia up to

London the day after tomorrow so I'll be back in town soon but, well. I'm going to need some more time off.'

'It's fine, Tom. Katherine's already said.'

'Can you talk to her though? I don't think I could face it.'

'I will, of course I will, but it's fine, Tom. She's already said: take as much time as you need.'

'Really? Oh. Well, great. Thanks. Tell her thanks.'

'There're some messages, Tom.'

'Just ignore them. They can wait.'

'Yes. Of course. But . . . there's one in particular.'

'What do you mean?'

'Why are you in Exeter, Tom? What were you doing down there in the first place?'

'What? Nothing. We were just . . . Why? What was the message?'

'You can tell me, Tom. You know you can.'

'Amy? What was the message?'

'It was a guy. Like, an older guy. My dad's age, probably. He said he thought you were on your way to see him.'

'He said what?'

'That he thought you were on your way to see him. He said he heard about the accident and he's glad you're okay and if you felt like talking you should give him a call. Whenever you were feeling up to it, he said. Just casual, even though he didn't sound casual.'

'What else did he say?'

'Nothing else. He left a number. Shall I give it to you? Tom? Hello? Are you there?'

'I'm here.'

'Where did you go?'

'Nowhere. I'm here. He left a number?'

'I have it here. Have you got a pen?'

'Just . . . just ignore it, Amy. It's not important.'

'What? Are you sure? It sounded important. I mean, it didn't but that's why it did.'

'Ignore it. Just ignore it. I've got to go, Amy. I've got to get back.'

'Tom? Wait. What's wrong? What's this about?'

'Thanks, Amy. And say thanks to Katherine. I'll call you soon.'

'Tom? Tom? Wait, I—'

He stands at the foot of the bed. He rests his good hand on the frame and looks at his knuckles. He can still see Julia's face, however. Even with his gaze turned away, he can still see the bandages that cover her hairline and her left eye and her left cheek, down to her neck and her collarbone and beyond. He can still see the tube that helps her breathe. He can still see the figures on the screen that are his only visible assurance that Julia is not already dead.

It is a risk. Because maybe it was the news of the accident, like he said. A woman named Priestley, a reporter from a political news site, a crash on an empty road on the route into Dartmoor. And they were close; they must have been. If they were not, the Audi would have kept its distance. So maybe it was the accident or maybe he knew already who they were and what they were doing. Like the men in the Audi, for instance.

He flexes his left hand and finds he still cannot. The pain, though, is a comfort. It is a reminder that he absorbed some of the impact at least. It is a reminder that Casper is unhurt, the tractor driver too, and that is two lives saved from the menace of Tom's stupidity.

Say he calls. Who would be listening? If they met, who would be watching? And what, anyway, could he possibly say that might mitigate the danger, might justify Tom taking this any further than he already has?

The pain is also his penance. It reminds Tom that he is not suffering enough, which is almost the hardest thing to bear. It is a reminder that, no matter how much he wishes, there is no bargain to be made that would allow Julia to hurt any less.

It is not his decision. He cannot, apart from anything else, be trusted to decide. Although in fact he does not have to because he knows already what Julia would say. It would be the toughest choice she has ever had to make but he knows exactly what she would say. And Arthur, if Arthur were here, would agree.

He unhooks Julia's chart. He stares at what is written as though there might be some hint in the cryptic shorthand that things are not as bad as they seem. He replaces the chart and moves around the bed to Julia's side. He lifts his hand to cover his face.

She would find a way though. Her decision would be to protect Casper but that would not stop her. So maybe Julia would be just as torn as Tom is. More so because her life is no longer just her own. That is what Arthur would tell her: you cannot risk your life because it belongs to Casper now too. And she would say, what about yours? How is your life any less important to Casper than mine? And she would be right, of course.

Arthur would argue but the argument would already be lost.

Which leaves him where exactly? Standing at Julia's bedside with his hand over his mouth and thinking about which lives he has the right, the responsibility, to put at risk. No further on, then, from the point at which he started.

'Amy. It's Tom again.'

'Tom.'

'Amy, listen. That message you mentioned. Have you got it still?'

'What? Yes. Of course. I have it here. Do you want me to—'

'On a piece of paper? Did you write it down or did you email me?'

'I wrote it down. Why? What does it matter? Do you want me to—'

'Burn it. Shred it. Swallow it if you have to. Amy? Are you listening?'

'I'm listening. But Tom—'

'You took the call, right? No one else took the call?'

'No, I took it. I told you, he sounded like—'

'Good. That's good. But the message: get rid of it. Amy? Promise me you'll get rid of it as soon as you hang up the phone. Forget you even heard it in the first place. I mean it, Amy: if anyone asks, you don't know what they're talking about.'

'Tom, please. You're scaring me. Tell me what this is about.'

'I can't. I absolutely can't. Just promise me, Amy.'

'Okay, okay. I promise. Jesus, Tom.'

'Good. Okay then. But Amy. Listen. Give me the number he left first.'

It is ludicrous that he should feel nervous. It is ludicrous that he should rub his palms and pick at his fingernails when his hands will at least wash clean. It is ludicrous that he should beat his heel and chew his lip, as though the man for whom he waits were someone worthy, someone notable – not a coward and a killer and a thug.

He makes to stand so he might pace. The guard, though, pushes him down. Arthur's chair scrapes against the hardwood floor as he lands and Graves's assistant raises his head. He looks at Arthur for a moment, then at the guard. The guard lifts his chin and stares ahead, his hands joined now behind his back. Burrows glances again at Arthur, then returns his gaze to the paperwork on his desk.

And making him wait. What is that but a means to some megalomaniacal thrill? Drag him from a graveside, have him watch a man die, then drop him in a chair and tell him, stay. Sit. Come to heel when I tell you. As though Arthur did not already know who was in charge. As though he felt any semblance of control as to his fate.

It is not nerves, he realises. This energy he feels, this urge in every muscle to twitch and tense: how Graves might come to wish it were Arthur's nerves.

'Priestley.'

Arthur looks up.

'He's ready,' says Burrows. 'You can go in.'

Arthur stands and approaches the adjoining door. He senses the guard following at his shoulder.

'Not you,' Burrows says and Arthur stops, turns. He feels himself frowning. Me? he is about to say but Burrows is looking at Knuckles. 'He doesn't need you, Percy. You can leave.'

Arthur twists and sees Knuckles give a scowl. The guard starts to say something, then clamps his jaw.

Burrows looks at Arthur and tips his head. 'Go ahead.'

It is not what he expected. The room itself is grand – outsized windows and double-height ceilings, as well as coving and walnut panelling – but Graves has set himself in a corner, as though shying, wincing, at the splendour. His desk is a table really, inexpensive and not particularly large. The computer atop it looks older than the PC Arthur and Julia set aside years ago to give to Casper. The rest of the table is clear but for a stack of plastic trays and a telephone and two mugs: one holding pens that have been chewed to varying heights, the other stained down the side with tear tracks of coffee. Behind the desk there is a black-fabric office chair, which appears to be missing an arm, and on Arthur's side of the table a large leather armchair. The armchair is ragged but imposing and gives the impression of having come with the room.

Graves is standing by the window. 'Mr Priestley. I'm sorry to have kept you. There was a crisis in the kitchens that required several phone calls. Not so much a crisis as a drama really but I—' Graves interrupts himself. 'Never mind. Come in. Sit.'

It is the sit that does it. As Graves speaks, he turns and takes his own chair, evidently in no doubt that Arthur will obey his command. Arthur remains standing.

'Can I get you anything?' says Graves. 'Some water? Coffee perhaps?'

Arthur has not had coffee since . . . No. It is not quite as long ago as he thought. He recalls the taste of the last cup his captors offered him and shakes his head.

'No,' says Graves. 'Very wise. I'm trying to cut down myself. Something to eat, then. We have some fruit, I believe. Would you like some fruit?'

'I don't want anything from you.'

Graves falls silent. He watches Arthur and seems to consider. He links his hands and rests his forearms on the edge of his desk and pulls himself upright in his chair. 'I heard about your friend. I understand the two of you had become close. I am sorry.'

Arthur intended to keep his expression impassive. Already, though, he finds himself sneering. 'You're sorry?'

'Yes, Mr Priestley, I am. I'm sorry, for one thing, that we could not help alleviate his suffering. I'm sorry we could not have done more.'

'You've done plenty,' says Arthur. 'Believe me. You've done more than I thought a human being capable of.'

Graves, this time, does not hold Arthur's eye. He seems to

notice the empty chair opposite. 'Are you certain you will not sit down? You would be more comfortable, I'm sure.'

'What do you want? Why am I here?'

'I . . . You wanted to see me. Didn't you? My assistant told me you had asked to see me.'

'I asked weeks ago. I asked every day and every day I got the same answer. Different answers actually, some more abrupt than others, but they all amounted to the same thing.'

'Yes,' says Graves. 'Well. I am here now. You are here now. I am listening if there is something you would like to say.'

Arthur feels his lip curl again and he cannot stop it. 'Are you bored? Is that what this is about? You're bored so you thought you'd have your guards rustle up some in-house entertainment?'

'Mr Priestley—'

'I'm not much of a dancer, I'm afraid. And I'm no Andrea Bocelli. Or perhaps it's a story you're after? Perhaps you just want to hear how fucked up my life is now so that you can feel a little better about yours?'

'Please, Mr Priestley, I—'

'I wanted to see you but don't pretend you don't know what I was going to say. Don't pretend there is anything I could tell you that is not right there on your computer.' Arthur lifts a finger and follows as it advances on Graves's desk. 'Because you know I don't belong here. I know you know. You know I don't have this thing, whatever this thing is, and you know there are others imprisoned here who don't have it either.'

'Mr Priestley. Please. There is no point—'

'And the sick. The people like my friend. You talk about

helping them but all you're really doing is hiding them. From what, I don't know. Why, I don't know. You do, though. You know what you're doing and why you're doing it and still you manage to sleep at night.'

Graves says nothing. He seems to be waiting for Arthur to finish.

'Do you know what you are?' Arthur has his legs pressed against the desk. He is pointing and he is leaning. 'Do you want me to tell you what you are?'

'If it would make you feel better, Mr Priestley. Please do.'

Arthur is shaking. He smiles and it is a wicked smile. 'You're a—'

'Henry? Is everything okay? Do you need some help?'

Arthur turns. Burrows is already halfway across the office. In his grip is a small metal tray, half raised at his side as though in preparation for a forehand. Arthur's anger threatens to vent into laughter.

'Shall I call Percy back, Henry? He'll be just outside the main door. I think I can hear him, in fact.'

Burrows says this so obviously for Arthur's benefit that this time Arthur cannot help but give a snort.

'Thank you, John. I appreciate your concern but we're fine. Aren't we, Mr Priestley?'

'Oh, absolutely. We're just fine, thank you, John.'

'But you might bring us some coffee,' says Graves. 'Two cups, if you would. One for me and . . . a spare.'

Burrows hesitates. He takes another step and collects Graves's mug. Then he backs from the room, the tray in one hand and the cup in the other. As he pulls the door closed, he watches Arthur through the narrowing gap.

The room falls silent. Arthur breathes and Graves waits. Neither man looks at the other.

'You were saying,' says Graves. 'You were about to tell me what you think of me.'

Arthur raises his head. The movement is suddenly an effort. 'I was about to. But I imagine you already know.'

Graves nods. 'I imagine I probably do. Indeed, I imagine it is not entirely dissimilar to what I have come to think of myself.'

Arthur feels his forehead crease. He looks at Graves, not quite believing that the man has said what Arthur heard him say. Graves is adjusting some papers in his in tray, just as though he did not speak at all.

There is a knock and Burrows enters once again. He is carrying the tray still, though this time it bears two mugs. He sets down the mugs and nods in acknowledgement of Graves's thanks. Then he retreats, scowling in Arthur's direction as he passes.

'You are right,' says Graves once Burrows has gone. 'I asked you here for a reason.' He pauses. He clears his throat. 'I have a dilemma, Mr Priestley. More than one, as it happens, but one in particular that should immediately concern us both.' Graves reaches for his coffee and slides the second cup to Arthur's side of the table. 'Drink it if you wish. I dare say I will if you do not.'

Arthur ignores the second cup of coffee. He keeps his eyes fixed on Graves.

'I don't know you,' Graves says. 'I have your file and I have

SIMON LELIC

been trying to get to know you but really – how could I possibly? So there is no way for me to gauge how you will react to what I am about to tell you. Or, in fact, whether you would want me to tell you in the first place. Given, that is, your . . . situation.'

Arthur takes a step. 'Tell me what? What are you talking about?'

'Sit down, Mr Priestley, I implore you. It is not a sign of weakness to accept a thing when it is offered. Some might even argue it is the opposite.'

Arthur ignores Graves's appeal. 'Tell me what?'

Graves links his hands and slides them into his lap beneath the desk. 'Your wife,' he says. 'Your son. There was an accident. A road-traffic accident.'

Arthur feels his head begin to shake. His lips, likewise, part of their own accord but the gap is too narrow to admit the dozens of questions that rush to be asked.

'Your son is unharmed. He suffered a concussion, I believe, but it was minor. Truly, he is fine.'

'And Julia? What about Julia? Is she . . .'

'She is alive. She is . . . hurt.'

'Badly? How badly?'

Graves rolls his lips. 'Quite badly, I am afraid. From what I understand she was driving and the car . . . it was an old car. A BMW?'

Arthur nods. 'It's a classic. She calls it a classic.'

'I think,' says Graves. 'I think that, because there was no air bag . . . That is, the steering wheel . . .'

Arthur closes his eyes. He curses: the car, Julia, himself, the car once again.

'She's unconscious,' Graves says.

'She's in a coma?'

'They didn't say that but . . . Maybe. I'm afraid I don't know. They said she was unconscious and that they were transferring her to a hospital in Hammersmith. They didn't say why. Something about a specialist unit but they didn't go into specifics.'

'They? Who's they?'

'The newspapers. The BBC.'

'What about the hospital? Did you speak to the hospital?'

Graves shifts. 'I . . . No, I . . .'

'Call them. Can't you? I'm her husband. I'll call them, for Christ's sake.' Arthur has started pacing and he stops. He looks at Graves. Graves lowers his eyes and Arthur gives a sniff. 'Or perhaps I won't.' He is beside the leather armchair and he reaches for the arm. He slides into the seat.

'I'm sorry, Mr Priestley. You can see my predicament, I hope. You can see why I was so unsure whether to tell you.'

'I feel for you,' Arthur says. 'It must have been tearing you up inside.' He slumps forwards, so that his elbows are on his knees and his eyes on the battered oak floorboards at his feet. After a moment he lifts his head. 'Why did you?'

'I'm sorry?'

'Why did you tell me?'

Graves swallows. 'I just thought . . . I don't know. I thought, if it were me, I would want to know.'

Arthur watches Graves and the governor does not squirm

as such but it is clear he is becoming uncomfortable. He reaches again for some papers and straightens the edges of the pile. Arthur feels his eyes narrow. Slowly, he sits upright. 'Why should I believe you? How do I know this isn't a trick?'

Graves looks up. His surprise seems genuine but the whole conversation, until now, has seemed genuine.

'What do you want from me? You're telling me this because you want something from me. You want me to spy for you, is that it?'

'Spy on whom, Mr Priestley? For what purpose?'

Arthur taps a foot, furiously. 'You're making it up. You're trying to provoke some reaction. What though? You want me to shout and scream, is that it? You want me to attack you? Is that why you sent Percy for a walk? You want an excuse to keep me locked up after all the other men are lying four to a grave.'

'Mr Priestley. Really. I do not want to sound callous but, given everything you have already witnessed, do you really think we would need a pretext to keep you here?'

'It's clever,' says Arthur, smiling. He is thinking suddenly about the thing he has begun to plan: that Graves, somehow, has foreseen what in effect is Arthur's escape and has devised some scheme to stop him, to keep him here, to prevent his fate falling into anyone's hands but Graves's own. 'It's clever because the obvious thing would have been to say Casper was hurt. Which perhaps I would have expected, so instead you say—'

'Mr Priestley.'

'—you say, Julia was hurt. When, really, you don't even know if Julia and I—'

'Arthur.'

Arthur stops talking. He stops tapping.

'Arthur, please. It is not a trick. It is not a trap. Much as I wish I were making it up, your wife has been gravely hurt. I wanted you to know because I would want to know. That is all. I swear to you.'

Arthur stares. He wills Graves to look away because then Arthur would know what he wishes he could believe. But Graves does not look away. He holds Arthur's eye and his expression is open, earnest. It is honest.

Arthur drops his head again. He speaks to the floor. 'Will she live?'

Graves sighs. 'They . . . they do not expect her to. But Mr Priestley. Arthur. You must not give up hope. You know how these things get distorted by the press. And doctors. Doctors, in my experience . . . Well. Doctors are not always to be trusted.'

Arthur does not answer. He continues to stare at the floor-boards. After a minute, he slides his palms to his knees and pushes until he is standing. 'I'm not grateful to you, Mr Graves. Do not expect me to thank you. You told me only what I had a right to know.'

Graves stands too, so that the two men face each other across the table. 'I quite agree.'

Arthur's eyes drift towards the office window: to the court-yard and the outer wall and the hills and the skyline beyond. They must have been digging for the entire afternoon because the world, as Arthur watches, is dimming.

Graves looks where Arthur is looking. His gaze lingers before he turns back. 'I am planning a short trip,' he says. 'I will ask John to keep you informed should anything change with your wife while I am away. He will be discreet, naturally. As, I am sure, will you.'

'Burrows?' says Arthur. 'The same man who, ten minutes ago, was ready to brain me with a tea tray?'

Graves lifts a shoulder a fraction of an inch; a corner of his mouth the same distance. 'He is a better man than his behaviour might sometimes suggest.'

Arthur looks again to the window. He breathes, as though the horizon were air. Then he turns and moves past the chair and across the oak floor and he almost reaches the door.

'Mr Priestley.'

Arthur stops.

Graves starts to speak but his voice lags. He tries again. 'I meant what I said before. There is always hope. For your wife . . .' Graves hesitates. 'For your wife but for you too.'

He walks in a non-denominational glow. The lights strung across the high street could be a tribute to stars generally, to candles and winter snow. Given that it is not yet December, let alone Christmas, they might as well be. And yet the shops Graves passes on Balham High Road are less shy in proclaiming the coming Advent than Wandsworth council. There are climbing Santas and wilting reindeer; webs of bulbs cast like fishing nets and bannered exhortations of festive cheer. One store seems to have forgone its regular fare entirely and dedicated itself instead to the tinsel and tat of the season. Another goes further: not content with pre-empting Christmas, it proclaims the opening day of its January sale. In November. Graves has to remind himself: it is still November.

He does not know this pocket of London. It is no distance, really, from Wandsworth Prison but it is removed enough that he never had cause to venture down here. Their home, when Graves was posted to Wandsworth, was in Battersea and even Battersea was to him simply a route – a roundabout here, a left turn there, a never-ending procession of speed humps –

that linked his private life to his real world. He might have eaten in the mess and slept in one of the cells for all the attention Graves paid to the places he otherwise inhabited. Indeed, it was in Wandsworth, if his ex-wife is to be believed, that what she called his Insularity – and somehow she always seemed able to pronounce the capital letter – reached its zenith. His career too but that was the point: the pinnacle for him was the nadir of their relationship. Wandsworth, ultimately, broke them.

Which is why he is surprised his daughter moved back to the area. At the time, she seemed just as eager to flee as he and Carol were. More so, actually, and certainly her determination carried her further. Carol did not leave zone two; a journey north of the Thames was enough of a break with the past for her. Graves ended up in Liverpool but only because that is where Her Majesty required him to be. Rachel, by contrast, escaped across borders. She chose Edinburgh, even though she had previously considered the university there a fanciful addition to her shortlist. Then, from Edinburgh, and like a spy who has been trained in the art of throwing off her pursuers, she seconded herself to Italy, and then France, and then, after her studies were finished, to New York. But now she is back beneath the capital's beltline. Almost, Graves thinks, as though she considers the place from which she escaped the last place anyone looking would think to find her.

Although that is hardly fair. It is tempting to believe that Rachel absconded from his life but the truth, at best, is that they absconded from each other's. More realistically, Rachel simply followed her father's lead. Even after Graves himself moved back to London, they tended to meet as frequently as they did when he was posted in Liverpool. Which, last year, was . . . what? Three times? Four? And, now, not since . . . not since . . . He cannot remember. Genuinely, he cannot remember the last time he saw his daughter. He recalls apple blossom. He remembers sitting in a pub garden, with a half of bitter and a view of apple blossom, but apple blossom would suggest April, May at the latest. And it is November. He reminds himself again: it is November.

In the haze of a streetlamp, Graves checks the printout he has taken of Rachel's most recent email – her response to his own telling her he was coming to London. He squints and moves to the opposite side of the pavement, where a chain of fairy lights in the window of a nail salon serves to spotlight Rachel's directions more clearly. He looks up, at the sign on the corner of the side road, and checks the email again. Then he folds the piece of paper and tucks it into the pocket of his overcoat. He takes the turning.

She did not say in her message whether Nick would be there. Is it wrong that he hopes he is not? Not because he dislikes Nick, more because . . . No. He does. He dislikes Nick. He acts his age, which technically is not a crime, but twenty-something seems younger to Graves these days than it used to. It is as though, as life expectations have increased, the phases associated with the path to maturity have stretched too. When Graves was twenty-four or twenty-three or however old Nick is – and he remembers he is younger than Rachel, which in Graves's mind is another mark against him, though he could not elucidate why; if Nick happened to be older, that would be a mark against him too – but when Graves was twenty-four he had been working for eight years. Nick went to school and then to college and then he had a year out, in the jargon, which from what Graves understands amounts to taking a break from taking a break, and after the year out, which in fact stretched into two, he started studying again – as though just the two decades being spoon-fed qualifications could not possibly be considered adequate time in which to settle on a career. Pick a job, work hard at it. Where is the angst in that? You would think, apart from anything else, that Nick might be embarrassed. Graves would be: if his girlfriend were paying for his flat, his food, his 'further education', Graves would struggle to look her in the eye. Certainly he would struggle to look his girlfriend's father in the eye. Not so Nick. On the few occasions he and Graves have met, Nick has been brazen in his familiarity. He called Graves – to his face, more than once – Mr G. Even Rachel was mortified by that, Graves could tell. Mr G. As though Graves were a rap singer or a cartoon character or a children's entertainer.

No, he does not like Nick. He would not say so to Rachel – he has not the right to say so – but he can certainly admit it to himself. And, apart from anything else, it would complicate matters if Nick were home. Graves would have to ask for some time alone with his daughter and he is not sure how his daughter, never mind his prospective son-in-law, would react to that.

Forty-six. Forty-four. He is on the wrong side of the street. Graves waits for a scooter to shriek past, then crosses to the opposite pavement. Thirty-nine. Which means thirty-one will be just a few paces further along. Graves checks his watch. He is five minutes later than he planned to be but still ten minutes early. He would wander for a while, yet he is loath to give himself any more time to think. Rachel will anyway be expecting him to be early. She knows him that well at least.

'I bought whisky. Would you like a glass?'

'Coffee would be fine, thank you. Just instant, just black. Don't go to any trouble.'

Rachel has the bottle of whisky in her hands. She directs the label towards the light and draws a strand of hair from in front of her eyes. Her hair was black the last time Graves saw her; today it is its natural rosewood. 'Are you sure? It's supposed to be good. Nick told me which one to get.'

'I'm sure it is but . . . You didn't buy it just for me?'

'You like whisky, don't you? I thought that's what you drank.'

'I do. I mean, once in a while. But it's early and I . . . Are you having any?' He says this breezily though inwardly he is horrified at the thought of Rachel drinking anything stronger than a white-wine spritzer.

Rachel, though, makes a face. 'God, no,' she says and Graves is relieved until she adds, 'I threw up on whisky when I was seventeen. Just the smell of it . . .' She shudders and turns the bottle over, as though it might look less foul from a different angle.

'You didn't buy it just for me, though? Whisky's expensive, Rachel.'

'I thought whisky's what you drank.'

'I do but . . . Can you take it back? Have you got the receipt?'

'Dad,' says Rachel and she makes another face. 'It's fine. Nick will drink it.'

'Nick?' says Graves. 'Nick drinks?'

This time Rachel does not reply. She rolls her eyes towards the kitchen and follows her gaze through the archway.

Graves sits and listens as the coffee-making ritual unfolds. As he waits, he surveys his daughter's flat. It is not his business how she spends her money but if she had asked – and he would never have expected her to ask – he would have advised against buying a conversion. It is one of six in the building, for a start, and she is on the middle floor – which means there will be noise above and noise below and noise either side as well probably because the walls in these places are invariably made of paper. Even more of a problem is the flat's size. The only part Graves cannot see from where he is sitting is the kitchen behind him and the bathroom – the shower room – which is only accessible through the bedroom. He tries not to think about how much it will have cost Rachel. He knows, were he to try and guess, that his daughter would tell him to double, triple whatever sum he arrived at. And she is so proud of it – he could tell she was the moment she showed him through the door. It is smart, he will grant her that. It is a young professional's flat, not the student digs he imagined. But there is no escaping Graves's central observation, which is that the flat, however well decorated and however well tended, is, fundamentally—

'You think it's too small.'

Rachel is at his shoulder. She sets a cup for him on the corner table at his elbow. 'What?' Graves says. 'No, I . . .'

'You do.' Rachel is smiling. She sits. 'It's fine. It is small. It's ridiculously small. Two hundred and fifty grand doesn't go very far, does it?'

Rachel springs to her feet and dashes back into the kitchen. She emerges with a tea towel. 'Here,' she says. 'Don't worry about the table. It's all over your suit. It's my fault, I filled the cups too high. Oh, look at your suit!'

Graves lifts the tea towel from his lapel and tugs it from Rachel's grip towards the table. 'I'm sorry,' he says. 'Don't worry about my suit. Your table . . .' But in truth he is not thinking about the table. Although he is, now. He is thinking, how many tables – how many suits – could you buy with two hundred and fifty thousand pounds? Two *hundred* and fifty thousand pounds. Two hundred and *fifty* thousand pounds.

He had no idea he was quite so out of touch. So out of touch, and so old. It is like every year beyond his fortieth has counted double.

They clear up the mess and they sit. They sip. Graves places his cup back on the coaster with surgical care.

'How long are you in town?' his daughter asks.

'Just a night. I'll be heading back some time tomorrow.'

Rachel nods. If she is considering whether to ask where he has travelled from, she resists. 'Where are you staying? You could sleep here, if you like. It wouldn't be any trouble.'

Graves's eyes sweep the flat. Where? he does not ask. 'It's kind of you,' he says instead, 'but I have a hotel room. Just around from the station. I left my things,' he adds, even though the briefcase at his feet is the entirety of his luggage and he has not yet settled on where he is staying.

It seems to satisfy Rachel, however. She drinks into the silence.

'Where's Nick?' says Graves. 'I was hoping . . . I was hoping to see him.'

Again the face, slightly tempered this time. 'He's working. He'll be home soon.'

'He's working? I thought he was – ' Graves endeavours to keep his tone even ' – studying.'

'He works for BAE,' says Rachel. 'He's a research consultant. He has been for the past six months.'

A research consultant. It sounds to Graves like just another euphemism for student. BAE, though. He cannot find fault with BAE. 'Good on him,' he says. 'Tell him from me: good on him.'

Rachel smiles. 'I will,' she says. Then, 'Thanks, Dad.'

Graves nods. There is a silence and it seems an opportunity. He clears his throat. He opens his mouth, then closes it again. He scratches at an unseen mark on his trouser leg. He attempts again to say what he came to say but diverts his words at the last. 'How's your mother?'

'Fine,' says Rachel, 'I think. I haven't actually spoken to her for a while.'

'You should call her. She worries when she doesn't hear.'

'Sounds like you know how she is better than I do.'

'Rachel,' Graves says, in a tone he has forgotten he possessed.

Rachel lifts the tips of her fingers from her knee. 'I know, I know. I should call her more. I should call you both more.' She slides forwards on her chair. 'Listen, Dad. I'm sorry I've been so slack. It's no excuse but . . . I don't know. It's been busy. With work and the flat and with Nick's new job. Time just seems to . . .' She opens a hand, gives a grimace.

It takes a moment for Graves to process what Rachel is saying. She is apologising, he realises. He did not expect her to apologise; he did not expect her to feel any need to. 'It would have helped, I'm sure, if I had given you a number on which to reach me. If I had told you I was leaving in the first place.'

Rachel gives a wry smile. 'It might have.' She glances at her father and then at her lap. This is it then: Rachel has got there before he could. Graves is shaking his head already as Rachel starts to speak. 'Listen, Dad. Can't you tell me at least—'

'I can't. Don't ask, Rachel, please.'

Rachel smiles again but this time when she smiles she looks all of a sudden like a girl again – like someone young and innocent and not a little frightened. 'Okay. It's fine. If you can't tell me, don't feel you have to.' Again she lowers her gaze to her lap. 'But I watch the news, you know. I've heard about this fac—'

'Rachel! Don't say it! Don't even think it!' Graves snaps before he can stop himself. Rachel stares as though he has slapped her. 'You don't know, Rachel. I mean it. You couldn't even guess if someone asked you to. If someone . . . If someone forced you to.'

'Dad, I—'

'I'm not kidding, Rachel. I'm not messing about.'

'Jesus, Dad. No shit.'

'And don't talk like that. We brought you up better than that.' Graves regrets saying it even as the words pass his lips. He tightens his jaw and stares at his hands and waits for Rachel's rebuke.

It does not come. When Graves looks up, the little girl he saw before has been replaced by the forbearing adult: the one who has learnt over her short years to endure the tantrums of her juvenile parents.

Graves shuts his eyes, opens them again. He should have stayed away. Coming here was a risk anyway, given what else he still has to do. It was selfish and short-sighted and most of all it was unfair.

He stands. 'I'm sorry, Rachel. I have no right to . . . It's not my place to . . .' He struggles to finish his sentence. Rachel speaks before he has to.

'Sit down, Dad. Please. Don't go.'

'I think perhaps I should. I have to get on and—'

'Stay for dinner. Have dinner with us.'

'Dinner? No, I . . . I really can't.'

'At least finish your coffee. Please, Dad. Sit down.'

Graves hesitates. He lowers himself to the edge of the seat. Rachel is silent again. She tries to say something but Graves forces himself to speak in order that his daughter does not have to.

'Rachel. Listen. I wanted to see you. That's why I came. But . . . But I wanted to warn you as well. To prepare you. It strikes me that you are perfectly prepared to deal with just about anything but I didn't want you to think . . . That is, I didn't want you thinking . . .' Rachel is the little girl again. It is her expression, Graves realises, one facet of her expression: the furrow that appears between her eyebrows whenever she is on edge. 'You're going to hear some things about me,' Graves says. 'On the news, in the papers. I can't tell you what exactly but it's to do with where I've been.'

'What things? What do you mean?'

'Just . . . stories. They will not be pleasant.'

'Made-up stories? Lies, you mean?'

'No,' Graves says. 'Not lies. And that's the point, Rachel. I can't explain. It really is vitally important that I don't. I wanted to see you, though. It was selfish, I suppose, but I wanted you to see me. I wanted you to hear from me that . . . That I was wrong. That I was wrong and that I know I was wrong. And that . . . Well. That I'm sorry.'

Graves tries to hold his daughter's eye. He cannot. He hears her instead: not speaking, not moving, barely breathing. He said he cannot explain but an explanation, in all likelihood, is hardly necessary. If she was unsure before it will be plain to her now. She will understand all she needs to.

She stands and Graves glances. She is not the little girl any more. She wears an expression that might be resolve; that might just as well be revulsion. She crosses the room and Graves assumes she is walking into the kitchen: a signal that, just as Graves suspected, she knows exactly what the stories will be about and that perhaps it is time for her father to leave after all. But she stops at his chair. She settles on the arm. She reaches a slender hand around his shoulders and she bends and she kisses him on the cheek. 'Okay,' she says.

Nick's keys are in the lock and his hand is outstretched and it seems they have plucked the keys from his grip. He beams through the open door. 'Mr G!' He is suited and – aside from the unfastened collar, the tie knot so constricted it must surely never have been unravelled – he looks almost like a man who works for a living.

'Nick,' says Graves, nodding.

'Hey, honey.' Nick leans to plant his lips on Rachel's. Rachel turns her cheek at the last moment, so that Nick meets the corner of her mouth. She glances at her father and she blushes. Graves looks to his feet.

'You're not going?' says Nick to Graves. 'We bought some whisky. Did you have a glass? It's a single malt, twelve years old. Recommended by a colleague of mine.'

Graves wishes now he had accepted some. It is clear that between them they have gone to some trouble to select a reasonable bottle. And, given his next stop, a nip of whisky might have done him some good. 'Rachel offered,' he says. 'Thank you, Nick. Perhaps next time. We'll have one together, shall we?'

'Absolutely,' says Nick, as though a drink together were the highest honour his girlfriend's father could bestow.

'Congratulations on your job, by the way. It sounds . . .' Graves finishes the sentence with an enthusiastic nod.

'Yeah, thanks. It's good. It's going well. It's just like uni, if I'm honest. Lots of, you know—'

Drinking? Sleeping? Partying? Don't ruin it, man.

'—reading.'

Again Graves nods. 'Good. Well. Stick with it.' He lifts a hand and, to his surprise and Nick's, it would seem, it settles on the boy's shoulder.

'Er . . . Thanks. I will. Good seeing you, Mr G.'

Rachel walks her father to the pavement. She has not brought a coat and she wraps her arms around her middle and hunches her shoulders against the cold.

'Get inside, Rachel. You'll catch pneumonia.'

'Are you sure you won't stay, Dad? Nick was going to make a curry.'

'Nick cooks?'

Rachel nods through a shiver. 'Most nights.'

Graves hesitates. He studies his daughter's smile. 'He . . . You seem happy. The two of you, I mean.'

'We are, Dad. You should get to know him. You'd like him, I know you would. Why don't you stay and eat with us?'

Graves reaches to button his coat. 'I can't. I would but . . . I have an appointment.'

'Next time then. Any time, in fact. I mean that, Dad. Let's not leave it so long.'

Graves takes hold of Rachel's shoulders and kisses her on the cheek. 'Get inside. Go and eat curry.'

Rachel nods and shivers again but she lingers. Graves can sense her watching as he begins his walk towards the high street. She calls after him.

'Dad,' she says. 'Take care, won't you?'

Graves raises a hand. He walks on.

'Graves. Henry Graves.'

Katherine shakes her head. 'Never heard of him.'

'There's no reason why you should have. Not unless there's something in your past you're keeping secret from the rest of us.'

'Excuse me?'

'Never mind,' says Tom. He is babbling. He knows he is. He pulls out the chair from behind Katherine's desk and thinks about sitting down. Instead he grips the back, taps the fingers of his good hand against the upholstery. He beams; he cannot help it.

'Tom? Are you sure you're okay? I said to Amy, tell Tom to take all the time he needs.'

'I'm fine. A bit tired. A bit wired. This bloke: he drinks a lot of coffee. I was matching him cup for cup and I didn't exactly get much sleep.'

'You met him? Face to face?'

'Uh huh.'

'And? What did he tell you?'

Tom leans closer. 'Everything,' he says. 'He told me everything. This is it, Katherine. You said I needed more and I got more.'

Katherine reclines in her seat. She regards Tom for a moment, then tips her chin towards the empty chair across from her. 'Sit down. Wait. Shut the door first.'

Tom crosses the room to close the door, then returns and slides into the seat. He is still smiling, he realises. He attempts a more sober expression but his features, the moment he stops concentrating, rebound.

'I don't need to ask you what you were doing on Dartmoor, do I?'

Tom shakes his head. He feels, and imagines he looks, like a schoolchild who has been caught doing something foolish but who has escaped the lesson he might have learnt.

'Is that where you made contact with Graves? Did you . . . did you find the facility?'

'Not exactly. We came close.'

'Hell, Tom. What were you planning to do? Walk up to the gates and lift the knocker? You realise what might have happened to you had you found it?'

He does. Although not to him so much as Julia, Casper. His smile falters.

'So you didn't find the facility but you found Graves? Is that it?'

'No. Graves found me, really. I only met him last night. I only spoke to him for the first time a few days ago.'

A light on Katherine's phone begins to flash. She ignores it. 'Okay,' she says. 'Who is he exactly? What did he give you?'

Tom shuffles as close to the desk as his knees will allow. 'He's in charge, Katherine. Not of the policy but of the place. The facility. He runs it. He practically built it. And the things he told me . . . I don't know where to start.'

'Pick somewhere. Pick a headline.'

'All right,' says Tom. 'How about this: government interns uninfected.'

Katherine raises an eyebrow.

'Okay,' Tom says. 'Maybe the headline needs work. My point is, there are at least eighteen people being held who have been tested for the disease and have come back clear. Including Arthur. You remember Arthur Priestley? The government knows, Katherine, but it won't let these people go. And Graves can prove it.'

'How? I mean, it's new, right? So how do they know their tests are accurate? And there's a thing. Isn't there? A window period. Isn't that what they called it?'

'It's a smokescreen. It can't hide the fact that there are people locked away who are no more infected than you or I.'

Katherine exhales through her nose. 'I don't know, Tom. The authorities could say they were just being cautious. Which, given the risk to public health, is entirely justifiable.'

Tom's expression curdles. 'Justifiable? You think it's justifiable that eighteen perfectly healthy citizens have been snatched from their families and thrown into a dungeon in the middle of Dartmoor? I mean, ignoring the fact that none of the others should be there either – that everything about the government's policy belongs to the dark ages.'

'A dungeon? Is that how Graves described it?'

Tom shifts. 'Not exactly. But it's a prison, Katherine. It's not a hospital. Just because these people aren't chained to a wall doesn't make it right.'

'I'm not disputing that, Tom. But it's my job to pick holes. If we're going to run it, it has to be watertight. This, what you're telling me: it's a bucket made of paper. It won't hold.'

'But with Julia's side of the story . . . With the background she's given us on Arthur . . .' Tom sees Katherine about to inter-ject and he raises a hand. 'Never mind. That's just for starters anyway. Wait till you hear about the testing.'

Tom outlines what Graves has told him, about Dr Silk's arrival and the trials that followed. He explains about the death of the first eight inmates the doctor selected and Silk's deter-mination to keep their fate hidden from the other prisoners. 'And he's operating with a direct government mandate,' Tom says. 'Just think about that. This programme: it's sacrificing lives on the say-so of some self-aggrandising charlatan.'

Katherine, for a moment, does not react. She taps a finger-tip noiselessly against the surface of her desk. 'Tom,' she says and immediately Tom is wary of her tone. 'Don't think, even for a moment, that I am condoning what you have just told me. But—'

'Jesus Christ, Katherine! You've got to be kidding me!'

'But,' Katherine continues, 'you told me yourself: they signed their consent. Probably I would have too. Probably, if I knew I was going to die anyway, I would give my consent regardless of what happened to the people before me.'

'You wouldn't know! If you were there, you wouldn't know

what happened to the people before you! You would be tricked, manipulated, lied to. Jesus, Katherine . . .'

'It's unethical. I don't dispute that. But, Tom: remember what I said. If we're going to run this, we need to be one-hundred-per-cent right. We need a story they can't counter, can't spin, can't comment on without digging themselves deeper into a hole.'

Tom sits back. He leans forwards again. He looks at Katherine and he stands. 'Okay,' he says. 'Fine.' He paces. He tells himself Katherine is only doing what she is supposed to be doing. She is the editor, after all; probably she is right.

She is not right. She is wrong. But in fact it does not matter. 'Forget the testing for the moment,' Tom says. 'Forget about the people there who don't have the disease. You want a headline.' He stops pacing. 'Right? You want a story they can't spin. How about this,' he says. 'How about the home secretary standing up in front of the British public and lying to save her career? How about senior government ministers colluding to conceal their negligence? How about,' Tom says, only vaguely conscious that he is talking too loudly, 'scores of British citizens dying of a disease they only contracted because the government let them?'

Katherine says nothing. The light on her phone is flashing once again and she watches it until it dims. She looks up and Tom thinks for a moment she is trying to gauge just how big a knock he took to his skull. But then she shakes her head, a fraction of a movement that is almost no movement at all. 'Talk me through it,' she says at last. 'But, Tom, keep your voice down.'

Tom glances behind him. The door is still shut but the walls of the office, Tom knows, are thinner even than those in his apartment. More than once, from his desk twenty paces away, he has heard Katherine tear apart a sub-editor, a sales executive, a politician who is refusing to co-operate with one of her reporters. It is not as though there is anyone in the newsroom that Tom does not trust but there is his arm, there is Julia: evidence enough of the price of being indiscreet.

Tom sits back down and shuffles the chair free of the grooves it has made in the carpet. He leans. 'You heard the home secretary's press conference, right? Of course you did.' He waves a hand to erase the question. 'Myers said the first man to die from the disease did so three months previously. There's no easy way of verifying that but it's unlikely that Myers was lying. The doctors involved: they would know. The other cases too: there would be a trail of reports from GPs' surgeries to the CMO. And that, for Myers, is where it gets tricky. Because she claimed they were monitoring things from the start. Right? From a month before the first victim died. She had to because she wouldn't want doctors coming forward and saying that they reported the disease but the government failed to react.' Tom smiles. 'You see?'

Katherine is looking at him like she is waiting for the punch line.

'The facility,' Tom continues. 'Myers claimed it had been standing ready long before the disease manifested itself. She said . . . what was it? That the facility was a core aspect of the government's strategy to prepare the country for . . .' Tom rolls a hand. 'Known unknowns. All that other crap.' He smiles again.

'I mean, you have to give her credit. She realised she was caught in a lie so she gambled and decided to push it just a little bit further. To lie in a way that would at least make her look good.'

'Tom,' says Katherine. 'I'm really not sure I—'

'It's bullshit, Katherine! All of it! The truth,' says Tom, a little more quietly, 'is that they came to Graves in a panic. A month after the first guy, patient zero or whatever Myers called him, died; two months after, according to Myers, the government actively started monitoring the course of the disease. The facility, until then, was a wreck. It was four walls and a leaking roof, which the government just happened to own. The only thing Myers and her cronies were monitoring until that point was the slump they had hit in the polls. Some doctors told them there was something new, that a handful of homosexuals, a prostitute here and there, were getting ill. That they were dying. But gay men, sex workers: these people are hardly this government's core constituents.' Tom leans forwards. 'They fucked up, Katherine: that's the bottom line. They ignored the disease because they didn't care about the people it was killing. Only when it became clear that their voters were dying too – that the disease worried less about political demographics than they did – did someone raise a hand and point out that maybe they ought to do something. So they did. They came to Graves. Because it was too late by then, they decided, to do anything else.'

Tom pauses, to give Katherine a chance to react. He is not sure what he is expecting because he finds his boss inscrutable at the best of times. So he is not sure what he is expecting, just that he is expecting something. She is looking at him now, however, as though she either does not understand what he is saying or simply does not care to.

Tom cannot help but fill the silence. 'It was clever,' he says. 'The way Myers managed the story, I mean; the way she moved it on. She gave us scapegoats, because everyone loves having someone to blame, right? She gave us a terrifying disease – which always makes for great copy – and she gave us new legislation. She gave us the civil-liberties angle too but she knew no one would be interested in that.'

Tom does not mean it as a rebuke but it is clear from Katherine's expression that she has taken it as such.

'My point,' Tom says, hurrying on, 'is the one angle she didn't concede. The one angle, in fact, that she did everything she could to conceal. Because the real story here, the one thing this entire policy is intended to camouflage, is that the British government is directly accountable for dozens – scores – of needless deaths. And they know they are. That's why they're going to the lengths they are now to get the disease under control.'

Katherine opens her mouth, then closes it again. 'They could argue,' she says finally, 'that they didn't know. They could say they had no idea it would be so serious. Someone would back them up, I'm sure. A doctor. An epidemiologist. They could argue that they can't fund everything. It's the standard political fallback.'

'Right,' says Tom. 'I'm sure you're right. It's what they did after Drax, after all. They blamed the previous administration, if you remember, because even though Drax happened on this government's watch, it was soon enough after they took power for them to shift the blame on to their predecessors. The previous government, they said, overspent: on social care, on education, on everything but protecting the country's infra-structure, on keeping Britain safe.' Tom scoffs. 'But they're reaching into their pockets now, right? Into ours, I mean. Into the taxpayers'. And they have to because the election's get-ting closer and they're teetering on thirty-six per cent. They managed to get away with it last time but no way they can sur-vive being accused of looking in the wrong direction twice.'

Katherine starts to answer but Tom cuts her off.

'However they try to explain it, Katherine, they can't get away from the single central fact: they lied. They lied and they're still lying. Here's another one, for instance,' he says and he lifts a finger. 'Myers said eighty-six people had been interned, right? Eighty-six and *no more*. Well, Graves can testify that another thirteen people arrived at the facility a week ago. It's still going on! They fucked up and they're lying to cover themselves and they can't stop. In the meantime, they're locking up innocent people using laws they said would protect us.'

There is a knock at Katherine's door and Tom turns to see Katherine's assistant poke her smile through the gap. 'I'm just running down to Starbucks, Katherine. Do you want—'

'Shut the damn door!' Katherine says and her assistant obeys so hastily – so decisively – that the partition walls quiver in her wake.

Katherine turns to Tom. 'What about Graves?'

'Graves can prove it. He has records, work orders: everything we would need to verify the timing of it all.'

'That's not what I mean. I mean, what does Graves get from this? Why is he talking to you in the first place?'

'What does he get? I . . . Nothing. He wanted a name or two kept out of it, a day at least to give him time to warn some of his staff. But other than that, I don't know. A clear conscience, I suppose. A decent night's sleep.'

'He knew though? He knew what the government was planning when he decided to take up the post?'

'He knew they were desperate. He knew they needed his help.'

'And he knew what he would be doing? He knew what the facility would be for?'

Tom nods. 'But he didn't know about the trials. And he didn't know that the people who tested negative would continue to be held.'

'But he's complicit. You realise that? *He* realises that?'

'He's not looking for a way out, Katherine. He knows he'll be blamed. He knows he is to blame. Probably he blames himself more than he actually deserves.'

Katherine makes a noise like she is not convinced.

'Katherine. Please. Just think about it for a minute. Think about why the government hasn't released the names of the people being held. Think about why they won't let the prisoners – the "patients", remember – see their families. Because this isn't swine flu. The risk of infection through anything but sexual contact or, let's say, a blood transfusion is virtually zero.' Tom has both elbows on Katherine's desk now. 'Remember Guantanamo,' he continues. 'Remember the orange jumpsuits. Do you think the outcry then would have reached anything like the pitch it did if the prisoners there had been kept from sight? That's one lesson this government has learnt. They've learnt that if they show it, they can't spin it. If they can't spin it, they can't control it. And if they can't control it, the truth will eventually come out: about what they're doing; about why they're doing it in the first place.' Tom leans back. 'The facility is a fuck-up, Katherine. It's the government cleaning up its mess and making a bloodier one in the process.'

Katherine sighs. She stands. She turns her back on Tom and faces the window. The sky beyond is a spectrum of grey. Precipitation spits itself against the glass: not quite rain, not quite snow – lazy, obese drops that seem barely able to decide whether to bother falling at all.

'We've got enough, Katherine. We've got more than enough. I hate to say this but, if you don't want to run it, then . . . I don't know. I guess I'll take it to a publication that—'

'Okay.' Katherine turns. 'There's no need for threats, Tom.'

'Okay?'

'Okay.'

'Okay as in you'll run it?'

'As in we'll run it. Tomorrow, if that's what you agreed with Graves.'

Tom grins. He gets to his feet. 'I'll get to work.'

'Not here. Go home and work on your laptop. I don't want anyone leaking this.' Katherine hooks her teeth across her lower lip. 'Who else have you told? Did you tell Amy?'

'No, I . . . No one,' Tom says. 'Just you. I saw Graves, I went home, I came to you.'

'Good. Keep it quiet, Tom. Get it done.'

Tom sets his jaw. 'I will. Thanks. Thank you.'

'And Tom,' says Katherine. She smiles. 'Good work.'

Tom stops at the hospital on his way to his flat. Pippa is waiting for him.

'You said you'd be here by ten, Tom. I told my friend I'd be back to collect Casper by ten.'

They are outside Julia's room. Tom leans past Julia's cousin to steal a glimpse through the glass panel on the door. He can make out just the end of Julia's bed, the outline of her upraised toes beneath the covers. 'How is she?' he says. 'What have I missed?'

Pippa makes a face, like she is annoyed at Tom for changing the subject. She cannot, though, repress a smile. 'She's . . . They say she's responding well. They say if there had been any complications from the surgery, they would have presented themselves by now.' Pippa folds her arms, as though annoyed at herself for allowing her irritation to dissipate. Her smile, at the same time, broadens. 'They say her chances are good.'

'Good?' Tom grips Pippa's shoulders. 'Good's good, right?'

Pippa laughs and it comes out as a sob. She reaches a finger to the underside of her eye and rolls her lips as though to stop herself beaming. 'It's still early, Tom. Don't get carried away.'

Tom reaches and wraps Pippa in a hug. 'Good's good, Pippa! Good is very, very good!'

Pippa tuts. The hug seems to have sobered her. 'You said you'd be here by ten, Tom. I need to collect Casper.'

Tom is leaning again to see through the glass. He tempers his grin and turns back. 'Listen, Pippa.' He guides Julia's cousin towards the wall. 'I need the day.' He sees Pippa's expression begin to harden and he rushes on. 'I wouldn't ask if it wasn't important. For Casper, for Julia. I just need the day and then . . . then they'll be safe.'

'You told me you'd help, Tom. You said one of us needed to stay with Julia and you wouldn't say why but I agreed. I'm doing what you asked but I can't do it on my own. There's Casper to take care of. There's my family to take care of. I have my own family, Tom!'

Tom nods. 'I know. You're right. But it's just this one day, Pippa. Please.'

Pippa exhales and her nostrils flare. She turns away from Tom and ends up facing the window into her cousin's room. She shakes her head. 'I need to call my friend. I need to call work. Do you think you can spare ten minutes?'

'Absolutely. Thank you, Pippa. Really.'

Pippa seems worried Tom is about to embrace her once more because she edges away. She scoops up her handbag from the chair outside Julia's door and marches towards the foyer.

'Pippa,' Tom says and she turns. 'Take twenty. I'd like to sit with her for a while.'

Pippa does not reply. She glares and then she is gone.

Inside the room, Tom drags a chair to Julia's bedside. He takes hold of Julia's hand. Very little about her appearance has changed. She is bandaged and motionless and she seems barely to be breathing. But, unless Tom imagines it, there is a colour below her cheekbone where before there was a pallor.

He runs the pad of his thumb across the contours of her knuckles. He leans close. 'This is it, Julia,' he says. He brings her hand to his lips and for a moment he holds it there. He smiles through a laugh and once again he kisses her fingers. 'We've done it.'

He was careful. His assistant knows he is away but only, as far as Burrows is concerned, to visit his daughter. It might seem odd perhaps that Graves, being Graves, has taken three days off now in the space of barely more than a week but that is what people do, is it not? They take a few days off. And it is not like the rest of the staff at the facility see him on a daily basis. His path and those of the majority of the guards barely cross. So it would take more than a twenty-four-hour absence to prompt questions, surely. And in London he has done exactly what he came to do: he spent an evening with his daughter. They talked and they drank coffee and at the end of her garden path he kissed her on the cheek and said goodbye. After that he made his way to his hotel, ready to catch the train back the following day. Maybe, on the walk from Paddington tube, he stopped for another cup of coffee but it was reasonably early still so there would have seemed nothing unusual about that. And no one was watching, he is certain. The journey he wove on the underground from Balham was so intricate that Graves himself almost got lost. Thereafter, above ground, he took enough detours and long cuts that anyone following might just as well have been wearing a high-visibility vest. No one, anyway, would have been waiting for him because no one knew he was staying in Paddington – Graves only knew for certain himself when he walked into a Best Western at twenty past midnight. So he was careful. Extraordinarily, paranoiacally careful.

Tom then. He does not know him. He has no reason to trust him. Except he does trust him, having met him. He was young, certainly – younger than the picture they used on the television suggested. But he seemed . . . he seemed . . . The word that occurs to Graves is wise, given his limited years. He seemed remarkably single-minded and remarkably resolute and Graves cannot help but respond positively to such char-acteristics, particularly when exhibited by someone who is still in their twenties. The humour was perhaps a touch facile but that, Graves assumed, was down to nerves. Because the boy was nervous, he could tell. To the extent that Graves had to point out that the surest way to attract attention is to act as though you have something to hide. At least Graves could be certain, though, that Tom would have taken the same pre-cautions before their meeting as Graves had. If anything, Tom would have gone to even greater lengths to ensure he was not being followed because he had already experienced the repercussions of being reckless – the cast on his arm attested to that. Besides all of which, Graves would not have agreed to the meeting at all if there had been any hint during their tele-phone conversation that Tom was not somebody he could trust. The boy had called him from a public phone and had spoken suitably guardedly, suitably obliquely. In the end, it was Graves who was pressing for the meeting and Tom who needed to be convinced.

They were each as careful as the other then: that is the upshot. Graves has done nothing that might be deemed suspicious and there is no reason for anyone to be watching him.

And yet they are.

They are seated at the table across from his and they are taking it in turns to glance across. It is a young couple and did not Tom mention a young couple, watching him in a cafe soon after he first started asking questions? And now here they are again, in a cafe, watching Graves this time as he waits for the departure of his train. It is too coincidental, surely, to be a coincidence.

Graves signals to a waiter for his bill and shuffles a finger through the change compartment in his wallet. The waiter slides a saucer on to Graves's table as he hurries past and even before it has ceased its clatter, Graves has loaded it with coins. He stands, knowing the couple at the table across from him will soon be standing. He picks up his briefcase – his one piece of luggage – and his copy of *The Times* and he slips through the crowd of tables and on to the station concourse. He checks his watch, not because he does not know the time already but to give him a moment to think. Also to send a message to his pursuers that he is not fleeing because fleeing, surely, would be the worst thing he could do. Better, in fact, to allow them to catch up because then he will not be left wondering, should it turn out that they do not follow him towards his train after all, whether they only failed to do so because he inadvertently gave them the slip.

He walks purposefully, with his chin high. He is hot suddenly but that is only because he is wearing his winter coat and there is less of a chill inside the station than in the breeze that sweeps the streets outside. It is all the people, probably. All the bodies, perspiring like his under their own multi-layers, rushing with suitcases or pushchairs or perilously stacked paper cups towards their trains. So it is not unusual that, when Graves pauses under the departures board, he dabs his forehead with his handkerchief. If he appears anxious, it might only be because he is worried he has mistimed his walk to the platform.

He has not, of course. He has twenty minutes until fourteen-o-six, which is when his train departs. It is listed on the board directly above him but Graves pretends he is still searching. Think, he tells himself. Think. But all he can do is read. Platform nine. Fourteen-o-six. Calling at Reading, Exeter St Davids, Newton Abbot, Plymouth, Liskeard, Bodmin Parkway, then on to Par, St Austell, Truro, Redruth, Camborne, Hayle, St Erth, Penzance. Four carriages. A trolley service on board. Platform nine. Fourteen-o-six.

He removes his coat. The reason he cannot think is that he cannot breathe. It is the thermal vest he wears that is the problem, he tells himself, but he can hardly remove that. It is fine, though: with his coat off he will quickly cool down and he will regain his reason and there will be no chance that the couple following will mistake his sweat for panic, his flush for fear. Although it occurs to him that a man in a hurry would not have paused to remove his coat so if he continues to act flustered, to dab his brow and tug at his collar, there would appear to those watching to be only one explanation for his behaviour. And then they will pounce.

Henry. For pity's sake, man. It was a couple drinking coffee. For all you know, that is all they were, all they are. You have not looked round since you left your table so you do not even know for certain that they are following.

He looks round, just as anyone might who was checking for the nearest conveniences, considering perhaps whether to make a final call before boarding. He sees the lavatories but not the couple. The lavatories are impossible to miss so now, as he continues scanning, it would be obvious to anyone watching that he is looking for something else. But he does not see the couple and it gives him heart. It emboldens him. He feels cooler suddenly and like a fool too but a gladdened fool. He folds his coat and picks up his briefcase and, with one final glance behind, takes a step towards platform nine.

He hits a pillar. That is what it feels like. But the pillar is a person and the person falls. Graves falls too but stops himself with his hands and for an instant the person with whom he has collided is pinned beneath him.

'Oh!' he says and his victim echoes his exclamation. Graves cannot see her face but he can tell from the pitch of her panic that she is a woman. He hears other cries too, from people standing close by. He realises he is gripping his briefcase still but lets it drop and struggles upright. A set of hands on each of his arms help him to his feet and immediately he bends to assist the woman sprawled on the concrete floor.

'I do apologise!' Graves says but the woman seems barely to hear him. She is a small woman, slight, of about Graves's age. She appears unhurt but dazed and it takes Graves and the outstretched hands of the person on either side of him to coax her to stand. There is a line of grime down the coat across her arm and Graves reaches a hand to brush it clean. 'I do apologise,' he says again, then realises he is brushing his own coat. Somehow it has ended up hooked around the woman's elbow. 'Um,' he says and he attempts to ease the coat free. The woman's instinct, though, is to cling tight. She is looking at Graves as though, as well as having assaulted her, he is trying to strip her of the clothes on her back. She says something, in Polish or Russian or something anyway that makes her words sound to Graves like a curse. 'Um,' he says again. 'I think that's my . . . Would it help if I took . . .' and still the woman does not let go. Graves smiles, apologises again and gives his coat another tug. This time the woman tugs back and turns to the faces surrounding them as though to plead for help. Graves turns too, meaning to explain, but it is not the faces nearest that catch his eye. He sees the couple, not ten yards away, making no pretence now that they are not looking right back at him.

Graves yanks and yanks hard. The woman stumbles and the coat comes free and Graves stoops to gather his briefcase. 'I do apologise,' he says once more and he casts a smile at the stunned expressions that surround him. 'I'm sorry,' he says to the woman, to the crowd. 'I really have to . . .' He raises his briefcase to point out a path. 'Sorry,' he says. 'Excuse me. Sorry. Excuse me,' and finally he has the space to expand his lungs. He glances behind and sees his victim, staring uncertainly now at her own coat, and several bystanders tracking his escape. And the couple. They are still there, still watching him – and they are moving in his direction.

Platform nine. Platform nine. Graves strides now with undisguised haste, his overcoat trailing on the ground and his tie, he can feel, wrenched towards his ear. He treads on his coat and almost trips and hoists his arm to lift the fabric from under his feet. Platform nine. Platform—

There. Just ahead. But there is a noise at his shoulder and Graves turns. There is a man in a dark suit and he is running – sprinting – towards Graves. Graves breaks into a trot. He would run but he cannot run because there are other travellers bunched tight in front of him as they slow for the barriers. Graves weaves. He hoists his coat. He glances behind and he sees the man and the man is almost upon him. Fool, Graves thinks. Idiot. Because why would the couple be alone? Why would they not have help? Why would there not be someone with them, someone like this man for instance, this man who is five steps behind now, four, three, who is panting and who is lunging and who—

Who runs right by. Past Graves and past the queue at the manned gate and on to platform seven, the expletives of his fellow travellers snapping at his heels.

Graves pauses. He watches the man in the suit fail to catch his train and hurl an expletive of his own towards the station roof. And as Graves watches, an idea finally occurs to him.

Turn round. Leave the station. Forget the train and forget Bodmin Parkway and forget the cursed facility. Forget Tom, too, as well as their plan – their agreement that Graves would go back, would carry on, would do nothing to engender suspicion until after the story breaks. Forget Priestley and Burrows and all the others he intended to protect. Think instead about Rachel. Think, for once, about himself. Because maybe the man in the suit was not following him. Maybe the couple – here now, beside him now, walking past him now – are doing just what they seem to be doing: drinking coffee, waiting for a train, watching Graves and glancing back at him only because he is behaving like an imbecile and everyone else is watching him too. So maybe Graves is free, right now, but in a day, two, what then? This is his chance. This is his one chance to escape the repercussions of his mistakes and his adolescent impulse to set them right.

Graves turns. He sees the coffee shop and, alongside it, he sees the doors by which he entered the station – the doors by which he might leave. He takes his handkerchief from his pocket and dabs his forehead and wipes the back of his neck. He folds the square of cotton and replaces it in his trouser pocket and then takes the time to brush the dust from his coat and fold it over his forearm. He straightens his tie. He lifts his briefcase. And then he follows his pursuers on to platform nine.

They share a carriage. There is plenty of space on the train but the couple are seated in the same compartment into which Graves steps and there is no reason, save his embarrassment, not to take a seat across from them. It will be his penance, Graves thinks. He will bear his smirk and her whispered, hair-shrouded giggling and he will remember, in future, the consequences of abandoning his head.

They alight at Reading. The first stop. Graves pretends not

to watch them go but he is more relieved than he would admit. With the couple gone and the compartment empty, he can forget his paranoiac display. He can dismiss it as an aberration, an inevitable and understandable outburst of anxiety that, in the end, caused no one any lasting harm. He can smile at it, even; shake his head at it. He can, in short, relax.

And he can: that is perhaps the strangest thing. Having allowed his fretfulness to erupt, he feels purged. He is not a big eater of fast food but it feels like that: like he has binged at a McDonald's for a day and discovered, afterwards, that his appetite for hamburgers has been extinguished. The train rolls and the buildings scatter and with the sunlight on his face, Graves feels at ease, almost tranquil. He has made his decision and it was the right one and the hardest part, actually, is behind him. Because the hardest part, for him, in any situation, has always been knowing that there is something still to do. It is planning for things, running through things, deciding how one thing will impact on another. But now it is done and everything that follows is beyond his control. Whatever happens now . . . Well, whatever happens now will just happen.

He laughs out loud. There is no one in the carriage to hear him but he would laugh out loud even if there was. This is it, he realises. This is what his wife has been begging of him. This, Graves tells himself, is letting go.

He wakes to a whistle. For an instant the panic returns because he does not know where he is, why he was asleep, who might be watching – but then a single answer announces itself and Graves is soothed: it does not matter.

Although it is possible he has missed his stop. They are pulling away from a station and Graves cannot see any signs. He shuffles upright in his seat and glances towards the electronic display in the carriage. It is thanking him for travelling First Great Western, reminding him to take with him all of his belongings. He looks again out of the window instead and though the station is behind them now, the signs too, Graves thinks perhaps he knows . . . He does. He knows exactly where they are. They are crossing the River Exe and there, beside the road that wraps itself round the incline beyond, are the university buildings that he and Carol came, a lifetime ago, to visit with their daughter. He has slept, then, from Reading to Exeter. Absurdly, he is proud of himself. Two hours, on a train – when these days he can barely manage two hours in a bed.

He peers along the aisle and sees the carriage is no longer empty. There is a lone businessman a few seats down and a pair of students in the next row along. Graves checks about him for his newspaper but realises, when he cannot find it, that its pages are most likely scattered around Paddington station. He settles back in his seat instead and allows his eyes to close. He does not sleep but he dozes and this, too, is a skill he thought he lacked. It comes easily, however, and the second half of the journey passes in a haze of half-formed thoughts.

As the train approaches his station, Graves gathers his things and moves to wait beside the carriage doors. The facility is closer to Liskeard than to Bodmin Parkway, which is why they have been instructed to disembark at the latter. It is part of the security arrangements that were established even before Graves first arrived: a train to the wrong stop, followed by one of five

309

routes by road back east. It is the part of the journey to which Graves has least been looking forward. He is not a confident driver and each of the prescribed routes is laborious, long-winded – unfamiliar, too, just like the Toyota that awaits him in the station car park. Also it is dark and in the dark the roads will seem narrower, more perilous than they already are. Graves thinks of Tom, of Arthur Priestley's wife, and for an instant his unease returns.

The drive, as it turns out, is uneventful. It is tiring though, as Graves expected, and takes as long as he feared. By the time he eases the Toyota to a halt outside the cottage, the evening has soured into night. A mist has settled on the moorland, obscuring the moon and the stars and even the tops of the trees. There is a light on in the main building but it is like a lamp in the far corner of a room viewed through curtains from the street outside. Graves kills the engine and waits for his eyes to adjust. He picks up his briefcase and tilts himself from the driver's seat. Standing on the muddy path he stretches, then reaches to shut the car door. He is staring up at the facility and his hand finds only air. He turns, to focus this time on what he is doing, and it is when he looks that he sees: a pair of eyes, glinting like shards of glass.

Graves gives a start. One hand finds his chest and the other tenses on the handle of his briefcase. He finds himself raising the case – whether as a shield or a weapon he could not say.

But he needs neither. He heaves a breath and forces a laugh. With his free hand he reaches again for the car door and when he slams it shut the fox darts into the bushes as though from a starter's gun.

Graves breathes again. He is exhausted, he realises, and not just from the journey. But rather than filling him with worry – with a weary appreciation that he is fated to not get the rest he needs – the realisation, this time, gives him cheer. Because tonight, he knows, he will sleep. Right away, in fact. He will not wash, he will not eat, he will not bother to undress. He will sleep and he will sleep and he will sleep.

And with that in mind, he digs his keys from his pocket.

With that in mind, he opens the cottage door.

With that in mind, he steps across the threshold and flicks the switch to the overhead light.

He wakes. He is awoken. His eyes open and he is on his elbows because the noise, whatever it was, was within his room. That is how it sounded. That, rather, is how it seemed to sound. But now there is nothing, just the echo of whatever he heard – and the echo could in fact be a memory, a fragment of an undispersed dream.

He sits upright. He stretches his eyes and frees his hands from the covers. He glances to the door, to the window. Both remain sealed. He looks across to the other bunk and Willis, his new cellmate, sleeps on. He has his shoulders rolled towards Arthur and they swell, shrink as he breathes. The man is sick but not that sick. If there had been the noise Arthur imagined, surely Willis would have heard it too.

That is it then: he imagined it. But Arthur looks again at the window and the glass, this time, seems to glow. Only faintly, as though with the setting sun. It is late though: well past lights out. It could be one, two, three o'clock in the morning for all Arthur knows, so the glow must be from a light somewhere else in the compound. Strange that he has not noticed

it on any other day. It is not as though he has never before
been awake, staring at the window, at one, two, three o'clock
in the morning.

He swings his legs, quietly so as not to wake Willis. He rubs
at the stubble on his jaw and attempts to swallow the dryness
in his throat. He stands and pads to the far wall, lifting himself on to the balls of his feet to try and get a view through the
glass. It is dappled, though, and criss-crossed with wire, so even
if Arthur could reach he would not be able to see. The window
is definitely glowing, though. There is a light burning somewhere and it is seeping into the cell.

On the bunk again, Arthur crosses his legs and leans against
the wall. He reaches between the plaster and the mattress and
allows his fingers to search for the thing he has hidden. He
pulls it free and sets it in his lap. He holds it, tracing its edges,
and taps it slowly, thoughtfully, against his wrist. Then, in the
marmalade glow, he unfolds the letter and starts to read.

Arthur's first thought, on seeing Burrows in the doorway, is of
Julia. It is the only reason he can think of that Graves's assistant might come to his cell. It is hardly discreet, however, and
Graves said Burrows would be discreet. And anyway he is not
alone. There are voices in the corridor beyond – guards snapping instructions and the undertone of prisoners mumbling as
they obey.

'Just you, Priestley,' says Burrows, when Arthur and Willis
both stand. 'Come outside. Get in line.'

It is light but it is early – too early for breakfast and too
early even for the morning bell. Arthur is dressed but only

because he could not get back to sleep after waking. Willis is a muddle of crumpled skin and ruffled hair. On being excused, he sits and slumps and slides his hands across his face.

'Burrows?' Arthur says. 'What's going on? Do you—' He looks at Willis but Willis is paying no attention. 'Do you have any news?'

Burrows jerks a glance across his shoulder, as though to make sure none of his colleagues would have heard Arthur's manner of address. 'Just come outside.'

Arthur reaches to his bunk for a shirt to cover his vest. He leans and slips a hand behind the mattress too. He wraps his letter to Julia in the shirt and transfers it to his trouser pocket as he stands. He is buttoning his shirt still as he steps into the corridor.

There are at least fifteen other prisoners – half a dozen women, the rest men – and four guards. Arthur takes a spot at the end of the line and, like the other inmates, faces the cell doors. He watches as Burrows walks back down the row, muttering and pointing as he passes each inmate. When he reaches the far end he turns and counts his way back. At the head of the line again, he nods to one of the guards and turns to Arthur and gestures for him to follow. He leads off.

'Burrows?' hisses Arthur.

Burrows does not so much as shift his bloodshot eyes. He walks half a pace ahead of Arthur and focuses on the approaching stairwell. Arthur checks behind. There is a gap of ten feet or so between him and the next prisoner; twenty between Arthur and the closest guard.

'Burrows. Have you heard anything? How's Julia?'

This time Burrows scowls, as though in remembrance of his obligation. 'They operated,' he says. It is all he says.

'And?' Arthur skips to draw level.

Burrows tries to ward Arthur back with a look. 'And she's alive. That's all I know.'

'That's all? How can that be all?'

Burrows acts as though he does not hear.

'Graves said you'd keep me informed. He promised me you'd—'

'Graves is—' Burrows cuts himself short. 'Graves isn't here.' He quickens his pace.

Arthur trails for a moment, watching the back of Burrows's head, then once again draws level. He reaches into his pocket and wraps his palm round the letter. He nudges Burrows's hip bone with his knuckles. 'Here.'

Burrows looks down. 'What?' he says. 'What is it?'

'It's for Julia. Take it.'

'What? No!'

They reach the stairs and begin their descent. Arthur matches Burrows step for step.

'It's not about the facility. It's just . . . Read it if you like. Just take it.'

Burrows shakes his head. He is smiling but not with pleasure.

'Burrows, please. Just take it, read it and, if you think there's anything incriminating, burn it. But I promise you there isn't.'

Still Burrows ignores him. They reach the bottom of the stairwell and turn to cross the entrance hall.

'Please, Burrows. John. She might die! Just take the letter. Please!'

Burrows, surely, sees the desperation welling in Arthur's eyes. For an instant he seems to consider. His expression begins to soften but then there is a noise behind and both men turn.

Someone has fallen. How far, Arthur cannot tell, but there is a prisoner in a bundle at the base of the stairs. Arthur does not think. He does not have time to. He slips the letter into Burrows's jacket pocket and frees his hand just as Burrows takes a step towards the staircase.

'What happened? Is he all right? Pick him up, then, for goodness' sake.'

Burrows turns back towards the front. He looks at Arthur and veers away, so that he walks now with three yards between them. Arthur follows in silence.

They pass the recreational area and enter a part of the building Arthur has never seen. It is just another corridor but undecorated. It smells of plaster and damp and something else – like a hospital but not quite as clean. Like a morgue, maybe. Like a morgue might smell.

There is a set of double doors ahead but Burrows stops before he reaches them. He waits in the corridor beside a smaller, single door and, without making eye contact with Arthur, directs the prisoners through.

They are a work detail, Arthur assumed, even though it is unusual for the male and female prisoners to be made to work together. In the room they enter, however, there is no work to be done. It is four walls – again undecorated, or decorated but with paper that has long since faded and begun to sag – and, in the far corner, a stack of chairs. There is another door opposite the entrance but it is closed and there is no indication as to where it might lead. The room into which the prisoners file, though, is clearly an antechamber of some sort. It has the feel of a secretary's office or, given the chairs, a doctor's waiting room.

'Sit down,' Burrows tells the inmates. 'Wait here.' He brushes past Arthur and opens the second door but, as he slides through, Arthur can see only darkness beyond. Two guards position themselves in front of the exit once Burrows has gone; the remaining two stand beside the door by which the prisoners entered.

They wait. There are only a dozen chairs in the stack, which means six inmates, including Arthur, have to stand. Eighteen men and women, then, according to Arthur's count. Some, like Arthur, might have been up and ready for hours; others wear shoes but not socks, shirts but with misaligned buttons, as though they have been roused before they were willing to wake. It is clear what they have in common, however. No one coughs, no one groans. No one shows any sign of suffering anything more serious than a lack of sleep.

There is always hope. Isn't that what Graves said? Is this what he meant, then? Is this why Graves went away – to make . . . arrangements? Arthur feels hope flood his gut but he swallows it down. He scans the faces of the other prisoners but they stare blankly, wearily; nervously, some of them. How would they know, though, what Arthur has reason to believe: that the man they assumed was indifferent to their fate is in reality striving

SIMON LELIC

to set them free? There is always hope. Those were his words.
And why would he say them – why would a man like Graves,
in Graves's position, say them – unless he expected that hope
to be fulfilled? Unless he *knew* it would be.

What then? Some form of debriefing? Some legal complex-
ities to cover themselves before Arthur and the others can be
released? An interview? Witness statements? Is it perhaps the
police beyond the door – the proper police, the people's police,
not the hoodlums who dragged him from the street? How long
ago that feels. How long ago life feels. How near, though, it
might be now. One threshold to cross and then he will be home.
He will see Casper, his adored son. He will see Julia, his beloved
wife. To think how close he came to losing them; to ensuring,
by his own hand, that they would be lost. Now even the letter
will not be necessary. There was no need to write it; there was
no need to ask Burrows to send it because he can carry the
words himself. And he will. The hospital is the first place he
will go. He will find Julia's room and he will crouch at Julia's
side and he will stroke her hair and kiss her lips and he will—

'No!'

It is Burrows's voice, from the room beyond.

'That's not what you said! That's not what I was told!'

Arthur stares at the door. He tugs his gaze away long enough
to see that everyone else in the room, the guards included, is
staring too.

There is another voice, a hiss really, and not one Arthur
recognises. The words do not carry but it sounds like someone angry, someone irritated – perhaps at Burrows for not
modulating his tone. Indeed, when Burrows speaks again, he

seems to mumble. After Burrows, the second voice returns, closer this time, and Arthur catches a fragment of what is being said.

'. . . like Graves, you mean? Honestly, man, do you think doing this is the reason I came . . .'

Then there is a click, like a door being shut, and the second voice, too, is cut off.

Silence, after that. The prisoners exchange glances. Those who before seemed still to be half asleep check about them now as though only just realising they are somewhere new. Arthur struggles to keep his own eyes from the door. Where's Graves? he wants to know. Burrows started to tell him – didn't he? – but all he said in the end was that Graves was not here. And that hiss, the voice Arthur heard: it did not belong to Graves, he is certain of that, but if Arthur did not know better, he would have said it sounded like the person in charge.

The door opens. Arthur is expecting Burrows but, instead, another guard appears. The guard is followed by a woman, Arthur's age or slightly younger, wearing heavy-rimmed glasses and cradling a clipboard in the angle of one arm.

'Adams,' she says, reading. Her eyes sweep the faces watching hers. 'Cynthia Adams.'

No one moves. No one looks anywhere but back at the woman.

She says the name again, through a slight frown now. This time a prisoner stands.

'That's me.'

Like the other men, Arthur looks across. He knows the face but it takes a moment for him to place it. It is the girl from the bus, from the day Arthur arrived. She was a mess then, Arthur recalls. Coughing and bruised and with the look of someone who had been dragged from a sleeping bag in a supermarket doorway. Now, although still a touch thin, she looks healthy: fit and well and clean. Arthur has not thought of her in weeks but if he had he would have assumed she was already dead. The facility, on the contrary, has been good to her.

The woman half turns and indicates that the girl should follow. The girl glances at the inmates around her, who offer no expression back, and then starts forwards. The door closes behind her.

· More waiting. More silence. Arthur strains for some clue as to what the next prisoner through the doorway might expect to find but he hears none. A voice, then another, but no words that carry. A laugh. Was that a laugh? It seems unlikely, incredibly so, but a laugh, of elation, is what it sounded like. After that, silence again. Until the door opens and the woman with the clipboard and her escort return.

'Daniels. Stephen.'

After Daniels it is Hamilton, Knight, Mahmood, and Arthur knows that his turn is approaching. There are seats now but he does not take one. He could not. It does not help his nerves that the prisoners who pass through do not come back but, in spite of the suspense, in spite of Burrows's exclamation, Arthur finds his optimism gradually returning. He has faith in Graves. He did not realise, until now, quite how much. Since their meeting, Arthur has not allowed himself to hope – he has been too concerned about Julia to expend any prayers other than on her – but he feels now like a man who has been deprived of water suddenly presented with a fire hose. So as he stands and drums his foot and worries what will happen when they call his name, he wishes too that his turn would come.

'Priestley. Arthur.'

Arthur hesitates. Like the prisoners before him, he looks to his fellow inmates for reassurance. One man nods. Another winks. The rest just watch and wait for him to go.

The room beyond turns out to be a corridor. It is only a few paces long and there is another open door at the far end. Arthur walks between the woman and the guard and only sees where they are heading when they arrive.

Burrows is there. He is seated against a wall with his head bowed. He makes no sign of having noticed Arthur enter the room. Arthur looks round and realises the room itself is actually a ward. There are eight empty beds, stripped of linen, and a pile of equipment either recently unpacked or ready to be boxed. There is a set of double doors – the doors, Arthur assumes, he saw before Burrows first ushered the inmates into the antechamber – and a guard standing on either side. The only other person in the room, except for the woman and the guard who escorted Arthur, sits at a small round table in the central aisle. Even seated, the man appears tall. His limbs seem somehow out of proportion with the furniture: he might be an adult crammed behind a table in a children's nursery. Across from him there is another seat, angled and offset as the patient's chair would be in a doctor's surgery.

'Mr . . . Priestley,' the man says, checking the notebook beside him. Then, as though to confirm what Arthur is thinking, 'I'm Dr Silk.'

The woman beside Arthur smiles and gestures to the empty chair with an upturned palm. The smile, Arthur notices, does not reach her eyes. It is hardly reassuring yet the doctor's words carry Arthur forwards. He moves warily and lowers himself into the seat. He scans the table, empty but for the notebook and a covered silver tray. He looks to Burrows once more and Burrows, this time, looks back.

'As you know,' says Silk, 'we have been working with a number of volunteers to identify a cure for the illness the inmates at this facility have contracted. I am pleased – delighted, in fact – to tell you that we have been successful.'

Silk does not look delighted. He looks more like a police officer who has been tasked with telling a family about the death of a relative than a doctor announcing a clinical breakthrough. He catches Arthur looking, though, and hoists a smile.

'We were successful,' he says again. 'We have a cure. Which means, Mr Priestley, that, subject to a period of quarantine and verification later by blood test, you will soon be free to rejoin your family.' Again he attempts a smile. He seems to be waiting for Arthur to speak. When Arthur says nothing, he lifts the cover from the tray. Beneath the cover is a row of hypodermic needles. 'Roll up your sleeve please, Mr Priestley. Either arm will do.'

Arthur, finally, finds his voice. 'Where's Graves?'

The question seems to throw Silk and he looks, when Arthur does, towards Burrows.

'Burrows?' says Arthur. 'Where's Graves?'

'Henry Graves,' says Silk finally, 'is unfortunately no longer with us.'

It is a phrase Arthur might once have used to explain to a patient the loss of a receptionist to a rival surgery. Something in Silk's tone, though – malice? Not quite. Fear then? – seems to convey something more . . . definite.

Again Arthur turns to Burrows. Graves's assistant is upright in his seat now, his hands on his knees and his lips slightly apart. Arthur recalls what Burrows began to tell him on the walk from the cells. He recalls the fragment of conversation he overheard in the room outside. He recalls, finally, the noise that woke him. The noise, like a blast; the glow, afterwards, like something ablaze.

He stands. 'What is that?' He flicks his chin towards the needle in Silk's hand. 'Get that away from me.'

'Please, Mr Priestley, calm down.' Silk is looking past Arthur's shoulder. Too late, Arthur realises why.

He spins but hands grab him. They wrench his arms and press his shoulders, forcing him back into his seat.

'Get off me! Let go of me! Burrows!' Arthur tries to turn. 'Burrows!'

There is a guard either side of him and the woman is there too, struggling to unfasten Arthur's cuff. He yanks his arm away and without meaning to, without caring that he has, he strikes her. The woman yells and falls away. A guard takes her place and, rather than bothering with the button, he grips the fabric of Arthur's sleeve and he tears.

'Burrows! Help me, for Christ's sake! John, please!'

The guard pins Arthur's hand to the arm of the chair. Even as Arthur struggles, he can see the veins bulging in his wrist. He can see Silk, lifting the needle and carrying it close.

'Dr Silk!' It is Burrows's voice. 'Don't,' he says. 'Please don't!'

'Get away, man. Can you not see what I'm holding?'

Again Arthur tries to turn but one of the guards has thrown a forearm around his neck. He can barely open his mouth to speak; he can barely open his throat to breathe.

'Silk, please! You're a doctor, aren't you? Don't do this!'

'Hold him still. For Christ's sake. Hold his arm. Hold his arm!'

'Dr Silk—'

Arthur can see Burrows now, behind Silk. The doctor is leaning, trying to time his lunge, and Burrows is reaching his hand to Silk's shoulder. Suddenly Silk spins. He shoves Burrows away.

'Get away from me! Get off me!'

Burrows shrinks and he slips and Silk is towering over him with the needle in his upraised hand.

'What do you suggest I do?' When the doctor speaks he spits. 'What do you suppose will happen to me if I refuse?'

Burrows tries to answer but Silk does not wait. He turns back towards Arthur. He grimaces as he leans in close. One guard has Arthur's arm and the other has his throat and all Arthur can do is watch. As Burrows stands and stumbles to the wall. As Silk lowers the needle to his arm. As his skin dimples and its resistance breaks and the liquid flows from the vial. As the doctor stands and snaps the needle and tosses it back on to the tray.

'There,' he says.

And it is done.

Welcome. Come in, sit down. Would you like some coffee? Muffin? They're yesterday's but they're fine. There's blueberry and chocolate and a lemon one with some kind of seed. Sesame, I want to say but my friend here's going to tell me poppy, is that right? Right, says his friend: lemon and poppy seed. His personal favourite. Low fat too, he adds and he winks. And they are looking at Tom as if it is all some game, as if they cannot understand why he seems so reluctant to play along. As if the cuts and contusions their associates have given him are all just part of the fun.

'Who the fuck are you? What the fuck do you want from me?'

Sesame flinches. 'Please, Tom. Language.'

Poppy Seed is standing behind his colleague's chair. He drops his eyes to the floor and shakes his head.

Tom smiles a bloody smile. He leans in to the table and props his cast on the surface. 'You realise people will be looking for me? You realise I'm not the only one who knows what I know?'

Sesame affects a look of concern. 'Our apologies, Tom. If

we'd known there would be people looking for you, we would
of course have kept them informed. Give us their names, if you
like. Tell us who you think might be looking for you. Tell us – '
and now Sesame is the one smiling, now Sesame is the one
leaning close ' – who knows what you know.'

Tom draws back. He presses his lips tight.

'Or,' says Sesame, 'I can tell you who I know won't be
looking for you. Would that help? Would that set your mind
at ease?'

There is a mug of coffee in front of Tom and he stares at it.
He says nothing, knowing he has already said too much.

'Your girlfriend,' says Poppy Seed and though Tom wills
himself not to, he cannot help but look. 'Jules. Do you call
her Jules?' Poppy Seed lifts his eyebrows, as though genuinely
curious as to Tom's response. Sesame, though, answers before
Tom can decide how to.

'I'm not sure they're quite at that stage. He calls her Julia.
Don't you, Tom? Jules sounds a little . . . post-coital.'

Poppy Seed snorts. He turns his attention to his fingernails.

'Julia then,' says Sesame. 'Julia won't be looking for you. Julia,
fortunately for her, is a little behind the curve. She is, anyway,
indisposed. But Julia has family. Doesn't she? She has a—'

'Don't you dare! Don't you dare hurt Casper!'

'—cousin. I was going to say, cousin.'

'Pippa? What? No, she—'

'Hold on,' says Poppy Seed. Suddenly his weight is on the
table. His hands – huge hands, Tom realises; hands like swollen
slabs of meat – are splayed on the surface. 'Casper's the boy,
right? You think we'd hurt a boy?' Poppy Seed twists to face

Sesame. 'Is that what he said? Is that what he – ' and he turns back to Tom ' – insinuated?'

Tom presses himself into his chair.

'Pippa,' says Sesame. He talks as though they had not been interrupted. As though a man with forearms the size of Tom's thighs were not leaning into the space between them and snarling as though ready to snap. 'I was going to call her Philippa but you're right, it's Pippa these days, isn't it? She hasn't been Philippa since she was a girl.'

Poppy Seed slowly stands upright. He is scowling at Tom and it takes all of Tom's self-control not to flinch as he stares back.

'Pippa, then,' says Sesame. 'Will Pippa be looking for you, Tom? Does Pippa, quote, know what you know?'

'What?' Tom is watching Poppy Seed still. 'No,' he says, jerking to face Sesame. 'Pippa doesn't know anything. I swear to you! All she knows about is the accident.' Tom sees Sesame's eyes tighten and he shakes his head. 'She knows we had an accident, that's all. She doesn't know . . . I mean, I didn't tell her how it . . . I didn't tell anyone about the . . . '

Sesame lifts a hand. 'Relax, Tom. Take a breath.'

Tom, in spite of himself, obeys. He fills his lungs and then exhales and he feels, afterwards, a little better; a little less as though he is steering himself, his friends, into oncoming traffic. He says, 'Pippa knows her cousin is hurt. She knows there was a car accident. She doesn't know what caused it.'

'So if we were to talk to her,' says Sesame, 'if we were to ask her—'

'She hasn't done anything! There's no reason for you to hurt her!'

Poppy Seed gives a sniff. He crosses his arms and angles his head and stares at Tom like he has just about had enough.

'Why would we hurt her?' says Sesame. 'If you're telling the truth, what possible reason would we have for causing her harm? You're thinking we'd bring her here.' He gestures to the walls around him, to the room that is a concrete cell. 'Am I right?' He seems to gather from Tom's expression that he is and he laughs: a chuckle that, in any other context, would sound kindly. 'There are degrees, Tom. There are shades of grey. You, for instance: you get charcoal. A long way from black but further from white. Pippa . . . Well. We'd start Pippa on . . .' Sesame keeps his eyes on Tom but directs his chin towards his colleague. 'What was that colour you painted your kitchen?'

Poppy Seed does not miss a beat. 'Chiffon.'

'Right,' says Sesame. 'Chiffon. We'd start Pippa on chiffon. Which, in my book, is a pleasant chat. With someone at the hospital maybe; a friend, perhaps, of a friend. She wouldn't even know what was really going on, not unless we escalated things to . . . Let's see. Oyster pearl, say. Antique lace.'

'What's the point then?' says Tom. 'If you're going to drag everyone through this, why bother asking me at all?'

Sesame smiles. 'So we know how far to drag them. So we know who to drag first.'

Tom swallows and tenses his jaw. 'I'm done.' He folds his arms. 'I've said all I'm going to.'

Poppy Seed takes a step towards him and Tom, involuntarily, drops a hand to the side of his seat to brace himself. Sesame, though, lifts a finger and his colleague stops mid pace. He holds his finger upraised for a moment, then lowers it to the table and taps. 'Graves,' he says, beating a rhythm. 'Henry Graves.' He is watching for some reaction and possibly he sees what Tom senses: his eyes widening, just a fraction, just for an instant. 'Graves won't be looking for you, Tom. Graves is . . . no longer with us.'

Poppy Seed tuts. 'Such a shame. Such a waste.'

'What was it?' Sesame says, turning once more to the man beside him. 'Some kind of accident, did they say?'

'Gas leak, I heard.' Poppy Seed tuts again.

'I don't know a Graves,' Tom says. They're lying. 'I don't know who you're talking about.' They have to be.

Sesame laughs through his nose. Poppy Seed cracks his neck.

'To Graves's credit,' says Sesame, 'the man was at least discreet. He had a daughter, you see. Did you know that?'

Tom says nothing. They're lying. They have to be. Please God let them be lying.

'And he saw her the same day he saw you. But Graves, it turns out, was discreet. Which is good news for his daughter. Not so good, perhaps, for you.'

He's dead. They killed him. They're not lying because why would they need to?

'So Graves, then. Graves's daughter.'

'Jules too,' says Poppy Seed and Sesame nods.

'None of them are looking for you,' he says. 'Does that make you feel any better, Tom? Does that set your mind at ease?'

The mug in front of him, Tom realises, bears a Peanuts cartoon, faded but just about visible. Charlie Brown is flat on his back; Lucy stands over him with the ball. That is the joke, Tom seems to recall: Charlie trusting Lucy to hold the ball so he can kick it and then Lucy snatching it away so that Charlie falls as he swings his foot. It is not funny. It is not remotely funny.

'Tom?' Sesame clicks his fingers. 'Are you still with us? I said, does that set your mind—'

'Katherine.' Tom looks up. 'I told Katherine Fry, my editor.'

Sesame inclines his head. 'Good. Now we're getting—'

'And she told you.'

Sesame falls silent. He locks his hands.

Idiot, Tom is thinking. How many chances did she give you to kill the story? How many hints just to let it lie? 'What have you got over her?' he says. 'I mean, I assume you have something over her, right?'

'Now why would you assume that?' says Sesame. 'Why not assume your boss is . . . patriotic, for instance? Law-abiding? Pragmatic.'

'Because I know her. I know what she stands for.'

Sesame lifts a shoulder. 'Maybe. Or maybe you don't know as much as you think you know. Maybe you don't know what it takes to get where Katherine Fry has got. Did you never question Ms Fry's extraordinary knack for sniffing out a scoop? Did it never strike you how far your little website has come – and how fast?'

'Not easy, in a market like this,' says Poppy Seed. 'With so much competition, so many vested interests. Virtually impossible, I would say, without bargaining for a little help.'

Tom looks from one man to the other, then lets his head drop. That's it, then. Without Graves, without Katherine: that's it.

'Let's talk about Amy,' says Sesame. 'Your little office buddy. You told Katherine. Did you tell Amy?'

'For Christ's sake. If I'd told anyone else, if I'd told Amy, how would I know it was Katherine who came to you?'

Again Poppy Seed starts to advance. This time Tom just watches as he draws near – uninterested now, uncaring what Poppy Seed intends to do. But the big man moves past him. He settles himself against the wall behind.

'Katherine,' Sesame is saying, 'might simply be the person, of those you told, you trust least.'

Tom scoffs. 'With good reason, right?'

Sesame's lips curl at one corner, as though to acknowledge the point.

'I'd like some water,' Tom says. He reclines in his chair.

'There's coffee,' says the voice at his shoulder. 'Drink that.'

Tom considers the coffee in the Charlie Brown mug. There is a sheen on the surface, glinting like diesel on wet tarmac. He pushes the mug away.

'Tell me about Amy,' says Sesame. He speaks with exaggerated patience, somehow conveying that his patience is in fact running out. 'Did you tell Amy, Tom?'

'Did you ask her?'

'I'm asking you.'

'Well, seeing as you'll get round to talking to her eventually, why don't you—'

Tom interrupts himself with a scream. There is pressure, suddenly, at the hinge of his jaw, so intense it feels like his skull is about to shatter. He reaches and finds himself flailing at Poppy Seed's wrists. He tugs but he might as well be tugging on oak.

'Answer! The! Question!'

'No!' Tom yells. 'The answer's no! Let me—'

Poppy Seed squeezes again and Tom screams again but then he is falling towards the table and the pressure is gone. He catches himself on his forearms and ordinarily the impact would jar his broken arm. He barely notices, however. The pain in his jaw consumes him. It wraps itself around his neck and seeps along his spine. He opens his mouth and stretches it wide and it is like tearing open a badly healed wound.

'You realise,' says a voice, 'that this will soon be over.'

Tom squints through the tears in his eyes.

'In a fortnight, I'd say. Less than that.'

The pain is an ache now: a steady throb that seems as much a part of him as the bones in which it resonates.

'The facility: it will be closed. It will be as though it never existed.'

'Closed?' Tom focuses on Sesame, though he is aware too that Poppy Seed is still behind him. 'What about . . . What about the prisoners? What about the people you locked up who aren't infected?'

Sesame frowns. 'I'm not sure I follow.'

'What, you're just going to shoot them? Lock them up some-where else?'

'Shoot whom, Tom? Lock up whom?'

'Arthur Priestley! Seventeen others! You could set them free, I suppose. Send them back to their families, tell them, sorry, it was all a mistake.'

'Tom.' Sesame folds his arms and rests his elbows on the table. 'They all have it, Tom. Every one of them.'

Tom shakes his head. 'Arthur Priestley doesn't have it. And there are others . . .'

'They all have it, Tom. Do you think they would have been quarantined in the first place if they didn't? Do you think the government would be planning to release their bodies if the cause of death were in any way . . . unclear?'

Tom stares and Sesame stares back, as though waiting for Tom to catch up.

'You gave it to them. Jesus Christ. You gave them the virus.'

Sesame does not reply. He does not need to. Tom feels disgust warp his features and watches delight being mirrored back.

'Forget the prisoners,' says Sesame after a moment. 'Think about what I'm saying. It will be over in a fortnight. The patients are dead; those who aren't quite soon will be. The facility will be closed and you, my friend . . .' Sesame smiles. 'You will be free.'

When Tom laughs it is a release. He splutters and then, as though some ignition has been tripped, the laughter follows in a steady chug. It is like breathing. It is like gulping in air when before there was none.

Sesame is smiling too but like a man who does not understand the joke. 'You don't believe me. Why, I wonder, would you not believe me?'

And this just makes Tom laugh more.

'We're not monsters, Tom. We won't keep you here if we don't have to.'

'You'll let me go,' Tom says, grinning. 'All I have to do is promise, I suppose, and you'll let me go and trust me not to run the story.'

Now Sesame laughs. 'Run it where, Tom? More importantly: what story?' He leans closer. 'Without Graves, what have you got? Without Katherine, where can you go?'

It is a trick. It is just a trick to convince him to co-operate, to say more than he otherwise might. 'There are plenty of other editors,' Tom says. 'And I still know what I know. I still have the information I have.'

'You're right. There are plenty of other editors. Although you might struggle to find one who is any less of a realist than your boss. And as for what you have . . .' Sesame presses his lips tight, shakes his head. 'You have rumours, Tom. Not even that. You have, at best, a theory.'

'A blog,' says Poppy Seed across Tom's shoulder. 'You could run the story on a blog.'

'Good idea,' says Sesame, pointing to his colleague. 'You could take your theory and you could post it online. On your own website, maybe. You could call it . . . Let's think. Conspiracy dot com. Lunaticleft dot net. Although, thinking about it, you might find those domain names are already taken. You might find your theory's been taken too.'

Tom tries smiling again. 'You'll take a chance then. For the sake of one more life; for the sake of, I don't know, avoiding tipping the tally into triple figures, you'll take a chance and let me go.'

Sesame's veneer of humour seems suddenly to peel away. 'Your life, Tom, is irrelevant. We'll take it. If we have to, if you give us no choice, we'll take your life and toss your body on the pile.' He glares and only gradually does his expression soften. 'But give yourself some credit. You are no John Doe.

You are no, let's say, Arthur Priestley. You have a name and, for what it's worth, a reputation. You've written about the facility; you've made your position clear. Were you to disappear suddenly, particularly in light of the accident that has recently befallen you . . . Well. Some people might actually start reading what you wrote. They might start wondering whether it is possible that Tom Clarke – journalist, activist . . . martyr – had a point.'

'On the other hand,' says Poppy Seed.

'On the other hand,' echoes Sesame, 'say we let you go. Say we let you write whatever you want to write. Who's going to take you seriously? Who is going to regard Tom Clarke as anything other than what you are about to become: a disgraced former hack with . . . I don't know. Let's say, a drug problem. An alcohol problem. Maybe even a taste for pre-teen boys.'

Tom says nothing. There is nothing he can say.

'I'm not trying to discourage you,' says Sesame. 'I don't want to knock your confidence. I just want you to be aware how many people are likely to believe you. And, more to the point, how many people who believe you are likely to care. Because it worked, remember?' Again Sesame smiles. 'Set against everything and anything you have to say will be the public's understanding that the facility worked. That they are safe. That the government took a stance and it was a tough one but, in the end, it was a policy that got this country through.'

Tom feels a hand on his shoulder and he flinches. 'It's just the age we're living in,' says Poppy Seed and he gives Tom's shoulder a pat. 'The means, these days, just don't seem as important as what they achieve.' He brings his other hand up too and lets both palms rest against Tom's neck.

'So that's it then,' Tom says. He squirms under Poppy Seed's touch but Poppy Seed holds him firm. 'You think that's it. You close the facility, you let me go, you win. What about when the virus comes back? Because it will, you know. Maybe you think you've got it under control but it's like . . . like terrorism. Isn't that what you want us all to believe? And you're right because the principle is exactly the same. You grip and you grip hard but the tighter you squeeze the more likely it is that something will slip through your fingers.' Tom twists. This time he breaks from Poppy Seed's grasp but only, it feels like, because he is allowed to. Immediately the man's hands settle again on Tom's shoulders. 'It was eighty-six initially,' Tom says. 'That's what Myers said, right? She didn't mention the most recent intake, did she? She didn't talk about the people you won't find, won't even realise you should be looking for, until it's already too late.'

Sesame bobs his head. 'She didn't. You are quite right. You're right, too, that the virus will come back. We've been thorough, I can assure you, but maybe we missed one or two. So maybe the virus comes back and maybe we have to start all over again. Maybe – ' and he chuckles, as though at an idea that seems outlandish but is not, perhaps, out of the question ' – maybe, if the virus comes back, we bring the facility back.' He pauses and angles his head, watching Tom for a reaction. Tom fails not to oblige.

'The point,' Sesame continues, 'is that here, now, on our watch, the facility worked. There is no panic, no epidemic. Ask yourself: as far as the public is concerned, could we possibly have done anything more? Could the British government be accused of acting anything other than decisively, discriminately, compassionately—'

Tom interrupts with a laugh. 'Discriminately? Compassionately, for pity's sake?'

Sesame affects confusion. 'Certainly we were discriminate. We were, I would argue, uniquely so. And compassionate: what could be more compassionate than instituting a dedicated medical facility to care for the afflicted? Than protecting this country from a savage contagion? Than returning to the grieving families the bodies of the victims in order that they might have closure, might understand, might finally . . . move on.'

'They'll never understand,' says Tom. 'They'll never be able to move on. Not until they know the truth.'

Sesame shakes his head. His manner is of a teacher tiring of a pupil who really should know better. 'You are a journalist, Tom. Surely you have learnt by now that truth is a matter of perception. They will understand. They will move on. And even if they struggle to, the rest of the country will move on for them. The rest of the country will realise that it could have been so much worse. If – when – the virus comes back, they will realise nature is the real enemy. Nature, and the morally depraved.'

Poppy Seed sniffs out a laugh. His breath hits the back of Tom's neck.

'So there you have it,' says Sesame. 'The facility has served its purpose. The families – even Mrs and Master Priestley, given time – will come to terms with their loss. The government, in due course, will win the general election; it might even be tempted to call it early should its lead in the polls since the start of this episode endure.' Sesame pauses. 'And as for you, Tom: you will be released, assuming you earn the right.'

Poppy Seed's hands feel heavy all of a sudden on Tom's shoulders. He writhes but this time there is no breaking free. 'What then?' he says, falling still. 'What do you want from me? You win. Right? No matter what I tell you, no matter who I might have told: you win.' He lifts his chin. 'Let me go. If you're going to let me go, let me go.'

Sesame offers Tom an indulgent smile. 'Now, Tom. There's no rush. You'll be with us another fortnight, remember? You'll be with us until the facility closes at the very least. Plenty of time to chat. Plenty of time to be thorough.' Sesame frowns suddenly at the coffee mug on the table. 'And look,' he says. As he slides Tom's coffee mug towards him, Tom feels the grip around his shoulders begin to tighten. 'You haven't even touched your coffee.'

Epilogue

Through the mist that has settled on the year, he watches. There is a tree beside him but he does not lean. He would like to; just a few days ago, he would have had to. The pain is fading, though, and his strength is returning and he is sick, moreover, of hobbling, of crawling, of trying to sit and collapsing, of trying to stand and failing. He is sick of wincing on everything but the shallowest breath and of rolling, between bouts of sleep, from bruise to bruise and then back again. He is sick, mostly, of being a man who has been beaten – when he knows he is not yet that.

He does not lean, then, he just watches. At first he does not see her. There is a crowd around the graveside and it is a uniform black and it is hard to tell one form from any other. But then the crowd breaks, or the boy does. Prematurely, it would seem, because heads turn but no one follows. Protocol pins them. Not her, though. She too breaks away and in five paces, ten, she has caught him. He struggles but she pulls him tight. She wraps her soul around his. From where he is standing he cannot hear her words but he can sense them. In the boy's ear, in his: he can almost feel them.

He would like to be there, by her side, but today is not the day. Even if it were safe, today would not be the day. This is her time, and the boy's, and Arthur's above all. And so he watches. He waits. He tells himself he is content to because the waiting, he knows, will come to an end. And really it is not so bad because seeing her standing, walking, even crying: for the moment it is enough. It is beyond what he would once have dared to wish for.

Though now, of course, he wants more. He does not deserve it perhaps but she does. The boy does. The man they should never have lost: he as much as anyone. So he wants more and he will get it because rumours, a theory – they forgot to list the thing they gave him. They forgot time. They forgot too, or possibly never understood, that there might always be something they overlooked. A name, for instance. Just a name and hardly, therefore, worth considering. Unless the name were of a man who knows what Graves knew; who was at Graves's side from the start and was there, unlike Graves, until the end. Unless the name were of a man Graves insisted was worth saving were the story to break. And if that is what Graves thought then surely this is a man worth finding. Surely this is a man who, struggling perhaps to reconcile himself with the truth, might in turn be willing to be found. And, when he is found, to come forward. To pass on the burden he carries.

Through the mist that has settled on the year, he watches. She stands and she holds out a hand and the boy reaches to take it with his own. She steps and the boy follows and, though he is not yet by their side, he is with them as they fade into the black.

It is a tale that bears telling,
so that it will never happen again,
to any people, anywhere.

Randy Shilts,
And the Band Played On
(1988)

Acknowledgements

I would not have written this book – nor any book – if my wife, Sarah, were not there to read it. Likewise, my extended – and extending – family: your love and support means more than you could know. I owe thanks (and more) to my friends, in particular to Sandra Higgison and Courtney Fingar, as well as to all at Macmillan, Penguin, the Zoë Pagnamenta Agency, Andrew Nurnberg Associates and Felicity Bryan Associates. A special mention for Kathryn Court, Zoë Pagnamenta, Maria Rejt and Caroline Wood: agents and editors extraordinaire.

AVAILABLE FROM PENGUIN

The Child Who

Twelve-year-old Daniel Blake stands accused of murdering an eleven-year-old girl. But who is truly responsible when one child kills another? With piercing psychological insight, Lelic examines a community's response to a hideous crime.

ISBN 978-0-14-312091-9

A Thousand Cuts

Detective Inspector Lucia May investigates a school shooting in which a teacher has killed three pupils, another teacher, and then himself. As Lucia begins to piece together the testimonies of the various witnesses, an uglier and more complex picture emerges, calling into question the innocence of all.

ISBN 978-0-14-311861-9

PENGUIN
BOOKS